ChangelingPress.com

Tiny/Rancor Duet

A Bones MC Romance

Marteeka Karland

Tiny/Rancor Duet

A Bones MC Romance

Marteeka Karland

ISBN: 978-1-60521-969-1

Publisher:
Changeling Press LLC
315 N. Centre St.
Martinsburg, WV 25404
ChangelingPress.com

Printed in the U.S.A.

Editor: Jean Cooper
Cover Artist: Marteeka Karland

The individual stories in this anthology have been previously released in E-Book format.

This book contains sexually explicit scenes and adult language which some may find offensive and which is not appropriate for a young audience. Changeling Press books are for sale to adults, only, as defined by the laws of the country in which you made your purchase.

Table of Contents

Tiny (Kiss of Death MC 9)
A Bones MC Romance
Marteeka Karland

A giant of a man with a shattered soul. A mother running on fear and fury. Love isn't even an afterthought.

Tiny -- Christmas meant nothing to me. Just cold nights and bad memories. Then *she* arrived at Haven. Penny. A woman who's already fought her share of battles. She and her girls light up this place like the most beautiful of Christmas lights. I never thought I'd crave my own family. But watching them hang ornaments and laugh? Feels like coming home.

Penny -- I don't believe in miracles. Not anymore. Not until I meet a man who looks like sin and loves like salvation. Tiny's scarred, quiet, and so gentle with my girls it breaks my heart. This Christmas, we're not running. We're starting over. All of us. Including Tiny. One kiss, one breath, one strand of lights at a time, I will build my girls a future to look forward to. And maybe, just maybe, my own Christmas miracle can withstand the storm about to crash down on us.

***Tiny* (Kiss of Death MC 9) is a gritty, emotional, and deeply romantic story of survival, redemption, and a protective alpha hero who would burn the world down to keep his family safe. Can be read as a standalone in the Kiss of Death MC series.**

Prologue

Tiny
Three Years Ago

I hunched over my beer in the corner of *Throttle,* trying to make my nearly seven-foot frame smaller in the wooden chair that creaked beneath my weight. The celebration swirled around me, brothers from the Kiss of Death MC shouting, drinking, and partying. All supposedly for me, but it felt like sandpaper against my frayed nerves. Fifteen years inside made noise hit differently. Made everything hit differently. The smoke hung thick enough to taste, mingling with spilled whiskey and the sweat of too many bodies packed into too small a space. Some of that I was used to, but it was still different. A bar in Nashville, Tennessee was a far cry from the barracks back in Terre Haute Prison. I ran my fingers down my long, thick beard, braided tight like a Viking's, and I kept my eyes down. Freedom was supposed to feel good. This just felt like drowning in a different kind of cell.

Someone raised a glass, shouted my road name. "To Tiny! Back where he belongs!"

The irony wasn't lost on me. Nothing tiny about me except the name they gave me when I first prospected, back when I was just a ridiculously tall kid with too much bulk and not enough sense. I nodded at the toast, took a swallow that burned all the way down, and wished again for the quiet of my cell. At least there, nobody expected me to smile.

A door clanged somewhere in the bar, and I flinched. The sound shot me straight back to Terre Haute as if I were still there. Time had seemed to stretch out like a road with no end until one day they let me out. Something about good behavior and being a model prisoner. As if fifteen years of keeping my head down could erase what I'd done.

I didn't regret killing the bastard. Not one fucking bit. The memory of my sister's face when I found her so bruised and bleeding, that animal on top of her. The way his skull felt beneath my hands. The sound it made when it broke. Some men needed killin'.

"You look like you'd rather be facing a firing squad than a homecoming."

I looked up. Knight sat across from me, sliding into the chair. His voice was smooth as honey, nothing like you'd expect looking at him. Tattoos covered nearly every inch of visible skin -- his face, his neck, his hands. Even the whites of his eyes looked colored in, giving him an otherworldly appearance in the dim bar light. But his smile was genuine, and of all my brothers, he was the one who might understand.

"Too much," I said simply, gesturing vaguely at the noise around us.

Knight nodded. "Takes time to decompress. Took me months after my three-year bit, and that was nothing compared to what you did." He kept his voice low, meant just for me. "Nobody expects you to be right as rain, brother. Xavier said to drink a few for him. Knuckles has him helping with something at Terre Haute. He should be out in six months tops."

"I didn't see him before I left. No one said he was comin' in. I could have stayed."

"Which is why we didn't tell you. Knuckles wanted you out of prison, so here you are. He wasn't expecting to send Xave in before you got out, but the timeline got moved up."

I took another drink. "How's it work out there now? World's different."

"Smartphones everywhere. Internet's in

everything. People take pictures of their food before they eat it." Knight's mouth quirked up. "But people don't change much. Still want the same things. Still hurt each other the same ways."

I thought about that. "Club changed?"

"Yeah. Things are stable and strong since Knuckles took over. We've been working closely with the Miles family. Guy's a real hardass, but he's fair. And we don't hurt innocents." He grinned. "We've been working with a judge and a lawyer in the city to bring Knuckles' people here. He said he wasn't risking the place going back to the way it was when Slash was alive." As intelligence officer, Knight's cyber skills kept us ahead of both law enforcement and rivals. No doubt he used those skills in helping to funnel the right people in our direction.

"Heard you were the one who found the loophole in my case. Got me out early." The words felt inadequate for the gratitude I felt.

Knight shrugged. "You did the work. All those GED programs you ran inside, the mentoring. I just made sure the right people saw the right paperwork."

A commotion near the bar pulled my attention. A drunk in a business suit, out of place in this bar, had his hand wrapped around a female server's wrist. She was trying to pull away, her face a mask of practiced patience cracking around the edges.

"C'mon, sweetheart, just one drink with me," the man slurred, yanking her closer. "You've been teasing me all night with that ass."

The server, Mike's niece, I remembered vaguely, twisted her arm. "Sir, I need you to let go. Now."

Something hot and familiar uncurled in my chest. I watched her gaze dart around, looking for help, but Mike was in the back and the brothers were too caught up in their own revelry to notice.

Knight followed my gaze. "Shit."

I stood. Didn't mean to make a scene of it, but when I unfolded to my full height, the conversations nearby stuttered to silence. I didn't rush. Didn't need to. My long legs ate the distance in a few strides, my shadow falling over both of them like night.

The drunk looked up, and up, and up, his mouth going slack as he registered my size. I could see the calculations happening behind his eyes. The Mohawk down the center of my otherwise shaved head, the full beard, the club colors, the muscles that strained against my shirt were all impressive, but mostly, I knew, he was seeing how easy it would be for me to break him in half.

I didn't speak right away. Just stood there, letting him stew in it. When I did speak, I kept my voice soft, almost gentle. "You're going to let go of the lady. Now." It wasn't a request. The drunk's fingers sprang open like he'd been burned. "We good here?" I asked the server, who was rubbing her wrist.

She nodded, relief plain on her face. "Thanks, Tiny."

I turned my attention back to the drunk, who seemed to be recovering some of his liquid courage. "Listen, man, I was just --"

"Leaving." I didn't raise my voice. Didn't need to. "And on your way out, you're going to remember that women aren't toys. They're not things you get to grab when you want to play."

"Who the fuck do you think --"

I leaned down, just a fraction, just enough to bring my face closer to his. "Fifteen years I've been away. Crushed the skull of a man who raped my sister. With my bare hands." I paused, letting my words sink in. "First night home, I'd hate to go back inside for something as insignificant as you." I smiled then, a gentle expression that never reached my eyes. "Especially since they might not find enough pieces to prove it was murder."

The bar had gone quiet around us, the celebration paused like a held breath. The drunk stood on wobbly legs, fumbled for his wallet, and threw some bills on the bar. "Fucking freaks," he muttered, but he kept his eyes down as he staggered toward the door.

I watched him go, the tension in my shoulders easing only when the door swung shut behind him. The server patted my arm lightly as she passed by, greeting a patron she hadn't seen in a while.

"This round's on me, Tiny. Welcome back." Mike, the bartender, must have come in on the tail end of things. Now he handed me a double shot of Jack and I nodded my thanks as I took a measured sip, embarrassed by the attention. As I made my way back to my corner, conversations gradually resumed, though I felt eyes following me.

Knight was grinning when I sat back down. "Some things don't change," he said, raising his glass in a small salute. "Still hate bullies."

I shrugged, uncomfortable with the praise. "Just didn't like how he was grabbing her. Especially when she told him to stop."

But as the celebration resumed around me, I felt something ease in my chest. Maybe there was still a place for me out here after all. Maybe some parts of me hadn't died in that concrete box. I took another sip of my whiskey and let the noise wash over me. Seemed a little less abrasive than before.

* * *

Penny
Present Day

I stuffed another sweatshirt into the duffel bag, my hands shaking so badly I nearly dropped it. The overhead light flickered like it always did, casting shifting shadows across the bedroom walls. Three duffel bags. That's all our lives added up to after twelve years of marriage. Three bags and two daughters and the thundering of my heart so loud I was certain he would hear it, even though his car wasn't in the driveway. Even though I'd watched him leave with my own eyes.

My ears still rang with what I'd overheard him saying on the phone yesterday. "She's twelve, but she looks and acts older. Pretty too. You'll like her."

There was a pause. His next words chilled my blood and filled me with more terror than I'd ever known. "Just to be clear, I give you Zelda, my debt's paid in full. Correct?" He said it like it was a demand rather than a question. Which didn't really surprise me. Andy liked to think he was always the one in control. Even when he clearly wasn't.

"Good. I'll bring her to you in the morning when I drop her off at school."

My daughter. My Zelda. He was going to give away my daughter. To pay a debt?

Andy left soon after and I knew this was probably the only chance we had of escape.

"Mom." Zelda's voice snapped me out of the dark memories. She stood with her fists clenched at her sides. Her dark eyes never stopped scanning the street below. "Someone's coming. Blue car and it's slow."

My heart seized. "Andy's car is silver," I said,

but my voice betrayed me with its tremor.

"It's not stopping," Kira whispered from the other window. Unlike her sister, she'd made herself small, nearly invisible behind the curtain. The threadbare stuffed rabbit she'd had since she was three was clutched against her chest, its missing eye and matted fur testimony to years of fierce love.

I tucked a stray hair behind my ear, a nervous habit I couldn't break. "Keep watching. Both of you." The full backpack sat where I'd hidden it, tucked behind the box of Christmas decorations we hadn't used in two years. Black, nondescript, with a broken zipper I'd safety-pinned closed, it contained two changes of clothing for each of us, a travel pack of various toiletries, and a burner phone with its charger as well as the girls' birth certificates and Social Security cards. I had put this pack together a month ago but hadn't yet worked up the courage to actually use it.

I was out of time.

I climbed up on one of the shelves in the same closet. At the top was the door to the attic. There wasn't a ladder or anything. Just an opening. I could get high enough to stick my head and shoulders through the opening. The crawlspace was close to the corner of the house. On the outside wall, shoved as far back as I could reach, was a small plastic box. Inside it was all the cash I'd managed to save for the past couple of months. Two hundred and sixty-seven dollars. That's what stood between us and a means to leave the maniac I'd married.

The faded tattoo of two stars on my wrist caught the light. One for Zelda, one for Kira. I'd done them myself the day after they were born, these miracle twins I'd made from horror. Fifteen and terrified in that foster home, with that man. But I'd worked hard to prove I could take care of the girls. Social services couldn't take them away from me unless I proved neglectful, though they really wanted Zelda and Kira. Regulated or not, the state adoption system was just as corrupt as everything else and infant girls whose mothers didn't have a history of drug addiction were a rarity, something the public defender assigned to me pointed out. While there was a bunch of outrage at his accusations, once he'd voiced them the judge had no choice but to give me a fair chance. No matter how much money he stood to lose. The girls were mine, stars in the darkness. The only brightness in a world that had never been kind.

Now Andy wanted to take one of my stars and hand her over like property.

Not as long as I was still breathing.

"He said he'd be gone until nine," I said, checking the clock for the hundredth time. "We need to be on the four-fifteen bus." I hadn't told the girls what I'd heard. Not the specifics. Just that we had to go, and go now, and never look back. "We've got thirty minutes to get to the bus station."

But Zelda knew. Somehow, she always knew. I'd seen it in her eyes when I woke them up thirty minutes before, whispering urgent instructions to grab only what they could carry. She hadn't asked questions. Just nodded and started organizing her sister, too adult for her twelve years.

"Mom," Kira's voice was barely audible. "What if he finds us?"

I climbed down from the shelves with my stash and knelt to tuck two-thirds of my roll of bills in one of the inner pockets of my backpack. The rest I put in my jeans pocket before I zipped the bag with a decisive tug. "He won't."

"But what if he does?" Zelda demanded, turning from the window at last. "What's the plan? We need a plan." She stood there, wiry and small for her age, jaw set in defiance, and I saw myself at fifteen, facing down a world that only wanted to use me. But the difference was, Zelda had me. And I would die before I let anyone hurt her or her sister.

"The plan is we get as far away as possible. I have a friend in Nashville --" I didn't really. Andy had systematically cut every person from my life, one by one, until there was no one left to notice the bruises he was careful to leave where clothes would cover. "We'll be fine. I have a place to go when we get there. Just for a few days, until I can figure out somewhere permanent."

Not a friend's place. A shelter for abused women. I'd spent the hours since I'd heard Andy talking trying to find some place a reasonable distance where I could still be far enough to hide from Andy. Nashville was three hours away. I'd found a family attorney with so many positive reviews I had to at least ask if they knew of a safe shelter in the area. Lana Thompson had given me the phone number of a shelter willing to give us time to get there without giving our space away. In fact, after I'd explained the situation to her, she'd said they'd be more than happy to hold us a space as long as we needed to stay.

"Will he be mad?" Kira asked, her fingers worrying at the rabbit's ear.

A hysterical laugh bubbled up in my throat, which I swallowed down. Mad didn't begin to cover what Andrew Harlow would be when he discovered we were gone. With what he owed to his business associates, the kind of men who'd accept a child as payment, our disappearance would be more than an inconvenience. It would likely be a death sentence. Whether for him or us was the real question.

"Doesn't matter what he feels," I said, slinging the backpack over my shoulder. "We need to move. Now."

Zelda took Kira's hand automatically, positioning herself between her sister and the door, a habit she'd developed years ago. I led them down the back stairs. At the kitchen door, I paused, scanning the small yard that backed up to an alley. Empty. For now.

"Stay close," I whispered. "If I tell you to run, you run. Understand? You don't stop until I say so." I took a deep breath, twisted the lock, and pushed open the door to the life I was leaving behind.

We slipped through backyards like shadows, avoiding the pools of light from streetlamps. The sodium glow gave everything a sickly orange tint, turning familiar landmarks sinister. Kira stumbled once over an unseen root, and I caught her before she fell, my heart hammering so hard I thought it might crack my ribs.

Three blocks. Four. Five. The backpack straps cut into my shoulder, but the pain was clarifying. It kept me moving forward when fear threatened to freeze my limbs. We emerged onto Main Street just as the bus pulled up to the stop, its brakes hissing like a warning.

"Go," I urged, giving Zelda a gentle push toward the doors. "Window seats. Back of the bus."

The driver barely glanced at us as we paid. Zelda claimed the rear corner, where she could see everything, pulling Kira into the seat beside her. I took the seat across the aisle, arranging our bags as a barrier between us and the rest of the bus.

The doors closed. The engine rumbled. And with a lurch that made my stomach heave, we were moving.

Away from the house that had been a prison. Away from the man who thought he owned us.

As the lights of our neighborhood faded behind us, I pressed my forehead against the cool glass and made a silent promise to my daughters, to my stars. No one would ever hurt them again. No one would ever use them as bargaining chips or punching bags or playthings. Not Andy, not his associates, not anyone. I'd failed them before, staying too long, believing things would change. But I wouldn't fail them again.

The bus picked up speed, carrying us into darkness and uncertainty. But for the first time in years, uncertainty felt like hope instead of dread. Not hope, exactly, but certain knowledge that, for good or for ill, our lives were about to change forever.

Chapter One

Penny

I stepped off the city bus with leaden legs, my hand automatically reaching back to make sure the girls followed. Four buses and nearly seven hours of travel with all the stops and waiting and… *stuff,* had left us hollow-eyed and jittery. Nashville sprawled around us, indifferent to our arrival, the late afternoon sun cutting between buildings to cast long shadows across unfamiliar streets. A woman with vibrant red hair waited by the bus stop, her pale blue eyes scanning the disembarking passengers until they found us. She raised her hand in a small wave, and something in my chest tightened. This was our contact. The shelter worker. The next step in our escape.

"Penny?" she asked, her voice gentle but carrying enough to reach me over the bus's idling engine. "I'm Violet. From New Beginnings. I believe we spoke on the phone earlier."

I nodded, my throat too dry for words. Violet looked nothing like I'd expected. No social worker beige, no clipboard, no practiced professional sympathy. Instead, she wore jeans and a simple green T-shirt, her vibrant hair pulled back in a loose ponytail. She looked a few years older than me, with pale skin that showed the ghosts of freckles across her nose. A simple name badge with her first name and a picture with the New Beginning's logo on it was the only way I knew she was here for me.

Zelda moved in front of Kira, her skinny shoulders squared, her small fists clenched at her sides. I recognized her posture, coiled tight, ready to either fight or run. Kira peered around her sister, clutching her threadbare rabbit against her chest, taking in everything with her quiet, calculating gaze.

"My car's just over here," Violet said, gesturing toward a small blue SUV parked against the curb. "It's not far to the shelter, but I wasn't sure if you'd be able to bring any of your things. Walking would almost be faster, but not if you had several things to carry." She smiled as she led us to her vehicle, unlocking the doors as we approached. The girls sat in the back seat while I climbed in the front. Violet fastened her seat belt once she was inside, turning over her shoulder to smile at me and the girls. "No matter what situation you guys came from, no one in the world can promise you everything will be OK. But I can promise you that you'll have the protection of both New Beginnings and our associates within the Nashville community."

"He'll search for the girls." I spoke softly, my voice rough. My heart pounded, the adrenaline hitting me unexpectedly. I'd really done this. I'd left Andy. The enormity of my situation threatened to crash over me, but I held myself tightly in check by sheer force of will.

"We'll be ready. There's a lawyer we work with. I believe she's the one who sent you our way. She does a lot of *pro bono* work for women who come to us." Violet reached over and patted my knee gently. "You're not alone, Penny. We'll help you in every way possible. We'll do that because, as the saying goes, it takes a village. We all have to help each other."

I nodded my head, not wanting to cry, but Violet offered more than anyone else in my life. "Thank you." The interior of Violet's vehicle smelled faintly of cinnamon and something citrusy. Clean. Normal. It made my head spin, how normal it felt after the hours of tense hypervigilance. I wanted to just close my eyes and sleep for a week, but I was wired on fear and caffeine.

"You must be exhausted," Violet said as she pulled away from the curb, her eyes flicking to the rear-view mirror. "New Beginnings is just around the corner. We've got a suite ready for you."

Her words floated around me like debris, not quite landing. Each concept required effort to process, and I had nothing left to give. I nodded again, my gaze fixed on the passing storefronts and street signs, mentally marking our route in case we needed to find our way back. I needn't have worried. We rolled through a chain-link gate not two blocks away.

My breath caught as the shelter came into view. What I'd expected was something… I don't know. Institutional? Cinder blocks, barred windows, maybe a fence topped with barbed wire or something at the very least. What loomed before us was a renovated warehouse, four stories of weathered brick with large windows that caught the late afternoon sun. It looked solid, permanent. Defensible.

The grounds surrounding it were modest but well-kept, with small patches of grass and a few sturdy benches. A tall, heavily muscled man in a leather vest stood near the entrance, casually leaning against the wall. My fingers tightened around Zelda's wrist.

"Don't worry," Violet said, following my gaze. "That's Riot. He's with the MC. They provide security and protection when any of our women need to leave the facility."

"MC?" I asked, the abbreviation unfamiliar.

"Motorcycle club. They're partners with New Beginnings. They help keep our residents safe. In fact, this is their property. They donated the building and helped with the renovations and security." She smiled at me in the rearview mirror. "Give them a chance. No one gets into Kiss of Death MC without being a good man. Their president, Knuckles, won't allow anything otherwise."

A biker gang. She was talking about a biker gang like they were the neighborhood watch. Had we jumped from the frying pan into the fire?

Sensing my disquiet, Violet reached over and squeezed my hand. "Look. I can see Lana didn't have time to explain everything to you. She probably thought you'd back out if you found out about Kiss of Death before you got here. Lana only sends us the women in the worst danger because the guys at Kiss of Death work with her to protect and support vulnerable women and children from abusive partners."

Violet parked the small SUV in front of the building. The thing was really huge. I had no idea how they had the place broken up into areas, but I had no doubt they could house at least a couple dozen women with children. Maybe more, depending on the room sizes.

"Here we are," Violet said, pulling into a spot marked *Staff*. "New Beginnings Women's Resource Center. We usually just call it Haven. Though we don't advertise for safety reasons, we have a few good friends in the local and semi local justice system. They send us women they believe we can help, usually ones with exceptionally nasty abusers."

I couldn't help the snort of derision. "Exceptionally nasty abusers," I echoed softly. "Pretty much sums up the situation."

We all exited the vehicle and followed Violet through double doors into a small lobby where a woman sat behind a reception desk protected by thick glass. She nodded at Violet, then buzzed us through a second set of doors. I watched Violet enter a code on a keypad.

"Have you eaten?" Violet asked, her voice cutting through the fog in my mind. "There's dinner at six-thirty, but I can have someone bring you something to your suite if you like. I know you'll all want to clean up and rest."

The thought of food made my stomach lurch. When had the girls last eaten? The vending machine at the bus transfer station, hours ago. A bag of chips split two ways and bottled water that the girls had sipped sparingly, making them last.

"We're fine," I said, my voice sounding strange to my own ears. Raspy. Distant. Anyone could tell I wasn't fine but there didn't seem to be anything I could do to fully engage. I was crashing. Hard.

"Mom's tired," Zelda said, her voice sharp with warning. Protective. Always protecting me when it should have been the other way around.

"Of course," Violet said, her smile kind and a little sad. "It's a lot, I know. Zelda?" I hadn't formally introduced the girls, but I was pretty sure the lawyer lady who'd gotten me into this place had given her a profile of sorts. It didn't surprise me Violet knew our names. When my daughter nodded, Violet smiled. "We'll get you settled, and you all can rest. I'll bring you a hot meal.

"Everyone who works here has an ID badge," Violet explained, tapping the plastic card clipped to her shirt. "All external doors are locked at all times, and the residents' wing has separate security. No one gets in without proper clearance."

The hallway opened into a common area with worn but clean furniture, a television mounted to one wall, and several doorways leading to other parts of the building. Signs pointed to a kitchen, classrooms, and a wing labeled "Residential." Overall, it seemed like the common room took up maybe a quarter of the ground floor.

"I'll show you to your room," Violet said, guiding us toward a lift just off the main area. "I got you guys a three-bedroom ready for you so the girls could have their own rooms." She continued to give me the rundown as we walked. "We got two full-size beds, two dressers, and two desks with a chair in their bedrooms and there's still plenty of room for anything else you need. The master bedroom has a king bed, as well as a couple of dressers and a workspace like in the other bedrooms."

"I'm sure it will be perfect." I thought my words might be slurring and I faced Violet. "I think I'm crashing."

"Oh, honey." She put her arm around me as we stepped off the lift. Violet guided us a short way down the wide hall and swiped a key card to open the door and we all filed inside. Violet helped me to the couch in the center of the room in front of a large television. "Let me get you some water." Violet hurried off.

Kira crawled up on the couch beside me, putting her thin arms around my neck. I pulled her onto my lap and hugged her tightly. Zelda fidgeted, seeming uncertain what to do as she watched Violet. The urge to break down was strong, but I held everything in. For now.

"I'm leaving a list of phone numbers on the table," Violet said as she handed me a glass of water. "It's basically a comprehensive list of people around the compound here and at the club you can call if you need anything. Me, Hannah, and Pippa are the main three, but all the women listed are more than happy to come to you at any time. If you have a security issue, call Knight and he will get someone on the way immediately." She sat on the coffee table in front of me. "It's a lot to take in," she said quietly. "I'm throwing a lot at you, and I know you're not in the frame of mind to remember anything and that's OK. Me and the girls will be checking on you tomorrow. I've got you guys some supper on the way, and I'll bring breakfast in the morning. Just get through the night knowing you and your daughters are safe. We've all got your back, and this place is like a fortress."

"I'm sorry to be so much trouble," I managed to get out. "Just… keep my girls safe."

"You're *all* safe." Violet gave me a soft, kind smile. "Get some sleep. By the time they get here, every woman who comes to us is exhausted. Mostly from trying to sleep with one eye open all the time."

"Thank you so much." My voice broke on the last word, but I cleared my throat. "Thank you."

"Get some rest. Food should be here in ten minutes. I'll be back. In the meantime, get settled. Maybe take a hot shower to wash the journey away. If you don't feel like eating, I'll pack it up and put it in the fridge. Got a fully functional kitchen in here if you want to cook, but most prefer to eat in the dining room. So you can reheat it if you wake up hungry before breakfast." She looked from me to the girls and back. "You're safe here, Penny. All three of you."

She gave me one more comforting smile before squeezing my hands briefly once again, then she left. As the door closed behind her, I looked at my daughters -- Zelda's defiant stance, Kira's watchful silence -- and wondered if any of us remembered what safety felt like, or if we'd recognize it when we found it.

* * *

It took us a couple of days, but the girls finally decided it was time to get out and explore our new temporary home. Just as she'd promised, Violet had brought the other women with her. They visited us each day and brought three meals a day as well as snacks and basic groceries. We'd all had a chance to sleep, bathe, and just… breathe. Now it was time for us to begin this journey.

The hallway smelled faintly of lemon cleaner and fresh laundry, scents so normal they seemed strange after the stale cigarette stink of the bus. I perched on the edge of a donated couch in what they called the "common room," watching Zelda and Kira case the place.

Violet appeared from around a corner, her red hair caught up in a messy ponytail. "Penny, girls, this is my son Caleb," Violet said, her hand resting lightly on the boy's shoulder. "He sometimes comes by after school when I'm working late. He's only ever in the front TV area so he's available if anyone needs him to run errands."

"Errands?" Zelda tilted her head to the side.

Caleb shrugged. "You know. 'Cause some of the moms here don't feel safe leaving. I try to keep the boys company and be around in case anyone needs something we don't have in stock."

"So, you're a gofer." Zelda raised a challenging eyebrow.

I thought the teenage boy would bristle at her comment, but he smiled instead. "Hey. Someone in this town's gotta show women not all men are assholes. Besides. Gofers are cute." He smirked and, for the first time in a very long time, I saw a spark of the mischievous kid Zelda was before Andy lost his Goddamned mind. Caleb had effectively thrown down a gauntlet Zelda couldn't resist picking up.

Caleb hitched his backpack higher. "I brought a breakfast pizza, if you're hungry." He directed this at the twins, his voice matter of fact. "Figured it'd be better than yogurt or oatmeal."

"What's the catch?" she demanded, the phrase so familiar it made my heart ache. How many times had I heard those exact words from her when someone offered help?

"No catch," Caleb replied with a shrug that looked too adult on a kid who was barely a teenager. "Just… breakfast." He headed back over to the L-shaped sectional where there was a large coffee table and plenty of room for the pizza box and the small paper plates.

Kira looked up at Zelda, who shrugged, but I knew she was trying to act indifferent. Both girls followed Caleb and the three of them dug in.

"Thank you," I said, the words feeling rusty in my throat.

Violet shook her head as she smiled. "That's all Caleb. He's got a thing about protecting women. Started with me. Bled over to the various women and kids who've filtered through here in the last few months since we opened."

I turned to look at the young man. He had a kind smile and didn't take offense at anything Zelda said to him, including her calling him a gofer. "I think this is the first time Zelda has engaged with another person other than me or her sister for months. Kira certainly hasn't been interested in being around others." Tears filled my eyes, but I choked them back. I didn't deserve to cry. Not over this. "I should have left months ago. The first time he hit me."

Violet studied me, her eyes filled with something

that looked more like understanding than pity. "You left when you could. That's what matters."

But was it? The weight of what Andy had planned to do with Zelda pressed down on me, suffocating. I'd almost waited too long. One more day, and my daughter would have been gone forever. "I heard him," I whispered, watching the kids from across the room. "On the phone. He was going to --" The words caught in my throat. "He was going to give Zelda away. To pay some kind of debt."

Violet's sharp intake of breath was the only indication she'd heard me. When I glanced at her, her face had hardened, a flash of something fierce crossing her features before she controlled it. "Then you got out just in time," she said, her voice low and steady. "And you're here now. We are more than capable and happy to help you. You're not alone anymore. Not if you don't want to be."

Across the room, Zelda had managed to hustle Caleb into giving her and Kira the largest slices of pizza. I watched as Kira actually smiled -- a small, hesitant thing -- when Caleb said something I couldn't hear.

"The girls seem comfortable with Caleb," Violet said, leaning against the edge of the folding table. "That's a good sign. He's got a way with the kids who come through here."

I nodded, running my fingers along a shelf of toiletry items. "Zelda doesn't trust easily. Neither does Kira." My throat tightened. "It's been a long time since they've had the chance to just be kids."

Violet smiled. "That's why we're here. To give you a safe place where you can rest, decide what your next move needs to be." She paused for a moment, hesitating before she continued. "You're probably wondering about the MC connection, right? Most women who come here do. The guys know and do their best to make small, frequent appearances so everyone gets used to them. Usually accompanied by a lot of food." She smiled as if remembering something amusing.

I hadn't asked directly, but the question had been gnawing at me since we arrived. A women's shelter backed by a motorcycle club seemed like a contradiction in terms. "It crossed my mind," I admitted. "When I think of bikers, I don't usually think 'women's advocates.'"

Violet's laugh was soft, tinged with something that sounded like hard-won wisdom. "I used to think the same thing. Until they saved me and Caleb."

I looked at her, really looked, and saw something in her eyes I recognized all too well. The shadow of someone who had survived when she didn't believe she could. I sucked in a breath, wanting to ask what happened but not being able to voice the question. I had a feeling I was going to hear a story similar to my own.

"Caleb's dad was… mean. He had money and thought his money would buy him whatever he wanted, basically. Caleb walked in on Doug one night when he was drunk, lost his temper, and beat me. My son heard and saw most of what happened and threatened to kill Doug if I didn't leave him that night."

I listened intently as Violet paused, gathering herself before continuing her story. There was something in her eyes, a haunted look I recognized all too well. The same look I saw in my own mirror on those rare occasions I dared to really see myself. She tucked a strand of her vibrant red hair behind her ear and took a deep breath.

"I grabbed what I could carry, took Caleb, and we ran." She glanced over at her son, who was still chatting easily with the twins. "That's when we met Riot. Lana Thompson, a local attorney, got us a hearing with a local judge about emergency custody. Riot came with us to the courthouse. He stood by Caleb while he faced his father in court." She gave me a watery smile as she brushed a tear from her cheek. "Anyway, they're all good men. Knuckles doesn't let anyone in he doesn't fully trust. And they are all super protective. They saved us," Violet said, her eyes warm with emotion. "Gave me and my son a home, and I couldn't have asked for better role models than these guys."

Just then, the side door burst open with a bang that made me flinch. "Sorry!" An enormous man shouldered his way through, arms laden with what looked like a dozen grocery bags. His massive frame seemed comically burdened as he balanced the precarious load, his biceps straining against his T-shirt sleeves. I couldn't see his face, but I was pretty sure it was Riot.

"Damnit, Vi," he grunted, staggering toward the kitchen area. "Next time make a smaller list or come help carry this shit."

"Or you could make two trips like a normal person," Violet called after him, not bothering to hide her amusement.

Riot deposited the avalanche of bags onto the nearest table with an audible sigh of relief. He turned to face us. What struck me most about the man from the first moment I'd met him was how his eyes softened when his gaze landed on Violet. This man adored her. And she felt the same about him.

"Two trips?" he said, looking properly

disgruntled. "That's quitter talk. There's a reason I bench four-fifty."

"To compensate for your stubbornness?" Violet teased, walking over to peek into the bags.

"To impress you, obviously," he retorted, the corner of his mouth twitching upward. He winked at Violet, and the gesture transformed his entire face from intimidating to almost boyish. "Did it work?"

"Always does," she replied with a laugh that sounded so free, so unburdened it made my chest ache.

In one smooth motion, Riot pulled Violet into his arms, engulfing her completely in a bear hug that lifted her feet off the ground. She melted against him, her hand coming up to rest on his cheek with such casual intimacy I had to look away, feeling like I was intruding on a private moment.

I couldn't remember the last time someone had held me like that, like I was precious, like they'd always keep me safe. The casual affection between Violet and Riot stirred something in me I'd thought was long dead. Not just desire for a partner, though God knew it had been years since I'd felt wanted in that way, but for that evident security. The knowing that someone had your back, completely and without question.

I glanced at my girls, still engaged with Caleb. Zelda was actually smiling now, a sight so rare these past few years that it made my throat tight. Kira had edged closer to the boy, her perpetual wariness easing just a fraction. They deserved a life where smiles weren't rare, where they didn't have to be constantly on guard.

"Sorry," Violet said, returning to my side after Riot set her down. Her cheeks were slightly flushed, her eyes bright. "He always insists on doing everything in one go."

"It's nice," I said softly, meaning more than just Riot's determination with the groceries.

Violet seemed to understand. "It wasn't always like this," she admitted. "Trust takes time to build. For both of you." She nodded toward Riot, who was now unpacking the groceries with the same intensity he'd carried them with. "He's a good man. They all are, in their own rough ways." I knew what she meant. I'd been wary of the idea of MC members being the security, but the men I'd met so far had been nothing but kind to both of us.

I watched as Riot noticed the kids and made his way over, offering Caleb a fist bump before nodding politely to my girls. He didn't crowd them or try to engage beyond that simple acknowledgment and a kind smile. He respected their space.

Maybe this strange alliance between bikers and abused women wasn't as contradictory as I'd first thought. Maybe sometimes safety came in unexpected packages. I didn't know if I could trust these men -- trust was a luxury I hadn't been able to afford for a long time -- but seeing Violet with Riot, seeing how she'd built a life here from the ruins of her old one, gave me something I hadn't felt in years. Hope. Fragile and tenuous, but there all the same. And for now, that was enough to get through one more day. One step at a time.

Chapter Two

Tiny

I ducked my head and turned slightly sideways as I stepped through the door of the large warehouse, a habit born from years of door frames too small for me. The club had renovated the structure several months ago because the club's old ladies demanded the place be secured for their new project. The shelter only accepted horribly abused women deemed high risk for retaliatory violence from their abusers. We'd started calling the shelter Haven. The girls all did their best to make it a haven. It also meant men my size weren't exactly welcome.

I smelled fresh coffee when I stepped inside, a stark contrast to the exhaust fumes that clung to my leather and clothes. Inside, the few conversations stuttered to silence as heads turned my way. The newer people stared at me with wide eyes and a touch of fear. I was used to it. Nearly seven feet tall, shoulders wide as a doorway, with a Mohawk and a beard you could lose a small animal in, I never entered a room without changing its atmosphere.

Violet spotted me from across the common area and waved me over with an enthusiastic smile. I moved carefully, each step measured, making myself as predictable as possible. Prison taught me how to move without threatening, how to exist in a space where sudden movements could get you shanked. Also taught me how to use my size to every advantage I could. Here, those same skills served a different purpose.

"Tiny, I'm glad you could make it," Violet said, her voice warm but pitched just loud enough that others nearby could hear. Deliberate. Showing them I was expected and approved of. Safe.

"Knight asked me to check the security systems," I replied, keeping my voice soft. When you're my size, everything about you can intimidate, even your voice. Especially when there were young children around. It's why I played Santa at Christmas. It helped the kids associate me with Santa so when they saw me out and about, they remembered. At least, that was my theory. It had worked pretty well last year, but the very nature of this place meant the kids didn't stick around long. Though, I was pretty sure the old ladies had invited every mother and child who'd come through this place in the last year to the Christmas party.

As I headed to the back of the big room where the security office sat nestled off to itself, I noticed three new faces huddled on the worn sofa near the window. A woman in her mid to late twenties with light brown hair and hazel eyes sat in the corner with a book while the girls played quietly on the floor with LEGOs. All three glanced up as I neared the office door.

The girls, though they appeared to be twins, had very different stances. One with fists clenched, shoulders squared, stood to put herself slightly in front of her sister. The other girl reached for a threadbare stuffed rabbit with one missing eye, clutching it to her tightly.

I recognized the signs as clearly as if they'd been written in neon. The way the woman's eyes darted to the exits, how she stood slowly, not making any sudden moves, to put herself between me and her daughters.

"This is Penny, and her daughters, Zelda and Kira," Violet said, gesturing toward them. "They arrived a few days ago. Penny, this is Tiny. He's with the same club Riot's with. They provide security for us here."

I nodded once, not approaching. "Ma'am."

The woman, Penny, gave me a tight smile that didn't quite reach her eyes. It was the smile of someone who'd learned to hide her true emotions.

"Tiny helps maintain our security system," Violet continued, her voice still carrying that deliberate lightness. "And he sometimes escorts our residents when they need to go to appointments or court dates. Tiny is an amazing friend to have in those kinds of situations."

"Yes," Penny whispered. "I imagine he is."

I thought Violet would move with me to the office where we could talk. Instead, she sat on the other end of the couch from Penny. There were two more couches in the area arranged in the shape of a U. Normally, I'd take a seat as far away from the women as I could, but I'd still be at a distinct height advantage even sitting down. So, I sank to the floor, sitting cross-legged with my back against the couch.

The change was immediate. I watched Penny's shoulders relax. The girl unclenched her hands, giving me a curious look. From my position on the floor, I was still eyelevel with most people standing, but the psychological difference mattered.

"Knight and I updated the cameras last week," I said to Violet, keeping the conversation normal, mundane. "But he thought one on the east side might have a small blind spot."

Violet nodded, following my lead. "That's the one near the service entrance, right? I noticed it seemed off when I checked the monitors yesterday."

As we talked, I kept my peripheral vision on the small family. Though Zelda had relaxed somewhat, she still kept a wary gaze on me. Kira watched me with cautious curiosity now. She clutched her rabbit tighter, its worn fabric testament to years of comfort sought.

Then it happened. The rabbit slipped from her grasp, falling to the floor and bouncing once before settling a few feet from where I sat. The girl froze, eyes wide with alarm.

I didn't move immediately. Instead, I telegraphed my intentions clearly. "Would you like me to get your friend for you, Kira?" My voice was soft as I addressed her directly.

The girl looked to her mother, who gave a barely perceptible nod. Only then did I slowly unfold one long arm, reaching for the toy. I kept my movements smooth and deliberate, picking it up with the gentlest grip I could manage.

I didn't extend it toward her -- that would force her to come to me. Instead, I leaned over, stretching as far as I could, and placed the rabbit gently on the floor halfway between us, then returned to my original position.

"Thank you," the woman, Penny, said when her daughter didn't speak.

The moment crashed into me like a wave, dragging me back fifteen years. My sister Julie, sixteen and broken, flinching from every raised voice after what that bastard did to her. The way she'd curl into herself when men came near. The stuffed horse she'd kept since childhood that she clutched at night when she thought no one would see.

The same stuffed horse that had been torn to pieces the day I came home and found her hurt and half dead.

I blinked away the memory. That had been the worst night of my life. I think it hurt just as bad as when she died a few days later.

"Tiny's road captain for the club. He also helps with security both here and at the clubhouse." Violet spoke to Penny and her voice pulled me back to the present. "He's been instrumental in setting up our security systems here."

I shifted uncomfortably at the praise, my vest creaking again with the movement. I understood why Violet was doing it. These women needed to know I wasn't a threat, but praise had never sat well with me. Not before prison, and certainly not after. "Just trying to help," I mumbled, examining the tattoo on my forearm to avoid meeting anyone's eyes.

"Tiny volunteers for most of the escort duties when our residents need to go to court," Violet continued. "He's been a huge help to many of the women who've passed through here."

I glanced up to find Penny studying me with a careful gaze. Not fearful anymore, but assessing. I recognized that look too. She was recalculating, reshuffling whatever assumptions she'd made when I first walked in. No doubt because she knew Violet had a point. I was a big fucker. The intimidation factor alone was generally enough to keep unwanted people at a distance.

"Good to know." Penny spoke softly, almost timidly. I got it and wasn't insulted. I didn't know their story, but to be here in the first place, there had to be some pretty horrific details.

The smaller girl had reclaimed her rabbit by now, holding it against her chest as she whispered something into its tattered ear. For just a moment, our eyes met, and I saw something there that squeezed my chest tight. Not fear, not anymore. Something closer to recognition.

I knew that feeling. The paradox of finding safety with someone who looked like they could crush you with one hand. I'd seen it in the eyes of younger inmates who gravitated toward me in Terre Haute, seeking protection in my shadow. It was a burden I carried willingly, both inside those walls and now here, in this shelter with its mismatched furniture and reinforced doors. I wasn't an overly religious person, but I'd always felt God put me on this earth with my size and strength to be a protector. It had started with my sister. Now I did my best to continue as much as I could. It took a while, but I could usually prove that sometimes safety came in unexpected packages. Like a giant with a Mohawk and prison tattoos, sitting cross-legged on the floor to avoid scaring a little girl and her stuffed rabbit.

That's when I noticed the small movement at the edge of my vision. Kira, the girl I'd handed back her stuffie, had moved in my direction. The stuffed rabbit dangled from her hand as she took one cautious step in my direction, then another. Penny was distracted, talking with one of the shelter staff, but her sister had noticed. Zelda's eyes narrowed and I could almost see the fierce protective instinct that sometimes rode me, too, envelop her. She stood but didn't immediately hurry our way.

I remained perfectly still, not wanting to spook either of them. The girl's approach reminded me of how stray cats would sometimes appear at the prison fences, wary and ready to bolt at the slightest provocation, but driven by some need stronger than fear. She stopped several feet away, her small fingers working nervously at the rabbit's worn fabric. Up close, I could see the careful stitches where someone had repaired a seam, the worn spot where fur had been loved away. A well-tended comfort object. Someone cared enough to keep fixing it.

"His name is Mr. Hoppers," she said, voice barely audible. The first words she'd spoken in my presence.

I nodded solemnly, giving the introduction the gravity it deserved. "Good name."

She studied me with an intensity that belied her age. Not the fearful assessment I was used to, but something different. Searching. Her eyes tracked from my hands to my face, then back to my hands again.

"You have big hands," she observed.

"Yes."

"But you were careful with Mr. Hoppers."

I understood then what she was doing. Testing a theory. "I try to be careful with things and people smaller than me." I shook my head slowly. "I don't like hurting people."

Her head tilted slightly. "My dad has big hands too. But he breaks things."

The simple statement hit me like a punch to the gut. I kept my expression even, though something hot and angry flared in my chest. "Some men don't know how to be careful."

She nodded as if I'd confirmed something important. Then, with deliberate care, she extended her arms, offering me the rabbit. The trust in that gesture staggered me. I held perfectly still, afraid that any movement might shatter this fragile moment. Then, with the same care I'd use handling a newborn, I accepted the offering, cradling the worn toy in palms that could crush a man's skull.

"He likes you," she said with the conviction of absolute certainty.

"I'm honored," I replied, meaning it more than

she could know.

That's when I saw it… the recognition in her eyes. Not of me specifically, but of something in me that felt safe despite appearances. I'd seen the look often but this was the first time I could say someone making that judgment had the right of it. I could be deceptively calm. Until I wasn't. But not with this girl. Or anyone here seeking shelter.

The moment stretched between us like a bridge, this strange connection forged in the quietest of gestures. I gently returned Mr. Hoppers to her waiting hands, and she clutched him close again, a half-smile ghosting across her face.

Then the spell broke when the very kind of man this little girl had been running from just walked into the Goddamned foyer.

"Let me in, you little bitches! I know she's in there!" The male voice exploded from outside the main area but still inside the warehouse, followed by the sound of something hitting the front door hard enough to rattle the windows. I wasn't certain how he'd gotten in but I knew at least two of the brothers wouldn't be far behind him.

Still, the reaction inside was immediate. Mothers gathered children to them, some retreating down hallways, others frozen in place. The volunteer at the coffee station fumbled her pot, dark liquid splashing across the counter. A woman with a cast pressed herself against the wall, face drained of color.

"My husband," she whispered, eyes wide with terror. "He found me." Her whimper tore at my heart, but more, fueled my anger toward the man outside.

The shelter coordinator, a tall woman with short gray hair, moved swiftly toward the security office, her face hard, showing no signs of panic. She'd hit the panic button that not only notified the local sheriff's office but would give them a live feed of our cameras so they could see what they were up against. This wasn't the first angry ex to show up, but something in her expression told me this one was especially dangerous. This was the kind of man the women coming to Haven had run from. And I hated every Goddamned motherfucking one of 'em.

"I just want to talk to her!" The voice outside rose again, followed by another impact against the door. "You can't keep my wife from me! I have rights!"

Kira scurried back to her mother and sister, who had both risen to their feet. Penny's face had gone chalk-white, her arm instinctively curving around Zelda's shoulders. Not their problem, but they recognized the threat all too well.

I rose to my full height in one fluid motion, unfurling from my seated position like a dark promise. My protective instincts surged, not just for the woman with the cast but for all of them. For Penny and her girls, for every resident who'd found temporary safety behind these walls. But especially for those who hadn't made it here.

"Stay here," I said to no one in particular, my voice calm despite the anger swelling inside me. I rolled my shoulders and popped my neck. I felt the leather of my vest stretch across my back over my T-shirt. "I'll handle this."

As I moved toward the door, residents parted before me like I was Moses at the Red Sea. This time, the fear in their eyes didn't pain me. This time, it had a purpose. Some men need to be feared. Others needed to fear. Those included men who think their fists give them rights over women and children.

I swiped my key card to open the heavy security

door separating the common area from the lobby. The women all had their own cards to get in and out, but we opted for a swipe on both sides to open the door to prevent the children from accidentally opening up the door to danger.

The door swung outward, into the reception space. I was careful to keep myself between the opening and the bastard currently being blocked by Griffin and Inferno. Griffin was usually pretty good at redirecting and deescalating, but Inferno could sometimes be a bit of a hothead. No pun intended. Stepping into the small reception space, I didn't open the door far and made sure it shut quickly. I braced myself in case the bastard got through my brothers.

The smell hit me first. Cheap cologne, mingling with the tang of cheaper alcohol. The man stood about five-ten, wearing a rumpled button-down and slacks that looked expensive despite the wrinkles. He was thickly built, kind of like someone who was athletic in college but hadn't yet realized his muscle was slowly being replaced by fat.

The guy whipped his head around, and for a split second, I watched the calculations play across his face as he took in my size. I knew what he saw -- nearly seven feet of thick muscle wrapped in a leather vest with the Kiss of Death MC patch prominently displayed. His eyes widened, then narrowed with the stubborn bravado of a man too drunk and too entitled to recognize real danger.

In prison, I'd learned there are ways to end conflicts before they start. I took a deep breath and let it out slowly, centering myself. This wasn't about me. This was about the women and children behind that door. About the woman with the cast on her arm who'd gone white as paper at the sound of his voice.

About Penny and her girls who'd already fled one monster.

I stood perfectly still, hands loose at my sides, blocking the path to the door without making any aggressive moves. Waiting.

"Who the fuck are you?" he demanded, his voice slurred but still carrying the crisp consonants of someone who thought themselves important. "This is between me and my fucking wife. Get out of my Goddamned way."

I didn't answer immediately. Instead, I took one step forward, letting my shadow fall over him. Another prison lesson. Sometimes, silence unsettles more than words ever could. When I finally spoke, my voice was soft, almost gentle. "You need to leave. *Now.*"

He puffed up, indignation overriding his initial wariness. "You can't tell me what to do, motherfucker. She's my fucking wife. I have a right --"

I took another step forward, quicker this time, a threat there was no way he was too drunk to miss. The bastard instinctively backed up, though his face flushed with anger at his own retreat. His eyes flicked to my patch, recognition dawning. "You're with that motorcycle gang. Heard every fucking one of you guys done time. You're holding me against my will. Bet that'll buy you a one-way ticket back to prison."

"No." I shook my head slowly, deliberately. "It won't."

His face contorted, and I could see the moment his anger overrode his caution. "You don't know anything about my marriage! She's lying about everything. She always does this, makes me out to be the bad guy when she's the one --"

"Don't care." My voice remained calm but raised

so I could be heard over him. "My job is to keep you out and them safe. Not to make judgments one way or the other."

"Ain't leaving without her. I'll get the police down here and you'll be on your way back to prison."

"You'll leave. And you won't come back."

"Or what?" He tried for bravado, but his voice wavered.

I smiled then, not a friendly expression. "Or you'll regret it. For the rest of your natural life. However short that might be." I leaned in slightly, just enough to let him feel how much bigger I was than him. "The sheriff's already been called. And when they get here, they'll find either an empty parking lot, or they'll find whatever's left of you. I might go back to prison, but you won't be alive to gloat."

Something in my eyes must have convinced him because the blood drained from his face. "You're insane," he whispered, but he was already stepping back.

"No," I said softly. "I'm restrained. Stick around. I'll show you what I'm like when I'm not restrained."

His retreat was almost comical, backing away with his hands raised as if I were pointing a weapon at him. In a way, I was.

Once he was outside, Griffin and Inferno could make sure he didn't come back. Griffin would keep him engaged until the cops got here to take his ass somewhere he could sober up before he tried to drive.

The rage that had built inside me during the confrontation needed somewhere to go, so I channeled it into deep, measured breaths. In prison, uncontrolled anger was a one-way ticket to solitary -- or worse. Out here, it wasn't much different. The last thing these women needed was to see me lose control, even in defense of them.

When I was certain my face showed nothing of the storm inside, I turned and re-entered the common area. The shelter coordinator gave me a small nod of thanks before disappearing down a hallway, probably to check on the woman with the cast. But it was Zelda's reaction that caught me off guard.

She stood apart from her mother and sister, her small frame tense but her eyes alive with something I hadn't seen there before. Now in addition to her wariness, a kind of fierce curiosity showed in her expression. She studied me openly, her gaze tracking from my hands to my face and back again, as if looking to see if I'd fought the guy. While anyone in this room could see out through the large picture window, it was one-way glass. The front was blacked out and looked decorative instead of what it actually was. If she'd watched, she knew I hadn't fought the guy, but she still looked like she didn't quite believe I hadn't settled the problem without violence of some kind.

Across the room, Penny's gaze met mine. The fear that had shadowed her expression earlier had shifted, not gone but different now. There was gratitude there, yes, but something else too. Maybe a reassessment of me. The look of someone seeing past the surface to something familiar underneath. Story of my life, except most people didn't bother to look deeper.

I cleared my throat, uncomfortable with the scrutiny. "Everything's OK," I said to the room at large, though my eyes lingered on Penny for a heartbeat longer. "I don't think he'll be back."

Violet appeared with Caleb, both ready to leave. I'd promised them a ride back to the clubhouse where Riot would be waiting. As I followed them out, I found myself already planning to return tomorrow to do preventative maintenance on… anything I could find that needed it in the next two or three months. Maybe stuff even that didn't need it. Maybe I'd see if Kira wanted me to check Mr. Hoppers in case he needed any more repairs after all his years of loyal service. It had nothing to do with wanting to see if Zelda's curiosity would win out over her caution. Or to see if Penny would look at me again the way she had just now, like maybe I wasn't someone to fear after all.

No. Nothing to do with any of that. At all.

Chapter Three

Penny

I chopped carrots into neat, even pieces, the rhythm of the knife against the cutting board oddly soothing. The kitchen at Haven hummed with quiet activity as Violet and I prepared enough vegetable beef soup to feed the four families currently staying here. Steam rose from the massive pot, carrying the rich scent of Italian seasoning, garlic, and onion throughout the room. For a moment, it almost felt normal, just two women cooking together on a quiet afternoon, but the weight of vigilance never fully left my shoulders.

"So, how are the girls settling in?" Violet asked, her red hair tucked up into the paper hair cover sported by both of us as she stirred the pot. Her voice was casual, but I'd learned that Violet rarely asked casual questions.

"Better than I expected," I admitted, sliding the carrots off the cutting board into a bowl. "Kira slept through the night yesterday. First time in months."

Violet smiled, the expression warming her pale blue eyes. "That's progress. Sleep is always the first thing to go and the last thing to come back."

"You sound like you're speaking from experience."

"I am." She added the carrots to the pot, the splash sending up a fresh cloud of fragrant steam. "It took Caleb three weeks to sleep more than two hours at a stretch after we left his father."

"How did you know when it was… safe? You know. To trust people again."

Violet paused, wooden spoon hovering over the pot. "I didn't. Not at first. You just take small steps. And you watch for the people who prove themselves trustworthy through actions, not just words."

I nodded, reaching for the celery. The steady chop of the knife filled the silence between us. Then I heard a sound so unexpected and precious that my hands froze mid-slice. Laughter. Zelda's laughter. Not the forced, hollow chuckle she sometimes produced to placate adults, but her real laugh -- open and unguarded. I hadn't heard that sound in... I couldn't even remember how long.

"Penny?" Violet's voice seemed to come from far away. "Are you OK?"

I blinked, realizing I'd been standing motionless with the knife hovering over the celery. "That's Zelda," I whispered. "Laughing."

Understanding crossed Violet's face. "Go," she said gently. "I've got this."

I set down the knife with trembling fingers and moved toward the sound, drawn by its magnetic pull. I followed the sound to the common room, stopping abruptly in the doorway. The scene before me was so unexpected that for a moment I wondered if I'd somehow stepped into someone else's life.

Tiny sat cross-legged on the floor like he had the first day we'd seen him here. He'd managed to fold his massive frame into an improbable position. His head nearly reached the height of the sofa, even seated, but his focus was entirely on the delicate structure of playing cards taking shape between him and my daughters. Both girls knelt across from him, Kira leaning forward with unusual eagerness, Zelda with her arms crossed but a smile -- an actual smile -- playing at the corners of her mouth.

"Careful," Kira whispered as Tiny reached forward with a playing card.

His enormous hands, capable of who knew what

kinds of violence, trembled slightly as he attempted to balance the card atop the fragile tower. His brow furrowed in concentration, the short Mohawk down the center of his head lending him an incongruous, almost comical appearance as he focused on this delicate task.

The card wobbled, then slipped, sending the entire structure cascading down with a soft patter. Kira dissolved into giggles, the sound so pure and unexpected it caught in my chest like a physical pain.

"Your hands are too big," Zelda said, but there was no malice in her voice, just the matter-of-fact observation of a child.

"I know," Tiny replied, his deep voice so soft it was barely audible from where I stood. "Good thing I've got you two to help me."

My throat tightened. When was the last time anyone had made my girls laugh like this? When was the last time they'd felt safe enough to simply be children? The realization that it wasn't me, that despite everything I'd sacrificed, I couldn't give them this simple joy, hit me like a physical blow.

I remained frozen in the doorway. My body hummed with conflicting impulses, relief at seeing my daughters relaxed and happy at the fore, followed closely by wariness about trusting this moment with a man I barely knew and a crushing guilt that someone else had accomplished what I couldn't.

Tiny gathered the fallen cards with careful movements, his huge hands looking absurdly gentle as he passed half the deck to Zelda. She took them without hesitation, already planning the foundation for their next attempt. The casual trust in the gesture made my chest ache.

"Mom!" Kira noticed me first, her face lighting

up. "Look what we're building!"

Tiny turned his head, his gaze finding mine across the room. Something flickered across his face before he nodded in acknowledgment. "Your daughters are teaching me patience," he said, his voice deliberately light. "I'm not very good at it yet."

"He keeps making the tower fall," Zelda informed me, but there was a hint of playfulness in her tone I hadn't heard in years. "But we're letting him try again."

We're letting him try again. The words echoed in my head. My fierce, wary daughter who trusted no one, especially men, was willingly spending time with this giant of a man with his intimidating appearance. And Kira, my silent, watchful sweetheart, was openly laughing.

I took a breath, trying to steady my racing heart. "That's… that's nice of you." My voice sounded strange, tight with emotions I couldn't fully process.

"Mom, come help," Kira patted the carpet beside her, inviting me into their circle. "Maybe your hands are steady enough."

But as I watched Tiny carefully place another card with exaggerated concentration, causing both girls to lean forward in anticipation, I felt something else beneath the fear and guilt. A tiny spark of hope, fragile as the card tower itself flickered inside me. Maybe this place really could be the haven its name promised.

I hadn't realized how long I'd been standing there until Tiny cleared his throat softly. A recognition flashed in his eyes as he met my gaze with his. With a deliberate slowness that spoke of someone acutely aware of how his size might be perceived, he unfolded himself from the floor, rising to his full height like a mountain slowly rising from the ground. I felt myself tense, an automatic reaction I couldn't control despite having watched his gentleness with my girls just moments before.

"Sorry," he said, his deep voice pitched carefully soft. "Didn't mean to scare you." He spoke softly, the pleasant timbre soothing me when I knew I needed to keep my guard up. There was something about Tiny that had me feeling secure when I didn't think I should. Not yet.

I shook my head. "You didn't. I just…" What? Just what? Just stood here watching a strange man play with my daughters and felt conflicted about it? "I was surprised to see the girls so… engaged."

He nodded, keeping a respectful distance between us. "They're good kids. Smart." His massive shoulders shifted slightly as he gestured toward the far wall. "I came by to check the east-side security camera. Knight noticed a blind spot in our coverage. Thought I'd check on it myself and adjust it." He seemed like he was stretching to find something to talk about, like he thought he needed to make conversation but had no idea how to go about it. Also, he seemed… nervous? Even now, as he spoke, a flush crept up his neck to his face.

"The one by the service entrance?" I asked, latching onto the neutral topic with relief. So, maybe if I ignored his discomfort, he'd ignore mine.

"Yeah. Angle was off by about fifteen degrees." His hands, so large they made the playing cards look like postage stamps, moved in a small arc to demonstrate. "Creates a dead zone where someone could potentially approach without being seen." I involuntarily glanced toward the window, an old habit from years of watching for Andy's car to pull into the driveway. "It's fixed now," Tiny added hastily, seemingly reading my concern. "And there's always someone on patrol, even if the cameras missed something."

The girls had returned to building their card tower, Zelda positioning the base with surprising precision while Kira sorted cards by their condition, setting aside the bent ones. They seemed so at ease, even with this enormous man standing just feet away. The contrast with their usual hypervigilance around men made my throat tight.

"They don't usually..." I started, then paused, unsure how to continue. "They're not usually comfortable around people they don't know. Especially men."

Tiny's gaze moved to the girls, then back to me. "I like hearing them laugh." He hesitated, then asked, "How are you settling in?"

"We're OK." The automatic response, practiced over years of deflecting concern. Then, surprising myself, I added, "Better than I expected, actually. It's been a long time since any of us slept without... without worrying."

He nodded, his beard shifting slightly with the movement. The intricate braiding was really cool, despite how the thick beard gave him a wild appearance. Everything about him seemed to exist in that contradiction. Intimidating, yet careful, massive, yet gentle.

"How'd you find this place?" he asked, the question casual but his eyes watchful.

I glanced at the girls, making sure they were absorbed in their building before answering. "A lawyer. She works with domestic violence cases. She called ahead for me when I told her we needed to leave immediately." I picked at the edge of my sleeve, worrying at a loose thread. "We took four different buses to get here. I was afraid he'd track the car."

"Smart," Tiny said, and the simple approval in his voice shouldn't have mattered, but somehow it did.

"Not smart enough," I whispered, almost to myself. "I waited too long. Almost too long."

Silence stretched between us, broken only by the soft sound of cards sliding against each other as the girls worked. The tower rose slowly, precarious but determined, much like my own resolve had been that day we fled.

"I had a backpack for us ready to run. I just hadn't been pushed to make the leap." I found myself spilling my story, the words flowing out like water through a crack in a dam. "I'd been saving cash for months, hiding it in the attic. Two hundred and sixty-seven dollars to start a new life." A bitter laugh escaped me. "Ridiculous, right? But it was that or… or…"

"Or stay and be hurt?" Tiny finished quietly. "It's never ridiculous to survive."

I looked up at him, really looked, taking in the weathered lines around his eyes, the tattoos visible at the edges of his shirt sleeves, the way he held himself with a controlled stillness that spoke of hard-won discipline.

"I heard him on the phone," I said, my voice dropping so low I wasn't sure he could hear me. "My husband. He was going to…" The words caught in my throat, nearly choking me. I swallowed hard, my eyes automatically seeking Zelda, reassuring myself she was still there, still safe. "He owed someone money. A lot of money, I think. And he was going to pay them with…" I couldn't finish, my voice breaking on the unspoken horror.

Tiny went utterly still. Not the relaxed stillness from before, but something dangerous, contained. His jaw clenched, a muscle jumping beneath his beard. His massive hands curled into fists at his sides, knuckles whitening before he deliberately, consciously relaxed them finger by finger.

"With Zelda," he said, the words flat, a statement rather than a question. "He was going to give her away. To settle a debt." His voice was controlled, too controlled, like something wild trapped behind steel bars. His eyes, when they met mine, burned with a quiet fury that should have frightened me, but somehow didn't.

I nodded, unable to speak past the knot in my throat. "How did you know it was her and not Kira?"

He didn't hesitate. "Because Zelda probably fought him. Maybe not physically, but I doubt she took his direction easily. If I was an asshole who thought he could do whatever he wanted, I wouldn't get rid of the girl who didn't cause me problems."

The silence that followed was electric, charged with an understanding that needed no words. I saw in his face, in the careful way he contained his rage, a reflection of my own desperate need to protect my daughters. Different circumstances, different demons, but the same essential truth. Some things were worth any sacrifice to prevent.

"He'll never touch her," Tiny said finally, each word precise and heavy with promise. "Either of them. You have my word on that."

It wasn't until that moment that I realized how desperately I'd needed to hear those words. Not just empty reassurances that things would be OK, but a concrete promise from someone who clearly had the will and means to keep it.

"Tiny!" Zelda's voice broke the moment. "We need your help. It's getting too tall for us to reach."

He glanced at me, something unspoken passing between us before he nodded once. Then, with the same careful deliberation I'd seen earlier, he lowered himself back to the floor, joining my daughters at their card tower.

"What do you need me to do?" he asked Zelda, his focus entirely on her now.

"Hold these steady while I add the next layer," she instructed, already trusting him with this delicate task.

I watched as his enormous hands hovered, steady now, no tremor betraying him as he supported the fragile structure my daughters had built. For the first time in years, something loosened in my chest. The feeling didn't completely let me go, but enough to draw a full breath without the constant pressure of fear.

From the kitchen doorway, I caught Violet watching us, a knowing smile touching her lips. She raised an eyebrow in silent question, and I gave a small nod in return. Was everything OK? Not by a long shot. But in this moment, watching this gentle giant helping my daughters build something beautiful and fragile, I could almost believe that someday it might be.

Chapter Four

Tiny

I wrestled the massive Fraser fir through the door of Haven, pine needles showering down my vest like green rain. Behind me, Xavier struggled with the base, his teenage arms straining against the weight. "Where do you want this monster?" I asked Violet, who was hurrying toward us with a look of barely contained excitement.

She pointed to the far corner. "Over there, by the big windows."

Perfect. The spot gave clear views of both the main entrance and the hallway leading to the residential wing. I nodded and maneuvered the tree across the room, careful not to knock over furniture with the tree or my wide frame. Xavier followed, carrying the stand and grumbling under his breath about pine sap on his favorite boots.

"It's not like they won't clean," Tillie, Xavier's woman, teased him before looping her arm through his and leading him off.

I'd missed my friend when we'd been separated after he'd been released. Finding out he was back on the inside just as I was getting out had been hard. Thankfully, he was back with me now, and with a woman he clearly adored.

"Mom said you'd need help with the decorations." Caleb grinned as he trotted over from the other side of the room. "The boxes are still in your truck."

"We'll get them after we set this up," I replied, positioning the tree exactly where Violet had indicated. The excited murmur of voices grew as residents began to notice our arrival. A few women gathered at a cautious distance, their children less hesitant as they darted forward, eyes wide at the enormous tree. I knelt to secure the trunk in the stand, my movements deliberate and slow, always mindful of how my size could intimidate.

"Is that a real tree?" A small boy, maybe six, inched closer, his curious eyes fixed on the pine.

"Sure is," I said, keeping my voice soft, my body hunched slightly to appear smaller. "Want to help me straighten it?"

He looked back at his mother, who gave a tight nod from several feet away. Her knuckles were white where she gripped her coffee mug, but she took a deep breath and smiled, nodding again at the child.

As I adjusted the tree, the door opened again, and several club members filed in carrying boxes of ornaments, lights, and garlands. Several of them pretended to juggle their loads like they were about to drop them when they stumbled, which delighted the kids to no end. Knight had organized this whole thing, insisting that Haven deserved a proper Christmas. The residents deserved it. The kids especially. We all agreed with him.

"Hey, big man," Knight called, setting down a particularly large box. "Got the whole North Pole in my truck. Need some elves to help unload."

I straightened up, rolling my shoulders to release some tension, and that's when I noticed her. Penny stood in the doorway to the kitchen, one hand resting lightly on the frame as if ready to pull back at any moment. Her eyes weren't on the tree or the decorations. They were on me.

I gave her a slight nod of acknowledgment. She returned it, a barely perceptible dip of her chin and a ghost of a smile before she slipped back into the kitchen.

Caleb returned with Zelda and Kira in tow, each carrying a small box of decorations. The twins had changed in the weeks since they'd arrived. Though still cautious, both girls looked less haunted around the edges. Zelda still positioned herself slightly in front of her sister, and Kira still clutched that threadbare rabbit when she felt uncertain, but they'd begun to unbend a little, like plants slowly turning toward the sun.

"Here," Knight said, thrusting a tangle of Christmas lights into my hands. "Make yourself useful."

I stared down at the snarl of green wire and tiny bulbs, my massive fingers suddenly feeling like blunt instruments. I'd been pretty Goddamned big my whole life and had basically taught myself to do intricate work. But there was something about these delicate strands of Christmas lights that made me acutely aware of my size.

"Maybe I should handle the heavy lifting instead," I suggested, looking at the mess dubiously.

"Nope." Knight grinned. "Consider it fine motor skill practice."

I sighed and settled on the floor, spreading the lights out around me. My boots were larger than some of the ornament boxes, my hands dwarfing the fragile bulbs as I carefully began to separate the strands. A few of the braver children edged closer, watching with fascination.

"Can I help?" Kira asked, her voice so soft I almost missed it.

I looked up, careful not to make any sudden movements. "I'd appreciate that. These fingers aren't made for untangling."

She knelt down several feet away. Close enough

to help, far enough to bolt if needed. Then she began working on one end of the tangle. We worked in silence for a few minutes, her nimble fingers making quick progress while mine fumbled with the tiny wires. It wasn't long before she was giggling at me. I winked at her, then gave a mock frown and she really started giggling.

More residents filtered into the common room, drawn by the carefree sound of Kira's laughter, and probably the promise of Christmas. One of the strand's plastic hooks snagged on my calloused palm, and I muttered "shit" under my breath before catching myself. "Sorry," I said quickly, glancing around to make sure no kids had heard.

Kira looked up, a hint of amusement in her eyes. "My mom says worse when she thinks we're not listening."

The casual comment startled a laugh from me, a deep rumble that seemed to surprise her as much as it did me. Her eyes widened slightly, but she didn't retreat.

Across the room, I caught Penny watching us again, her gaze traveling from her daughter to me and back again. There was wariness there still, but something else too. Something that looked almost like hope, fragile and uncertain. Our eyes met briefly, and I felt a strange tightening in my chest. I looked away first, suddenly finding the Christmas lights absolutely fascinating.

"There," Kira announced, holding up her now-untangled section with a grin. "All fixed."

"Thanks," I said, genuinely grateful. "You've got a real talent there."

The faintest smile touched her lips before she ducked her head, but not before I caught it. Small victories. Sometimes those were the only kind worth counting.

As the common room filled with the sounds of excited chatter and Christmas music, I continued my silent watch, even as I helped arrange ornament boxes and move furniture to accommodate the decorating. Protecting this small pocket of safety, ensuring these women and children could experience one Christmas without fear might not be my redemption, exactly, but it felt like a good purpose.

Now, I stood on the step ladder, stringing lights around the upper branches of the tree, when I felt someone watching me. I glanced down to find Zelda standing a few feet away, a glittery star ornament clutched in her hand. Her stance was different than usual, less defensive and more uncertain. She shifted her weight from one foot to the other, her dark eyes studying me with wary intensity.

I finished securing the strand of lights I was working on, then slowly descended the ladder, making each movement deliberate and predictable. With Zelda, as with many of the people here, sudden movements could shatter fragile trust in an instant.

"Need some help?" I asked, keeping my voice low enough that only she could hear. Private communication, no audience, no pressure.

She didn't answer immediately. Instead, she examined the ornament in her hand, a five-pointed star covered in silver glitter that caught the light with each small movement. Finally, she looked up at me. "It's too high," she said, gesturing toward a specific branch about halfway up the tree. "I want it right there."

Her directness surprised me. Not "Can you help me?" or "Would you put this up?" but a simple statement of what she wanted. No room for refusal, no vulnerability in asking. Smart kid.

"I can reach that," I said, matching her matter-of-factness.

She held out the ornament, and I cupped my palm beneath her hand, letting her drop it into my waiting fingers rather than taking it from her. But instead of the quick release I expected, her fingers brushed against mine as she carefully placed the star in my palm. The contact lasted only a second, but its significance wasn't lost on me. From a girl who flinched when men came within three feet of her, this deliberate touch felt monumental.

I closed my fingers gently around the ornament, careful not to crush the delicate hook. "This spot right here?" I confirmed, pointing to the branch she'd indicated.

She nodded, watching intently as I reached up, positioning the star exactly where she wanted it. The branch was sturdy enough to support the ornament's weight, situated where the light from the windows would catch its glitter throughout the day. Not a random choice at all.

"Perfect," I said, stepping back to view it.

"It's not perfect," Zelda replied immediately, but there was no bite in her words. Then, so quietly I nearly missed it, she added, "But it's good."

Something tightened in my chest, an unexpected swell of emotion I hadn't felt in years. It wasn't just about hanging an ornament. It was about being trusted with something she cared about, being allowed to help rather than being seen as a threat. For a kid who'd learned the hard way that men weren't safe, this small act of inclusion hit me harder than I was prepared for.

I cleared my throat. "Got any more you want up high?"

The question hung between us for a moment. Then, miracle of miracles, a small smile tugged at the corner of her mouth. Not a full smile, nothing that would crack her careful composure, but real nonetheless. "Maybe," she said, and turned toward one of the ornament boxes, a clear invitation to follow.

I moved behind her at a respectful distance. Zelda led me to a box filled with glass balls and figurines, squatting down to sort through them with the seriousness of someone selecting weapons for battle. I crouched nearby, despite the protest from my knees.

"This one," she decided, extracting a delicate glass icicle. "And this." A small bird with iridescent feathers joined the icicle. "And --"

A sudden blast of "Jingle Bell Rock" cut through the room as someone turned the volume dial far higher than necessary. The abrupt wall of sound made me tense and whip my head around. But it wasn't my reaction that mattered. Across the room, Kira froze mid-decoration, the ornament in her hand trembling visibly even from where I stood. Her eyes darted rapidly around the room, her breathing quickening as her small chest rose and fell in an accelerating rhythm. I recognized the signs immediately, the rigid posture, the unfocused gaze, the slight tremor in her hands weren't just discomfort with noise, but the beginning of a full-blown panic attack.

My sister Julie had looked exactly the same way the first time I'd taken her to a mall after the attack. The crowd, the noise, the sensory overload had triggered something primal and terrifying. I'd learned then that removing her from the situation only reinforced the fear. What she'd needed was a safe space within the chaos, a controlled environment where she could regulate without feeling singled out or further traumatized by her own reaction. At least, that's what the shrink had told me. All I knew was my actions with Julie had hurt her. So I'd try what the doc had suggested with Kira.

No one else seemed to notice Kira's distress, caught up in the festivities. Both Penny and Violet were making cookies in the kitchen so they weren't immediately available. But I saw her distress. I remembered, and I knew I didn't have long before the girl either shut down completely or bolted.

"Zelda," I said quietly, "does your sister get overwhelmed sometimes? With noise?"

Her head snapped up, eyes instantly suspicious, but then understanding dawned. She looked across the room at Kira and gave a short nod.

"I'm going to make a quiet spot," I said. "Can you help me?"

Without waiting for an answer, I moved across the room, not directly toward Kira but to a stack of blankets. I selected two large fluffy ones, then made my way to a relatively unused corner where two overstuffed armchairs sat at right angles. I draped the blankets over the chairs, creating a small tent-like structure with an opening facing away from the main activity. The arrangement blocked most of the light and dampened the sound without making it obvious that was its purpose. Plus, what kid didn't love a blanket fort? Zelda had followed me, watching curiously.

"Could you get those pillows?" I asked, nodding toward some throw pillows on a nearby sofa.

She gathered them without question, bringing them to me as I adjusted the blankets. I arranged them inside the makeshift fort, creating a comfortable nest in the sheltered space.

"One more thing," I said, and moved to the light switch that controlled this section of the room. I dimmed it slightly, not enough to be obvious or disrupt the decorating, but enough to reduce the sensory input in this corner.

Then I made a small gesture toward the fort for Zelda's eyes only. Zelda nodded several times before hurrying over to her sister and whispered something in her ear. After a moment's hesitation, Kira slipped away from the main group and toward our created sanctuary, Mr. Hoppers clutched tightly to her chest. She paused at the entrance, her gaze finding mine with a question in them.

"It's quiet in there," I said simply. "Sometimes our brains need a break from all the noise and lights. Mine does all the time."

A flash of relief lit her face and she ducked inside. I heard her small sigh as she settled into the pillows and covered up with another fluffy blanket I'd tossed in while Zelda had gone for her sister.

Zelda remained beside me, her expression unreadable. "You knew how to help her and not embarrass her," she said finally. "How?"

I considered my words carefully. "My sister was hurt once. After that, sometimes the world got too loud for her. Too bright. Too much." I kept my voice neutral, factual, though the memories still cut like glass. "I learned how to help her. Figured it couldn't hurt to try with Kira."

Zelda absorbed this, her eyes studying me with new consideration. She opened her mouth as if to ask something more, then closed it, apparently thinking better of it. Instead, she said, "I should work on the tree."

"We should," I agreed, recognizing the deliberate change of subject.

"No. Not you." She pointed to the tent. "Stand guard."

I nodded slowly, understanding and absurdly pleased. If Zelda trusted me to watch over her sister, I was teaching her not all men were abusive assholes. I positioned myself two steps in front of the opening where Kira could see me but I wasn't crowding her.

"Do I have to get out soon?" The small voice came from the fort.

I didn't bend down or look in on her. Instead I turned my head to the side so she could hear me. "You don't have to come out until you're ready. If you need your mom, Zelda will get her."

"No. I'm OK now." There was a pause. "You won't leave, will you?"

"Not if you don't want me to, Lil' Bit."

Again, there was a short silence. "I think I want you to stay there until I'm ready to come out."

"You can tap my leg to get my attention if I don't hear you. Otherwise, I'll stay here as long as you need."

From within, I could hear her breathing gradually slow, the rhythm evening out as the protected space did its work. Not a solution to whatever haunted her, but a temporary respite, a moment to gather strength before facing the world again. Sometimes, that was all any of us could hope for. One quiet moment at a time.

Kira only needed fifteen or twenty minutes before the sounds of the other kids having fun and singing Christmas karaoke finally coaxed her out. The scent of gingerbread cookies wafted through the room also, which probably contributed to helping soothe her with the warm, spicy fragrance. After that, she went back to helping her sister and eating cookies.

Now, I untangled a length of pine garland, the artificial needles scratching against my palms as I worked out the knots. Somehow, I'd been assigned garland duty with Penny, both of us standing at the long folding table that had been set up against the wall. We worked in silence for several minutes, the kind that wasn't quite comfortable but wasn't exactly uncomfortable either. Like we were both testing the waters, feeling each other out. She worked deftly with nimble fingers whereas I fumbled with the delicate work. I admit, I might have been distracted. Penny was a very beautiful woman. I'd never dream of touching her, but I liked admiring her from afar.

"Sorry," I muttered as I accidentally yanked a section she was untangling. "These hands aren't made for delicate work."

She glanced up at me, that same assessing look I'd noticed before. "They seem to do just fine with the girls."

The observation caught me off guard. I busied myself with straightening a particularly mangled section of garland. "Kids are tougher than they look." I glanced up. "Sorry if I did something wrong. I don't want to scare anyone here, but especially not the kids."

"You didn't," she said quietly. "And you're right. They are tough." We worked for another minute before she spoke again, her voice pitched low so it was hard to hear her. "The girls have never had a real Christmas. Not one they can remember, anyway."

I kept my movements steady, not wanting to interrupt this rare moment of volunteered information. "No tree? No presents?"

She shook her head, eyes fixed on her hands.

"There was a tree the first Christmas after me and Andy got married, when the girls were just toddlers. They wouldn't remember it." Her fingers stilled on the garland, and when she continued, her voice had a distant quality to it. "Their father…" She faltered, then pushed on. "He destroyed any decorations I tried to put up. Said it was all a waste of money and in his way. He hated anything being what he considered 'in his way.' Basically, anything unusual within his field of vision. Including, sometimes, me and the girls."

The casual cruelty of it made something dark and familiar stir in my chest. I concentrated on breathing evenly, on keeping my hands gentle on the garland even as I imagined what I'd do to a man who robbed children of something as simple as Christmas decorations.

"The first year, he just threw everything in the trash," she continued, her voice so soft I had to strain to hear it. "The second year, he broke the ornaments. One by one. Made us watch." She swallowed hard. "After that, I stopped trying."

A muscle worked in my jaw as I clenched my teeth against the words I wanted to say, against the rage that threatened to bubble up and spill over. I thought of Zelda's face when she'd handed me that star ornament, of Kira's careful retreat to the quiet space I'd made. Of all the small moments of trust they'd shown despite everything.

"This Christmas will be different," I said finally, my voice deliberately gentle despite the storm gathering inside me. I wasn't making empty promises. I meant every word. "Whatever you and the girls want to do for Christmas, whatever traditions you want to start, it'll happen."

She looked up at me then, and the naked hope in

her eyes almost undid me. "I don't even know what they'd like. What normal families do." Her laugh was soft and bitter. "What kind of mother doesn't know what her kids want for Christmas?"

"The kind who's been fighting battles most people can't imagine," I replied immediately. "Your priority had to be keeping your daughters safe and getting them out of a horrible situation. And that's the kind of mother you are."

Color touched her cheeks, and she looked away. "Thank you," she whispered. "For understanding."

"I understand more than you might think." I thought of Julie, of what happened to her, of my own hands covered in blood. Some kinds of understanding came at a high cost.

We lapsed back into silence, but it felt different now, like something had shifted between us. Not trust, exactly. Not yet. But something adjacent. I glanced across the room to where Kira carefully hung a candy cane on a lower branch of the tree. Zelda stood nearby, keeping watch as she always did, but her posture was less rigid than usual. Both girls looked like they were experiencing real enjoyment.

"They're doing OK," I said, nodding toward them. "Taking it at their own pace."

Penny's eyes softened as she watched her daughters. "I forgot they could look like that," she said, her voice catching. "Just… like kids. Normal kids." Her words pierced me with an unexpected ache.

We finished with the garland and carried it over to the tree. I reached up to drape it around the higher branches while Penny handled the lower sections. Working together, we created a spiral that wound from top to bottom. When the garland was secured, I stepped back, and our gazes met briefly. A kind of sad wistfulness and longing shone almost as brightly as the tears glistening in her eyes. I wanted to pull her into my arms and tell her everything would be all right because I was going to hunt down her soon-to-be-dead husband and kill him the same as I had Julie's attacker…

I took a breath, needing to get myself under control. The last thing I wanted to do was let my emotions bleed through to my expression. Penny wouldn't understand and I found the thought of her fearing me literally made me nauseous. I wanted to protect this woman. I wanted to protect her daughters. Sure, I felt something of that protectiveness toward everyone in Haven, but these three were different. I didn't just want to keep them safe. I wanted the right to defend them.

I stilled, not wanting to catch Penny's attention but needing to catch my breath after the thought dancing on the edge of awareness. The girls. Penny. All three of them were… *mine*.

The moment broke when I caught sight of Zelda whispering to Kira, their heads bent together in conspiratorial closeness. Kira's eyes widened at whatever her sister was saying, then darted toward me before quickly looking away. Both girls seemed to reach some kind of agreement, nodding before approaching one of the decoration boxes.

They rummaged through it, pulling out several strands of tinsel and some colorful beaded garlands. Then, with what could only be described as mischievous grins, an expression I'd never seen on either of their faces, they approached me.

"What's this?" I asked, immediately suspicious of the gleam in Zelda's eyes.

"Come sit over here," she commanded, taking

my hand and leading me to a spot on the floor closer to the boxes of decoration where there was plenty of room.

Before I could ask why, Kira had darted behind me and draped a length of silver tinsel across my shoulders like a glittering cape. Zelda, bolder now, stepped forward and hung a string of red beads around my neck.

"What are you --" I began, but Kira cut me off with a giggle as she tossed another strand of tinsel over my head.

"You're nearly as tall as the tree," Zelda explained matter-of-factly, as if that clarified everything. "You need decorations too."

I stood frozen, afraid that any movement might disrupt this fragile moment of play. The girls circled me, adding more tinsel to my arms, draping beads across my shoulders, even attempting to attach a small ornament to my beard. I must have looked ridiculous as the girls transformed me into a human Christmas tree, complete with what smelled like a candy cane now tucked behind my ear.

And then something unexpected happened. A laugh bubbled up from deep in my chest, a genuine sound of amusement I barely recognized as my own. The sensation was foreign but felt good.

The girls paused in their decorating efforts, startled by the sound. Then, miracle of miracles, they both smiled. Zelda, still obviously reserved but unable to not share our amusement, flashed a real, honest-to-God, smile. Kira's grin spread across her face like a sunrise.

"More," Zelda decided, returning to her task with renewed determination. "He needs more sparkles."

Penny watched us with a complex mixture of emotions I couldn't fully decipher. Gratitude and fear and something warmer all tangled together in a soft look of wonder as she watched us. Our gazes met over the heads of her daughters, and I saw tears glimmering in her eyes, though none fell. I understood. Some joy cuts as deep as sorrow when you've been without it for too long.

I remained perfectly still as the girls continued their work, allowing myself to be transformed into the world's least intimidating Christmas giant. The weight of tinsel on my shoulders was nothing compared to the weight of the trust these two girls had placed in me. Trust was a heavy thing, especially when it came from those who'd learned the hard way that the world wasn't safe. I'd carry the weight proudly, though.

"There," Zelda declared finally, stepping back to assess their handiwork. "Now you match the tree."

"Sparkly," Kira added solemnly, clutching Mr. Hoppers to her chest.

"Very sparkly," I agreed, my deep voice rumbling through the tinsel. "How do I look?"

"Like a Christmas giant," Zelda said with unexpected frankness, and then, even more unexpectedly, she smiled again, a full, unguarded expression that transformed her entire face.

My laughter filled the room once more, joined now by Kira's softer giggles and even a small chuckle from Zelda. Penny pressed a hand to her mouth, her eyes never leaving her daughters.

This Christmas would be different for them. I'd make damn sure of it. Whatever it took, whatever they needed.

Chapter Five

Penny

I carried the plate of Christmas cookies through Haven's common room, the warm cinnamon, sweet aroma wrapping around me like a comfort I'd almost forgotten. For a brief moment, I allowed myself to savor this slice of normal life we'd carved out here. I knew it was only temporary, but Violet had promised I could stay as long as I needed. She said to not even think about leaving until my lawyer, Lana Thompson, said it was safe to do so. Violet said Ms. Thompson had helped her and Caleb when she'd left her own abusive husband. It had taken us a while, but I thought we were all feeling better about the situation.

I glanced out the window… My heart stuttered, my chest constricting painfully. A silver BMW crawled past the building, moving slowly, deliberately. Andy's car. My husband had found us. The plate trembled in my hands. My lungs seized, each breath a conscious effort as the car rolled past the shelter a second time.

I set the cookies down on the nearest surface, my fingers suddenly numb and clumsy. Crumbs scattered across the tabletop as the plate clattered louder than I'd intended. A woman reading nearby glanced up, her eyebrows drawing together in concern, but I was already moving, my body operating on instinct honed through years of danger.

The girls. I needed to find my girls.

I hurried through the common room, scanning each corner frantically. The familiar weight of dread settled in my stomach, heavy and cold. Three weeks. We'd had three weeks of safety. I should have known it wouldn't last.

I spotted the girls by the back window, sunlight

catching in their hair as they hunched over a board game with Caleb. Laughter bubbled from Kira, actual unguarded laughter that sent a jagged pain through my chest. Zelda was smiling, her perpetual wariness momentarily set aside as she moved a game piece across the board. The sound of their happiness was a cruel counterpoint to the terror clawing at my throat.

"Mom?" Zelda looked up, her smile fading as she registered my expression. She could always read me.

I forced my voice to stay steady. "Time to head back to our room for a bit."

Caleb glanced between us, his young face showing wisdom beyond his years. "We can finish the game later," he said easily, already standing as if he, too, sensed my fear.

My hand shook as I fumbled with my phone, turning slightly away from the children as I pulled up Violet's number. The device felt slippery in my sweating palm.

"Penny? Everything OK?" Violet's voice came through clear, concerned.

I turned farther away, dropping my voice to an urgent whisper. "He's here. Andy found us." The words burned my throat like acid.

The silence on the other end lasted only a heartbeat. "Where are you right now?"

"Common room. With the girls and Caleb. I was going to go up to our room."

"Good. Stay inside Haven. You'll be safe as long as you stay inside the building. I'm contacting Knight at the compound right now." Her voice shifted, becoming brisk, professional. "Don't go near the windows. Keep the kids away from them too. I'll be there in five." I ended the call, tucking the phone into my back pocket where I could feel it vibrate if necessary.

"Mom?" Kira's small voice pulled at me. "What's happening?"

I knelt before them, checking the nearest window with a quick peripheral glance. "We need to go up to our room. Just for a while." I gave them a smile I knew had no hope of being reassuring because tears burned my eyes.

Zelda's studied me for a long moment. "Is it him?" she whispered, and I hated that my twelve-year-old daughter knew to ask that question.

I didn't answer directly. "Caleb, do you think maybe you could move the game upstairs to keep us company?" My gaze met his and I saw understanding flash across his features.

"Absolutely, Ms. Penny." He guided Kira back toward the game and two of them returned the game to its box. Zelda hesitated instead, her gaze never leaving my face.

I squeezed her shoulder gently. "It's going to be fine. Violet's calling for help and I'm not letting anyone get to you or your sister."

She nodded once, jaw set in a determined line too adult for her young face, then followed her sister and Caleb to the lift. I wanted to follow them but couldn't seem to make myself move forward. I heard the lift close and start upward but I still couldn't make myself follow. I needed to know what happened, if Andy stopped or if he kept going.

True to her word, five minutes later Violet entered the building, Riot close behind her. Her face was composed, but I recognized the tightness around her eyes. She'd been through this before with other women who'd come to Haven. She'd also been through it herself.

"Knight's on his way with some equipment," she said quietly as she reached for me, pulling me into a brief, fierce hug. "Tiny's with him. Everyone here will protect you."

Something in my chest loosened marginally at the mention of Tiny's name. I hadn't realized how badly I'd wanted to hear that until she said it.

"Has he tried to come in?" Violet asked.

I shook my head. "Just driving by. Slowly. Like he's casing the place."

"He probably is," Riot said, his voice low. "Testing our security, seeing who's around."

"How many times did he pass by?" Violet asked.

"Twice that I saw." My voice sounded strange to my own ears, too calm for the storm of panic inside me.

My phone vibrated in my pocket.

Andy: *I see you found some new friends. They won't help you. They're using you and the girls. We need to talk.*

My hand tightened around the phone until my knuckles turned white. How had he gotten my number? Andy always knew exactly how to get under my skin, how to plant seeds of doubt when I was most vulnerable. But this time was different. This time, I wasn't alone.

I heard the rumble of motorcycles approaching as several more members of Kiss of Death rolled into the parking lot. The thunder of motorcycles was more comforting than I'd ever thought possible. Looking out the window separating the lobby and the common room, I watched as Tiny's massive frame approached the double doors from the parking lot to the lobby.

The woman at the desk pressed a button as Tiny reached for the door handle. The door unlocked and

Tiny strode inside. He went straight to the inner door separating the common room from the lobby. There was a click, and the door opened.

The sight of him as he entered, his broad shoulders nearly brushing both sides of the door frame made a weight lift from my chest. Relief crashed through me so powerfully my knees almost buckled. Knight followed close behind, a duffel bag slung over his shoulder, his face set in grim determination. Tiny's gaze swept the room, finding mine immediately across the space. Something in his expression shifted when he saw me. I thought I saw relief followed quickly by concern. He gave me a slow nod, and I saw a quiet resolve fill his expression as he registered my rigid posture.

I watched Tiny conferring quietly with Violet and Riot near the entrance. His presence seemed to expand beyond his physical form, somehow making the room feel both smaller and safer at the same time. I couldn't hear their conversation, but I saw Tiny's shoulders stiffen at something Violet said, his massive hands curling into fists before deliberately relaxing.

Knight moved with purpose, setting his duffel bag on a nearby table and unzipping it to reveal an arsenal of technical equipment. Cameras, monitors, cables spilled out as he organized them with practiced precision. "I checked the feeds on the way over," Knight said, his voice carrying across the now quiet common room. "I can patch the blind spots today. Add a few more cameras, upgrade the motion sensors." His tattooed fingers worked deftly with the equipment as he spoke. "We'll have overlapping coverage everywhere outside this place within a couple hours."

Tiny broke away from Violet and made his way toward me. "Andy definitely knows where you are," he said quietly when he reached me, his deep voice pitched low enough that only I could hear. "Me and Knight did a quick scan of the video footage. That same car got flagged from our security system's AI. Knight had been keeping tabs on him so he's pretty sure Andy has been watching for a few days."

My throat constricted. "He texted me. Just now."

Tiny's eyes darkened, but his voice remained steady. "What did he say?"

I swallowed hard, showing Tiny my phone. I hated how Andy's words could still worm their way inside me. "He wants to talk. How did he even get this number?"

"If he knows anyone with any kind of skills, he could find you by process of elimination once he knew which building you were in."

"But how did he find me?" I knew I sounded on the verge of a full breakdown, but I kind of was.

"Honey, a decent hacker who knew an approximate time you left and what you looked like could easily track you through public service cameras."

"I wasn't careful enough." I could feel panic rising inside me. I absolutely could not let him take my daughters.

"He's not getting near you or the girls," Tiny said. For the first time since meeting the big man, the gentleness he always showed us here was gone. Steel would have looked softer than this man's expression right now. "Not while I'm here."

The rest of the afternoon stretched on, every minute pulled taut by the memory of Andy's car circling the block. Kira asked if we could stay up late and watch a movie. I agreed before realizing it was an avoidance tactic -- she didn't want to be alone, even in our own room. Neither did I.

Tiny walked me up to our apartment. As soon as we stopped at the door, Tiny turned to me. "You have my number. Right? Violet gave it to you?" I nodded my head. "If you need me… er… anything, you call me. Text me. Whatever you're most comfortable with. I'll stand between you and the girls and whatever is trying to harm you."

I searched his expression for any hint Tiny was playing me. All I found was sincere concern and fierce determination. "Thank you." My voice was soft. Even I could hear the fear, but I took a deep breath and let it out slowly. "Just your presence is reassuring. I hate to be a bother --"

"You're not." He held my gaze with his steady one. "Use my number. I'm only a phone call away. Even if all you want is for me to sit outside your door." He gestured to our apartment door. "I'll sit out here between you and the hallway. No one's gettin' past me to you guys."

I sucked in a breath as tears spilled over my eyes and down my cheeks. I hastily turned away and brushed at my face. "I know. Thank you, Tiny. I owe you and Violet and Caleb more than I'll ever be able to repay."

"Just stay away from the windows as much as you can, honey. Keep the girls away too. We've all got your back, but I will always stand between the three of you and any danger. No matter who or what." I'd never had anyone make that promise I thought might keep it. I knew absolutely without question Tiny would live up to his promise.

Before I could think about it too much, I reached for him. I intended to give him a hug, but even on my tiptoes, I had trouble getting my arms around his neck. Tiny leaned down and enveloped me in those impossibly large arms and immediately, all the tension left my body. He was warm and strong and so Goddamned gentle as he protected me from the outside world. It was only a brief moment, but I knew I'd always remember how safe I felt for those precious few seconds.

When I pulled away, I couldn't help but look up at him. While I dreaded seeing a look of pity, there was a small part of me inside begging to know if he felt this same pull toward me I was feeling for him. He looked down into my gaze and suddenly, I was falling forward. Or maybe he was leaning down toward me.

I sucked in a shuddering breath a moment before our lips met in a gentle press. That was all it was, but I felt the impact all the way to my toes. Sure, there was more than a spark of lust inside me, but mostly, I wanted to sag against him in relief. Not because I was kissing him or could still feel arousal after everything I'd lived through with Andy. Because an overwhelming sense of safety and peace enveloped me when his lips touched mine and I knew in my very bones this man would always put himself between me and the girls and any threat headed our way. Whether we were a couple or not. It was all there in that chaste kiss.

Now I was afraid, pure and simple. Not of Tiny. Never him. I feared for myself. Because, if he continued to see us every day like he had been, I couldn't imagine a scenario where I didn't miss him for the rest of my life when he left.

Once inside the apartment, I pulled the blinds tight and triple-checked the window locks. The twins watched me intently. Kira shed her shoes, then pressed her back to the wall and kept her eyes fixed on the door. Zelda, arms crossed, watched me instead. She probably wanted to ask something but didn't want her sister to hear.

I went through the motions of preparing for bed. All the while, I strained to hear any noise from the hallway or outside, certain I'd catch the metallic purr of the BMW's engine or the telltale staccato of Andy's angry footsteps on the stairs even though I knew he couldn't get inside the building, let alone up to my apartment.

When I heard movement outside our door, I froze, fingers tightening on the edge of the Formica table. A gentle knock. I nearly came out of my skin.

"It's me," Violet called softly through the wood.

I cracked the door and saw her standing alone, concern etched deep into her pale features. "Knight's almost finished tinkering with the cameras," she said. "He and Tiny will be here most of the night. Riot's watching the gate. They've even got a few of the brothers keeping watch on the only road in or out of this area. He's not getting past us now." Her gaze flicked past me, toward the twins. "You can sleep easy tonight, Penny. We've all got your back."

Sleep easy. The phrase sounded obscene. "Thank you," I managed. "Is he still out there?"

She shook her head. "Not since dusk. But we're not taking chances."

"Can I..." I didn't finish the question. I didn't want to leave the girls alone, but I also didn't want them anywhere near Andy if he came back. "Never mind."

Violet nodded, as if I'd said something important. "If you want, I'll stay in the room with them. I can bring a laptop and get some work done while they sleep."

I hesitated, glancing at the twins. Kira was

watching cartoons on mute, but Zelda's eyes were on me, waiting. I nodded, not trusting myself to speak.

Violet followed me back into the apartment and set up at the kitchen table, her laptop glowing blue in the half-dark. "Go on," she said quietly. "If you need anything, just knock on the wall."

I slipped out and walked the halls. On the main floor, the common area was empty except for Tiny, who stood by the entry with his arms folded and his gaze fixed on the darkened window.

He didn't look up as I approached, but I saw his jaw clench. "You all right?" he asked, still watching the lot outside.

"Not really," I said, because there was no point in lying to a man who'd already seen me at my lowest. "Is he coming back?"

"Don't know," Tiny said. "Probably. When he does, he and I are havin' a come-to-Jesus meeting, so let him come."

I peered out the window beside him. Nothing moved on the lot. "He's never been this direct before," I said quietly. "I thought he'd try to charm his way in. Talk to the staff, pretend he was worried about the girls. This is new."

Tiny snorted. "Sometimes, when a guy knows he's about to lose, he doubles down on the crazy."

We stood in silence for a while, his presence comforting. I found myself leaning toward the warmth that radiated from his body, letting it shore up the places inside me crumbling under the pressure.

The moment shattered when the phone in my pocket buzzed again.

Andy: *The girls need their father. You're traumatizing them. If you make me come up, I'll call the police. How do you think this looks?*

I felt the rage crawl up my throat, sour and choking. I held out the phone so Tiny could read it. He read the text, then looked at me, his expression unreadable. "He's going to try to scare you into coming out by making you look unstable."

"He's good at that," I said, bitterness slipping out. "Used to have me doubting my own memory. There were times I thought I was going crazy."

Tiny's phone buzzed in his back pocket, and he pulled it out, reading the text. His jaw tightened, but there was an almost maniacal gleam in his eyes. The man was looking forward to whatever was about to happen. "You do exactly what I say. Understand?" His expression was firm, a man expecting to be obeyed. Strangely, I'd seen the same look from Andy, but… different. Tiny was most definitely capable of violence. A man his size who'd been in prison would have to be. The difference was subtle, and I couldn't quite put my finger on it. But I thought maybe I felt differently because this dangerous mien he showed now meant he was intervening on my behalf rather than wanting to hurt me.

I nodded. "What's happening?"

"He's here. And I'm going out to meet him."

The intercom in the lobby crackled. "Uh, Ms. Penny? There's a man at the door? He says you called him and told him to meet you here."

I felt myself go cold. "No," I said, but my voice was too soft for the mic to pick up.

Tiny turned sharply and started toward the lobby. "Motherfucker's got balls. Or, more likely, thinks he can bribe us." He gave me one more firm look. "Stay here, honey." His voice was gentle as ever, which belied the anger in his movements.

I followed anyway, moving without realizing I

was going to. By the time I caught up, Andy was at the glass. He'd ditched the suit for designer jeans and a Henley that still managed to look expensive. His hair was perfect, not a strand out of place, but his face was red with fury. He pounded on the glass with the flat of his hand, making the whole door rattle in its frame.

"Penny." His voice echoed through the empty lobby. "I know you have my girls in there. I have a right to see my kids. Don't make me get a judge involved." It was a threat. I knew Andy had judges back in Memphis in his pocket. It wasn't a stretch to think some of his judge pals knew judges in Nashville and had sway here. If he chose to, I had no doubt he could take both my girls from me.

I shrank back, instinctively looking for cover. But Tiny just squared his shoulders and shoved open the door. Since the windows were one way, Andy couldn't see inside. So when Tiny took two steps out the door, placing himself between Andy and the only entrance on this side of the building, he didn't say a word. He just… stood there. Unmoving.

Andy took a couple of steps back, startled by the sight of the giant in his club colors blocking his view inside the building. For a moment, Andy looked afraid. His eyes got wide, and I could actually see a sheen of sweat appear beneath the lights in the parking lot. Then the calculation began. He smiled. "What 'cha got there, Penny? You get your own goon squad now? That's cute."

He shifted, catching sight of me behind Tiny's bulk. Then he looked up at the larger man. "You really think this muscle-bound retard's going to keep you safe?" he jeered. "You think I don't know how to get through a bunch of dumb, criminal bikers? That's who you're trusting with my daughters?" He looked back at me. "Let me see my daughters. You owe me that much."

Tiny's voice was so calm it barely seemed real. "Go home. You're not getting in tonight. Or any other night."

Andy sneered. "Is that what this is about? You think you can scare me with your bulk and your attitude, fat motherfucker? I could buy and sell you, you piece of shit." Then Andy shifted tactics, dropping his voice and trying to sound reasonable. "Penny, be sensible. You know this isn't a good look for you. The judge isn't going to like it if you keep my children from me. I'm not the enemy. I just want to work things out." His eyes flicked back to Tiny, and then he laughed. "Jesus Christ. Penny, you realize who you're dealing with, don't you? Ask any cop what happens to women who hang around biker gangs. You think you're escaping a nightmare, but you're just walking into a worse one."

My hands shook, but I held my ground. The world had taught me that men like Andy always got their way, always talked their way back in, but right now I had a wall of muscle and stubbornness between him and us. Tiny didn't move. He waited until the only sound was Andy's heavy breathing as he looked at me.

Finally, Andy seemed to give up, but I didn't need his warning to know it was only a temporary retreat. "This isn't over," he snarled, turning away. "You'll regret this, Penny. You will."

He stalked back to his car. As I watched the taillights retreat down the road, my whole body trembled so hard I thought I'd collapse. Tiny didn't look at me right away. He waited until the sound of the engine faded, then turned, his eyes searching my face. "You good?"

I let out a laugh that was closer to a sob. "Not even close," I whispered. "But I will be."

He reached out, as if to touch my shoulder, then seemed to think better of it and let his hand fall. "If you want to hit something, I can get you a pillow," he said softly.

I snorted, surprised at the absurdity of the offer, and a real laugh broke through the haze of fear. "Sounds like really good therapy."

He nodded, then jerked his chin toward the elevators. "Let's get you back to your girls."

I followed, numb but moving, and didn't even notice until we were halfway to my floor that he was walking just behind me the whole way. I wanted to turn and say thank you, but the words stuck in my throat. If I spoke now, I knew I'd break down in front of this man, and I couldn't do that. Not yet. Maybe not ever.

Once inside the apartment, Kira was already in bed, curled around Mr. Hoppers, but Zelda was waiting in the dark by the window, watching the street. She saw me come in and asked, "Did he go away?"

"For now," I said, and knelt beside her. "We're safe. Tiny made sure."

She nodded, pressing her face against my shoulder. "He doesn't scare easy, does he?"

"Who, Tiny?" I asked.

"Yeah. He's not afraid of Dad."

"He really isn't," I confirmed with a small smile. "Let's get some sleep. Violet said Caleb was coming by in the morning to take you down for breakfast if you and Kira want to go ahead."

"I like it here, Mommy." Zelda spoke softly, sounding almost vulnerable. "No one's scary to us.

Only to people like Dad."

"I know, baby. I like it here too."

Zelda wrapped her thin arms around my waist, and we hugged each other for a long time before she let me go. Then she went to bed, but in her sister's room. No doubt she'd sleep in there for several days until she felt certain the threat was over. Zelda would always protect her sister. No matter what.

As I passed by Kira's room, I heard her ask softly, "Can we leave the bathroom light on tonight?"

I moved into the doorway. "Of course, sweetheart." I kept my tone light.

"He's not coming in," Zelda said with conviction. "Tiny won't let him." OK, Zelda caught me off guard with that one. When had my fiercely suspicious daughter developed such faith in the giant biker?

"You're right," I agreed, surprising myself with how much I meant it. "Tiny and Knight and the others will keep us safe."

Kira nodded solemnly. "Tiny promised. He doesn't break promises." Christ, this girl. Kira was only twelve, but she could read people better than any adult I'd ever met. Sure, she played like a kid sometimes, but she was growing up too Goddamned fast, and I had mixed feelings about it.

Once the girls were in bed, I lay awake in my own bed, staring at the ceiling as sleep refused to come. Every time I closed my eyes, I saw Andy's face, his perfect hair and expensive clothes masking the monster I knew lurked beneath.

I turned onto my side, pulling the blanket tighter around me. When we first met, Andy had seemed like salvation. A stable, successful man who wanted to take care of me and my twin girls. After struggling alone, working multiple jobs while being a new mother to twins, his attention had felt like the biggest relief.

Now, I realized how carefully he'd groomed me, how patiently he'd waited until I was fully dependent before the mask began to slip. Until the first full-blown rage that left me cowering in a corner, wondering what I'd done wrong. By then, my friends were gone, my independence surrendered, and my self-worth so eroded I believed I deserved everything he wanted to dish out.

I closed my eyes, but the darkness only made the memories sharper. I forced myself to focus on something else. Something good. My mind drifted to Tiny, standing between Andy and the door, immovable as a mountain. In the weeks since we'd arrived at Haven, I'd watched him with my daughters. The careful way he held himself when they were near, the gentle rumble of his voice when he spoke to them, the genuine care in his eyes when Kira had that panic attack.

The image of him sitting cross-legged on the floor, letting the girls drape tinsel over his massive shoulders, flashed across my mind. He'd been gentle as he steadied the card tower for Zelda. When Kira offered him Mr. Hoppers, that sacred threadbare rabbit she barely let out of her sight, he'd cradled it with such reverence, understanding the trust implicit in her simple gesture.

Andy'd never understood my daughters. They were possessions to him; extensions of himself when it suited him, annoying inconveniences when it didn't. But Tiny saw them. Really saw them, their fears, their needs, their small, brave hearts.

I shifted again, restless with conflicting thoughts. Wasn't this how it'd started with Andy too? Hadn't I once thought he saw me when nobody else did? The fact that I was lying here, considering trusting another man after everything, made me question my own judgment. What if I was making the same mistake? What if the warm safety I felt around Tiny was just another trap waiting to spring?

But something deep inside me rejected the comparison. Andy had isolated me from day one, subtly cutting me off from friends and family, positioning himself as my sole protector. Tiny did the opposite. He facilitated connections. Like with Violet and the other women at Haven, and the entire support system of the club. Andy had demanded control. Tiny offered choices. Andy used my fears against me. Tiny acknowledged them without judgment and promised to protect me from them.

I traced my finger over the faded twin stars tattooed on my wrist, remembering the day I'd given them to myself. Sixteen and terrified, with newborn twins and no idea how to be a mother. I'd been determined to mark my body with this permanent symbol of my love for them.

I couldn't go back to Andy -- that much was clear. Even if the club, Haven, and Tiny himself all disappeared tomorrow, I'd sleep in my car, under bridges, in shelters across the country before I'd take my daughters back to that house. But running forever wasn't a life. The girls deserved stability, safety, normal childhoods if such a thing was even possible after what they'd been through.

Maybe Tiny was our best hope for that. Not because I needed a man to protect us. I'd learned the hard way depending on someone else for safety was its own kind of trap. But because he represented something I'd thought was a fairy tale. He was a good man who used his strength to shield rather than to harm.

I checked the door one more time, making sure the electronic lock and the deadbolt were both engaged. On impulse, I pressed the security monitor to look outside the room. There, on the other side of the hall directly across from our door, Tiny stood guard between us and whatever came next. The knowledge settled over me like a blanket, heavy and warm and real. I remembered that hug, how safe I'd felt in his arms. I wanted to feel that safety again. I had no idea if he was interested in me beyond friendship, but the more comfortable I grew with Tiny, the more I wanted to be around him.

Tiny had promised to watch over us. I wasn't sure if it was a hero complex or Zeus Instinct, but I thought I might need to find out if that kiss affected him the same way it affected me. Was I stupid for even thinking about getting involved with not only another man, but an ex-con to boot? Possibly, but I didn't think so. There was too much proof to the contrary.

Sleep beckoned at last, and I surrendered to it. My last conscious thought was that Tiny could keep us all safe. And, if he was willing, I would let him.

Chapter Six

Tiny

I leaned against the wall in Haven's common room, watching the morning light spill through the windows. Caleb had brought over his gaming system, and now he sat cross-legged on the floor with Zelda and Kira, all three hunched forward with controllers in hand, faces lit by the glow of the television. The twins were different kids when they played. Kira's perpetual wariness softened, and Zelda's defensive posture relaxed. Actually, Kira could be vicious when she didn't win which surprised me enough to laugh. She glared at me and I had to cough to cover my humor. Something in my chest tightened at the sight. *This* was how kids should look.

Penny stood in the kitchen doorway, cradling a mug of coffee between her hands. Dark circles shadowed her eyes from another restless night, but she smiled as she watched her daughters. That smile hit me like a physical blow. It transformed her face, made her look younger and less haunted. I wanted to see her smile like that every day.

The security door separating the reception area and the common room opened. Knight strode in, his arms loaded with equipment cases, his face set in grim lines. He scanned the room, caught my eye, and jerked his chin in a silent summons.

"Everything OK?" I asked as he set down his burden on a nearby table.

"Need to talk," he said, his voice low. "You and Penny. Now."

I straightened, every protective instinct on high alert. Knight wasn't one for drama. If he was concerned, there was good reason. I caught Penny's eye across the room and motioned her over. Her smile vanished instantly, replaced by the wary expression of someone who believed, because of life experience, unexpected news was rarely ever good.

Knight glanced at the kids, then positioned himself so he could keep them in his peripheral vision while we spoke. Smart. No need to alert them to trouble if we could avoid it.

"Found some shit while setting up the monitoring equipment," Knight said, keeping his voice low. "Been digging into that ex of yours." He directed this at Penny, who went rigid beside me. "He's got gambling debts. Big ones. To people you don't want to owe money to."

Penny's fingers curled into fists at her sides, her knuckles going white. "How bad?"

Knight pulled out his phone, tapped the screen a few times, then turned it so we could see. "Three hundred and fifty thousand, at least. Probably more. I just started looking, so I'm positive I've not found it all."

I let out a low whistle. "Shit."

"These aren't casino debts," Knight continued, tucking the phone away. "These are private games. Underground. The kind run by people who don't exactly file paperwork when you don't pay up."

"That explains a lot," Penny whispered. Her voice was steady, but I could feel the tremor running through her body as she stood beside me. "He was desperate for money those last few months. Always on the phone, always locked in his office." She closed her eyes and gave a little shake of her head. "More violent, too."

Knight nodded, his eyes darting back to the kids for a moment. Caleb had just scored some kind of victory, judging by the way he punched the air and Kira's angry grunt followed closely by a giggle as if she couldn't maintain her ire. They remained absorbed in their game, oblivious to our conversation.

"Here's the thing," Knight said, turning back to us. "Guys like this don't just write off debts. And they don't care how the money gets paid, just that it does."

I'd seen it before inside Terre Haute. Men who'd gotten in too deep with the wrong people, who'd offered up anything and everything to clear their debts, including their wives and daughters. The thought of Andy trying to trade Zelda to settle a gambling debt made bile rise in my throat.

"You said you heard him on the phone," I said to Penny, keeping my voice carefully neutral. "About Zelda. About trading her to settle a debt."

She nodded, her face so pale I worried she might pass out. "I thought he was just… selling her. To some pervert." Her voice cracked. "I didn't know it was to pay off gambling debts. Does that make a difference?"

"Maybe," Knight said, already unpacking one of his equipment cases. "Means he's under pressure from multiple angles. Desperate men make mistakes."

"Or they get more dangerous," I countered.

Knight gave a grim nod. "That's why I'm upgrading everything today. Setting up facial recognition hardware on the cameras, tying it directly to alert systems. If he comes close enough for the camera to get a good view of him, it will send us an alert in real time."

Penny's breath hitched. "He'll keep trying, won't he? To get to us."

"Yeah," Knight said. "Not gonna try to sugarcoat it. But we'll be ready." He gripped Penny's shoulder briefly. "No one's gonna get to anyone in this place.

But especially not you three."

Penny nodded, but her eyes had that thousand-yard stare. Fear and anxiety shone through clearly.

"Hey," I said softly, putting my arm around her shoulders and squeezing gently. "We've got this."

Her gaze shifted to mine, and something in her expression shifted too. Not quite trust; she'd been burned too many times for that, but maybe something adjacent to it. Hope, maybe. Or at least a willingness to believe it was possible.

"The club's sending extra security," Knight said, not looking up from his work. "Round-the-clock patrols, two-man teams. No one gets in or out without ID and being cleared by the resident they're here to see."

"What about the girls?" Penny asked, glancing at her daughters. "They can't stay inside forever."

"Let us worry about that," I said. "We'll figure out safe ways for them to get fresh air."

I wanted to insist they move to the compound, but I knew as much as I wanted her safe, I couldn't risk terrorizing her by throwing her in an enclosed and locked compound with a bunch of big, rough-looking bikers. Who were also ex-cons.

Knight nodded. "I'm not just upgrading Haven's systems. Installing panic buttons in everyone's apartment, setting up secure communication channels, the whole fuckin' works, thanks to Tonio Miles." He glanced up from his laptop, looking Penny directly in the eyes. "This isn't our first rodeo. Won't be our last. The club protects its own. This whole place is getting a serious upgrade, starting with your space."

I watched Penny absorb this, saw the slight trembling of her lower lip before she pressed them together firmly. "Thank you," she whispered.

"Don't thank us yet," Knight said, turning back to his equipment. "Thank us when that bastard's no longer a threat."

I knew what Knight wasn't saying. There were ways to handle threats that didn't involve law enforcement. Ways that ensured problems stayed solved permanently. I'd been down that road once. The results had cost me fifteen years of my life, but I'd do it again in a heartbeat if it meant keeping Penny and her girls safe.

"I should check on the girls," Penny said, her voice stronger now.

"Go ahead," Knight said, nodding toward the children. "We'll finish up here."

As she walked away, Knight looked up at me, his gaze knowing. "You're in deep, brother."

I didn't bother denying it. "Yeah."

"Knuckles know?"

"Probably. Pretty sure the whole Goddamned club knows by now."

"You know what this might lead to," Knight said, his voice even lower.

"I do," I answered, watching Penny settle on the couch behind her daughters, her hand absently stroking Kira's hair. "And I'm OK with goin' back to prison if it means that fucker goes to hell." Whatever came next, I was all in. For her. For those girls. For all of them.

After Knight left to finish installing equipment in the security office, Penny and I drifted toward the far corner of the common room. We settled into the worn armchairs angled to face each other, still within sight of the kids but far enough away that our conversation wouldn't carry. The morning sun cast long shadows across the floor between us. I leaned forward, resting my elbows on my knees.

"You have questions," I said, keeping my voice low. Not a question, but an observation. I'd seen the way she watched me since our kiss yesterday, a mixture of curiosity and uncertainty in her gaze.

She nodded, tucking a strand of hair behind her ear. "Knight mentioned Terre Haute. You were there?"

"Fifteen years," I confirmed.

Her eyes widened slightly, but she didn't recoil. "What… what were you in for?"

I took a deep breath, steadying myself. I'd told this story before, but it never got easier. "I crushed a man's head with my bare hands."

She sucked in a breath, her eyes going wide. I might have gone for the shock factor to push her away. I shouldn't have kissed her, knowing there was every possibility I was going to kill her husband. To my surprise, she didn't look scared. Not in the way I thought she would be. "There has to be more to it than just some random guy who farted in the wrong direction." I recognized morbid humor for what it was and smiled. Likely, she was holding herself together with the barest of threads.

"My sister Julie. She was sixteen." I paused, gathering my thoughts. Penny reached out and took one of my hands, lending support when she knew the tragic ending and probably suspected what happened in between. "She was attacked and raped. I came home and found him still there. Still… hurting her." Penny's fingers tightened on my hand but she remained silent, letting me continue. "I pulled him off her…" I looked down at my hands, these massive instruments that had once taken a life. "Didn't even think about it. Just… reacted."

I glanced up, expecting to see fear or disgust in

her eyes, but found only a fierce understanding. "He deserved it." Her voice was a mere whisper, and she added her other hand to mine.

"I'm not proud of how I lost control," I continued. "But I'm not sorry he's dead. Julie deserved better than she got." The words felt like stones in my throat. "I was charged with second-degree murder. Could've been a worse sentence, but the prosecutor had a sister too. Understood, I guess."

"Fifteen years," Penny whispered. "For protecting your sister."

I shrugged my massive shoulders. "System doesn't care why you kill someone. Just that you did. And they're right. I got no problem with killin' someone who needs killin'. But if it means enough to me to do it myself, I'm fully prepared to accept the consequences. I don't know any other way to be."

"I don't know what you were like before, but I would have thought prison would have made you more aggressive. Not less."

"Prison changes you. Teaches you to watch everything. Everyone." I met her gaze directly. "But it also taught me control. How to channel anger, how to de-escalate instead of react. Had to learn that to survive. Otherwise, I'd be the biggest target in the yard. Literally. With my size, winning fights could be a detriment. I couldn't always avoid a fight, but I prevented more than I participated in." I shrugged. "I called it a win."

Penny nodded slowly. "I understand that." Her voice softened. "Living your whole life on high alert."

"It's different now," I admitted. "With my club. I found purpose. Found people worth protecting." I hesitated, then added, "People like you and your girls."

Her eyes flicked toward the children, still absorbed in their game. "I'm afraid all the time," she confessed, her voice barely audible. "Not just of Andy finding us. I'm afraid of making the wrong decisions. Of trusting the wrong people." She looked back at me. "Of failing them again."

"You didn't fail them," I said immediately, the words coming out more forcefully than I'd intended. "You got them out. You're keeping them safe. Most of all, you brought them here. There is no place you could be safer than with the men and women in Kiss of Death. The old ladies are just as much a part of everything as we are. They will all stand with you."

"I waited too long," she countered.

I shook my head. "Leaving an abuser isn't simple. You know that. You left when you could. When you had to."

"But at what cost?" Her eyes glistened with unshed tears. "They're so damaged, Tiny. Zelda doesn't let anyone near her. Kira barely spoke before we got here. They jump at shadows. They've seen and heard things no child should." She pressed her palms against her eyes. "And now I'm what? Dragging them into a world of outlaw bikers and ex-cons? What kind of mother does that make me?" I sat very still, absorbing her words. She'd put voice to the exact fears that had been plaguing me since our kiss yesterday. Since I'd started feeling things for her I had no right to feel. Hearing her mirror my own thoughts still hit me like a dick punch.

"Andy said something to me yesterday," I said carefully. "About how a judge would see you associating with people like me. People with records." I let out a slow breath. "He's not wrong."

Penny dropped her hands, looking at me with

sudden intensity. "Don't."

I shook my head, slow and deliberate. This time, I reached out for her hand. She didn't hesitate. She turned her palm up, curled her fingers tight and locked them around mine. "Haven works closely with a lawyer named Lana Thompson. Lana probably has more pull with family court than any other attorney in the system here. Not because she's on the take or anything. She's a by-the-book kind of lawyer. She's smart, she's more than a little bit devious, but she has earned the respect of every family court judge in the county. Ms. Thompson knows the guys in the club. She uses us to help support children who are testifying against their abusers. She knows we are the best protection the three of you could have. Judge Whitmore does too. She and Ms. Thompson sometimes work together when they need to remove a child from a home. Judge Whitmore has an uncanny ability to cut through red tape in the legal system when she needs to." I took a breath, looking into her eyes and holding her gaze. "So, yes. There is always a chance being near me could hurt you. What I'm asking…" I deliberately paused, needing her to understand I meant every Goddamned word I said. "What I'm asking is for you to trust me. I know it's a lot, but I'm still asking."

Penny studied me for a long moment, her gaze studying me intently. "Do you know what Zelda said to me last night? When we thought Andy might come back?"

I shook my head.

"She said 'Tiny won't let him in. Tiny promised.' My daughter who trusts no one, who questions everything… She believes in you." The knowledge hit me like a physical blow. I thought of Zelda's fierce protectiveness of her sister, her suspicious nature, her careful distance from everyone -- especially men. The thought that she trusted me enough to believe I'd keep my word. "And Kira," Penny continued. "You saw how she gave you Mr. Hoppers. That rabbit is her most precious possession. Her only comfort through years of fear. And she handed him to you without hesitation."

I remembered the weight of that threadbare toy in my hands, the solemn trust in Kira's eyes as she placed it there. "They're good kids," I said roughly.

"They see something in you," Penny said. "Something real. Something I see too." She leaned forward in her chair. "I've spent years being afraid, Tiny. Years looking over my shoulder, anticipating the next blow, the next insult, the next threat. I don't want to live like that anymore. And neither do my girls."

I wanted to believe her. God, how I wanted to. But doubt still gnawed at me. "I'm not exactly father material," I said. "Never thought I would be. After Julie… after prison… figured that part of life wasn't for me."

"I'm not asking you to be their father," Penny said. "They had one of those. He was a monster." She shook her head. "If you don't want us, if you don't want me, that's one thing. But please don't decide for us what's best. We've had enough of that to last a lifetime."

I looked across the room at the twins, at Kira's small smile as she concentrated on the game, at Zelda finally acting more like the kid she was. Then back at Penny, with her stubborn chin and eyes that had seen too much pain. They deserved better than what life had dealt them so far. Better than Andy. Better than me. But sitting there, watching Penny's quiet courage, I knew I couldn't walk away. Not unless she told me to.

We sat in silence for a moment. I watched

Penny's face, trying to read what was happening behind those guarded eyes. Her thumb brushed over my hand absently and the contact sent a jolt through me, unexpected and electric. I stared at our joined hands, her delicate fingers against my scarred knuckles, the contrast striking.

"Your hands," she said softly, tracing a callus with her thumb. "They're so strong." I swallowed hard, fighting the urge to pull away. Not because I didn't want her touch, God knew I did, but because her delicate touch felt undeserved. These hands had taken a life, had hurt people, had done things I wasn't proud of. And now they were being held with such tenderness. "Yesterday," she continued, her voice steady despite the pulse I could see fluttering at her throat, "when you hugged me. That was the first time in years I've felt truly safe. Not just physically safe. But… at ease." Her gaze met mine, direct and unflinching. "I didn't have to be on guard. I didn't have to be wary about what might set you off, what might trigger a storm. I could just… breathe." Christ, she was gutting me. And that I'd been the one to give her that feeling, however briefly. It humbled me.

"I've never wanted to hurt anyone who didn't deserve it," I said, my voice a low rumble. "And I've never wanted to protect anyone the way I want to protect you and your daughters."

She nodded, her gaze dropping to our joined hands. "I know. That's what scares me. Because I want to believe in that. In you." She looked up, her eyes vulnerable but determined. "And I haven't wanted to believe in anything, or anyone other than my girls, for a very long time."

I hesitated, searching her face for any hint of doubt or reluctance. Finding none, I leaned forward slowly, giving her every chance to pull away. She didn't. Instead, she met me halfway, her free hand coming up to rest against my cheek, brushing her fingers over my beard as she leaned in. The gentle touch nearly undid me.

Our lips met, and this time there was nothing tentative about it. Not like yesterday's brief, chaste contact. This was deliberate, deep, a seal on something unspoken but understood. Her lips were soft under mine, yielding yet demanding in their own quiet way. I cradled the back of her head with one hand, careful of my strength.

Time seemed to stop as we kissed, the background noise of the video game and the children's occasional shouts fading to a distant hum. I felt the slight tremble in her fingers against my face. There was hunger in the way she kissed me -- hunger, and a willingness to put herself in my care.

When we finally broke apart, I pressed my forehead against hers, our breath mingling in the small space between us. Her eyes remained closed for a moment, dark lashes fanned against her cheeks, and I memorized the sight, wanting to remember her exactly like this, open and unguarded.

"I don't have much," I said, the words rumbling up from deep in my chest. "Never did. But everything I do have is yours and the girls'. I'll take care of you." I brushed a strand of hair from her face, tucking it gently behind her ear. "Provide for you. And protect you with my life."

It was a vow, as binding to me as any oath I'd ever taken. More so, because it came not from obligation or expectation, but from something raw and real that had been growing inside me since the first moment I'd seen her with her daughters.

Penny's eyes opened, meeting mine with a clarity that took my breath away. "I believe you," she whispered. Three simple words, but coming from her, they might as well have been a declaration of love.

In the background, the video game continued, electronic music punctuated by sound effects and the occasional happy shout. I liked the sense of normalcy the kid's noise created. It made me feel like maybe I could have a family of my own. Maybe.

I glanced over Penny's shoulder and caught Zelda's gaze. She'd turned away from the game, her controller temporarily forgotten in her lap as she watched us. For a heartbeat, I expected to see disapproval or suspicion in her eyes. Instead, I found something that looked remarkably like… relief? Maybe even approval.

She held my gaze for a moment longer, her expression thoughtful. Then she gave me a small, deliberate nod before turning her attention back to the game. That tiny gesture hit me with the force of a physical blow.

I looked back at Penny, who was watching me with a mixture of hope and caution that made my heart ache. "Your daughter just gave us her blessing," I said softly, a hint of wonder in my voice.

Penny glanced over her shoulder just in time to see Zelda fully absorbed in the game again, though a small smile played at the corners of the girl's mouth.

"She likes you," Penny whispered. "God knows why. She doesn't like anyone." The attempt at humor didn't quite mask the emotion in her voice.

"I don't know either," I admitted with a grin. "But I'll spend every day trying to be worthy of her acceptance." I squeezed her hand gently. "Of all three of you."

Penny leaned forward, resting her head against my chest. I pulled Penny onto my lap and wrapped my arms around her. I wasn't sure if she'd let me, but she not only went willingly, she wound her arms around my neck and actually snuggled close.

Whatever came next, I was ready. I'd faced down some of the worst of the worst in prison, survived fifteen years in a hellhole. I never thought there was anything I could encounter that would rattle me. But nothing had prepared me for the fierce, protective love I felt for this woman and her daughters. And yeah. I was ready to call it love. I'd loved my sister. So Goddamned much. It was nothing compared to the emotional tie I was developing for Penny and her daughters. Nothing had prepared me for the weight of their trust, or the determination I felt to be worthy of it.

I held Penny a little tighter, silently renewing my vow to her, meaning it with every breath in my body from now until the day I died. *Everything I have. Everything I am. It's all yours now.*

Chapter Seven

Penny

I awoke with the memory of Tiny's arms around me, the echo of his promise still humming through my veins. For the first time in years, I fell asleep without lying awake listening for footsteps in the hall. One night of actual rest had left me feeling different, somehow lighter, as if an invisible weight had shifted on my shoulders. The girls had sensed it too, Zelda watching me with curious eyes over breakfast, Kira actually humming as she brushed her teeth. We had changed, all of us, by the simple act of being believed. Of someone actually giving a damn about what happened to us.

The morning had started like any other at Haven. Violet had brought in fresh bagels from the bakery down the street. Kira sat cross-legged on the floor sorting through a box of art supplies while Zelda sat with another resident's child and helped the young girl with a coloring page, encouraging her to color outside the lines because that's what rebels do.

A soft, chiming alarm sounded. At first, I didn't think much other than to wonder what the noise was. I honestly thought someone had set an alarm on their phone or something.

But it didn't stop. It didn't take long before the few people in the common room were looking around trying to figure out what was going on.

"Mom?" Zelda urged her sister from where they now played a video game. Apparently, the young girl had lost interest and gone to her mother. Both girls hurried to me.

"It's OK." I smiled, trying to reassure them, pulling them both in for a hug. "It's just an alarm.

Probably nothing."

Violet entered through the back, probably from the rear entrance. They kept the door locked and on a swipe card entry, but no one but residents and staff used that door. She had her phone pressed to her ear, her other hand gesturing urgently for everyone to move back the way she came. Which meant that back door. They were sending us outside?

Her voice was steady but strained as she spoke. "Yes. I'm moving everyone there now." Her eyes met mine across the room, and something in her expression made my stomach clench.

There were only two other women and one toddler besides me and the girls. Violet helped the three of them out as I followed with Zelda and Kira. Everyone else had either found a safe, permanent home or their abusers had been arrested. Or were otherwise out of the picture. Which I didn't ask too closely about lest I be tempted to ask for something I wasn't willing to have anyone here pay.

The doorway darkened as Tiny's massive frame filled it. My heart stuttered, relief and fear tangling together at the sight of him. His gaze found mine immediately, as if pulled by some invisible tether. The steady calm in his gaze anchored me even as the alarm continued its assault. If I hadn't known before this moment how much I needed and wanted Tiny in our lives, I knew it now.

"We need to evacuate," he murmured as he urged us to follow Violet. "Knight traced a bomb threat to a burner phone. He did some computer shit to find where the phone was when the call was made. Did more computer shit and found Andrew Harlow on a security camera within five meters of where Knight pinged that cell. Could be nothing, but we're not taking chances."

"Oh, God." I glanced down at the girls, but they held hands as Zelda urged Kira after Violet. I snagged our coats before turning to look at Tiny. I was sure my eyes were wide with shock.

"Don't worry, honey. Knight's all over this shit."

"I know." And I did. "You all are. Aren't you?"

Tiny held my gaze for a second before seeming to remember the urgency of the situation. He cleared his throat gruffly. "Yes. We need to go."

I nodded. "Yes. Sorry."

"Are the girls up ahead?"

"Yes. Zelda had Kira's hand and they followed Violet. I just stopped to get our jackets."

"Good. Come on. We'll catch up to everyone."

We hadn't gone far when we heard a small whimper, followed by a frantic cry from the child's mother up ahead. Tiny stopped and listened. "Go on, Penny. I'll find little Rita and bring her out. Let her mom know."

Tiny knelt to look under the big table next to the kitchen entrance. "Hey, there." He held out his hand for the child. "Want me to take you to your mom?" His voice was gentle, almost tender, as he spoke to her. The child nodded, wiping her eyes with the back of her hand.

"That's my brave girl." Tiny reached for the child.

I saw her mother and flagged the woman down. She sobbed in relief.

"Your mom's right here, and I'm watching out for both of you." The child crawled from under the table and threw herself at Tiny, crying as he held her.

Something twisted in my chest at the simple kindness of the gesture. It also didn't escape me that the child had gone to Tiny with no fuss at all. Rita clung to Tiny as he brought her to her mother. The girl didn't want to let go so Tiny guided us all out of the building. He didn't rush us but kept us moving as quickly as possible. It was like his energy was so calm it spilled over to the rest of us.

Outside, the morning sun seemed absurdly bright. There was a police vehicle just inside the gated drive at the side of the building. Knight had a tablet he held in front of the officer, pointing at something. I heard something overhead and looked up to see a drone fly overhead to the opposite end of the building.

Tiny kept us moving until we reached a grassy area under a big maple tree on the far inside corner of the property. About a hundred yards in the distance, I could see the compound of Kiss of Death adjacent to us. The fencing surrounded us too, but there was a separate chain-link fence between the two buildings.

"Stay here," he said, his voice low. "I need to go back and see what Knight needs. Violet has the key to the gate lock leading to the compound. If she takes you guys there, go. OK?"

I nodded. "OK."

Fear clutched at my throat. "Be careful," I whispered, unable to stop myself from reaching for his hand.

His fingers closed around mine for a brief moment, warm and strong. "I will be." His eyes held mine briefly and he smiled. Then he was gone, moving back toward the building with purposeful strides.

I realized how drastically my world had shifted. I had someone to stand between me and the girls and anyone who wanted to hurt us. Which is why I was never going to ask what had happened to the abusers who'd been rumored to have gone missing. Because unless I read the man completely wrong, Tiny would absolutely kill Andy. If he did, I'd never see Tiny again. He'd go to prison and they'd throw away the key.

At the thought, I had a need to be near my girls. I glanced around and saw Zelda headed my way, a panicked look on her face. My heart stuttered and I actually clutched my hand to my chest from the panic building rapidly inside me.

"Mommy! I can't find her! *Mommy*!" Zelda was full-on snot crying. I knew how she felt because I was seconds away from the same direction.

"Kira?" My voice cracked as I called her name, rising in pitch as panic clawed its way up my throat. "Kira!"

"She was right beside me!" Zelda's voice cracked as she continued to cry. "She let go of my hand when we got outside and I thought she was right with me!"

"It's OK," I gasped out. Shock was rapidly replacing the panic as my mind shut down the possibility of losing my daughter. "Stay with Violet, OK? I'll find her."

Violet saw us and took one look at my face before hurrying to my side. "What's wrong?"

"Kira's missing," I choked out. "Keep Zelda safe for me."

"Do you think she went around the front of the building?" Violet pulled out her phone as she looked in the direction she'd indicated. "But why would she leave Zelda? The girls are always close together."

Zelda gasped and her hands flew to her mouth, her eyes wide in horror.

"Zelda, honey?" I knelt in front of her, gently grasping her shoulders. "What's wrong?"

"She didn't have Mr. Hoppers."

"Oh, God. She went back inside for Mr. Hoppers!"

"I'm calling Knight," Violet said. But I turned and sprinted back toward the building.

I reached the police line but was stopped before I could get past. "Ma'am, you can't go in there." A police officer stepped into my path, his hand raised. "The building hasn't been cleared yet."

"My daughter is in there!" I tried to push past him, panic giving me strength I didn't know I possessed. "She's twelve years old, she's alone --"

"I understand, ma'am, but I can't let you enter. The bomb squad is working --"

"That's my baby!" My voice broke as tears blurred my vision. "Please, you have to let me --"

A shadow fell over us as Tiny appeared beside me, his presence suddenly filling the space between us and the officer. "I'll find her, Penny. Go back to Zelda and keep her calm, please."

The officer hesitated, glancing up at Tiny's imposing figure. "Sir, I can't authorize --"

But Tiny moved past him without looking at him. "Ain't asking permission."

Before the officer could stop him, Tiny was through the doors, disappearing into the building that might or might not contain an explosive device. I watched him go, heart in my throat. I felt Zelda's hand slip into mine as Violet put her arm around me and guided us back to the others. Rita and her mother were there along with three large men from the club. One of them sat cross-legged on the ground playing with Rita while the other two watched silently at a short distance. All the guys from the club we'd met were good about giving us space.

"He'll find her, Mom," Zelda whispered, and I

wasn't sure if she was reassuring me or herself.

* * *

Tiny

I moved through the common room, keeping my breathing even despite the urgency pounding in my chest. Knight had found something. They couldn't be sure what it was until the bomb squad got here, but it was concerning enough I didn't want Kira to be in here a moment longer than strictly necessary.

I called her name softly as I searched the common room. I found Mr. Hoppers where he'd fallen between two chairs when I kicked him with my forward stride. I'd bet my life this was what the child had been looking for.

I picked him up, then headed to the lift. When I reached their floor, I went straight to Penny's apartment. I rang the bell so she could see me through the security screen. "Kira? It's Tiny. You in there?"

The bomb squad hadn't cleared the building yet. The raw terror on Penny's face resonated with me. Because I kind of felt the same way when I saw her arguing with the police outside the tape.

"Kira? I need you to come out now, honey."

She opened the door, tears streaming down her face. She was sweating and trembling. "I can't find Mr. Hoppers, Tiny."

"I found him for you, honey." I handed her the rabbit and the poor thing burst into tears. The girls were both a heartbreaking mix of adult and child. Probably because their childhood hadn't been easy.

I didn't wait for her to calm down, scooping her up and holding her close as I left the apartment and headed back to the lift.

"Your mom and sister are pretty worried." I did

my best to reassure Kira, and I must be doing something right because she'd stopped shivering and wasn't nearly as tense. "They're waiting outside where it's safe and that's where we're going too."

Her lips trembled. "I -- I had to get Mr. Hoppers," she whispered, her voice barely audible. "I couldn't leave him."

"I know, honey." And I did. I remembered Julie and her stuffed horse, how it had been her one constant companion through the worst times. "He's your friend."

"I'm scared, Tiny." Her voice sounded small against the noise of the lift as we descended.

"Hey." I looked down into her upturned face. "I'm here with you, Kira. I will do everything I can to keep you safe." I held her gaze, willing her to believe me. "That's a promise. And I don't break promises."

Something shifted in her expression then, a flicker of trust breaking through the fear. She nodded up at me. "OK."

The lift stopped and I shoved open the gate. "Let's go find your mom and Zelda?"

She nodded, still clutching Mr. Hoppers with one arm while she bunched her other fist in my shirt. "You know what?" Kira's small voice broke the silence as we neared the back exit.

"What's that?"

"Mr. Hoppers says you're his favorite giant."

I felt a smile break across my face, wide and unexpected. "Well, that's an honor. Tell him he's my favorite rabbit."

She giggled softly against my neck, the sound washing through me like a healing balm. As I pushed open the door to step outside, I knew I'd walk through fire to hear that sound again. To keep this child, her sister, and their mother safe. "Thanks, Tiny. For coming for me but also for not making fun of me. I know I act childish sometimes, but it's how I keep from being terrified all the time."

"No one said you acted childish. Far as I can tell, you're a pre-teen hanging on to a childhood you never got to enjoy. Now you're free." I shrugged. "Laugh and play all you fu -- er -- flippin' want."

As we emerged outside, Kira really did let out a laugh. "I'm telling Caleb you said flippin' instead of the F-bomb."

I frowned down at her. "Little imp. You do and I'll tell him you're the one who put blue food coloring in his body wash the other day."

Her eyes got wide and her mouth formed an "O" of surprise. "You wouldn't!"

I smirked. "I might. You know. If you tell him I couldn't make myself drop the F-bomb in front of you."

She gave a disgruntled sigh and lay her head against my chest as we approached the rest of the group, including Penny and Zelda. "Fine. I won't tell. This time."

"I hear you. Next time, I'll censor myself at my own peril."

Some things were worth turning in my man card for. And I'd just found three of them.

* * *

Penny

I watched the door to the back exit, praying to see my daughter and Tiny when I saw Tiny reappearing with Kira in his arms. Riot wrapped his hand around my upper arm gently, holding me back while Violet did the same with Zelda, leaning down to whisper to her. The police were still securing the area, though no one stopped Tiny as he came our way. My heart hammered against my ribs as Tiny approached, Kira's small frame nestled against his massive chest like she weighed nothing at all, Mr. Hoppers clutched tightly in her hand.

"Wait until he's through the tape," Violet murmured, her grip firm but gentle on my arm. "We need to stay a safe distance away. In fact, we should move farther back."

Every second felt like an eternity. Tiny's eyes found mine across the distance, and something in his gaze helped me breathe. He said something to Kira that made her smile.

When they finally cleared the police line, Tiny knelt and set Kira on her feet. I broke free from Violet's hold and rushed forward, Zelda right beside me. We collapsed into a trembling group hug, my fingers tangling in Kira's hair as I pulled both girls against me.

"I'm sorry, Mom," Kira whispered against my neck. "I couldn't leave Mr. Hoppers."

"Don't ever do that again," I choked out, unable to keep the tremor from my voice. "Nothing -- no toy, nothing -- is worth your life, baby."

"Tiny found him for me," she said, holding up the ragged rabbit like it was made of gold. "He wasn't even mad at me."

I looked up at Tiny, who stood watching us with an expression I couldn't quite read -- relief mixed with something deeper, something that made my chest tighten. "Thank you," I mouthed over the girls' heads.

He nodded, a small smile lifting the corner of his mouth. I wanted to say more, to throw my arms around him like I had yesterday, but Knight approached with a grim expression that made my blood run cold again.

"We found something," Knight said quietly to Tiny, holding out a tablet. "Front corner of the building. The facial recognition software notified me of the hit a minute after I got the bomb threat, so I didn't pay attention to it until I knew we had everyone safe." He looked frustrated. Likely with himself.

"And thank God you did, Knight," I interjected. "The time it took you to answer an alert might have made a difference in the outcome of this if this thing is real."

"As it turns out, it wasn't a bomb." Knight scrubbed the back of his neck in agitation. "I'm pretty sure he was gauging our response. What we prioritize and which way we moved everyone. Maybe even confirming how many people we had in this building." He shared a look with Tiny. "Putting Haven this close to the compound was the best thing we could have done for this place. The closer Haven is, the faster our guys can get here in an emergency."

On impulse, I looked over at the expanse of warehouses about the length of a football field away from us. Standing at the gate were several men from the compound. I recognized all of them, and that's when I realized they'd likely been doing small errands and showing up for short amounts of time every couple of days to get us all used to seeing them. So we'd know they were safe.

Christ, I felt like I'd fallen down a rabbit hole and into an alternate universe where men weren't abusive assholes and actually protected people precious to them.

Riot and Violet exchanged quick looks. "We need to move the other residents immediately," Violet said. "I'll call our sister shelter in Memphis. They should be able to take Rita and her mother tonight. Andrea's sister is supposed to meet her at the airport in a couple of hours, so she'll be safe."

Riot nodded. "Got it covered."

I ducked my head, shame washing over me in a hot wave. "This is my fault. I brought this down on everyone."

"No." Tiny's voice was firm, leaving no room for argument. "This is on him. No one else. This is exactly why Ms. Thompson sent you to us. Most of the time, intimidation works great. Occasionally someone like Andy comes along and we have to get a bit more… firm than we'd like, but we're not squeamish about it either."

Tiny moved closer, placing a gentle hand on my shoulder. "Can I talk to you for a minute?" he asked quietly. "Just over here."

I nodded, glancing at the girls. "Stay with Violet," I told them. "I'll be right back."

Tiny guided me a few steps away, just far enough that we couldn't be overheard. He surprised me by dropping to one knee so our gazes were closer to eyelevel, his massive frame folding down to meet mine. The gesture struck me as deeply intimate, a man of his size making himself smaller, more accessible.

"Listen," he said, his voice low and urgent. "Haven isn't safe anymore. Not until we get permanent eyes on this guy."

I nodded, blinking back tears. "I know."

"Come to the compound," he said. "To Kiss of Death. We have space. There's several three-bedroom apartments for you to choose from. Violet and Hannah can let you pick one you like. You'd be inside a locked compound in the middle of hard men who will defend you to the death. You'll be safer there than you could possibly be anywhere else." I stared at him, caught off guard by the directness of the offer. "Honestly, it's not just about safety," he continued, his eyes never leaving mine. "It's about giving us time. Real time together. To figure out what this is between us without looking over our shoulders every minute."

My heart pounded as relief washed over me at the possibility of true safety, but I hesitated, the old fears rising up. "The girls… surrounded by so many men they don't know…"

"Mom?" Zelda's voice came from behind me. I turned to find her standing a few feet away, her expression uncharacteristically vulnerable. She must have followed us, listening to our conversation.

"Zelda, honey, I told you to stay with Violet --"

"I don't want to sleep here anymore, Mom." Her voice was small but firm. "Neither does Kira. We want to be near Tiny."

I stared at my daughter in disbelief. Zelda, my fierce protector, my suspicious, wary child who trusted no one, was asking to go with Tiny. The significance of it staggered me.

"You do?"

She nodded, her eyes flicking to Tiny before settling back on me. "He keeps his promises." She stated it as if it were the simplest, most obvious truth in the world. She shrugged. "Also, Kira said Mr. Hoppers likes him, so…"

A surprised laugh escaped me, sounding almost like a sob. "Well, if Mr. Hoppers approves…"

I turned back to Tiny, who was watching Zelda with a mixture of surprise and something that looked suspiciously like pride. "You're sure about this?" I asked him quietly. "About us?"

"I've never been more sure of anything in my

life," he said simply.

I took a deep breath, feeling something shift inside me, my fear dissolving like mist. "OK," I whispered. "We'll come."

His face broke into a smile that transformed his entire countenance, making him look younger, lighter. He rose to his feet and turned to Zelda. "Thank you for your trust," he said with utter sincerity. "I won't let you down."

She lifted her chin, studying him closely. "You better not." Tiny winked at her.

I reached for her hand, squeezing it gently. "Let's go tell your sister." As we walked back to where Kira waited with Violet, I felt the weight of the decision settling over me -- not as a burden, but as a foundation. Something solid to build upon.

For the first time in years, we were moving toward something instead of running away. It terrified me and thrilled me in equal measure. But one glance at Tiny walking beside us, his presence both protective and patient, told me we were making the right choice. Whatever came next, we would face it together.

Chapter Eight

Penny

The Kiss of Death compound loomed before us, a series of massive warehouses forming a grid. My daughters pressed against me as we approached, Kira's small fingers twisting into the hem of my jacket while Zelda looked around us with an odd mixture of wariness and wonder. Tiny gripped the steering wheel loosely as we drove through the gate. A chain-link fence seemed to surround the entire property. I knew it was at the lower end next to Haven, but really, the compound was really massive. The walkways between the buildings were covered with camo netting, and there were guys lounging next to buildings shooting the shit. Except when I looked closer, they were actually on pretty high alert. Made me wonder if the whole posture happened by design.

Tiny drove us in a large Bronco past the first warehouse, down the gravel path between the buildings to what had to be the center of the compound. There was a grassy courtyard-like area with a few small trees, flower gardens, and stone benches under the shade of the trees. He'd assured me we'd all love it here, but I had learned not to get my hopes up.

Once out of the vehicle, Tiny led us inside the warehouse in front of the courtyard. Other than the reception area, the place looked pretty close to Haven. Made sense. I got the feeling there was more to the relationship between Haven and Kiss of Death than was widely known. And in the most positive of ways. I'd bet my last dollar most of the funding came from the club in the form of money and, more importantly, labor and security.

"The bottom two floors of the outer warehouses are for club business," Knight explained as we walked inside the building. "Upper floors are apartments. The inner buildings are all residential."

"It's like a fortress," I murmured.

Tiny glanced back, a small smile lifting his beard. "That's the idea."

We passed three men inside the main room, painting the back wall by the lift. I recognized Griffin and Ranger but was unfamiliar with the third guy. They paused to acknowledge Tiny and all of us with subtle nods and friendly smiles. None of them stared or made any attempt to engage beyond the quiet, friendly greeting. Their restraint surprised me. Andy's friends had always demanded attention, inserting themselves into my personal space without permission.

"Everyone knows you're under our protection," Tiny said quietly, as if reading my thoughts. "No one will bother you unless invited to. But every single one of them will do anything you ask of them. They're all good men."

The knot in my chest loosened slightly at his words. "Is this place even real? Are we going to wake up one day and find we fell out of the frying pan into the fire?" I knew I sounded more than a little crazy, but there had to be a downside here. I never got this lucky.

Tiny chuckled, not taking offense in any way. "It's real, honey. We won't…" He trailed off before closing the lift and set it to go to the third floor. "We won't, but more importantly, *I* won't let you down, Penny. You and the girls are my first priority. The club knows this, and they will back me with anything I need."

"He's right, Penny." Knight stepped off the lift,

looking back over his shoulder. "Ain't a person in this place wouldn't help you in any way necessary. And I don't mean just the men. The old ladies already love you and the girls. Expect them to bring groceries and essentials as well as a few housewarming gifts."

"I hope we won't be in your way too long," I said as we followed him to the apartment they were letting us use. "We're causing you so many problems…" I trailed off, still upset over not being able to find Kira.

Knight glanced from me to Tiny and raised an eyebrow. "Oh, I don't think you'll be leaving. You might have to fight Tiny for closet space, but I have a feeling you'll work something out. Besides, you aren't the problem. None of this is your fault. If you believe nothing else any of us tells you, believe that, Penny." He gave me a gentle smile. It took me a few days to get used to Knight's appearance when we'd first met him. Pretty much every spare inch of visible skin was covered in tattoos. Even the whites of his eyes had been tattooed black. I'd heard of sclera tattooing but never seen it. While I admitted he looked really cool *now*, when I'd first met him I had trouble meeting his gaze head-on.

Knight coded our key cards and showed us how to use them. The girls had rolled their eyes at him and done it themselves while Knight looked contrite before breaking into a grin, making Kira actually laugh.

"This one's yours, if you like it." Knight gestured at the open living room. "Go take a look. If you think you'll be comfortable here, I'll let you set a PIN for the door and the security system."

"We need a security system inside here?" I know my expression was confused. Then it dawned on me, and I actually felt my face go red. "You have security so we feel safe. Like it really was a leased apartment."

Tiny shrugged. "We don't want anyone here who doesn't want to be here. And we don't take people under our protection we intend on harming in any way. We know this. The women who've come here over the last couple of years didn't always feel safe with strangers. As I'm sure you don't." He wasn't wrong. But the fact was, I did feel safe.

"It never even crossed my mind I wouldn't be safe in this apartment. I feel safer with everyone in your club than I have my entire life."

"Do we each get our own room, Mom?" Zelda rested her hand on her hip as she stood outside one of the bedrooms. Kira was at the door to the room across the hall from the one Zelda had apparently claimed even if she pretended to ask.

"I suppose that depends on how many bedrooms there are."

"Three." Knight said without hesitation. "Master bedroom is on the other end of the apartment.

"Wow. This place would cost a fortune to rent. It's really nice," I said, meaning it.

The kitchen/dining area was an open plan with a large picture window leading to a balcony. Heavy drapes could be pulled for privacy or to block the sun if necessary.

"The windows are bulletproof," Tiny said, "as well as tinted so no one can see inside. It would be best if you pulled the curtains at night if you've got the lights on, and to not go out on the balcony until we've taken care of this guy."

"You'll get no arguments from us. We will do exactly what you tell us to." I met Tiny's gaze, wanting him to know I meant what I said. "I trust you, Tiny. You and your club."

"Mom!" Zelda snapped her fingers impatiently.

"Do we get our own room or not?"

I sighed and closed my eyes, even as I smiled. "Yes, Zelda. You and Kira can each have your own room." That was the only permission they needed. Each girl claimed her room and started making herself at home.

"The women brought care packages to all of you. There's clothes and toiletries. Make me a list of everything you need, and I'll make it happen.

"I'll leave you guys to it." Knight smiled at me, excusing himself.

Tiny shifted his weight, uncharacteristically hesitant. "The apartment across the hall is vacant," he said, his deep voice pitched low. "I was thinking I might take it. Just to be close. In case you need anything."

I blinked, surprised by the suggestion. "You don't live here already?"

He shook his head. "My apartment's in the east building. But I thought… you know, with everything that's happened…"

I understood what he wasn't saying. He wanted to be near enough to protect us without crowding us. The thoughtfulness of it struck me, but I hesitated. Having him so close felt like a commitment to whatever was growing between us.

"I don't know," I began, my voice uncertain. "The girls --"

"I think it's a good idea," Zelda said from the hallway, startling both of us. She stood in the doorway to her newly claimed bedroom, arms crossed over her chest, but her voice held none of its usual suspicion.

"You do?" I couldn't keep the surprise from my voice.

She nodded, her eyes flicking briefly to Tiny

before meeting mine again. "If Dad shows up here, I want Tiny close enough to stop him."

"Me too," Kira added, appearing beside her sister. She hugged Mr. Hoppers to her chest. "Mr. Hoppers feels safer with Tiny nearby, too."

I glanced at Tiny, who looked as stunned as I felt by this vote of confidence from my usually wary daughters. His expression softened, the hard lines of his face gentling into something that made my chest tighten in an entirely different way.

"OK," I said finally. "Because if it makes Mr. Hoppers feel better, then it has to be done. Right?"

Relief flashed across his features, and he smiled down at me. "I'll get my stuff moved over today, so I'll be there tonight."

Knight returned with our few belongings from Haven. It wasn't much, but it was ours.

"Give me a couple of hours and I'll have some more things for you and the girls," Tiny said. "I'll get you all a key and your own code to my door. In case you need me."

"You coming back tonight or what?" Zelda gave Tiny an impatient look, like she was put out with him or something.

Tiny blinked at her, clearly confused. "Well, once I got my stuff moved I thought I'd come back and spend some time with you guys before bed. Too soon?" He looked from Zelda to me, clearly confused.

Zelda gave him a level look. "It's movie night. You need to bring junk food. Don't come back if you can't do your part." She scowled before heading back to her room.

"Well." Tiny scratched the back of his neck and grinned. "Guess I have my orders."

* * *

The knock at the door came just after seven. At the monitor panel on the wall beside the door, I saw Tiny standing in the hallway, his arms loaded with what looked like movie night supplies. He peered around an enormous basket piled so high he was having trouble seeing around it. He turned to the side and directed a strained smile at the security monitor.

I opened the door and as he turned to face front, three chip bags tumbled to the floor. He jerked in reaction, likely thinking he'd catch one or more of the bags. Why I have no idea, because movement of any kind guaranteed the whole thing would topple like the house of cards he'd built with Zelda and Kira.

As expected, it did. The only thing he managed to not drop were the cans of soda in the bottom of the basket. Microwave popcorn, chips (of course), various bags of candy, salsa (in a plastic jar, thank God), and a list of apps and passwords for any kind of streaming service the girls could possibly think up. The ordinary domesticity of the situation struck me as absurdly endearing. This enormous man, clutching a laundry basket full of junk food for movie night like precious cargo. Except most of it was now on the floor.

Tiny stood there looking as shocked as a man could. I had to cover my mouth to keep from laughing. Which lasted until I heard Zelda heft a loud, exasperated sigh. "I mean, at least you didn't bring lame junk food. Like celery sticks and apples with peanut butter or something."

Tiny gave a sigh of relief as he knelt to pick up the dropped snacks. Of course, I helped him. Zelda just looked down at him with her hands on her hips taking in the junk food smorgasbord. "You get a pass for dropping all the stuff since you got a good variety, but don't let it happen again."

Kira punched her sister in the tit as she hurried to help.

"Hey! Why'd you do that?"

"Don't be mean to Tiny," Kira said as she knelt to help us pick up the various bags. "Just because he didn't prove to be as lame as you thought and bring pseudo-junk food doesn't mean it's his fault."

Tiny gave Kira a solemn look. "I spent fifteen years in prison. Junk food ain't peanut butter and celery." As if that explained the whole thing.

Kira broke out in an absolutely beautiful smile. "I knew you'd understand!"

The girls scooped up all the stuff Tiny had brought and headed to the kitchen, jabbering and bickering good naturedly as they went.

"Why did you look so relieved when Zelda preferred real junk food instead of healthy food?"

Tiny glanced around, leaning to the side so he could see around me, probably to see where the girls were. Then he turned back to me and whispered. "Because I had a fruit and veggie tray. Caleb plucked it out of my hands and replaced it with that basket right before I knocked. Didn't say anything other than 'You're welcome' and kept going." I actually snorted a laugh before Tiny gave me a pained look and hunched his shoulders. "Shh!" he hissed out. "If Zelda hears, I'll never live it down."

"Why would you bring a veggie tray? Fruit, I could see. But vegetables?"

"I thought you might not approve of real junk food." He looked so distressed now I couldn't help but wrap my arms around his middle and hug him.

Just like that, I fell completely for this big man and his even bigger heart. There were obstacles to work out, for sure, but this was a man I desperately needed in my life for so many reasons I couldn't list them all. The fact he cared about my feelings with regard to something as simple as what my girls ate told me he'd be more of a father to Zelda and Kira than Andy had ever been.

It didn't take long for the girls to pick the silliest, most annoying rom-com in the whole entire universe. While the opening credits were going, they spread out everything Tiny had brought on the coffee table and sat on a quilt in front of the big TV.

When everything was ready, Tiny settled on one end of the couch. The message was clear. I could sit as close or as far away as I wanted. I smiled at him. Despite knowing Andy still had to be dealt with, despite the terror from earlier, I hadn't felt this contented in my entire life. There was nowhere I wanted to sit other than right next to Tiny.

So I sat next to him, tucked my legs under myself, and snuggled against Tiny. I looked up at him as he gazed down at me, happiness radiating from him. Slowly, probably to give me time to change my mind, Tiny moved one arm around my shoulders and pulled me close. His whole body relaxed, and he slouched comfortably in the cushions. I was pretty sure if I Googled the phrase "satisfied expression" there would be a picture of Tiny with the exact look on his face he was wearing now.

I was sure Tiny would hate the movie they picked out. Likely that was why they chose it. Instead, he surprised us all by laughing through the whole movie, commenting occasionally when one of the girls did. By the end of it, I was certain he'd enjoyed the movie more than the girls had, while Zelda, Kira, and I got our entertainment from watching Tiny.

"Never would have pegged you for the chick

flick kind of guy." Zelda sighed and shook her head. "I really thought we'd get at least a groan out of him."

"What about slasher films?" Kira tilted her head to the side studying Tiny. "Yeah. I think maybe we need to watch a horror movie next."

Tiny's eyes got wide and he shook his head slightly. "Um, aren't the two of you a little young for horror movies?"

Zelda rolled her eyes. "We're twelve. Not two."

Right.

At the end of the film, both girls were up on the couch with us. OK, so they were on the couch, one on each side of Tiny, squealing at the scary parts and burying their faces in the vicinity of his armpit. Every time they squealed, he laughed. Christ, that deep chuckle warmed my heart. I had my arm around Kira, and she alternated between me and Tiny for comfort. It was a magical moment.

"Maybe we should call it a night." Tiny reached for the remote, but both girls let out outraged protests, Zelda snatching the remote and shoving it in the couch cushion.

"Touch the TV, you'll find blue food coloring in your body wash." Zelda snarled her remark but didn't take her focus off the television. When the creepy killer struck, they both screamed. Popcorn and M&Ms went flying. Tiny pulled both girls close and chuckled through the blood and gore. Both girls turned away, though Zelda turned her head to the side so she had one eye on the screen.

When my laughter joined Tiny's, Kira turned to me and hid her face against my shoulder, hanging on to my arm for dear life. "I really thought you two were past the stage where you'd have nightmares from scary movies, but I'm beginning to wonder."

"Mom," Zelda said, poking her head up again. "The threat of nightmares is half the fun."

"Yeah?" I raised my eyebrows at her. "What's the other half of the fun?"

She smirked. "Waking you and Tiny up at zero-dark-thirty when we have those nightmares."

Beside me, with her face mashed into my side, Kira giggled. It struck me how sickeningly sweet all this was. And I loved every fucking second of it. This was the family I should have had. It was the family I wanted. A protective man who was willing and able to keep us safe instead of being the one to cause the harm.

I felt myself grinning at Zelda, laughter threatened to bubble up from deep inside me, but I held back. Not because I didn't want to show my humor, but because the image that popped in my mind was… not something I wanted to try to explain to my daughters since my face felt hot. And, yeah, I fully admit that Zelda had likely said what she had on purpose. I probably glowed like a firefly's ass. "That's it. Time for bed."

The girls grumbled and groaned, but ultimately left giggling, both of them going to Kira's bedroom. Then Kira opened the door, poked out her head, and addressed Tiny. "You're not gonna leave. Right?"

"I'll be right across the hall. Moved all my stuff there this afternoon." Tiny gave her a reassuring smile as he stood as if to leave.

There was a flurry of whispers and lowered voices as the girls conversed. It quickly became obvious they were arguing about something. The whispered conversation continued, escalating. I thought I heard slapping and a thump or two before everything suddenly stopped. I glanced at Tiny who shrugged slightly, shaking his head, a puzzled look on his face.

Kira stepped outside her room once again, glancing back at her sister before giving Tiny a pleading gesture. "Will you stay here tonight?" She glanced back inside the room but didn't move.

"Uh." Tiny glanced at me, a puzzled look on his face. "I mean, yeah. If you think I need to. Couch is pretty comfortable."

There was more whispering, this time mostly on Zelda's part. Kira looked back and forth from us to Zelda before finally twisting her fingers together tightly, something she did when she was nervous.

"Well, um…" She glanced back at Zelda. Again.

"Spit it out, honey." I had to fight the smile. Last thing I wanted to do was to make Kira think I was making fun of her, but I knew in my heart whatever was about to come out of her mouth was, A) a lie, B) had been Zelda's idea, and C) Kira knew she was about to say something Zelda thought we'd buy more coming from Kira rather than her. And Kira was nervous about it.

Finally, Kira sighed and shook her head sadly. "I'm really sorry, Mom." She took a breath, then looked at Tiny. Her expression was so earnest and concerned I was starting to get worried. "Tiny, Mom has this thing about scary movies. She'll be terrified if she stays by herself. Do you think that, maybe you wouldn't mind sleeping in her room? With her? You know. In case she wakes up screaming in terror. The screams can sometimes be blood-chilling…" Her voice broke on the last word as if she were driven to tears by the whole thing. The child actually covered her mouth with the back of her hand like she was some delicate feminine flower faced with unspeakable horror.

I was speechless. Like, I opened my mouth and

nothing came out. I heard Zelda's small giggle, then Kira pursed her lips before ducking her head.

"I'm so sorry!" Kira sobbed, putting her hand over her face in despair. "It's so horrible when she has those dreams, I'm terrified zombies are just down the hall." Oh, the little imp was good. "Just promise you won't leave her tonight, Tiny. Please. For me and Zelda. We really need our beauty sleep."

Apparently, that was all Zelda could take. Peals of laughter rang out from Kira's bedroom. Kira ducked inside and slammed the door shut.

Tiny plopped back down on the couch beside me. We sat there in silence. Until Tiny snorted out a laugh. Then chuckled. Then we were both laughing so hard tears were rolling down our cheeks. I slumped against Tiny and he wrapped his arms around me and pulled me sideways onto his lap as we continued to laugh.

Chapter Nine

Penny

"I'm so sorry." I covered my mouth with my hand to hide the smile. There was no way I could hide otherwise.

Tiny scrubbed the back of his neck with his hand. For the first time I noticed a tinge of pink on his cheeks above the beard. "I mean, I expected that from Zelda. Not Kira." The sight of the poor man looking so confused and slightly embarrassed made me give in to the mirth inside me. The earlier bout of laughing had my belly still sore, but it felt so good to laugh. So fucking good.

Tiny tightened his arms around me and rested his chin on my head. "Might be at my expense, but I'll take it. Anything to hear you laughing like this."

I smiled up at him, out of breath and smiling so much my face hurt. "I swear I'm not laughing at you. I swear. It's…"

"I know. The girls." He sighed. "I have the feeling life is never going to be dull with them around. Just promise you won't hold it against me if I have to violate my parole when some knucklehead comes around trying to date one of them. I'm not sure it's going to go well when that happens."

That got me laughing again and I hugged Tiny tight, nuzzling his neck with my face. His skin carried a faint scent of clean sweat and maybe gasoline mixed with a hint of evergreen. Like he'd been fiddling with the Christmas tree at Haven. "I'm sure your brothers here will keep you out of trouble. Besides, you honestly think Zelda is going to stand for anyone trying to date her sister?"

"Right. I forgot who I was talking about. Because

any boy brave enough to try to date Zelda has bigger *cojones* than I do."

Again, I laughed. When was the last time I'd felt this carefree? Like one of those Goddamned Christmas movies the girls kept on from November until January. As I smiled up into Tiny's face, I saw so much affection and satisfaction on his face I almost thought maybe he felt as much for me as I did for him. Maybe he did. He'd promised to take care of us.

Unable to stop myself, I reached up and stroked his beard. The big man leaned into my touch, his eyes shutting as if in bliss. When he looked down at me with what looked almost like euphoria, I thought maybe this man needed me as much as I needed him. I smiled back, urging him to meet me halfway with his kiss. He did.

His kiss was at once rough and gentle, like he fought hard for control and feared he was losing the precarious hold he had. The rumble in his chest vibrated against me as he grunted his approval. His strong arms felt so good as he squeezed me tight while he kissed me. It wasn't sweet. It was hunger and need and the kind of desperation that made me melt for him instantly. I moaned into his mouth, clutching at his neck, digging my fingers into the solid muscle there.

Then he seemed to remember where we were. Which was a good thing because I was really too far gone to care. He pulled back slightly, pressing his forehead to mine, his breathing as ragged as mine. "Christ, Penny. Not here. Those little hooligans are probably watching."

As if to illustrate his point I heard, "Get a room, you two," from the vicinity of Kira's bedroom door.

"I swear to God, Zelda, one of these days you and I really need to sit down and have a serious discussion about boundaries."

"Says the woman lip-locked to the biker. Go do whatever icky stuff you adults do and seal this deal. Kira and I want Tiny to be our dad, so we've decided to force the issue."

"Christ, my life," I muttered. "Just keep thinking of it as icky stuff and everything will be fine."

"Whatever." She waved her hand dismissively as she turned back to Kira's room and shut the door once again.

"Guess we have our marching orders." I grinned up at Tiny.

He grunted, then stood with me in his arms. The guy didn't seem to strain at all. I mean, I knew he was strong, but this was on a whole other level. There was no way to deny the thrill I got from his casual show of strength as he carried me to the master bedroom. On the other end of the apartment from the girls.

Once safely inside the bedroom with the door shut -- and locked -- Tiny laid me gently on the bed before covering me with his deliciously large frame. He settled himself between my thighs and I squeezed his hips reflexively. He kissed me once more before resting his weight on his forearms and stroking my hair as he looked down into my face.

"I never expected this," he said quietly. "When you showed up at Haven, I just wanted to help. I didn't expect to… care so much. About all three of you."

The admission hung between us, honest and vulnerable.

"I'm afraid to trust this," I admitted, my voice barely audible. "But I'm going to trust in you. I've was wrong before. When I chose Andy. So wrong. If I'm wrong about you, I honestly don't think I'll ever be able to trust anyone ever again."

Instead of being annoyed or even angry at a suggestion he'd do something to break my trust, Tiny smiled down at me. "I'll earn your trust, baby. Until then, give me the benefit of the doubt. I swear I will protect you and the girls. Body and heart."

My gaze traced the contours of his face, his thick beard, and his gentle eyes that belied his intimidating appearance. I felt safe with him in a way I hadn't with anyone in years.

"Penny," he said, his voice dropping lower. "Can I kiss you again?" The directness of his question, the way he sought permission instead of assuming when I'd already kissed him before, made my heart swell. This wasn't a man to ever hurt any of us. Hadn't he already proven he would protect us with his life when he went to find Kira?

I nodded, unable to form words around the sudden tightness in my throat. Tiny leaned down, closing the distance between us with careful deliberation. His hand came up to cup my cheek, his touch featherlight. And then his lips were on mine again, and the world narrowed to just this, to his gentle kiss and the feeling of finally coming home.

What began as a gentle kiss quickly transformed into something deeper, hotter, as if a dam had broken inside both of us. His beard tickled my skin as his mouth moved against mine, no longer tentative but hungry. I surprised myself with how much I fought for this, sliding my hands up his massive chest to grip his shoulders, feeling the solid muscle beneath his shirt. I'm not sure I'd ever felt this level of desire and raw lust, of enjoying the simple pleasure of being touched by someone who treasured rather than hurt.

I shoved my hands under the hem of his shirt, tugging the soft material upward with trembling hands. I wanted to see him, all of him. Tiny helped me, pulling the fabric over his head and tossing it aside. The sight of his bare chest made my breath catch -- broad and powerful, covered in a tapestry of scars and tattoos as well as a dusting of light hair trailing from his chest to his navel.

I knew he wouldn't strip me without my express permission. Not this first time. Not until he was certain I was all in with him. That's who Tiny was.

Smiling up at him, I wiggled out of my T-shirt and bra, leaving my chest bare. It felt right. I loved the hunger in his gaze as he shifted his weight off me so he could touch me easily without resting his full weight on me. While I appreciated the thought, I was certain I'd be demanding otherwise at some point. Maybe not today, but someday.

"God, you're beautiful," he whispered, his eyes never leaving my face even as my bra was revealed, then discarded. The Viking-like braids in his beard swayed slightly as he leaned in to place a gentle kiss on my collarbone.

I'd never felt small before, not in the way I did with Tiny. His hands could span my waist completely, his shoulders twice the width of mine. Our size difference was almost cartoonish, yet somehow, this disparity didn't frighten me. Instead, the sense of safety I felt with him told me exactly how much I trusted him subconsciously. Maybe it was time for the rest of me to catch up.

I moved my hands to the waistband of his jeans, popping the button free. "Off," I commanded softly, and he smiled, moving from the bed to shed them along with his boxers.

I couldn't help the small gasp that escaped me at the sight of him fully naked. He was proportional in every way, impressive and intimidating. Instead of calling a halt or pulling things back slightly, I found my mouth watering for a taste.

As if sensing my thoughts, Tiny knelt on the bed, keeping a small distance between us. "We go at your pace," he said. "Always."

That simple promise unraveled something in me. I stood, shedding my remaining clothes. There was a strangely powerful feeling in my nakedness as his hungry gaze took me in. I placed my hands on his chest and guided him back to the bed. When the backs of his knees reached the mattress, I pushed gently. He went willingly, lying back against the pillows, his gaze never leaving mine as I climbed over him, straddling his waist.

He found my hips with his strong hands, the calluses on his palms an erotic abrasion against my skin. I leaned down to kiss him, my hair falling around us like a curtain. His beard tickled my skin as our mouths met. Slowly, I rocked against his cock, my clit sliding over the thick base with each thrust of my hips. His cock pulsed in readiness beneath me. My pussy responded eagerly, wet and ready for him in a way I'd never experienced. He hadn't done more than cover my breast with his big hand and look at me like I was the most beautiful, most precious thing in his world. I experienced genuine desire. The need to get some kind of physical release I knew would fundamentally change who I was forever.

"You're in control here," he murmured against my lips. "We don't do anything you don't want."

"I want you to fuck me, Tiny. I think I need it."

"There should be condoms in the nightstand. I've never had unprotected sex and… well, no one was foolish enough to try and make me his bitch in prison, but this first time, since we haven't talked about it..."

I barked out an unexpected laugh. "Yeah. No life-changing decisions on the spur of the moment."

I stretched to open the nightstand drawer. Sure enough, an unopened box of condoms lay inside. Once I had the box opened, I pulled out a packet and opened it, moving back to rest on his upper thighs as I rolled the thin barrier over his cock. Then I shifted higher up on his body to straddle his hips once more. Reaching between us, I guided him to my entrance and slowly sank down onto him. The stretch was intense, almost overwhelming, but not painful. My eyes fluttered shut as I took him fully inside me, my body adjusting to his size. His hands on my hips remained steady, not pushing, not pulling, just supporting.

I set a slow pace at first, rising and falling in a gentle rhythm. Tiny watched me with hooded eyes, his breathing ragged but controlled. Every time I moved, his fingers tightened slightly on my hips, then relaxed, as if he was reminding himself to let me lead.

The sensation built slowly, like waves lapping at a shore. I leaned forward, changing the angle, and a jolt of pleasure shot through me. "Oh," I gasped, surprised by the intensity.

"Good?" he asked, his voice as strained as mine sounded.

I nodded, increasing my pace slightly. The feeling of control, of setting the rhythm, of seeing this powerful man yielding to me... The experience was intoxicating.

As my pleasure grew, my movements got faster. I rose and fell, snapping my hips forward as I leaned over him. I braced my hands on his chest as I continued to fuck him as best I could. I had experience with sex, but never in a dominant position.

"Tell me what you need, baby." Tiny kept pace with me. His voice was strained and the veins stood out in his neck. His hold on my hips was firm but gentle.

I nearly sobbed with relief. "I need to come, but I can't!"

He gave me a startled laugh but held my hips still. "I can help with that, but I'm gonna need a second. Otherwise, I'm gonna come before you and that ain't fuckin' happening."

I smiled down at him. "I should probably be embarrassed and maybe that will come later. But I…" I bit my lip as I trailed off. "OK, maybe I am embarrassed."

Tiny pulled me back down for another slow, gentle kiss. One filled with longing and hunger to match my own. "How many times has a man actually made you come? And don't tell me you don't know because I know you do."

I narrowed my gaze at him. "None."

"There's a lot we've got to talk about. Probably should have before we started this. But I swear, I'll do everything in my power to make this good for you."

"Then do it. Because I feel like there's something inside me trying to explode, and if it doesn't, I think I'll die!"

With careful movements, he rolled us over, keeping us joined. He supported his weight on his forearms, his massive body caging me in without crushing me. I expected to feel trapped, to feel the familiar panic rise, but it didn't come. Instead, I felt… settled somehow. I sighed in relief because I could tell the instant he felt me relax. He got a soft look on his face and he settled more of his weight on me.

"You good?"

I smiled up at him, hoping he could see the wonder on my face. "I've never been better in my life."

He lowered his face to mine again and kissed me as he began to move. He was careful at first, thrusts measured as he sweated above me. It was obvious he needed more, that he was desperately trying to hold himself back. Whether to keep from hurting me or to keep from coming, I had no idea. But I appreciated his restraint more than I could express.

Once I relaxed Tiny leaned down and kissed me again. "Tell me if you need me to slow down or stop. OK? I don't want to hurt you."

"Of all the things I have to worry about, Tiny, you hurting me is not even in the top fifty."

"Good. Hang on." His movements quickened to deep, commanding thrusts that made me gasp. His movements were controlled, deliberate. He watched my face intently, adjusting his angle when I moaned. "You feel so fuckin' good," he murmured, his beard brushing against my neck as he lowered his head to kiss my throat. "So fuckin' perfect."

I wrapped my legs around his waist, drawing him deeper. I explored the broad expanse of his back, feeling the muscles flex with each movement. The contrast between us was striking. I wasn't exactly a small woman, but Tiny absolutely dwarfed me in size. No one was getting around Tiny to either me or the girls unless he let them. And he wasn't letting anyone near us who meant us harm. Including Andy.

My hypervigilance, the constant alertness that had been my companion for years, began to melt away. For the first time in longer than I could remember, I wasn't bracing for pain, wasn't watching for warning signs. I was simply here, present in my body, feeling without fear. And, oh, my God, I felt so fucking good right now.

The realization brought tears to my eyes, not of sadness but of relief. Tiny noticed immediately, his movements stilling. "Penny? Did I hurt you?"

I shook my head, cupping his face in my hands. "No," I whispered. "Just the opposite. Please don't stop."

He grunted his approval and kissed me deeply, resuming his movements. His powerful body moved with mine in perfect harmony, building toward something I could feel approaching like a storm on the horizon. I surrendered to it completely, to him, to us, to this moment. And for the first time ever, surrender felt like freedom.

Tiny's movements grew more urgent, his hips driving forward with increasing power. Despite the growing intensity, his touch remained gentle, his eyes locked on mine as if constantly checking that I was still with him, still wanting this. The contrast of his restraint and his obvious need was intoxicating.

"Faster," I whispered, my hands sliding down to grip his hips, urging him on. My body arched beneath him, seeking more of the pleasure he was giving me. "Please, Tiny. More. Take what you need because I'm gonna come."

He responded immediately, adjusting his rhythm to match my demand. His breathing grew heavier, hot against my neck where he pressed his face. "God, Penny," he murmured, the words vibrating against my skin. "How the fuck have I survived without you in my life for so fuckin' long?"

The heat between us built with each movement, my skin slick with sweat. His too. I gasped, my fingers digging into the solid muscle of his shoulders.

"Yes," I breathed, my voice barely audible over

the sound of our ragged breathing and the rustle of sheets beneath us. "Now, Tiny. Now!"

His rhythm changed, each thrust hitting exactly where I needed him. One of his massive hands slid between us, finding my clit with surprising ease. The dual sensation was almost too much.

"I've got you," he murmured, his voice a deep rumble that I felt as much as heard. "Come for me, honey. I've got you."

My body responded to his command without my permission. The building tension in my belly had my muscles tightening around him. I was dimly aware of the sounds I was making, of the breathy moans and half-formed pleas, but I was beyond caring. The world had narrowed to just this man, just this building wave of pleasure threatening to crash over me.

"Open your eyes," Tiny whispered. "Look at me when you come. Know who's giving you this."

I hadn't realized I'd closed them. I forced my eyes open to find him watching me with such intense focus, such overwhelming tenderness that it almost pushed me over the edge instantly. His pupils were dilated, his breathing harsh, his movements becoming less controlled as he neared his own release.

"You're beautiful," he said, his voice strained. "So beautiful, Penny."

The orgasm that hit me was both terrifying and beautiful. I screamed and Tiny's hoarse shout was nearly as loud. The pleasure broke over me in waves, my body arching and trembling beneath him. I cried out again, unable to contain the intensity of the sensation. His body shuddered powerfully against mine, inside mine, as we rode the wave of pleasure together.

For several minutes, neither of us moved. I

thought his weight on top of me would feel suffocating or, at the very least, be pretty damned uncomfortable. But I could breathe just fine and I loved how his weight pressed me into the mattress beneath me. I sighed against him happily, going completely limp. I felt his heart thundering against my chest, matching the frantic rhythm of my own. Slowly, carefully, he lowered himself to the side, keeping one arm wrapped around me to draw me against him. I turned willingly into his embrace, my body still trembling with aftershocks.

We lay tangled in the sweat-dampened sheets, my head nestled against his chest, his massive arm draped protectively across my waist, the other wrapped around my body holding me against him like he never wanted to let me go.

"You OK?" he asked after a while, his voice a low rumble in the quiet room.

I nodded against his chest, too content to form words just yet. I felt his lips press against the top of my head, then move to my temple, my cheekbone, my shoulder. Tiny kisses, gentle and reverent, as if he was mapping my skin, committing it to memory. "More than OK. I can never remember being this..." I searched for the right word while my brain had gone on hiatus a long damned time ago. "Contented? Like the worst is behind us?" I took a breath, smiling up into his concerned face. Reaching up, I stroked his bearded cheek. "Like I'm finally where I belong."

He shifted slightly, adjusting our position so he could place soft kisses along my collarbone. The tenderness of the gesture after such intense passion made my chest tighten with emotion. His beard tickled my skin, but I didn't mind. The slight scratch of it was just another reminder that this was real, that he was real.

"Sex was never something I looked forward to." I admitted quietly. "It never felt anything like that, from start to finish."

He pulled back slightly to look at me, his expression serious. "Like what?"

I frowned, struggling to find the words to explain. "Safe," I finally said. "I felt safe tonight, even when I wasn't in control. Even when you were…" I gestured vaguely, feeling my cheeks warm. "You didn't hurt me. You did everything you could to *not* hurt me."

Understanding dawned in his eyes, followed by a flash of anger that I knew wasn't directed at me. He pulled me closer, pressing his lips to my forehead. "That's how it's supposed to be," he said firmly. "Always. You should never feel afraid with someone who claims to love you."

Love. The word hung in the air between us, neither acknowledged nor denied. I wondered if he meant to say it, if he realized what he'd implied. From the sudden stillness of his body, I suspected he had.

"Sorry," he murmured. "I didn't mean to --"

"It's OK," I interrupted, placing my palm against his chest, feeling his heart beat steady and strong beneath my hand. "I know what you mean."

"No," he muttered. He sounded like he was talking to himself more than me. "I don't really think you do." He sighed, relaxing slightly. "I just want you to know that you deserve to feel safe. You and the girls."

I nodded, settling more comfortably against him. His body was like a furnace, radiating heat that seeped into my bones. For the first time in years, I felt myself truly relaxing, the hypervigilance that had become second nature finally, blissfully quiet.

Neither of us spoke for a long moment. I thought maybe he'd gone to sleep, so I tested him. "Tiny?" My voice was a thread of sound.

"Yeah, baby?" His voice was rough. Either from sleep or his shouts during sex I had no idea.

"I was kind of hoping you were asleep." I had no idea why I said that, but once I had I knew he'd want to know why. I figured now was as good a time as any.

He chuckled. "Figured. Give me two minutes, honey. I need to clean up, then you will tell me what's on your mind." I looked up at him, and he gave me a serious look. "You will."

I couldn't help the grin tugging at my lips. "I'd argue, but I'm not sure there will ever be a good time."

"OK. I'll clean us both, then you can tell me what you need to."

It didn't take him that long. He even brought a warm, wet cloth to clean me up. Once he'd finished with me, he knelt to place a kiss over my pussy before tossing the rag toward the bathroom and climbing back into bed.

Once he had me settled, he kissed the top of my head briefly. "Now. What's goin' on, honey?"

I couldn't help but smile. "You are… perfect, Tiny. Perfect for me. For the girls. I appreciate everything you've done for us, and I will never take anything you do for us for granted. However long you let us in your life."

"Penny" -- he pulled back slightly so he could look at me -- "I'm not leaving. I'd never hold you against your will, but I will do everything in my power to keep you happy and to do right by Kira and Zelda in every way I can. You know that. Right?"

I smiled up at him. "Yes. I think I do. But that's

not what I need to tell you."

"I'm listening, baby."

"My mom was a drug addict. I think I took care of her for more of my life than she took care of me." That part hurt almost as much as the rest of it. "She OD'd when I was eight, and the state took me in." I paused to take a couple of fortifying breaths before I continued. "Zelda and Kira aren't Andy's daughters. I had them when I'd just turned sixteen. It was one of my foster fathers. The last one, actually." Tiny didn't say anything, but I was pretty sure I felt a growl deep in his chest. "I ran away. The police took me back to CPS. They didn't believe me and put me in a group home with other kids they consider unplaceable."

"Sounds like the fuckin' system let you down from the get-go." His voice was tight, and I knew he was holding on to his anger, though not at *me*. On my behalf.

"Yeah, well, I didn't like it there."

"What did they do to you, Penny?" He spoke softly but I could hear his anger. He ran his hand up and down my back and I wasn't sure if it was to soothe me or himself.

"They wouldn't let me have an abortion, but they didn't want me to keep the baby either. In fact, when I got there, and they got my lab work back, they insisted I sign away my rights and give the child up for adoption."

"They wouldn't let you have an abortion?"

"No. They tried to keep me on lockdown, knowing I was out of there the first chance I got. Unfortunately for them, I'd spent my entire life surviving on my own. I ran away the next day. Tried to get an abortion, but I was fifteen and the state required consent from a guardian."

"Which was the state."

"Yep. I tried to get what they called a judicial bypass, but that was only available when the minor didn't have a guardian. I had one. But the state wouldn't grant me an abortion. At the time, the judge actually told me he wasn't going to allow abortion to be used as a form of birth control just because I got myself in trouble."

"The fuck?" Tiny actually jerked back from me, looking down at my face in shock.

"My lawyer had pretty much the same reaction, but her hands were tied. The state simply didn't have a provision for a minor in state custody to get an abortion, even if I could have proven I was raped by my foster father. By the time the whole mess was sorted out, the kids would have been a couple years old or better."

"So you had the girls. Obviously you didn't give them up for adoption."

"Nope. Not for lack of trying on the part of the state."

"I'm not going to like this part either, am I?"

"Likely not. They tried to make me stay in the group home. But I split. Left Memphis and came to Nashville."

"Why Nashville?"

"I'm not really sure. It just… seemed like a place I could get a fresh start. I was also away from that bastard of a judge and the state's attorney handling my case. Besides, it was the farthest bus trip I could take with the money I had. I put three hours between me and those bastards, hoping it would buy me enough time to get a job, have the baby, and show I could provide for both myself and my child. Except for the fact I had two babies instead of one."

"Why do I get the feeling having twins made you even that much more determined to succeed?"

"I didn't ask to get pregnant, Tiny. I've never told the girls that story and I never plan to. But once I realized I didn't have a choice in the matter, when I knew I was going to have to pay for what someone else did to me regardless of what I wanted, I was all in. I wasn't about to let someone use my body as a baby factory for some rich couple who could pay a couple hundred thousand dollars. Fancy lawyers would happily take my baby and be as falsely sympathetic as they could be as they cashed that big fat check and moved on to the next poor kid raped by a foster parent." I took a deep breath. "I kept the twins I wasn't expected to keep. I think the social worker assigned to my case left Memphis for Nashville the second the hospital notified the state of my arrival."

"Because you were a minor."

"Yes. I had the right to seek my own prenatal care and to do anything to get the babies care, but once I was the patient, I still had to have a guardian's permission to treat me. Anyway, that doesn't matter. I already had a job. I had my own studio apartment. I met Lana Thompson when I gave birth to the girls. She got my emancipation pushed through in record time. I have no idea how and I don't really care. She told me then if I ever needed anything to call her. Anything at all. So when I needed to leave Andy, she's the one who told me to come here."

"Then I have Lana to thank for sending you my way." He smiled down at me before sobering, giving me a tender look. "Honey, never again. No one is ever going to take advantage or hurt you again. Not without some serious repercussions they won't like. From now on, I've got your back. Those girls?" He sighed and shook his head slightly. "I never thought I'd have a family, Penny. Not one of my own. I want you and the girls to be my family. I want the right to protect you all."

The smile tugging at my lips came without hesitation. "I think we'd all like that."

"Good." He pulled the covers higher over us, turning so that my back was to his front. Those strong arms of his closed around me in a blanket of warmth. The feeling was so wonderful I just closed my eyes and rode on that peaceful current.

As sleep began to pull at me, I found myself thinking about his slip. Love. Such a small word for something so enormous. I'd been so careful with it, so protective of it after Andy had twisted and perverted its meaning. Yet here, in the protective circle of Tiny's arms, it didn't seem so frightening.

I felt his breathing deepen, his body going slack with approaching sleep. My own eyes grew heavy, my thoughts becoming hazier as exhaustion claimed me. In that space between wakefulness and dreams, I found the courage to whisper the words I'd been holding back.

"I love you," I said, my voice soft but clear in the quiet room.

I felt him stir, his arm tightening around me for a moment. I wasn't sure if he'd heard me, wasn't sure if I wanted him to. But as I drifted off to sleep, I felt his lips press against my hair, and his whispered response followed me into my dreams.

"I love you too, Penny. You and those girls. More than I ever thought possible."

Chapter Ten

Tiny

The Bronco's heater fought against the December chill as I navigated the morning traffic, one hand on the wheel, the other resting protectively on the console between Penny and me. Her fingers occasionally brushed mine, those small touches still sending sparks through me even after several days together. In the rearview mirror, I could see Zelda and Kira huddled over Kira's phone, giggling at something on the screen. The sight warmed me more than any heater could. Two days before Christmas, and for the first time in fifteen years, I had something to celebrate beyond just making it through another day.

"We need to hit at least three stores," Zelda announced from the backseat, the self-appointed logistics coordinator of our Christmas shopping expedition. "I want to stop at that bookstore Kira likes, and then --" She lowered her voice to a conspiratorial whisper. "You know, that place for Mom's present."

I nodded solemnly. "Mission parameters received, commander."

This earned me a snort from Zelda and a giggle from Kira. Small victories, but each one mattered when it came to those girls. They'd been at the compound for nearly a month now, and while I wouldn't say Zelda fully trusted me yet, she tolerated me. OK, so, more than tolerated. She'd started leaving little notes on my desk when I was working, mostly sarcastic comments about my taste in music or suggestions for "less embarrassing" clothes. Coming from Zelda, this was practically a declaration of love.

And Kira… Christ, that kid had attached herself to me like I was her personal bodyguard or something.

She'd taken to sitting between me and Penny during movie nights, her small body gradually leaning into mine until she'd eventually fall asleep. The first time it happened, I'd frozen, terrified of moving and waking her, of breaking whatever fragile trust had formed between us. Since Penny had also fallen asleep, I'd sat there for three hours, arm tingling with numbness. I felt happier than I could remember being since before Julie died.

There had been no incidents since the bomb threat at Haven. Knight had upgraded our security systems twice more, and we'd established new protocols for leaving the compound. Today was the first time we'd ventured out without additional backup, but I'd thoroughly vetted the route, and I'd done three separate passes by the mall over the last week to check for suspicious activity. Nothing. Andrew Harlow had gone quiet. Too quiet for my liking, but Penny needed this. The girls needed this. A normal family Christmas shopping trip.

"This feels like a dream," Penny said softly beside me, her voice barely audible over the radio playing Christmas songs. "Being in a car, going to the mall two days before Christmas like a normal family." She looked at me, her eyes bright. "I never thought I'd have this again. I never thought I'd want it."

Something caught in my throat. I squeezed her fingers gently. "You deserve normal," I said. "All three of you do." I cleared my throat and raised my voice. "Even if I do have to listen to 'All I Want for Christmas Is You' on repeat for the next three days." That got a laugh from all my girls.

Penny leaned over and kissed my cheek, her lips warm against my skin. Behind us, Zelda made a gagging noise, but there was no heat in it. Just a kid being a kid, embarrassed by adult affection. Normal, like Penny said. The kind of normal I'd kill to protect.

We'd been on the road for about ten minutes when I noticed the dark sedan following too closely behind us, its windows tinted beyond what was legal in Tennessee. My gut tightened, the way it always did when trouble was brewing. I'd felt that same tension countless times in the yard at Terre Haute, right before everything went to hell.

I kept my face neutral, not wanting to alarm Penny or the girls. The sedan dropped back slightly but remained behind us through the next three turns. Coincidence, maybe. But I didn't believe in coincidences, not when it came to protecting what was mine.

"You know what?" I said casually, "I think we might swing by that coffee place you like first. Get some fuel for shopping."

Penny glanced at me, her brow furrowing slightly. She knew me well enough now to sense the shift in my tone, subtle as it was. Her eyes flicked to the rearview mirror, then back to me, a silent question.

I gave an almost imperceptible nod, then reached for my phone on the console. Knight needed to know we had a tail. My fingers had just brushed the screen when the world exploded into motion and noise. The sedan sped up, ramming us from behind, the impact jolting us forward violently. Penny screamed as did the girls. I gripped the wheel with both hands, fighting to maintain control as the Bronco fishtailed.

"Hold on!" I shouted. Before I could recover, two more vehicles appeared, one cutting in front of us, the other alongside, boxing us in. The maneuver was professional, coordinated. Not random road rage. A planned attack.

The vehicle beside us swerved sharply, forcing us off the road and onto the shoulder. The Bronco skidded over gravel and dirt, the tires fighting for purchase. I managed to bring us to a controlled stop before we hit the ditch.

As dust settled around us, I saw Andrew Harlow stepping out of the lead car, flanked by two men built like linebackers, but not as big as me. Harlow's face bore none of the polished businessman mask he'd worn at Haven. His expression was pure rage.

"Stay in the car," I told Penny, softly. "Lock the doors when I get out."

"Tiny, no --"

But I was already moving. The rage I'd kept carefully banked for years rose inside, familiar and almost welcome.

Andy's eyes locked with mine as I opened the door, and I saw recognition there. Not so much of who I was, but of what I was. Andrew Harlow knew I represented a big fucking threat to him. I was also the thing standing between him and what he wanted. What he was never going to get.

I charged out of the Bronco as the first attacker reached for the rear door where Kira sat. Penny screamed as a second man yanked open her door when she didn't get them locked fast enough. Zelda let loose an enraged scream, fierce as any battle cry I'd ever heard. The cold air bit at my skin, but I barely felt it.

The attacker reached for Kira's door, likely thinking he'd taken me out with the kick he'd delivered to my thigh when I'd staggered. He'd just managed to get his meaty fingers on the door handle when I slammed into him with the full force of my body. The impact drove the air from his lungs in a satisfying whoosh. Pretty sure I heard a rib snap. I didn't hesitate, following through with an uppercut that snapped his head back. The familiar crunch of cartilage under my knuckles told me I'd broken his nose.

"Tiny!" Penny's voice cut through the air, sharp with terror.

I spun to see the second man had her by the arm, trying to drag her from the passenger seat. Her feet scrabbled against the floor mat as she fought him, her free hand clawing at his face. The sight of him on her sent a fresh surge of rage through me.

Zelda appeared like a demon from the back seat, her small body launching over her mother's shoulder. She latched onto the man's arm, teeth sinking into his wrist while her fingernails raked across his eyes. The man howled, his grip on Penny loosening just enough for her to wrench herself partway free.

"You little bitch!" he snarled, backhanding Zelda hard enough to snap her head back.

Something primal broke loose inside me at the sight of her head rocking back from the blow. I lunged toward them, but the guy I was fighting grabbed me from behind, his arm locking around my throat. I drove my elbow back into his solar plexus once, twice, three times until his grip slackened.

"Get off my mom!" Zelda screamed, her voice cracking with rage and fear. On the other side of the Bronco, I caught a glimpse of Andy yanking open the rear door. He reached in, grabbing for Zelda's ankle as she kicked wildly at his face. Kira's terrified shriek filled the air as she scrambled across the seat, away from Andy's grasping hands.

"Kira, lock the door!" I shouted, then grunted as this guy landed a blow to my kidney. I spun, delivering a headbutt that connected with his already broken nose. Fresh blood sprayed between us, hot against my skin as it painted my face. He staggered back, giving me a precious second to assess the situation.

Penny was half out of her seat now, still struggling with her attacker. It looked like the only thing keeping her in was her seat belt. Zelda had been pulled from the vehicle, her small frame twisting like a wildcat in Andy's grip. Kira remained in the back seat, Mr. Hoppers clutched to her chest, her eyes wide with terror. I needed to end this fast.

I grabbed my attacker by his jacket and drove my knee into his groin, following with a right hook that dropped him to one knee. Without pausing, I pivoted toward Penny and her attacker, aiming a kick at the back of the man's knee that buckled his leg. As he faltered, Penny wrenched free of his grip and scrambled backward.

"Get back in the car, lock the doors!" I yelled to her.

But Andy had already circled around, dragging a struggling Zelda with him. "You really thought you could hide from me?" he sneered at Penny. "You think this fucking gorilla can protect you?" He yanked Zelda's arm hard enough to make her cry out in pain. "Tell your boyfriend to back the fuck off before I break her arm."

Zelda's eyes met mine over Andy's shoulder, wide but determined. I saw the calculation there, the decision forming before she made her move. Smart kid. She went suddenly limp in Andy's grip, dropping her weight so unexpectedly that, even though she was slight of build and still a growing adolescent, he had nearly lost his hold. In the split second he needed to adjust his grip, she twisted, driving her heel into his instep and breaking free.

"Zelda, run!" I shouted at her. Of course, Zelda darted, not away, but toward her mother.

Penny's attacker had regained his footing and was reaching for her again. In a move that would have made any action hero proud, Zelda launched herself onto the man's back, her arms wrapping around his neck, fingers clawing at his eyes. The distraction gave Penny the opening she needed. She drove her knee up between his legs with enough force that I almost winced in sympathy. Almost.

I turned back just in time to see the guy I'd just dropped with a dick shot charging me again, this time with something glinting in his hand. A knife, the blade catching the winter sunlight. I sidestepped, grabbing his wrist and twisting until I heard the bones snap. He screamed, the knife dropping to the ground. I kicked it under the Bronco, then delivered a blow to his temple that saw the man drop like a stone. This time, he didn't get up.

A sharp pain exploded across the back of my head. Stars burst behind my eyes as I staggered forward, catching myself on the hood of the Bronco. Andy's third man, the one I'd missed, had circled behind me, a crowbar in his hand. Warm blood trickled down my scalp as I turned to face him. He must have had shit aim and caught me with a glancing blow or I'd have been knocked out at the very least. Dead if he'd had any arm strength whatsoever. "You should've minded your own business," he growled, swinging the iron again.

I caught it mid-swing, the impact jarring up my arm. "They *are* my business." I yanked the iron from his grasp, then swung it like a baseball bat straight into his solar plexus. The guy gasped in pain before sinking to the ground, struggling to breathe. With any luck I'd ruptured his diaphragm, taking him out of the fight completely.

Blood dripped into my eye from a gash on my forehead, blurring my vision. I wiped it away with the back of my hand, taking stock of the situation. Penny had managed to break free from her attacker, who was now doubled over and cursing. Andy was advancing on Zelda again, murder in his eyes.

Another car screeched to a halt and two more men climbed out and managed to tackle me to the ground before I could make it to Penny and Zelda. The impact knocked the wind from my lungs. I rolled, trying to throw him off, catching glimpses of the scene around me. Penny pulled Zelda toward her as Andy's face contorted with rage.

"You think I'm going to let you walk away?" Andy shouted at Penny. "After everything you've cost me? You and those fucking brats?"

I drove my elbow into my attacker's face and shoved him off, struggling to my feet just as the other one joined the fight, grabbing me from behind. I felt myself tiring, the blow to my head making the world swim in and out of focus.

"Penny!" I roared, catching her eye as I grappled with both men. "Take the girls and run! NOW!" I bellowed, throwing one attacker into the other, buying Penny and Zelda a few precious seconds.

Penny grabbed Zelda's hand, reaching back into the Bronco for Kira. She yanked both daughters close and turned toward the woods that lined the roadside.

Blood streaming down my face, I planted myself between them and their pursuers. Andy's face twisted with fury as he watched his quarry escaping. He started after them, but I managed to get a foot out to trip him up. He face-planted on the gravel at my feet, and it was all I could do not to laugh at the bastard.

Andy wiped blood from his split lip, his eyes narrowing as he glared at Penny. "I'm sick to death of you and your brats," he spat, his polished facade completely gone. "Do you have any idea what you've cost me?" Behind him, his men regrouped, circling like wolves. I felt a familiar heat building in my chest -- the same protective fury that had erupted fifteen years ago when I found Julie with that bastard. The rage that had cost me a decade and a half of my life. But this time was different. This time, I had something to fight for, not just against.

"Let them go, Andy," I growled, widening my stance. Blood from the gash on my forehead trickled into my eye, and I blinked it away. "This isn't going to end how you think."

He laughed, the sound sharp and ugly. "Look at you -- bleeding, outnumbered. You think you're going to walk away from this?" His gaze shifted to Penny, who was backing toward the tree line with the girls. "You stupid bitch. Did you think I wouldn't find you? That I'd just write off what you stole from me?"

"I didn't steal anything!" Penny shouted back, her voice steady despite the fear I could see in her eyes. "Everything I took was mine!"

Andy snapped his fingers, and the man with the tire iron lunged toward Penny, catching her arm before she could retreat farther. She cried out in pain as his fingers dug into her flesh, and something in me -- something I'd kept carefully controlled since the day I crushed a man's skull with my bare hands -- broke free.

I moved without conscious thought, my body responding to a threat against what was mine. Three long strides brought me to the man holding Penny. My fist connected with his jaw with a satisfying crack that vibrated up my arm. He staggered, his grip on Penny loosening. I didn't give him time to recover, delivering a knee to his midsection that doubled him over.

"Keep going!" I shouted at Penny when she turned to look over her shoulder.

One of the guys I'd already injured recovered enough to charge me from the side, driving his shoulder into my ribs. The impact sent us both sprawling onto the ground. Pain exploded across my torso where I likely had at least one cracked rib. I rolled, using my size to my advantage, and pinned him beneath me. Three rapid punches left him dazed, but one of the other men was already back on me, wrapping his arm around my neck in a chokehold.

Through the struggle, I caught glimpses of Penny pulling the girls toward the tree line. Zelda was half-dragging Kira, who looked paralyzed with fear. They were almost there. Almost safe. I just needed to buy them a little more time.

I drove my elbow back into my attacker's sternum and broke his hold, spinning to face him. Blood dripped steadily into my eyes now, my vision swimming in and out of focus. My breath came in ragged gasps, each one sending shards of pain through my ribs.

"Shouldn't have gotten involved," the big guy snarled, spitting a tooth onto the ground between us. "This ain't your business."

"Family is always my business," I growled back, keeping my body between them and the retreating figures of Penny and the girls. That's when I noticed Andy wasn't engaging in the fight. Instead, he'd circled around, moving through the brush to cut off

Penny's escape route. I watched in horror as he emerged from the trees directly in Penny's path, grabbing Zelda by her jacket before they could change direction.

"Let me go!" Zelda screamed, twisting in his grip like a wild animal. "Mom!"

Penny lunged for her daughter, but Andy shoved her backward hard enough to send her sprawling to her ass on the ground. Kira stood frozen, clutching Mr. Hoppers to her chest.

The sound that emerged from my mouth didn't sound human. I fought with renewed desperation, needing to get to my girls. The three men tried to hold me back, one catching my arm while another landed a blow to my already injured ribs. The third one hopped on my back, wrapping his arm around my neck in a choke hold again. Pain exploded through my body, but I pushed through it, breaking free with a surge of strength born of pure unadulterated rage.

Three long strides brought me to Andy. He turned just in time to see my fist before it connected with his face. The impact lifted him off his feet, sending him staggering backward. He lost his grip on Zelda, who scrambled away immediately, running back to her mother and sister.

Andy's face contorted with hate. "You think this changes anything?" he spat. "I'm taking Zelda with me. You can do whatever you want with the other two bitches, but I need Zelda."

By that time, however, his men were back in the game once again, cockroaches down but not out. A sharp pain exploded at the back of my skull -- the tire iron again. My knees buckled, the world tilting dangerously. I caught myself on one hand, refusing to go down completely. I'd never been so thankful someone had shitty aim in my life. That was twice I should have been dead. Lord knew my head was hard, but though I might not be out, I was definitely down. Through blurred vision, I saw Penny and the girls reaching the edge of the woods. Almost safe.

Andy's foot connected with my ribs, sending fresh agony through my body. I rolled with the kick, trying to get back to my feet, but one of the remaining men landed a blow to my temple that sent stars bursting across my vision once again.

"Should've stayed in your lane, convict," Andy sneered, standing over me as his men closed in. "You think a piece of shit like you gets to play house with my wife? With my kids?"

I spat blood onto the frozen ground. "They were never yours," I managed, each word sending fire through my broken ribs.

Another kick, this time to my back. I grunted, absorbing the blow, focusing through the pain to check the tree line. Penny and the girls had disappeared into the woods. Good. They knew to head east, toward the compound. Knight would have people out looking for us already, alerted by the tracking app on my phone when we deviated from our route. I just needed to buy them more time.

With a surge of effort that sent black spots dancing across my vision, I lunged upward, catching Andy's jacket and driving him into his men. All three went down in a tangle of limbs. I staggered to my feet, my body screaming in protest.

Andy was the first to regain his feet, his face twisted with hatred. "You're a dead man," he snarled.

"Maybe," I agreed, bracing myself as all three charged me at once. "But they're alive. That's all that matters."

Once I stood, after the blows to the head, my world began to fade around the edges, my vision narrowing to pinpricks of light. I kept fighting, though I was slowing drastically. Another blow to the head sent me sprawling onto my back. Through dimming vision, I stared up at the winter sky, gray and endless above me.

Andy's face appeared in my field of vision, his lips moving, but the words were lost in the roaring that filled my ears. It didn't matter. Nothing he said mattered anymore. Penny and the girls were away, running toward safety. Running toward home.

As darkness closed in around me, a sense of peace settled over me. They were safe. My family was safe. And that was worth any price. My last conscious thought was of Penny's smile that morning, of Zelda's grudging approval, of Kira's small hand in mine. Of family. Of home.

Of love worth dying for.

Chapter Eleven

Penny

I crashed through the underbrush, one hand clamped around Zelda's wrist, the other reaching back for Kira. My lungs burned with each ragged breath, the December air stinging my throat and lungs as we plunged deeper into the unfamiliar woods. Behind us, the sounds of the fight still reached us. I knew each grunt of pain came from Tiny and no one else. I was about to lose my mind and I had no idea what the hell to do. Worst of all, hearing Tiny's voice growing weaker but still defiant as he bought us time to escape.

"Mom, take Kira and head deeper into the woods." Zelda gasped for breath, tugging at my grip and determined. "I'm going back to help Tiny."

"Believe me, honey, there's nothing I want more, but if one of us gets hurt trying to defend him, Tiny would never forgive himself." Then my ass-cheek buzzed and I gave a startled yelp before reaching back to pull my phone from my pocket. "Why the fuck didn't I think to call someone for help?"

Zelda snorted. "Who would we have called before now? The police? Call someone at the club. They'll come for Tiny." She said all that as I answered the phone and the man on the other end -- Knight -- heard.

"You tell Z we'd come for all of you. Like right now."

"Knight!" I sobbed and sank to my knees in the dead grass, leaves, and mud. "I-I can dr-drop you a p-pin." My voice trembled and my whole body started to shake as well.

Through a gap in the trees, I caught a glimpse of the Bronco, its door still hanging open. And Tiny...

God, Tiny was on the ground, blood streaming from his face as one of Andy's men kicked him in the ribs. Another blow landed, and yet somehow, impossibly, Tiny struggled to his feet again.

"Don't worry, Penny. You should be able to hear the bikes any second now. Drop Caleb a pin. He's headed your way too and I'd feel better if he was with the three of you."

I whipped around and saw Andy and one of his associates breaking away from the main group, peering into the trees where we'd entered the woods. Andy's face was contorted with rage, blood streaming from his nose where Tiny had struck him.

"We're safe for now, but Tiny's still back there," I choked out. "He's fighting them alone. There are at least three men, Knight. They're beating him, and I just left him there! I just --"

"You got your girls to safety," Knight cut in firmly. "That's what Tiny wanted. That's why he fought. We're rounding the corner now and we've got Tiny's back. Just focus on keeping the girls safe until we get the situation under control."

I pressed my fist against my mouth to stifle a cry as Tiny finally fought his way back to his feet when one of them swung the tire iron again, catching Tiny on the shoulder. He staggered but didn't fall. I watched as he spun, delivering a devastating blow to his attacker's face that sent the man sprawling. But there were too many, and Tiny was already injured, already slowing.

My entire body shook with the need to help him, to run back and fight alongside him. I'd made my choice the moment I pulled them into the woods. Their safety had to come above all else, even above the man I'd come to love.

The unfairness of it burned like acid. We'd been

so close to normal, a simple Christmas shopping trip, the kind of mundane family outing I'd thought was forever lost to us. And now Tiny was bleeding, possibly dying, while I cowered in the woods unable to help him.

"He's still fighting," Zelda whispered beside me, her eyes fixed on the road. "Look, Mom. He won't stay down."

As if I could force myself to look away. I watched as Tiny somehow regained his footing after another blow. Blood matted his beard and streaked his face, but his massive shoulders squared, his stance wide as he positioned himself between Andy's men and the woods where we hid. Even now, even as they continued to beat him, he was making sure they couldn't follow us.

Zelda squeezed my hand, her gaze never leaving the group in the fight just ahead of us. Her jaw was set, her slight body tense as a coiled spring. Terrified as she must be, my fierce daughter was ready to fight.

A sudden cry from the group drew our attention. Andy staggered backward. Tiny stood at full height, proud and tall like he hadn't been knocked silly by a fucking crowbar. He stood over Andy, not trying to make himself smaller. In fact, now, it looked like Tiny was using his full height to intimidate, his shoulders back. Far off in the distance I heard the faint rumble of motorcycles.

"I hear them, Mom," Kira whispered excitedly. "They're coming to save Tiny."

"They're here to save more than Tiny." Caleb was a short distance away, but close enough to hear the conversation.

Both girls immediately ran to him, hugging him tightly between them. They were close enough in age the girls should see him as an equal, but I got the feeling he was more like an annoying older brother to both of them. The three of them had grown even closer over the last few weeks. I was glad because not only was Caleb as solid as they came, he was just as protective as the other men in Kiss of Death. He was devoted to his mother, and he'd extended his protective nature to my girls.

"They'll be coming around the building in a couple seconds." Caleb jerked his chin in the direction he'd indicated. Sure enough, eight bikes charged from around the bend and straight to the fight.

One of the guys around Tiny swung a bat at his chest but Tiny caught it with surprising ease. A strangled sound escaping me despite my best efforts. I couldn't take anymore.

"Caleb, stay with the girls. You keep them safe. Promise me."

Caleb straightened, his chest going out with pride. Even as a young teen, he was tall. He wasn't filled out, but he was wiry and strong. And incredibly cunning. "They'll be safe with me, Ms. Harlow." Yeah. Caleb was a good young man. I'd already told Violet how fond I was of her son, but I thought I needed to tell her again. And Caleb.

Where the sound of the bikes had started like distant thunder at first, now the rumble grew until it vibrated through the frozen ground beneath our feet. I pulled the girls closer to me as the noise grew louder, resolving into the unmistakable roar of multiple motorcycle engines approaching fast. Through the bare winter trees, I caught flashes of movement on the road, and then the woods filled with the deafening sound of bikes tearing through the underbrush toward us.

I watched through the trees as the first

motorcycle burst into view, followed by another and another. The road suddenly swarmed with Kiss of Death cuts, leather, and righteous fury. Knight led the charge, his tattooed face a mask of cold rage as he drove his bike straight at Andy's men. Riot followed close behind, with Griffin and several others I recognized fanning out in a practiced formation that immediately cut off any escape routes.

Andy's face transformed from triumph to panic in an instant. His men scattered like roaches when the light comes on, dropping their weapons and bolting for their vehicles. Knight skidded his bike sideways, cutting off two men trying to reach the sedan. Riot and Griffin cornered Andy himself, forcing him back against his car with nowhere to run.

Without waiting for a response, I pushed through the underbrush and back toward the road. My heart hammered against my ribs as I ran, branches slapping against my face and catching in my hair. I barely felt them. All I could focus on was Tiny, still on his feet somehow despite the blood covering half his face, despite the beating he'd endured to buy us time to escape.

Pain dismounted from his bike in a fluid motion, medical bag already in hand as he rushed toward Tiny. The club's doctor moved with the quick, confident stride of someone who'd patched up worse injuries than these, though my stomach clenched at the thought.

"Jesus Christ," Pain muttered, reaching Tiny just as the big man finally allowed his knees to buckle. Pain caught him before he hit the ground, supporting him with a strength that belied his leaner frame. "Thank God you've got a hard head, Tiny," he said with gruff affection.

"Never been so grateful for it my own damned self," Tiny grunted, wincing as Pain helped him sit on the ground. His voice sounded rough but strong, nothing like the fading calls I'd heard during our escape. Relief flooded through me so intensely my legs nearly gave out.

"Tiny!" I couldn't help the sob that tore from my throat. His head jerked up at the sound of my voice, his gaze finding mine. He opened his arms as I skidded to a halt and threw myself at him. His arms closed around me and I sobbed. *And sobbed.*

"Penny," he breathed, his voice breaking before he cleared his throat. "You're OK. The girls --"

"They're safe," I assured him. "They're with Caleb at the edge of the woods."

Tiny held me for a long time. I cried into his neck and clung as tightly as I could. He didn't protest.

"I thought --" I choked on the words, tears streaming down my face. "I thought they were going to kill you."

He cradled the back of my head, stroking gently over my hair. "Takes more than a few cheap shots to put me down," he murmured, though I could feel the slight tremble in body, the unsteady rhythm of his breathing betraying how close it had been. "Just needed to buy you some time until the boys got here." He rubbed the back of his head. "They got in a few good licks."

"Damned lucky those fuckers didn't take your fuckin' head off with that crowbar," Pain muttered, his expression a mixture of exasperation and understanding. "Let me check him out properly before you squeeze those ribs any tighter," he said, not unkindly. "He's probably got at least one or two cracked."

I immediately loosened my grip, though I couldn't bring myself to move away completely. Tiny kept his arm around me as Pain quickly examined the gash on his head, shining a small penlight into his eyes to check his pupils.

"Concussion for sure, but nothing that won't heal," Pain announced after a moment. He gently pressed along Tiny's ribs, noting where Tiny flinched. "Two, maybe three cracked ribs. You're one lucky son of a bitch, Tiny."

Tiny's lips quirked in a half-smile despite the blood still matting his beard. "Told you those assholes couldn't fight worth shit."

"Let's get you back to the Bronco," Pain said, helping Tiny unsteadily to his feet then slid a shoulder under Tiny's arm to support him. "We'll clean you up at the compound."

I turned to look for the girls, needing to make sure they were still safe. They had emerged from the trees with Caleb. Riot joined them, talking quietly with his stepson and the girls. They hung back, watching the chaos with wide eyes. Knight had Andy and two of his men on their knees, hands behind their heads. Griffin stood guard over the others, his face a study in controlled violence as he watched them.

Tiny followed my gaze, his body tensing at the sight of the girls. "They really OK?" he asked, his voice tight with concern.

"They're fine," I assured him, squeezing his hand. "We were all so scared for you."

"They shouldn't see this," he muttered, gesturing vaguely toward the blood on his face. "Don't want to scare them more."

The protectiveness in his voice, even now when he was the one bleeding and injured, made my heart swell. "Hate to break it to you, big guy, but they're already running this way."

Zelda reached us first, Kira half a step behind her. They both threw themselves at him and Tiny, bless his heart, caught them each in one arm and held them close. Zelda's expression hardened into a mask of fury that reminded me so much of my own I almost laughed despite everything.

"Did you at least hit him back?" she demanded, her hands clenched into fists at her sides. "Did you break his stupid face?"

Tiny's laugh rumbled through his chest, though it cut off sharply as the movement jostled his injured ribs. "Yeah, Zelda. I got him good."

"You can call me Z," she said, lifting her chin. "Blame Knight. Heard him call me that when he talked to Mom."

Kira's eyes brimmed with tears as she stared at the blood on Tiny's face. "Are you gonna be OK?" she whispered.

Tiny's expression softened as he looked down at her. "I'm gonna be just fine, darlin'. Nothing a little rest won't fix." He winked at her, the gesture so incongruous with his battered face that a watery giggle escaped her.

Knight approached us, his tattooed face set in grim lines. "Cops are on their way," he said without preamble. "We need to get out of here. Now."

"What about him?" I jerked my chin toward Andy, who was still kneeling on the ground, blood running from his nose and split lip. The hatred in his eyes as he glared at me made my skin crawl.

"He's not going anywhere," Knight assured me. "Got some anonymous tips headed to the right people about his dealings. Couple files might have found their way to the feds too." He shrugged, a cold smile playing at the corners of his mouth. "Andy Harlow's about to have a very, very bad day, and it's only going to get worse."

Relief washed through me, so intense I swayed slightly on my feet. Tiny's arm tightened around my waist, steadying me.

"Let's get you all back to the compound," Knight said, his gaze softening slightly as he looked at the girls. "The girls and Caleb can ride with me, Riot, and Griffin. Penny, you ride in the Bronco with Tiny and Pain."

"I want to stay with Mom," Zelda protested immediately, her expression mulish.

Knight knelt down so he was eyelevel with her. "I need you to help me keep an eye on your sister," he said quietly. "And Tiny needs your mom right now. Can you do that for him? After what he did for you today?"

Zelda's eyes flicked to Tiny, who was still leaning heavily on Pain's shoulder, then back to Knight. After a moment, she nodded reluctantly. "Fine. But I get to ride with Riot."

Knight's lips twitched. "Sure thing, Z."

Kira hesitated, looking uncertain until Griffin approached her, his usually stern face softening into a gentle smile. "Want to see how fast my bike can go?" he asked, and Kira's eyes widened with a mixture of fear and excitement.

"Is it scary?" she asked in a small voice.

Griffin shook his head solemnly. "Not when you're with me. I'll keep you safe."

After a moment's consideration, Kira nodded. "OK."

As Knight led the girls toward the bikes, Pain

guided Tiny toward the Bronco, which had somehow survived the entire ordeal with only a few new dents. The tire tracks in the gravel where we'd been forced off the road were still visible, a reminder of how quickly our simple shopping trip had turned into a nightmare.

We were passing the man who'd hit Tiny with the crowbar when Tiny suddenly stopped, pulling away from Pain's support to stand on his own. Blood still streaked his face, but his eyes were clear and cold as he stared down at the man who'd knocked him to the ground.

"Next time," Tiny said, his voice carrying easily in the sudden quiet, "make sure your fuckin' swing counts. Any bitch-ass motherfucker who can't kill a man with two blows to the head with a crowbar has got to be a fuckin' pussy."

The man glared up at him but flinched when Tiny took a step closer. One of Andy's other men actually chuckled, earning himself a murderous look from his compatriot.

"He's right though," the man said with a shrug. "You hit a man in the head with a crowbar, he oughtta be dead."

Pain stepped forward, placing a hand on Tiny's shoulder. "Save it for later, brother. Need to get your girls."

Tiny held the man's gaze for a moment longer before nodding once, a gesture so full of contempt that the man looked away first. I couldn't help but feel fierce pride at the sight of Tiny standing tall despite his injuries, unbroken and unbowed.

Pain helped Tiny into the passenger seat of the Bronco, then turned to me. "You OK to drive?" he asked, his shrewd eyes assessing me for any signs of shock or injury.

I nodded, surprised to find my hands steady as I took the keys he offered. "I'm fine. I wasn't hurt at all."

"I'll follow behind," Pain said, already moving back toward his bike. "We'll have him patched up in no time."

I climbed into the driver's seat, stealing a glance at Tiny as I started the engine. His head was tipped back against the headrest, eyes closed, the harsh winter sun highlighting every bruise and cut on his face. The sight of him so battered made my throat tighten, but I swallowed hard against the emotion. He needed me steady right now.

"You sure you're OK to drive?" Tiny asked without opening his eyes, his voice roughened by exhaustion.

"I promise," I assured him, reaching across to squeeze his hand gently. "Just focus on breathing through the pain."

He turned his head slightly, opening one eye to look at me, a small smile on his face. "Not in pain when you're next to me."

The simple statement, delivered in that deep, matter-of-fact rumble, unraveled something in my chest that I'd been holding tight since the moment Andy's car had rammed us. I managed to put the Bronco in gear and pull back onto the road, following Knight's bike as he led the way back toward the compound. The girls were secure, perched behind Riot and Griffin, their small arms wrapped tight around the bikers' waists.

We'd only gone a mile when a sob escaped me, so suddenly I couldn't hold it back. I quickly pulled onto the shoulder, putting the Bronco in park before I lost control completely. Tiny's arm came around me immediately, pulling me across the console and onto his lap despite his injured ribs.

"Hey," he murmured, his hand coming up to cradle my face. "It's OK now. We're all OK."

"You almost weren't," I choked out, clinging to him as the tears I'd been fighting finally broke free. "You almost died protecting us, and I just left you there. I just ran --"

"You did exactly what you were supposed to do," he interrupted firmly. "You got the girls to safety. We both had to keep them safe. They're what mattered."

"You mattered too," I whispered fiercely, pulling back to look at him through my tears. "You matter to us. To me." I took a shuddering breath, suddenly needing him to know, needing to say the words in case I ever lost the chance again. "I love you, Tiny. I love you so much it terrifies me."

His thumb brushed away a tear from my cheek, his eyes never leaving mine. "I love you too, Penny," he said softly. "You and those girls. Nothing on this earth could make me stop fighting to get back to you. Nothing."

I pressed my forehead to his, careful of his wounds, breathing in the scent of him. Blood and sweat mingled with the faint hint of pine that always clung to his skin. My fingers traced the uninjured side of his face, memorizing the feel of him, solid and real beneath my touch.

"Take me home," he murmured against my lips. "Then we'll do some online Christmas shopping."

It took me a second to realize what he'd said, then a snorted laugh broke free, prompting him to chuckle. I nodded, pressing one more gentle kiss to his mouth before shifting back to the driver's seat. As I put the Bronco back in gear and pulled onto the road, I glanced in the rearview mirror at the line of bikes following us. The one behind us had pulled over with us. They hadn't intruded or done anything other than wait patiently. They had come for us. They had my daughters safe among them. These were fierce, loyal men who'd come when we needed them most and I would be forever grateful to them.

The compound was waiting for us, and beyond that, a future I never thought I'd have. A future with a man who'd fight through hell itself to keep us safe. A future with an unexpected family, one I'd found when I needed them. My family. Perfect in all its dangerous, beautiful chaos.

Chapter Twelve

Tiny

The central warehouse of the Kiss of Death compound had transformed into something I barely recognized. Colored lights hung from the rafters and wound through the camo netting overhead, casting a soft, festive glow that danced across Penny's face as we stepped inside. My ribs protested with a sharp stab of pain when I reached to hold the door open, but I swallowed the wince before it could reach my face. Tonight wasn't about my healing wounds. Tonight was about giving Penny and the girls the Christmas they deserved.

"Holy shit," Zelda whispered beside me, her eyes wide as she took in the massive tree that dominated the far corner, its branches heavy with ornaments that glinted in the light. Kira clutched Mr. Hoppers to her chest, speechless as she stared wide-eyed up at the spectacle in awe.

I rested my hand gently on Kira's shoulder. "What do you think, darlin'? The guys might've gone a bit overboard."

"It's beautiful," she breathed, and something in my chest loosened at the wonder in her voice. The warehouse had been completely transformed. Tables lined the walls, laden with plates of homemade cookies and steaming crockpots that filled the air with the scent of mulled cider and hot chocolate. The usual hard edges of the compound had been softened with greenery and ribbon, making the space feel almost cozy despite its size.

And lights. *Lots* of lights.

The ambush two days earlier had only reinforced my need to keep them protected. I'm not sure I would ever lose that need and I hoped I never would. My head throbbed where the stitches were still healing, a constant reminder of how close we'd come to losing everything.

Knight spotted us from across the room and made his way over, his black sclera tattoos making his grin look even wider by contrast. He wore a Santa hat, and I bit back a smile at how the red and white clashed with his otherwise intimidating appearance.

"About Goddamn time you showed up," he said with a grin, clapping me on the shoulder. The impact sent a fresh jolt of pain through my cracked ribs, but I managed to keep my expression neutral. "We saved you some grub before these animals ate it all."

"Hey, Z." Knight grinned at the girl. Strangely, neither Zelda nor Kira had ever blinked at Knight's appearance. In fact, I kind of think Zelda admired him. Didn't mean she didn't give him shit like she did everyone else. "Violet made those sugar cookies you like. The ones with the icing that turns your tongue blue."

A hint of interest flashed across Zelda's face before she masked it with practiced indifference. "Whatever. I guess I could try one."

Knight winked at her and straightened up. "They're over by the tree. Better hurry before Griffin finds 'em."

As Knight led the way, I glanced around the warehouse. My brothers, the people I trusted with my life, along with our growing families. Children from Haven and other women's shelters in the area and their mothers darted all over the place, their laughter echoing off the high ceiling. Our women chatted in groups, some wearing sparkly Christmas sweaters that contrasted sharply with their husbands' leather cuts.

Heresy or not, I was pretty sure someone had bedazzled Chains and Pain's vests on the back. Around the club emblem no less.

Everyone was here. Caleb and several of the kids played a new video game, trash talking and razzing each other good naturedly. Did my heart good.

Penny slipped her hand into mine, her fingers warm and small against my palm. "You doing okay?" she asked quietly, her eyes searching my face. "We can leave early if your ribs are bothering you."

I squeezed her hand gently. "I'm fine, honey. Nothing's gonna keep me from giving you all a proper Christmas." I grinned down at her. "Besides, I think I need this as much as I want to give it to the three of you."

The smile that spread across her face was worth every aching bone in my body. "I think it's already the best one we've ever had."

We followed Knight to a table near the tree where Violet greeted Penny with a warm hug. The girls hovered nearby, Zelda pretending not to care while Kira edged closer to the plate of cookies Knight had mentioned.

"Go ahead, honey," Penny encouraged her, and Kira reached for a star-shaped cookie frosted in bright blue. Then she snagged the whole plate and took off to the other kids in the corner with the video game. I couldn't help but chuckle.

I hung back slightly as Violet and Pippa brought Penny into their exclusive club of the biker old ladies within Kiss of Death, positioning myself where I could see both exits while still watching the girls. My gaze swept the room for threats. Another prison habit that had saved my life more than once and I couldn't seem to break no matter where I was.

"They're safe here," Riot said quietly, appearing at my side with two cups of spiced cider. He handed one to me. "No one's getting past our security."

I nodded, taking a sip of the cider. Spiked with something I was sure would help me relax. The warmth spread through my chest, easing some of the persistent ache in my ribs. Probably help with the pain too. "I know." I groaned in relief. "Just can't turn it off."

"Nor should you," he replied, his voice low enough that only I could hear. "But maybe dial it back to eight instead of eleven. It's Christmas Eve."

Steam rose from the cup in my hand, carrying the scent of cinnamon and cloves and the healthy, bitter tang of whiskey. Jack and apple cider was just wrong. Good, but wrong. Across the room, Caleb approached the girls, showing them something on his phone that had both of them laughing. Real laughs from both of them, not the guarded, half-hearted chuckles like they'd had when they'd first come here. Penny watched them from a few feet away, her eyes bright with unshed tears.

I knew what she was seeing. Her daughters acting like children for once, not the hypervigilant, guarded little adults they'd been forced to become. The knot in my throat tightened as I watched them. This was what I'd fought for, what I'd take a hundred more crowbar hits to protect.

Griffin passed by wearing reindeer antlers, a striking contrast to the full sleeve tattoos visible beneath his rolled-up flannel shirt. A little boy sat perched on Griffin's shoulders, his tiny hands clutching the antlers for balance. The sight made me smile despite myself.

"Never thought I'd see the day," I muttered to

Riot.

"What's that?"

"All of this." I gestured with my cup to encompass the room, all the battle-hardened bikers in Santa hats passing out presents, the children running between tables, the women laughing together over cups of eggnog. "Our own version of normal."

Riot followed my gaze to where Zelda and Kira finally relaxed enough to laugh and joke. No small thanks to Caleb. Even now, the young teen stayed close to the pair. Since the incident a couple of days ago, he'd been even more protective. Kid believed in taking care of the women in his life and I respected the hell out of him for it. I was also glad to see he'd included Kira and Zelda in his circle of family. They needed him to reinforce the idea not all men were evil pricks.

The girls' usual defensive posture had softened, their shoulders no longer hunched against expected danger. Kira moved to sit cross-legged under the tree with another girl from Haven, both of them examining ornaments with solemn concentration. When I'd first met Kira, she'd never have initiated interaction with another child. She might not have rebuffed anyone, but she'd preferred to hang back with her sister.

"Ain't nothing normal about us," Riot said with a quiet laugh. "But that's what makes it work."

Penny caught my eye from across the room and smiled, a private smile meant just for me. Something in my chest expanded, pushing against my injured ribs in a way that had nothing to do with pain. I was also reminded it had been two days since I'd had sex with her and as beaten as I was, I was ready to see how much I could get her to do before she realized I might not be up to the task just yet. I thought I could get her to do most of the work if I teased her enough.

As I made my way back to her side, navigating through the crowd while keeping an eye on the girls, I realized Riot was right. There was nothing normal about our family. Nothing normal about ex-cons feeling safer than stepfathers. Nothing normal about colored lights strung across camo netting or outlaw bikers wearing Santa hats. But as Penny leaned into my side and I carefully wrapped my arm around her shoulders, I knew I wouldn't trade our version of normal for anything in the Goddamned world.

I was nursing my second cup of nicely spiked cider when I caught Zelda and Kira huddled together by the decoration table, whispering and casting glances my way. That particular combination -- Zelda's plotting expression and Kira's barely suppressed giggles -- signaled the best kind of trouble. They broke apart when they noticed me watching, approaching with exaggerated innocence that immediately set off warning bells. Zelda had her hands clasped behind her back, rocking on her heels in a way that reminded me of a cartoon bomb about to go off.

"What are you two up to?" I asked, narrowing my eyes in mock suspicion.

"We need you for something," Zelda announced, her tone making it clear this wasn't a request but a command. "A surprise."

Kira nodded enthusiastically, bouncing slightly on her toes. "Please, Tiny? It's for Christmas."

Those words, "for Christmas", had become a magical incantation over the past two days, one the girls had quickly learned I couldn't resist. I set my cup down on a nearby table, already resigned to whatever fate they had planned for me.

"All right, what's this surprise?" I asked, knowing full well I was walking into a trap.

"First," Zelda said, holding up one finger, "you need to sit in the middle of the room."

"On the floor," Kira added helpfully, pointing to a spot near the tree. "You're too tall for a chair."

I glanced at the hard floor, then took stock of my still-healing ribs. Pain had warned me to avoid sudden movements and awkward positions, but I had no hope in hell of denying them when they gave me those big eyes, wide and full of excitement. Which made the decision for me.

"Lead the way," I said, resigned to my fate as I gestured for them to go ahead.

They both took my hands and led me to the spot they'd chosen. I braced one hand against my side where the worst of the bruising remained and went to my doom willingly. The movement sent a sharp jab of pain through my torso that nearly took my breath away. I managed to control my expression, but a hiss of discomfort escaped through clenched teeth.

"Are you okay?" Kira asked immediately, her brow furrowing with concern.

"Just a little sore still, darlin'. Nothing to worry about." I finished lowering myself to the floor, crossing my legs in front of me. The position pulled at my healing ribs, but it was bearable. "See? I'm fine."

Zelda studied me skeptically, her eyes narrowed. "You're still hurt from fighting Dad."

"Not your dad anymore," I corrected gently, meeting her gaze. "And I'm healing up just fine. Now what's this surprise you've got planned?"

The girls exchanged a look, communicating in that silent way they had, before Zelda nodded decisively. "Stay right there. Don't move." They darted back to the decoration table, and I saw them gathering materials with the serious concentration of artists selecting their medium. When they returned, their arms were full of tinsel, battery-powered string lights, and sparkly beads that had been draped on smaller trees around the room.

"We had so much fun last time, we're going to turn you into a Christmas tree again. Besides, Christmas trees are an important thing this time of year," Kira announced, her voice solemn as though imparting great wisdom.

I raised my eyebrows, looking from their expectant faces to the pile of decorations now scattered around me on the floor. "Again?"

"Yep," Zelda clarified, already sorting through the tinsel. "You're big enough even sitting down. And it's much more fun to decorate you than a stupid old tree." Yeah, I heard the humor in Zelda's voice.

A laugh rumbled up from my chest, making my ribs protest again, but I couldn't help it. "Can't argue with that logic, I suppose." I heaved out a sigh. "Fine. I guess Christmas only comes once a year."

"Except for Christmas in July," Zelda added, not even looking at me as she focused on her task.

Kira beamed at me, clearly taking my response as enthusiastic consent. "You did pretty good last time, but you have to remember to hold really still," she instructed, carefully unwinding a strand of battery-powered lights. Again.

Fuck my life.

On second thought, no. If the girls wanted to turn me into a human Christmas tree every night until next Christmas, who was I to argue? Especially when it made them look and act so carefree.

I settled more comfortably on the floor -- or rather, as comfortably as possible with cracked ribs, and prepared myself. Zelda approached first, draping a length of silver tinsel around my shoulders like a scarf. She stepped back, head tilted critically to the side, then adjusted it slightly.

"Your beard needs decorating too," she decided, picking up a handful of smaller tinsel strands. With surprising gentleness, she began to weave them through my braided beard, her tongue poked between her lips in concentration. Meanwhile, Kira had circled behind me, carefully wrapping a string of colored lights around my upper arms.

"Is this okay?" she asked softly, her eyes serious as she checked my face for any sign of discomfort.

"It's perfect," I assured her, and was rewarded with a smile that lit up her whole face.

I sensed rather than saw our audience forming. A few chuckles reached my ears, followed by the distinctive click of phone cameras. Out of the corner of my eye, I spotted Knight with his phone raised, a shit-eating grin on his face that told me these photos would be circulating among the club members for years to come.

"The great James 'Tiny' Reeves, brought to his knees by two fierce young women armed with tinsel, lights, and beads." Griffin teased, passing behind Knight.

"I'm sending this to my sister, Susie. Her husband, Stunner, will sympathize." Gunnar stood at the edge of the crowd, snapping pictures.

"Perfect timing," Hannah, Gunnar's twin and Knuckles' wife laughed as she looked at her phone.

She turned it to Gunnar who snorted cider out his nose, coughed several times, and wiped his nose on the back of his sleeve before collapsing into a nearby chair because he was laughing so hard. "I swear to God, that never gets old."

"What never gets old?" Zelda asked, turning from her task to walk over to Hannah. To my consternation, every kid in the place came over and got a hand in this whole human Christmas tree project like someone had thrown up an emergency flare.

Zelda squealed, snagged Hannah's phone and ran to Caleb. And I got a sinking feeling in the pit of my stomach. Especially when Gunnar snorted another drink out his nose. This time, he just let the drink drip into his short beard while he outright guffawed.

When Zelda and Caleb returned, Caleb was wearing the biggest shit-eating grin I'd ever seen. Zelda was carrying a bucket as she hurried over.

Again, like some kind of invisible signal went up, the kids abandoned me to gather around the bucket and Zelda. Meanwhile, Caleb went to stand with the others, watching with varying degrees of amusement.

"Ah, hell," I said under my breath. "I got a bad feelin' about this."

The feeling intensified when Zelda held up a can of hair spray. Before I could really appreciate what was about to happen, the group of them descended on me with… something. I couldn't really see, but they used the hairspray on my beard. They used… a *lot* of hairspray. On my beard.

Ten minutes later, there were pictures being taken by every fucking brother in the club. The kids were laughing and squealing and my ribs hurt like a motherfucker, but I stayed still, growling occasionally just to get the kids to giggle. Which they did. Continuously. I knew the pictures were going to be epic and I'd never live them down, but I wouldn't trade this moment for anything in the world. Not when it put such joy on the faces of all my girls.

"Perfect," Zelda declared, standing back to

admire her work.

A strand of tinsel slipped down, tickling my nose, and I couldn't suppress the laugh that rumbled up from my chest. The pain in my ribs was worth it for the delight on the girls' faces.

"Will someone at least give me a mirror so I can see how fu -- er, friggin' jolly I look?"

More laughter and this time I was pretty sure Gunnar was gonna manage to drown on the amount of cider he aspirated. Hannah stepped over to her brother and whacked him on the back several times while wiping tears from her own eyes as she laughed herself.

Through the growing crowd, I caught sight of Penny. She stood a few feet away, one hand pressed to her mouth, the other clutched tightly at her chest. Even from this distance, I could see the sheen of tears in her eyes, but they weren't tears of sadness. The smile that broke through as our eyes met was pure joy -- unexpected and overwhelming in its intensity.

I held her gaze, trying to communicate everything I couldn't say aloud in that moment. *I love you. I love them. I would endure far worse than decorated dignity for the sound of their laughter.* She seemed to understand, nodding slightly as she wiped at her eyes with the back of her hand, her smile so fucking beautiful I knew there would never be a time in my life when I didn't miss her smile any time I couldn't see her lovely face.

The crowd had grown, other children watching with wide-eyed, joy-filled fascination as the fearsome biker was transformed into a gaudy Christmas creation. A few of the smaller kids giggled behind their hands, while the adults made no attempt to hide their amusement.

"Stand up," Zelda commanded once she was

satisfied with her decorating. "Slowly, so nothing falls off."

Rising from the floor with my injuries was going to be even harder than sitting down had been, but I wasn't about to disappoint them. I braced one hand against the ground and pushed myself upward, gritting my teeth against the sharp stab of pain in my side. The lights and tinsel shifted but mostly stayed in place, thanks to the girls' careful arrangement. I thought I saw glitter dust falling as I disturbed some of the more textured garland they'd wrapped around me. Had to be. Right? Sweet, God, what had they put in my beard?

Once I was on my feet, Zelda tugged at my hand. "Now you have to bend down so we can get on your shoulders."

I crouched carefully, allowing first Zelda, then Kira to climb onto my shoulders. The added weight sent fresh pain through my ribs, but I locked my knees after I'd straightened slowly, supporting each girl with one hand to keep them balanced. Yep. It was as difficult as it sounded.

"Ladies and gentlemen," Zelda announced to the gathered crowd, her voice ringing with pride, "we present… the Christmas Tiny!"

A cheer went up from the crowd, followed by applause and more camera flashes and I knew Caleb, the little shit, had been recording the whole fucking mess from the second he returned with Zelda and that fucking bucket. I stood there, tinsel tickling my neck, lights blinking against my chest, beads tangled in my beard, and two nearly teenage girls perched triumphantly on my shoulders. As ridiculous as I must have looked, the wonder on Penny's face as she watched us made me feel ten feet tall. And I still didn't know what they'd put in my beard. OK, so maybe it was more denial than ignorance. Because, I absolutely knew I was going to have to shave after tonight.

Penny gave me a look of sympathy which she ruined by turning her lips inward as she tried valiantly to suppress a laugh.

"Go ahead and laugh," I told her, mock irritation in my voice. "I'll get my revenge." I snapped my teeth at Penny. Which delighted the girls to no end. And everyone else. Whoops went up all around and everyone laughed until I thought more than one of the kids had to go pee. Couple of my brothers too.

"The best Christmas tree in the whole compound," Knight declared, raising his cup in a mock toast. "Glitter beard and all." There wasn't a single person in the common room with us who didn't roar with laughter.

"Stunner says to tell you he recommends at least three shampoos the first day." Hannah gave me a serious look, like she wasn't talking about something as serious as desecrating a man's beard. "He said you could probably cut back to two after that. Says it takes a good month to get it all out."

Penny did something with her phone, then turned it around so I could see the picture of myself, the girls sitting on my shoulders, wrapped in Christmas lights, tinsel, icicles, garland… and the biggest, sparkliest glitter beard in red, gold, and green in the whole Goddamned world. I fucking loved it. Of course, I couldn't let them know how much I loved it. So I was appropriately outraged. Which caused more laughter.

Kira leaned down, her mouth close to my ear. "Are we too heavy?" she whispered, concern evident in her voice.

I turned my head slightly to meet her worried gaze. "Not even a little bit, darlin'."

The smile she gave me was worth every twinge, every ache, every bit of discomfort. As I stood in the center of the room, surrounded by my brothers and decorated like a Christmas spectacle, I realized I'd never felt more at home.

Chapter Thirteen

Tiny

The apartment was quiet when we finally made it back, the girls practically sleepwalking after all the excitement. I headed to the shower in my apartment across the hall from them. I'd been staying over most nights, but as much as I loved all three of them, even though I hadn't been around many women for fifteen years, I wasn't stupid enough not to realize that sometimes, one apartment simply wasn't big enough for three women. So I'd kept the suite, and it worked out now. I didn't want to get glitter everywhere in Penny's bathroom.

Good call, too, because when I hit the lights in my bathroom, I looked like a fucking disco ball. There were streaks of rainbow glitter in my beard, plastered to my arms and even my Goddamn eyebrows. Beard was nearly solid with so much hairspray, and I left a sparkly trail everywhere I went. Guess that was what happened when you let a pack of feral children douse you in art supplies.

I turned on the shower and undressed. The quicker I could wash this shit out the quicker I could go find Penny and sweet talk her into fucking me. Because, honestly, I had very little gas left in the tank.

"They're out cold," Penny's voice came from the doorway. She stepped inside and shut the door as I stepped into the shower. "I don't think Santa himself could wake them up tonight."

"Come here," I said, holding out my hand to her. "Help me wash out this shit. Then I want to fuck you."

She grinned up at me. "Wasn't sure you'd be up to it."

"Oh, baby. I'm definitely up to it." And I was.

My cock pulsed and ached, standing at complete attention, needing her touch.

She stepped in the shower with me and reached for my cock. When she wrapped her palm around my dick, I groaned in reaction, my hips thrusting subtly at her.

"Christ, woman," I growled. "Always need your touch."

"I need your touch too," she whispered, leaning into me as warm water cascaded over us both. "But I don't want to hurt you."

Thank God, the shower in this master bath was huge because there was no way to fit my big body into the shower in my old apartment with Penny in there with me. With my bruised ribs screaming with every breath, I doubt I could have managed but right now, I didn't give a good Goddamn about my fucking ribs. Penny pressed against me to avoid the spray, her soft skin warm against mine, and nothing else mattered. The bruises Andy's men had left, the ache along my ribs where they'd landed their hardest blows, were worth every second of pain if it meant she was safe. And in this shower. Here. With me.

"You could never hurt me," I murmured, letting my hands skim down her sides with all the delicacy I could muster. Touching her required such care. She was infinitely precious, breakable in a way that terrified me. "Not unless you leave me."

My hands trembled slightly, partly from the pain that shot through me when I moved, partly from the overwhelming reality that she was letting me touch her like this. The bruises didn't matter. The pain didn't matter.

"You're in pain," she said.

Our eyes met. No point lying to her. She saw

through me too easily. "Worth it."

Two words. The truest thing I'd ever said. I'd taken that beating to protect her and her girls, and I'd do it again without hesitation. This pain was something I'd bear proudly because I'd protected my girls. My family.

"Let me," she whispered, reaching for the soap. "Let me take care of you for once."

My chest tightened as she began washing me, her hands careful around my worst bruises. Until she tackled my beard. Stunner had been right. It had taken all of three washings. I could probably have used a fourth, but I was eager for Penny to continue touching the rest of me.

"You're always taking care of me," I said, the words rumbling up from somewhere deep. "Every day since you walked into Haven."

She smiled, pressing a kiss to my chest that made my heart stutter. "That goes both ways."

Her hands moved lower, washing away glitter I'd probably never fully get rid of. When her fingers wrapped around my cock again, I couldn't stop the sharp intake of breath, my head falling back against the wall. Fifteen years I'd waited for this woman, and she still reduced me to trembling need with a single touch.

"Penny," I groaned, my hands finding her hips. "Need to touch you."

I could see the concern in her eyes, worry about my injuries, but I couldn't not touch her. My fingers slid between her legs, finding her wet and ready.

I pushed two fingers inside her carefully, my thumb finding her clit with practiced ease. I'd learned from our nights together because I'd never leave Penny unsatisfied after sex. My free hand cupped her breast, thumb brushing her nipple in rhythm.

"God, look at you," I murmured, unable to tear my gaze away. "Most beautiful thing I've ever seen."

She flushed under my attention, still not quite believing how I saw her. Andy had been a blind fool. Penny wasn't something to possess, she was a precious, perfect woman and mother, someone to cherish, to worship, to protect with everything I had.

My breathing grew labored, the arousal mixing with pain as my ribs protested every movement. My hand trembled against her breast and I moved my arm around her back to pull her closer to me. When I leaned forward to kiss her neck, the movement pulled at my injuries hard enough to make me wince.

"Baby," she whispered, catching my face between her palms. "We can wait until you're feeling better."

I felt my expression shift, half amused, half determined. She didn't understand. "Not waiting another day, Penny. Two was enough."

When she giggled, burying her face in my chest, I curled my finger inside her, finding that spot that made her knees buckle. She clutched at my shoulders, careful even now to avoid my bruises. I held her weight effortlessly despite the lingering pain.

"See?" I said, smiling as her body responded. "Some things are worth a little pain."

Her laugh sent warmth through my chest. "Stubborn man."

"Yours, though," I answered. The truest words I'd ever spoken.

I reached behind her to shut off the shower without removing my hand from between her legs. She shivered -- from the cold or from my touch, I couldn't tell, didn't care. I pulled her against me, feeling her breasts press against my chest, her nipples hardening.

When I bent to kiss her, my ribs screamed in protest, muscles tensing involuntarily.

"Bed," she said firmly. "Now."

"Yes, ma'am," I replied, grinning. I loved when she got bossy. "But only if you come with me."

She toweled me dry with gentle strokes that felt more intimate than anything I'd experienced before. When we were both dry, I scooped her into my arms, ignoring her protests about my ribs. She weighed nothing and carrying her felt right. She protested, but I thought it was halfhearted at best.

I laid her on the bed with exquisite care, then stretched out beside her, propped on one elbow to look down at her body. Raw hunger coursed through me. Fifteen years of wanting, of dreaming, and I'd finally found the woman meant to be mine. "You're incredible," I whispered, my hand tracing the curve of her hip. My touch stayed light.

She reached up to stroke my beard, her smile making my chest tight. "You're not so bad yourself. Even covered in glitter."

I groaned, dropping my head to her shoulder. "Never gonna live that down, am I?"

"Not for at least a year. Tiny," she said softly. "You don't have to push through this. We have our whole life. You can take time to heal before we have sex again."

"You giving me orders again?" I asked, loving the way she tried to take care of me.

"If that's what it takes to make you take care of yourself."

I smiled, tender but determined. I slid my hand over her stomach, my fingers dipping between her legs again. "What if this is exactly what I need?"

Her body arched into my touch, and satisfaction

roared through me. "Then I guess I'd better let you have your way," she breathed.

I leaned down to kiss her, and she opened to me completely. This woman, this incredible, strong, beautiful woman, trusted me with her body, her pleasure, her safety. With her heart. And she was worth every single fucking second. That, more than anything, was the true miracle of Christmas.

Her fingers stroked over my cheek as she petted my beard, and I could see the concern in her eyes. Fuck, I hated that she could read me so easily. My ribs were screaming at me, the position pulling at muscles that shouldn't be moving like this, but I'd be damned if I'd let pain stop me from touching her.

"The hot water would help your muscles," she said. "Why don't we go back to the shower?"

I raised an eyebrow, letting a slow smile spread across my face despite the ache in my side. "You trying to get me clean or dirty?"

"Both," she admitted with a little laugh, pressing a kiss to my jaw that sent heat straight to my cock. "Definitely both."

I chuckled, feeling the rumble in my chest. With more grace than most people expected from a man my size, I rose from the bed and pulled her up with me. My gaze locked with hers as I led her back toward the bathroom, her small hand disappearing completely in mine.

The bathroom was still thick with steam when we entered, moisture clinging to every surface. I turned on the shower again, adjusting the temperature until it was hot enough to ease the knots in my muscles.

"Come here," I said, my voice coming out low and rough.

She stepped into the shower, water immediately streaming down her perfect skin. Water cascaded over my back and shoulders, hot enough to sting the fading bruises. Droplets caught in my beard, but I barely noticed. I was too focused on her.

"You're so fucking beautiful," I murmured, pulling her against me. My cock pressed hard against her stomach, and there was no hiding how much I wanted her, and I didn't even try.

Her hands ran up my chest, and I noticed how careful she was around my injuries. "So are you."

I laughed softly, my hands sliding down her back to cup her ass. The contrast of her soft curves against my calloused palms never got old. "Not sure beautiful's the right word for a man like me."

"It's exactly the right word," she insisted, rising on tiptoes to kiss me.

I responded immediately, claiming her mouth with a hunger I could barely control. I cradled the back of her head with my hand, fingers tangling in her wet hair as I deepened the kiss. My tongue stroked against hers, demanding but gentle. She deserved gentle more than any woman I'd ever known.

Without breaking the kiss, I maneuvered us so her back was against the cool tile wall. I needed her pinned there, needed to feel her trapped between the wall and my body. The move was about protecting her, possessing her in the best possible way. I always wanted my body, honed in the fires of battle under the most brutal of conditions, between her and the world.

"Hold onto me," I murmured against her lips.

Her arms wrapped around my neck as I gripped her thighs, lifting her effortlessly. She weighed nothing to me; I could hold her like this for hours if she'd let me. Her legs circled my waist, ankles crossing behind my back, and the feel of her pussy sliding against my cock nearly made me come right there.

"You sure?" she asked, those worried eyes searching my face again. "Your ribs --"

"Are fine," I finished, pressing my forehead to hers. The ribs could go fuck themselves. "I need you, Penny. Need to be inside you."

She nodded, and relief flooded through me. Her small hand reached between us, guiding my bare cock to her entrance. Which, again, nearly made me come.

I pushed forward slowly, gritting my teeth against the urge to slam into her. She was always so fucking tight, and I had to give her time to adjust. "Fuck," I groaned as I seated myself fully within her. "Love how fuckin' tight you are. Love the feel of your hot, slick pussy around my cock." My body trembled with the effort of holding back. Every instinct screamed at me to pound into her, to take her hard and fast, but I kept myself leashed.

"Move," she whispered, digging her heels into my lower back. "Please, Tiny. Fuck me!"

Her needy demand snapped my control. With a grunt, I began to thrust, shallow at first, testing. When she didn't flinch, I went deeper. The angle was perfect, I could tell by the way her breath caught, the way her pussy clenched around me. Water streamed down my face and chest, and my muscles flexed and bunched with each movement. The pain in my ribs was still there, but it was distant now, drowned out by the pleasure of being inside her.

Steam swirled around us, and the bathroom echoed with our breathing, mine deep and ragged, hers high and desperate. The slick slide of our bodies coming together was the perfect accompaniment to our erotic dance. Christ, I'd never get enough of this.

"So tight. So fuckin' perfect."

My words seemed to push her closer, and I felt her nails score over my shoulders.

"God, Tiny," she moaned, and the sound of my name on her lips nearly undid me. "Right fucking there!"

I adjusted my angle slightly, making sure to hit that spot with each thrust. My gaze never left hers, watching every reaction, cataloging what made her gasp, what made her moan. It was worship. And I wanted her to always know how much I loved her. I would never be a man of pretty words, but I could give her this. I could show her how much I loved her with my body.

The familiar tension built in my spine, but I wasn't going there without her. I moved one hand from her thigh to slide between us, my thumb finding her clit.

"Come for me, baby," I urged, my voice rough and strained. "Want to feel you squeezing my cum from my dick."

She came apart in my arms, her back arching off the tile as pleasure crashed through her as she screamed. Her pussy clenched around me rhythmically, milking my cock, and she screamed my name. The feeling of her coming around me was the most beautiful thing I'd ever experienced.

My movements became more urgent, my rhythm faltering as I chased my own release. With a final, deep thrust, I buried myself completely inside her and groaned her name, my cock pulsing as I emptied myself into her. Wave after wave of pleasure rolled through me, and I felt her trigger again, trembling in my arms.

For a long moment, we stayed joined, both of us

breathing hard as the water continued to beat down on us. I rested my forehead against hers, eyes closed as I tried to recover. When I opened them again, the emotion welling up inside me was almost too much to contain.

"I love you," I said simply. The words felt inadequate for what I felt, but they were all I had.

"I love you too," she whispered back.

Carefully, I lowered her to her feet, making sure she was steady before letting go completely. I cupped her face with my big hands and stroked her cheekbone with one thumb. "You're everything to me," I murmured. "You and Kira and Zelda."

She turned her head to press a kiss to my palm, and the tenderness of the gesture hit me square in the chest. "And you're everything to us."

* * *

Penny

We dried each other with tender care, the mundane act somehow intimate in the afterglow of our shower. Tiny winced slightly as he bent to dry my legs, a reminder of the injuries he'd sustained protecting us. I took the towel from him, finishing the job myself.

"Let me take care of you," I said, guiding him back toward the bedroom.

The sheets were slightly rumpled, the room warm and inviting in the dim light. Tiny sat on the edge of the bed, his massive frame making the king-size mattress look almost small. Despite having just found release in the shower, his eyes darkened and his cock pulsed with renewed desire as I stood naked before him.

"Come here," he said, his voice a low rumble that I felt in my bones.

I approached slowly, savoring the way his gaze traveled over my body. When I reached him, I placed my hands on his broad shoulders and gently pushed him backward until he was lying on the bed. His eyebrows rose in surprise, but he went willingly, a smile playing at the corners of his mouth.

"My turn," I told him, climbing onto the bed and straddling his hips. "You've done enough work for one week."

His hands found my thighs, sliding upward to grip my hips. "Not fighting you on this, baby."

I leaned down to kiss him, my hair creating a curtain around our faces. He responded immediately, his beard tickling my skin as his lips moved against mine. When I pulled back, his eyes were hooded with desire, pupils dilated so only a thin ring of blue remained. Despite his recent release, his cock pulsed like mad and I could feel the dampness of his precum on my belly. I rocked against him experimentally, drawing a groan from deep in his chest. His fingers tightened on my hips, but he made no move to take control, allowing me to set the pace.

"Ready for me already?" I teased, grinding against his growing erection.

"I think I'll always be ready for you," he answered, his voice rough with want.

I reached between us to guide him to my entrance again, then slowly sank down, taking him inch by inch until he was fully seated inside my cunt.

Tiny's focus never left my face as I began to move, rising and falling in a slow, deliberate rhythm. His hands on my hips supported but didn't direct me, letting me find the pace that pleased me most. I placed my palms flat against his chest, careful to avoid the worst of his bruising, and used the leverage to ride him more firmly.

"Fuck," he breathed, his head tipping back slightly. "The way you fuckin' move!"

I watched his face, memorizing every flicker of expression, the way his brow furrowed when I squeezed around him, how his lips parted on a silent gasp when I took him particularly deep, the intensity in his eyes when they locked with mine -- all of it. I never wanted to forget one blessed, blistering second of making love with Tiny. This mountain of a man, so feared by others, lay vulnerable beneath me, his pleasure entirely in my hands. I'd never felt more powerful in my life. Until this very moment, I never realized how much I needed to feel like I had the power. The feeling now was intoxicating.

Sex had been about Andy's control and dominance, selfish greed even. With Tiny, even when he led, there was always care in his touch. His pleasure seemed inextricably tied to mine, as though he couldn't enjoy himself unless I was satisfied first.

I increased my pace, chasing the building tension low in my belly. Tiny's hands slid up to cup my breasts, thumbs brushing over my nipples in time with my movements. The added stimulation pushed me closer to the edge.

"That's it, baby," he encouraged, his voice strained as he fought to hold back his own release. "Take what you need."

My rhythm faltered as pleasure built to an almost unbearable peak. "Tiny," I gasped, my thighs trembling with the effort to maintain my position. "I'm coming!"

"I know," he murmured, his eyes never leaving mine. "Let go. I've got you."

Those words, so simple, yet carrying the weight

of a promise I knew he'd always keep, sent me hurtling over the edge. My back arched as the orgasm crashed through me, my inner walls clenching around him rhythmically. Through the haze of my own pleasure, I felt Tiny's control finally snap. His hips bucked upward as he groaned my name, his release pulsing deep inside me.

I collapsed onto his chest, mindful of his injuries even in my boneless state. His arms came around me immediately, holding me close as we both struggled to catch our breath. For a long moment, we lay tangled together, my head tucked under his chin, his heartbeat thundering against my ear.

When I could move again, I shifted to lie beside him, my head pillowed on his uninjured shoulder.

"Do you hurt much?" I asked, my touch featherlight over a particularly angry-looking bruise on his ribs.

He caught my hand, bringing it to his lips. "Nothing I can't handle. And any pain I might have felt was overshadowed completely by pleasure."

I frowned, unconvinced. "You don't have to be stoic with me. I saw what they did to you."

His expression softened. "Honestly? It hurts like a bitch. But it's getting better." He pressed a kiss to my palm. "And it was worth it. I'd do it again in a heartbeat. All of it."

"Thank you," I whispered, my throat tight with emotion. "For protecting us. With your body. And your heart."

Tiny's eyes held mine, serious and sincere. "I'd endure it a thousand times to keep you safe. All three of you."

I believed him completely. This man, who'd spent fifteen years in prison for protecting his sister, understood the fierce, primal need to safeguard those you love. He'd taken on Andy and his men without hesitation, putting himself between danger and my family without a second thought. I was glad they'd found a way to make Andy pay for what he'd done and intended to do to Zelda without anyone getting into trouble.

"What's going to happen to Andy? I don't want him to come after Zelda again."

"He's going to prison for a long fuckin' time. Knight's makin' sure the evidence is solid. Knuckles told me Tonio Miles has some pull with several judges in the system. We do work for the Miles family that's critical to them, so he was more than happy to help put an evil bastard like Andy Harlow in hell." The smile on his face turned slightly sinister for a brief moment as he said, "I have it on good authority the poor bastard won't last long enough to have to sign divorce papers." Then he shrugged. "If he does? Well, Knight can do all kinds of things he's not supposed to do. I have no doubt he can make shit happen."

"I never thought I'd find this," I admitted, my voice barely audible even in the quiet room. "Someone who makes me feel safe. A home. A family who would protect my girls if I couldn't."

His arm tightened around me. "You deserve to feel safe, Penny. All of you do."

I rested my head on his chest again, listening to the steady thump of his heart. The sound was reassuring, solid and strong, just like the man himself. I traced the outline of a bruise near his collarbone.

"I keep waiting for the other shoe to drop," I confessed. "For something to go wrong. It's hard to believe this is real."

Tiny's hand stroked gently up and down my

spine. "It's real," he assured me. "I'm real. And I'm not going anywhere."

I pressed a kiss to his chest, right over his heart. "I believe you."

And I did, that was the miracle. After years of broken promises and betrayals, I believed this man completely. I trusted him with my safety, with my daughters. With my heart. I'd sworn never to entrust it to anyone again after Andy, but I now wondered how I hadn't seen through Andy from the very beginning. I was absolutely safe with Tiny. No question about it.

Outside the window, snow had begun to fall, large flakes drifting past in the darkness. Christmas was tomorrow, but I already felt like I'd received the greatest gift possible, a man who made me feel completely safe for the first time in my life and the promise of a future filled with the kind of love I thought existed only in fairy tales.

Tiny's breathing had deepened, his body relaxing toward sleep. I snuggled closer, drawing the covers up over us both. Tomorrow would bring Christmas morning with the girls, presents under the tree, and all the chaos of a holiday with family. But for now, in the quiet darkness of the bedroom in the apartment across the hall from my girls, I was content to simply be held by the man who had changed everything.

"Merry Christmas, Tiny," I whispered, pressing one more kiss to his chest.

His arms tightened around me briefly. "Merry Christmas, Penny," he murmured, his voice thick with approaching sleep. "First of many."

I closed my eyes, letting his heartbeat lull me toward dreams. First of many. The words settled in my chest, a promise I would hold onto, whatever challenges lay ahead. We'd face them together, this unexpected family of ours, built not from blood but from choice, from love, from the fierce determination to protect what was precious to us.

And *nothing* had ever felt more precious than this.

Rancor (Kiss of Death MC 10)
A Bones MC Romance
Marteeka Karland

A broken man, a wary woman, and a past that wants blood -- love has never been more dangerous.

Cora -- Survival is my full-time job. Delivering groceries to the Kiss of Death MC should've been just another stop... until Rancor stepped out of the shadows and looked at me like he already knew my secrets. His quiet strength is wrapped in scars and heat. He's the kind of man who could break the world but touches me like I'm the only soft thing he's got left. I should run. Instead, I keep driving through those gates, craving the one man who makes me feel safe in ways I don't dare say out loud.

Rancor -- I buried my heart years ago. Grief, violence, and prison killed anything left inside me, and I was glad. It meant I didn't have to feel anything. Then Cora walked into the compound and cracked me open with a single glance. She's brave without meaning to be, a storm in a small frame, and the first woman to make me feel anything since the night my life ended. One touch, and I knew I'd protect her with my last breath. One kiss and I knew I'd kill for her. I've already lost too much to lose her, too. Especially not to the same family who already ruined my life.

Chapter One

Cora

The gates of the Kiss of Death MC compound loomed ahead, iron and rust and threat. I knew the place was called Kiss of Death because there was a big-ass sign on the gate. I tightened my grip on the steering wheel of my beat-up sedan. No one wanted to deliver here, and for good reason. My second delivery here felt even worse.

The first time I could blame on ignorance, on not knowing better. This time I drove through those gates with full knowledge of what waited inside. At least, I hoped I did. The people inside these gates had been nothing but kind to me. Tipped well, too. I still found it hard to let my guard down in a place literally named Kiss of Death.

The sedan's engine coughed as I pressed the accelerator. The sound seemed too loud, even in a place that could get noisy. The rumble of a bike starting up had me jumping. As the guy caught sight of me, he froze and shut down the bike. Next thing I knew he was rolling backward, pushing the bike with his feet until he returned to the inside of the garage. I rolled forward, past the gates.

Camo netting stretched between the buildings, creating shadows in the afternoon light. The warehouses formed a perfect square with some kind of military precision in the architecture. If I didn't need the money, I definitely wouldn't be here.

The main building rose ahead. I'd been directed there last time, so I aimed for the same spot. I thought about the envelope from my first delivery. Cash, all of it, with a tip that equaled half the order total. That money had bought groceries for a week, gas for two. It had been the difference between making rent on time and asking my landlord for another extension I wouldn't get.

The parking area materialized ahead. I pulled in next to a row of motorcycles, their chrome catching the filtered light through the netting. My sedan looked all kinds of wrong among them.

I shifted into park and killed the engine. The silence felt worse than the noise. Now I could hear everything. Distant music from somewhere inside the compound. Male voices, laughing. It all sounded so normal I wanted to laugh at myself. Obviously they'd been grateful to get someone to deliver here and had treated me well. The phone app tracked my movements, kind of like a safeguard, so I really had little to worry about. I hoped.

My fingers fumbled with the door handle. Metal, cold against my palm. I pushed it open and the hinges squeaked, announcing my presence to anyone within earshot. The air outside tasted different than in my car. Heavier. It carried scents I couldn't identify; motor oil and something sharp underneath, something that made my lizard brain want to run.

Movement from the clubhouse caught my eye. Hannah bounded out waving as she hurried to me. She'd been the one to meet me last time.

She hurried toward me with an easy confidence and a bright, genuine smile I envied. Her dark hair caught the filtered light, pulled back from her face in a way that revealed high cheekbones and striking hazel eyes. She wore jeans and a simple T-shirt, and a black leather vest. I'd noticed last time the vest was similar to her husband's, though the back proclaimed her as "Property of Knuckles" where his simply said "Kiss of Death MC" and "Nashville, TN". It sounded barbaric, but this woman didn't seem oppressed in any way. In fact, when I met her the last time, her husband had dropped a kiss on top of her head as he'd passed her and hadn't let Hannah carry anything from the car.

I raised a hand in an awkward wave, immediately feeling stupid for the gesture. But Hannah's expression softened further, and she picked up her pace. I moved to the back of my car and lifted the trunk lid, ready to help her unload.

"You came back." Hannah's voice held a warm welcome that seemed impossible in this place. She stopped a few feet from my car, close enough to be friendly but far enough to respect boundaries. "I wasn't sure you would."

"The order came through." I tried to keep my voice steady, professional. "Same as last time."

"And you accepted it." Something shifted in her expression, a subtle approval that made me stand a little straighter. "Most drivers reject anything with our address. The guys haven't done anything, but this many ex-cons in one place makes people nervous, I guess." She frowned. "People tend to overlook the good they do. Not everyone guilty of bad things is a bad person."

I tilted my head to the side. "You know, I never thought about it that way. But you're right. I shouldn't judge people unless they give me reason to." I looked away, suddenly ashamed of myself. "I'd be in a world of hurt if people judged me by what they saw on the surface."

"Hey." Hannah moved closer, reaching out to touch my shoulder gently. "I wasn't trying to make you feel bad. We truly are grateful someone is willing to give us all a chance." She smiled, squeezing my shoulder gently before dropping her hand.

"Um, can I ask a question?" I didn't know why I asked her, but once I had, I intended to follow through.

"Of course." She looked pleasantly curious.

"I saw a guy when I first came in today. He came out of that building," I pointed back the way I'd come. "But he turned off his bike and rolled back into the shadows." I swallowed hard. If I'd gotten too nosy I might well have crossed a line I shouldn't have. But it was odd! Also, I might be feeling a little paranoid. But to my surprise, Hannah only smiled.

"The guys know this place isn't everyone's cup of tea. They also know that some people are scared of the noise, to say nothing of the men themselves. There's not one of them who doesn't look scary as hell." She grinned. "But every single one of them sat through and energetically participated in the Christmas party they had for the women and children in the shelter they help protect. The kids adore them all."

Before I could respond, movement behind her drew my attention. Another figure emerged from the clubhouse, moving with a deliberate slowness that made every step feel intentional.

My breath caught. He was big. Tall and broad-shouldered, big in the way that suggested power held in careful check. His shoulders stretched a gray T-shirt to its limits.

His head was shaved clean, and somehow, the man was more intimidating for its starkness. But it was his face that made my fingers tighten on the grocery bag I still held. Weathered. Lined with stress that had carved deep grooves around his mouth and between his eyebrows. He looked like a man who'd forgotten how to relax, if he'd ever known.

He approached with that same measured pace,

each footfall deliberate. The way he moved reminded me of documentaries I'd seen about predators. Not rushing. Never rushing. Because predators didn't need to hurry when they knew their prey couldn't escape. My heart, which had just started to calm, kicked back into overdrive.

"Cora, this is Rancor." Hannah gestured between us, casually as if introducing neighbors at a barbecue. Thank God she didn't notice my discomfort because how embarrassing would that be? "He's going to help with the groceries."

His gaze met mine, and I forced myself not to look away even though every instinct screamed at me to drop my gaze. His eyes were dark, nearly black in the shadow of the camo netting, and he studied me with an intensity that made my skin prickle.

"Ma'am." His voice was quiet and rough, as if he didn't use it much.

"Hi." The syllable came out higher than I wanted. I cleared my throat. "There are a lot of bags." Brilliant conversational skills, Cora. Truly impressive.

But Rancor just nodded, a single dip of his head, and moved past me to the trunk. He smelled like soap and motor oil, the combination oddly intriguing. I stepped back, giving him room.

He reached into the trunk and pulled out several bags at once, hoisting them like they weighed nothing. His forearms flexed, muscles shifting under skin decorated with what looked like a burn scar. Then he turned and walked toward the clubhouse at that same deliberate pace.

"So." Hannah's voice pulled my attention back to her. She'd moved closer, filling the space Rancor had vacated. "You deliver every day?"

"Most days." I watched Rancor's back as he

walked away, the way his T-shirt stretched across his shoulders. "Depends on the orders."

"That's a lot of driving." Hannah leaned against my car, comfortable in a way I envied. "You like it?"

Did I like it? I liked eating. I liked having electricity. I liked not being homeless. My job met those ends.

"It's fine," I said. "Flexible schedule."

Hannah's smile widened. Not mocking. Understanding. "Money talks?"

"Sometimes, I guess." No point in pretending otherwise. My car was clean, inside and out, and I took care with my appearance. I didn't have anything fancy, nor did I know how to do makeup or whatnot, but I kept myself clean, my clothes washed and pressed. Obviously, I didn't have much, but I had my pride.

Rancor emerged from the clubhouse, empty-handed now, heading back toward us. My pulse quickened at his proximity. Stupid. His presence made my pulse jump and my body betray me. I'd seen good-looking men before, both nice guys and dipshits. For some reason, though, this guy just did it for me when he shouldn't. Story of my life. Wanting things I had no business dreaming about.

He reached the trunk and grabbed another few bags. This time when he lifted them, his eyes cut to mine briefly. Just a flicker of contact, there and gone, but it jolted through me like touching a live wire. I looked away first. Examined my shoes as if they held the secrets of the universe.

"Where are you from?" Hannah asked, still making conversation like this was normal, like we were normal people in a normal place.

"Here. Nashville." I shifted my weight. "Well, just outside the city."

"You grow up here?"

"No." The word came out clipped. I didn't elaborate. Hannah didn't push. She seemed to have a way of paying attention to my body language and feeling me out.

Hannah glanced toward Rancor, who was emerging from the clubhouse again. When she looked back at me, something knowing glinted in her hazel eyes. "I'm glad you came back. Hopefully I can make a friend because you did."

Rancor collected the last of the bags. His fingers brushed the trunk's edge near where mine rested. We weren't touching, but we were close enough that I felt the heat of his skin.

He straightened with the final bags and paused. Looked at me full-on, not just a glance but actual eye contact that held for three long heartbeats. Then he walked away, and I remembered how to breathe.

When I finally brought my attention back to Hannah, I found her watching me with that same knowing expression, approval written in the curve of her mouth. I felt exposed in a way that had nothing to do with danger and everything to do with desire I had no business feeling.

Rancor must have set his load down somewhere because he now stood near the clubhouse door, hands loose at his sides, watching us. Watching me. The weight of his gaze pressed against my skin like humidity before a storm.

Hannah shifted closer, close enough that her voice dropped to something almost conspiratorial. "You know," she said, quiet enough that Rancor probably couldn't hear her. "You couldn't pick a better protector than any of the men from Kiss of Death."

The words hit me wrong. Too direct. Too

knowing. Like she'd reached inside my head and pulled out thoughts I hadn't fully formed yet. "I'm just delivering groceries." I kept my voice light, aiming for casual and probably missing by miles. "I don't need protection."

But even as I said the words, I felt the lie in them. I was one bad day's work away from being homeless. I lived in a really shitty part of town because I couldn't afford anything better.

Hannah's smile suggested she heard everything I didn't say. "Of course." I didn't know what to do with the implication hanging between us. That I needed protecting. That I might *want* protecting. Or, more aptly, that the men here, Rancor specifically, could provide the safety I longed for.

The idea should have offended me. I'd spent years learning to protect myself, to need no one, to be self-sufficient in every way that mattered. I'd always been stubborn. At least, I had been after I left my parents' sphere of influence.

"I should probably get going." I glanced at my phone, checking for new orders. Nothing yet. "Other deliveries." I hated lying to them, but I felt more than a little vulnerable.

"Sure." Hannah didn't move, didn't make space for me to leave. She looked over at Rancor, then back to me. "He's getting your tip."

Right. The tip. The reason I was here in the first place. The only reason I should care about being here. But my gaze drifted to Rancor anyway. He'd moved from the door, heading back toward us. He carried an envelope, white against his tanned skin. My throat went dry and I could practically hear myself gulp as he approached.

Hannah made a small sound, almost a laugh,

barely vocalized. When I glanced at her, she was smiling with unconcealed amusement. Caught. She'd caught me staring and we both knew it. Heat flooded my face. I looked away, studied the camo netting overhead like I'd never seen anything so fascinating.

Rancor reached us. Close enough now that I caught his scent again. Clean. He smelled clean and masculine and entirely too appealing. "We all pitched in for a tip." He held out the envelope. His voice maintained that quiet, measured quality, each word separated by space. Like he thought carefully before speaking. Like words cost something. "Appreciate you deliverin' supplies." He was definitely a man of few words.

I reached for the envelope. Tried to take it without touching him and failed. Our fingers brushed during the exchange. Just the barest contact, his skin against mine for less than a second. But static sparked between us. It jolted through me and I hissed in a breath, jerking my hand back as my breath caught in my throat.

Rancor met my gaze steadily. Up close his eyes weren't quite black. More a very dark brown, almost the color of coffee without cream. They studied me with that intensity I'd felt before, but now I was close enough to see something else in them. Something that looked almost like curiosity. Or hunger. Or both.

I took the envelope. Clutched it against my chest like a shield. "Thank you." My voice came out breathless. Stupid. "For the tip. I mean… thanks. And from last time, too. I can't remember if I thanked you guys or not." I shifted my gaze from Rancor back to Hannah. "Stop talking, Cora," I muttered to myself. "Stop talking right now."

Rancor's expression shifted. Not quite a smile.

Just a slight relaxation of the tension in his jaw. "You came back." A pause. Long enough that I almost jumped in to fill it. "When others wouldn't."

"It's just groceries." I shrugged, tried to seem casual. "Not a big deal."

"It is." Another pause. His eyes never left mine. "To us."

This wasn't just about the groceries. This was about respect. I understood that more than I wanted to admit. Being rejected. Being seen as not worth the trouble had been something I'd struggled with all my life. Still did.

"Well." I cleared my throat. "If you order again, I'll probably take it."

Probably. Like I didn't know I absolutely would. Like the generous tip was the only reason. Like I wasn't already hoping to see that address come through my app again. Besides, I kept thinking about what Hannah had said about judging people on the surface. I'd spent more than my fair share of time in homeless shelters and on the streets. I knew full well decent people did things they wouldn't do under normal circumstances.

"We will." Rancor's quiet certainty made it sound like a promise.

Hannah stepped back, creating space. "Drive safe, Cora."

"Thanks." I moved toward my car door, hand fumbling for the handle. The envelope crinkled in my other hand. When Hannah gave me another of her open, friendly smiles, the band around my chest eased.

She was genuine. I'd been on the street long enough to know when someone played me. The only vibe I caught from Hannah was an open friendliness I found refreshing. She lacked artifice, though I could tell she had a spine of steel. I admitted I knew Hannah was the real thing within the first minute after I met her. I guess I'd just feared trusting my gut when something seemed too good to be true.

I opened my door, and the hinges squeaked their protest. I slid behind the wheel and the seat wrapped around me with familiar comfort. Strangely, I found I didn't really want to leave. The realization hit me as I pulled the door closed. I didn't want to go. I wanted to stay here in this compound. Maybe I was simply building a fantasy around a sexy man. Wouldn't be the first time I'd done something equally stupid.

Stupid. Dangerous. Reckless. Story of my life.

I started the engine. It turned over with a rough cough that sounded more than a little judgmental. Through the windshield I could see Hannah and Rancor standing together. Hannah said something I couldn't hear and Rancor's attention shifted to her. Just for a moment. Then his gaze came back to me, tracking me through the glass.

I put the car in reverse. My hands felt steadier now on the wheel. I should have been relieved to leave. Should have felt that weight lift as I backed away from the compound. The envelope sat on the passenger seat where I'd tossed it. The small packet felt like a promise. Or maybe an excuse to come back.

I adjusted my grip on the wheel as I drove through those imposing gates. They looked less threatening from this side. Kind of like they kept out all the bad things in the outside world. Funny, because I think I felt more dread passing through them leaving than I did going in.

Behind me, the compound disappeared in my rearview mirror. Hannah and Rancor disappeared. That pull in my chest remained. I drove away with a heavy sigh, already hoping they'd forgotten something and needed me to come back.

And maybe I liked flirting with danger. Just a little bit.

Chapter Two

Rancor

The soil slid between my fingers, dark and moist against my scarred knuckles. Morning light filtered through the compound's camo netting, casting dappled shadows across Sarah's garden. My garden now. Six years since I'd buried her, and I still thought of these neat rows of herbs and flowers as hers. The mint had grown wild again, encroaching on the rosemary's territory. Sarah would have laughed at that.

Just like you. Always trying to take up more space than you're given.

I reached for the pruning shears. This morning ritual represented a kind of penance I performed to always remember. If it hadn't been for Knuckles, Oktober, and Ranger, I'm not certain I'd have kept my sanity.

I knelt on the worn rubber mat I'd placed between the rows, careful not to compress the soil. The burn scar on my right forearm caught the light, puckered flesh a shade paler than the surrounding skin. A memento from my construction days, from before everything changed. Before the night they broke into our home. Before Sarah's blood on our bedroom floor. Before I beat a man to death with my bare hands.

The mint surrendered beneath my shears, trimmed back to give the rosemary room to breathe. I collected the cuttings in a small basket. The mint would be dried, stored in the glass jars that lined my kitchen window. Sometimes I imagined I could still smell her on my fingertips after working with the herbs she'd loved. She said her herbs helped her create meals for her hardworking man. She said she grew them for me, but I knew better.

She found therapy in her garden. It never mattered what she had going on in her life, Sarah could come to her little garden, kneel in the cool earth, and tend her plants with loving care while peace filled her. She called it finding her calm. I never understood why digging in the earth and helping plants to grow filled her with so much satisfaction. Fucking shame it took her dying for me to figure it out.

"Dirt therapy again?"

I didn't startle at Knight's voice. I'd heard his footsteps approaching, the particular rhythm of his gait distinctive among the brothers. I didn't look up, continuing to trim with the same measured pace.

"Not dirt." I paused, scissors hovering over a particularly unruly stem. "Soil."

Knight chuckled, the sound gentle despite his intimidating appearance. His tattooed face and colored eyes made strangers cross the street to avoid him, but the brothers knew better. Beneath the ink and modifications was a man who'd hack government databases without hesitation but couldn't stomach killing a spider in the clubhouse.

"Soil therapy, then," Knight conceded, shifting his weight. "Sorry to interrupt your" -- he waved his hand vaguely at the ground – "soil time, but we got a delivery at the gate."

My hands stilled. Something shifted in my chest, a subtle change in rhythm I hadn't felt in years. "The woman from last week?"

"Yep, Cora. The one with the blue eyes that had you looking like you'd seen a ghost." Knight paused, immediately regretting the word choice. "Jesus. Sorry, man."

I set the shears down with deliberate care, wiping my hands on the towel tucked into my belt.

"Hannah handling it?"

"She's with the kids at the shelter today. Knuckles took her." Knight watched me stand. "I can take care of it if you're busy."

"No." The word came out more forcefully than I intended. I moderated my tone. "I'll get everything inside and put it away."

Knight's mouth twitched, a knowing look crossing his features. "Thought you might say that. She's waiting at the gate." He stepped back as I moved past him, giving me space. Knight always seemed to understand the need for physical distance, for the bubble of emptiness I maintained around myself.

"I'll be right there." I glanced in the direction of the front gate. I hadn't meant to give away more interest than Knight already knew I had for the girl, but I'd never had much of a poker face.

I walked to the hose coiled neatly against the wall of the warehouse, where I lived in an apartment on the first floor in order to be close to the garden. Turned on the spigot, washing the dirt from beneath my fingernails, from the creases of my palms. The water sluiced over the burn scar, momentarily cooling a phantom itch that sometimes plagued the damaged nerve endings.

Knight pulled out his phone, sending a text to whoever was manning the gate, most likely. I moved toward my bike, parked in its designated spot beside my door. The machine gleamed in the filtered sunlight, meticulously maintained like everything in my life.

I started the machine and the motor rumbled to life beneath me. I guided the motorcycle through the compound, past the inner ring of warehouses, toward the gate. The wind rushed against my face, cooling skin that felt unexpectedly warm. I hadn't felt this particular sensation in a long time, this anticipation.

I'd watched Cora drive away last time, the envelope of cash clutched in her hand, and found myself hoping she'd return. Not just for the convenience of having someone willing to deliver to our compound, though that was rare enough. But because something about her had pierced the carefully constructed numbness I'd maintained since Sarah died.

The gates appeared ahead, the metal barrier standing open. Beyond it, I could see her car. And beside it, Cora herself, one hip leaned against the driver's door, her posture attempting casual confidence but betraying tension in the set of her shoulders.

I slowed the bike, approaching with deliberate care, not wanting to startle her with the engine's roar. She straightened as I drew near, those striking blue eyes meeting mine for a brief moment before sliding away. The ghost of a smile touched her lips like an instinctive reaction quickly suppressed.

A feeling I thought long dead bloomed in my chest, an emotion I hadn't allowed myself to feel since Sarah's murder. If I embraced the emotions and let things progress naturally, I feared the danger I'd be putting my heart through.

I stopped my bike and killed the engine. I parked a building away to keep the noise to a minimum. The women thought we kept quiet so we didn't scare newcomers or people around us who might not like noise or were afraid of bikers in general, but the truth was, we knew the less attention on us the better. I found myself uncertain of what to say next, because as I approached and Cora straightened, her gaze focused squarely on me, something inside my chest snapped like an overstretched rubber band. I knew beyond anything reasonable and sane, the woman standing in front of me would be mine.

She stood straighter this time, looking less timid. The morning sun caught in her auburn hair, highlighting copper strands I hadn't noticed before. Her gaze met mine for a heartbeat longer than last week before darting away. The blue of her eyes reminded me of a clear winter sky. Today she wore jeans and a light blue T-shirt that seemed to match the color of her eyes perfectly. Christ, could the woman be any lovelier?

"Hey," she said with a small wave of her fingers.

I nodded, acknowledging her greeting without words. Silence had become my refuge in prison, a weapon and a shield. Six years inside had taught me the power of stillness, of making others fill the void with nervous chatter. But with Cora, I found myself wanting to speak.

She shifted her weight, one hand resting on her car door. The other played with her keys, a restless movement that betrayed the composure she tried to project.

"Hannah's not here today?" she asked, though her gaze didn't break from mine.

"She's at Haven." I was aware my voice was rough. I cleared my throat and tried again. "She helps at the women's shelter on Tuesdays."

Surprise flickered across Cora's features, quickly masked. "It's... really kind of her." A pause, her gaze dropping to the ground between us. "Of all you guys. To help there. I've heard a couple of the women you've helped talk about how they'd never felt safer than when they stayed at Haven."

I nodded solemnly. "We don't like bullies here. Especially when they hurt women and children."

She held my gaze for long moments before

nodding. "You know, I think maybe I believe you."

The space between us seemed charged, electric with a feeling I couldn't really name and wasn't sure I really wanted to try. I cleared my throat, tried to remember how normal people conducted conversations. Sarah had been the talker in our relationship. I'd been content to listen to her voice fill our home.

"Follow me." I gestured toward the compound interior. "To the kitchen. Around back."

Relief softened her expression. Instructions. A clear path forward. Something concrete to focus on rather than this strange, unexpected tension humming between us.

"Sure." She nodded, already moving around to the driver's side of her vehicle. "Lead the way."

I mounted my bike again, hyperaware of her watching me, of the engine's rumble breaking the silence between us. Through the side mirror, I saw her slide into her sedan, both hands gripping the wheel. I pulled away slowly, conscious of her following at a careful distance.

I led her to the back of the main clubhouse where the kitchen entrance was, and led straight to a long counter I could set everything on before putting them away. I parked near the entrance and killed the engine, watching as she pulled in beside me.

When she emerged from her car, she moved with more confidence than before, popping the trunk and starting to unload.

"This is different," she said, surveying the kitchen building. "I delivered to the main place last time."

"Easier here." I moved toward her trunk, noting the stacks of grocery bags. "I got it."

I reached for the bags nearest to me, lifting several at once. Our fingers didn't touch, but I felt her presence like a physical force, a gravity pulling at senses I'd thought long deadened. She grabbed bags of her own, following me to the kitchen's rear entrance. I had the door propped open so she didn't feel trapped. I noticed her hesitate briefly before entering.

Inside, industrial stainless steel gleamed under fluorescent lights. Walk-in refrigerator, freezer, commercial ranges. All donated or acquired through channels best not discussed with outsiders. Knuckles kept us in whatever equipment we wanted and, as it turned out, a few of the old ladies liked to cook. No one objected.

I set the bags on the center island, turning to take more from her. This time, our fingers did brush, a momentary contact that sent a jolt up my arm. Her eyes widened slightly, telling me she'd felt it too.

"Is all this for the club?"

I shook my head. "Some for here. Some to the shelter. Some to local families or homeless who need it."

She paused, tilting her head as she studied me. "You feed people outside the club?"

"Yeah." I didn't elaborate. Didn't explain about the families of incarcerated men we supported, the women rebuilding lives after abuse, the children who would otherwise go hungry. The club's reputation served its purpose, but the reality was more complex than outsiders knew.

We fell into a rhythm, moving between her car and the kitchen, unloading, sorting. I doubted most delivery drivers helped unload beyond setting everything on the nearest flat surface, but the only time she hesitated was when she actually entered the clubhouse. Which is why I'd left the door open.

"You been doing deliveries long?" The question surprised me as much as her. I rarely initiated conversation and never with strangers.

She glanced up from a bag of onions she carried. "About three months. Since I lost my other job."

I waited, giving her space to continue if she wanted. When she didn't, I respected the boundary. We all had stories we kept to ourselves.

She'd worn a light jacket last time, but today in just the T-shirt, I could see lean muscle in her arms. Not gym-built. The kind that came from work. She moved like someone accustomed to carrying her own weight, expecting no help but competent enough not to need it.

When she set the last bag on the kitchen counter she pushed a strand of auburn hair behind her ear. The gesture shouldn't have caught my attention; instead, it made my fingers itch to follow the same path.

"That's everything," she said, dusting her hands against her jeans. Her gaze met mine fully now, more direct than before. She didn't look quite comfortable, but no longer truly afraid.

I followed her back to her car. I have no idea why. She could make her way out of the compound on her own. Instead I found myself moving slowly after her, just… watching.

She reached up to shut the trunk of her car when she paused. Leaning in and reaching far in the back of the trunk, she dragged out two large boxes of eggs and hurried back to the kitchen entrance.

I stepped back from the door to give her room, but she stumbled. I'd intended to reach for the eggs, but it was either catch her or the box. Gravity took over from there. The floor caught the eggs. I had my arms full of warm woman.

"Shit!" Cora gasped, looking up at me in shock. "I'm so sorry, I didn't mean…" She trailed off, her eyes wide as she gazed up at me.

I shook my head, not really sure why, only that I never wanted her to be sorry for being in my arms. No matter what the reason. I knew I should let her go. Thing was, she wasn't fighting and I didn't have the willpower to let her go on my own. She fit against me in a way that made my chest tighten. Warm. Solid. Real. Her hair smelled like vanilla and clean, bright sunshine that made me want to keep breathing her in. Her hands rested lightly on my shoulders, her fingers curling around the muscles she found.

I knew I should have stepped back the moment I caught her when I'd ensured she had her footing. I should have released her. Instead I held on, arms wrapped around her so she was secure and held like something precious to me. And she still didn't fight. She didn't push away or stiffen with fear. She simply looked up at me with those impossibly blue eyes, breath coming fast, and her lips parted.

Around our feet, broken eggs spread in a yellow pool punctuated by shards of white shell. The mess didn't matter. Nothing mattered except the weight of her against me, the warmth seeping through my shirt into my very soul… the realization that I might not be as completely dead inside as I thought.

Her gaze traveled over my face with an intensity that made my pulse quicken. Her expression shifted. Softened. Something that looked almost like pain flickered across her features.

She lifted one hand with a slow, deliberate movement and reached up toward my face with fingers that trembled slightly. I held perfectly still, not breathing, as those fingers made contact with my skin just below my right eye on my cheek bone.

The touch was featherlight. Gentle in a way I hadn't experienced in years. Her fingertips traced the small scar there, a pale line about two inches long that I'd stopped noticing a long damn time ago. Courtesy of a shiv in Terre Haute's exercise yard, a fight that had established early in my sentence that I wouldn't be an easy target.

"Who hurt you?" Her voice came out barely above a whisper, rough with an emotion I couldn't identify. She stared at the scar like it personally offended her, like the mark on my face caused her actual pain.

My chest tightened with emotion. Maybe I felt this so much because I hadn't felt anything in such a long fucking time. But I felt like Cora had caused some kind of fissure in the concrete I'd poured around everything soft and vulnerable around my heart after Sarah's death.

The moment stretched, elastic and charged. Her fingers lingered on my skin, warm and impossibly soft. I couldn't remember the last time someone had touched me like this. With care. With something that looked dangerously close to tenderness. Then awareness seemed to slam into her. I saw it happening, watched her eyes widen as she realized what she'd done. She snatched her hand back like my skin had burned her, color flooding her cheeks in a rush that made the slight smattering of freckles scattered across her nose stand out.

"I'm sorry." The words tumbled out fast, breathless. "I didn't mean to -- I shouldn't have --"

She pushed against my chest and this time I let her go. Released my hold and stepped back, giving her the space she suddenly seemed desperate for. But I watched her face carefully, needing to make sure she was truly all right. She didn't look scared. Not the way people usually looked when they realized they'd gotten too close to me, when they remembered my reputation or the violence I was capable of. Cora looked intrigued. Her gaze kept darting back to mine, curiosity and unabashed interest bright in those blue eyes despite the embarrassment coloring her cheeks. She looked like someone who'd discovered something unexpected and wasn't quite sure what to do with the information.

"It's from prison." I pointed to my scar. I don't know what made me volunteer the information because I never talked about Terre Haute. But I wanted her to know. Wanted her to understand exactly what she was dealing with. "A fight. Six years ago."

She absorbed this with a slow nod, processing. Her tongue darted out to wet her lips, a nervous gesture that drew my attention to her mouth. "Did the other guy look worse?"

The question surprised a sound out of me. Not quite a laugh, but I felt my lips tugging upward. I don't think the smile made it very far, but I couldn't be sure. "Yeah."

"Good." She gave a satisfied nod, as if my answer was exactly what she'd expected to hear.

We stood there in the kitchen entrance, broken eggs congealing between us, awareness humming in the air like a physical thing. Then she seemed to shake herself, looking down at the mess we'd created. "Shit." She crouched, reaching for a piece of shell. "I'm so sorry. I'll pay for these."

"No." I moved to the storage area where cleaning supplies lived, returning with paper towels and a small bucket. "You won't."

I knelt beside her, and we worked in silence. The task should have given me something to focus on besides the tension stretched between us, but I was pretty sure not filling the void with conversation only enhanced my awareness of her. And wouldn't my brothers have a laugh if they found out I actually considered getting chatty?

"You always this helpful?" Her voice held a lighter note now, teasing almost.

"No." The truth came out flat, honest. I shrugged to take away any sting I might have caused her. "But I think I like you. I help people I like."

She smiled at that, a small curve of her lips that transformed her face. Made her look younger, less guarded. "I feel special?"

I met her gaze directly, letting her see the sincerity. "You should always feel special." There. I managed to string more than three words together. Progress.

The color returned to her cheeks, deeper this time. She looked away first, ducking her head and letting the thick wave of auburn curls partially cover her face.

We finished the cleanup quickly after that, disposing of the ruined eggs and soiled paper towels. "Um, I should get going." She hiked a thumb over her shoulder. "Will I see you next time?"

I moved to the counter where I'd left the envelope earlier. The brothers had pitched in again, probably more than was reasonable. But no one had objected when Hannah suggested increasing the amount. I walked back to where she stood near her car, envelope in hand. She watched me approach, her hand on the door handle, but she didn't get inside the car.

"Yours." I held it out.

Her eyes widened when she felt the weight of it. "This is too much."

"No." I kept my voice firm. "It's not. Everyone chipped in. They're grateful." I cleared my throat and swallowed. "Me, too."

She stared at the envelope, then back at me. Something worked behind her eyes, emotions I couldn't quite read. Finally, she nodded, tucking the envelope into her back pocket. "You guys order a lot?" The question came out casual, but I heard the real question underneath. *Will I see you again*?

"We do. Your first delivery was the only time anyone ever showed up. Usually gets cancelled for us after a couple hours." I paused, knowing I should leave it there. Knowing I should let her go without pushing, without revealing too much of the desperate hope that had taken root in my chest. But I couldn't seem to stop myself. "You planning to keep taking our orders?"

Her expression shifted, softening into something that looked almost like relief. That genuine smile returned, the one that made something warm unfurl behind my ribs. "Looks like I'll be your regular driver, then."

The words hit me with unexpected force. Regular. She'd be back. I'd see her again. Christ, I was so fucked. "Good." The word came out rougher than I intended, loaded with more meaning than I should have let show.

She held my gaze for another heartbeat, something passing between us that felt like acknowledgment. Like she understood exactly what I wasn't saying. Then she slid into her car, started the engine with that familiar rough cough.

I stepped back, giving her room to reverse.

Watched through the windshield as she adjusted her mirrors, tucked hair behind her ear with fingers that still trembled slightly. She glanced up once before pulling away, catching my eye, and I saw my own recognition reflected back at me.

Her car disappeared toward the gate. I stood there long after the sound of her engine faded. My hand came up without conscious thought, fingers finding the scar she'd touched. More in remembrance of her touch than how I'd gotten the scar.

Those few minutes had shifted my insides. Holding her had shoved me headfirst into a world I wasn't certain I was ready for or deserved, but a fundamental change burst through me and I felt the alteration in every cell. The numbness I'd maintained for so fucking long, the careful emotional distance I'd constructed to survive my grief, developed a crack. And through that fissure, something dangerous had crept in. Interest. Attraction. The first genuine spark of feeling I'd experienced since Sarah's murder.

I should have been terrified. Should have recognized this as the threat it was to my carefully maintained equilibrium. But standing there in the compound with my skin still warm where Cora had touched me, I found I couldn't muster fear. Only anticipation and the certainty that everything had just changed, and there was no going back.

She'd come to me again. And I'd be waiting, this spark she'd ignited already burning brighter than it should, already threatening to consume the careful walls I'd built around what remained of my heart. I knew these feelings weren't rational and I felt like some kind of stalker fixating on a young woman who'd showed me a kind smile. And maybe that's all it was on her part.

I needed to take a step back, stay away from her anytime she came around but I knew I wouldn't. Dangerous and reckless didn't begin to describe how that scenario would play out. But inevitable. For the first time in six years, I looked forward to tomorrow. And I'd be Goddamned if I willingly gave up the reason my soul finally showed signs of coming back to life.

Chapter Three

Cora

Week three, and I had made at least four runs a week to the compound since the first run. With the cash tips -- which usually equaled a hundred percent or better -- I made more from them than I did the rest of my runs combined. Turns out, part of the club's territory included the New Beginnings women's shelter. I'd known they protected the place but had no idea they'd actually donated the building. The more I learned about this place, the more I realized how very much everyone in the whole of the Goddamned city misjudged these people.

As I pulled through the gates, I waved at the two men manning the gate. Griffin and Diesel each raised a hand as I rolled through. I'd made a few friends and gotten to know several of the men and women inside the compound. Every single person I'd met was either pleasant or grumpy on the outside but marshmallows on the inside. To a man, the guys protected the women, especially at New Beginnings or Haven, as they called the shelter.

The compound looked different today. I realized about a week ago I'd started seeing the place as more of a kind of safe haven. I loved coming here because no one leered, played grab-ass, or made sexual innuendos every single fucking time I stepped foot inside the place. Which was way the fuck more than I could say about some homes I delivered to. The strange part wasn't that I kept coming back, but how relieved I felt when the delivery app pinged with their address.

I parked in what I now thought of as "my spot" near the kitchen entrance. Two women I hadn't seen before looked up from a conversation, their eyes tracking my movement as I got out of the car. One nodded in recognition though we'd never met.

I popped the trunk and it opened with a familiar squeak. I'd started unloading bags when one of the women approached. She was petite with light brown hair tucked behind her ears.

"You must be Cora." She had a friendly smile, just like the other women I'd met here. "Hannah told me about you. I'm Pippa." She held out her hand in greeting, and I took it automatically. "You have no idea how much we appreciate you taking our orders. We make regular runs, but I swear the guys around here are bottomless pits, to say nothing of the children at the shelter we feed."

"You're one of the few places I don't deliver beer." I have no idea why I made the observation but there it was. "I figured with as many men as you had here, I'd be delivering a lot of beer."

"You'd think, huh?" The other woman grinned as she extended her hand. "I'm Penny." I took her hand briefly. "It's not that we don't have beer, it's that the guys prefer to get their own. I don't think a single one of them drinks the same kind. It's just easier."

I helped carry the impressive haul to the kitchen. All the while, the two women chatted away, engaging me as easily as if we'd been friends for years.

The warmth inside was cozy and comfortable. Not just in temperature, but atmosphere. Hannah and Pippa each hugged me before going back to the car to bring in more stuff. Four times a week and they filled my trunk to overflowing. I'd actually started using my back seat sometimes, too.

"What's an old lady?" I'd been meaning to ask them for the last couple of weeks but hadn't worked up the courage. The last thing I wanted to do was offend these people when they'd been nothing but nice to me.

Instead of offense, I got laughter. "You'll have to ask the guys why they call us old ladies." Pippa grinned at me. "But, if you want to know the truth, I'm not a hundred percent sure even they know why the term is 'old ladies'. We're their women. Wives or girlfriends. And old lady is a woman in a permanent relationship with one of the men here."

"Archaic, I know." Hannah's laugh was infectious and I found myself smiling. "And to be honest, sometimes I feel like these guys are one step up from cavemen. My dad's the same way."

"Is your dad in a motorcycle club, too?" I set the last of the bags on the counter. The other women had started putting things away as they chatted, so I helped. Not exactly something I'd consider doing anywhere else, but this place almost felt like home. I'd only known these people three weeks. I didn't want to even think about what that said about my life.

"Oh, yeah." Hannah nodded her head several times. "He owns a paramilitary company. All the guys in Bones MC work at ExFil. Dad was the president until a few years ago. Now he mostly lets my brothers run the place."

"Mostly?" I raised an eyebrow.

Hannah shrugged. "Yeah. Dad has a bit of a control problem, but Mom says he's working on it."

"Yeah?" I raised an eyebrow. "How long has he been working on it?"

"Oh, I think maybe since she first met him." Everyone laughed.

"Heard that, Sis. I'm tellin' Dad." Gunnar, Hannah's brother, walked up behind her, placed a kiss on her cheek, and snagged a grape from the bunch she'd been going to put in the fridge. He popped it in his mouth with a grin.

"You know that snitches get stitches. Right?" I loved the easy way Hannah and Gunnar were with each other. Everyone was the same way. It felt like one big family and I found myself living for these moments, even if I wasn't directly a part of them.

"You love me too much to make me need stitches." Gunnar grinned before trotting over to Pippa and pulling her into his arms and giving her a hard, welcoming kiss. She squealed, then giggled as he tossed her over his shoulder. "Hate to run and eat so I'm taking her home."

"That's eat and run, you ape!"

"Yeah, not doin' that either. I'm gonna eat, then we're gonna have dessert." He swatted her ass as he carried her out of the kitchen. Yet another thing I loved about this place. There was no *vaguely* naughty anything. They were in your face, raw to the max, while managing to not be offensive or creepy about anything. The men stuck with their women and vice versa. So not my experience with anything related to family or any kind of personal relationship. Soon after, all the women except Penny and Hannah left, each of them giving me a warm hug.

When it was just me, Hannah, and Penny, Penny gestured to the coffeepot on the counter. "Coffee?" A wonderful smelling dark brew had just finished dripping into the glass bowl. "We almost always have a fresh pot on."

I shrugged. "Sure. You guys were my final run. I save you for last because I don't have room for anyone else. If your orders keep getting bigger I'm going to have to rent a U-Haul to get it all here in one trip."

That got a burst of laughter from Penny. She

filled a mug with coffee and handed it to me. I wrapped my fingers around the ceramic cup, the heat seeping into my cold hands. "I fucking hate this time of year," I muttered. "I never wear the right clothes for the weather."

"I can relate." Penny took a sip of her coffee.

"How'd you end up here?" I asked before I could stop myself.

The women exchanged glances. Penny's expression remained neutral. "The usual way," she said lightly. "Needed help, found it here." She glanced up at me, and I could see pain there. "My ex-husband… wasn't a good person. I actually met everyone through Haven."

"Makes sense." I reached out and gripped Penny's hand. "I'm glad you got away and that you found people to have your back."

"Oh, they most certainly have my back. When Andrew found us, if I'd been anywhere other than Haven, I'm sure he'd have gotten exactly what he wanted. Me and my daughters would still be in hell." I thought she'd sound sad or look haunted as she spoke. Instead, she smiled like she was the most contented person in the world. "I can't imagine willingly living anywhere else. These people are my family."

"I'm not too proud to admit I envy the happiness you've obviously found here. I've been on my own most of my life. I prefer it that way, but I'd like to have a companion. You know. Sometimes." I caught sight of the clock on the wall and straightened. "I should get going," I said, setting down my mug. "It's getting late and I've got chores to do at home."

"Of course," Penny said. "But come back when you're not working and can stay. We'd all love to bring you into our circle. There's plenty of room if you ever need a place to crash."

I blinked. "That's very kind. I appreciate the offer. And I'd love to come hang out sometime."

"Great!" Both her smile and enthusiasm were contagious. "I gave you my phone number. Right?"

"Yes. I have yours and a couple of the others'. I'll text and maybe we can plan something in a few days?"

"If you don't text me, I will definitely text you."

Before I could respond, footsteps sounded from the doorway, heavy and deliberate. My pulse quickened as I turned toward the sound, somehow knowing who I'd find.

Rancor filled the doorway. He was an imposing figure on the best of days. Probably because he didn't really talk much. The whole dark, mysterious vibe he had going on worked for him when it might have made other men seem aloof. The dark gray T-shirt he wore strained against his chest, shoulders, and arms. I was certain the man bought his shirts two sizes too small intentionally. His worn jeans and heavy motorcycle boots completed the look. And, Lord, the way his gaze seemed to devour me every time he looked at me turned me on way more than it should have. But Goddamnit, the man was wearing down my defenses with nothing more than good manners and persistence. He always made sure to see me every time he knew I was going to be here. Hannah said he asked her every single day if she'd put in a grocery order. She'd told me to put him out of his misery and give him my phone number already, but I hadn't worked up the nerve yet.

Penny glanced between us, a smile playing at her lips. "Well, would you look at that timing." She picked up her coffee mug and shot me a look that spoke volumes. I saw amusement and a healthy dose of encouragement. "I just remembered I need to check on something for the girls."

"Yep." Hanna grinned. "I promised to help.

Penny waved as she and Hanna left. "You two… catch up."

She squeezed my arm as she passed, then patted Rancor's shoulder. He stepped aside to let her through, then returned to filling the doorway.

And there we were. Alone.

"Hi," I said, the word coming out softer than I intended. Why I suddenly felt shy was beyond me. I wasn't one to be coy or play hard to get. If I wanted something, I went after it and wasn't ashamed. But everything about Rancor felt different. I had genuine affection for him. I liked being around him. Despite his size and appearance, the man gave off this soothing vibe I couldn't explain. But not all the time. I'd seen him outside as I pulled inside the compound. I could always tell the instant he saw me because his whole body seemed to lighten. He stood straighter with his shoulders back proudly. When he did that, Rancor was truly a sight to behold.

"You came back," he said, the words hanging in the quiet kitchen. He always made the same simple statement. I thought maybe he felt as unsure of himself as I did. Maybe I wasn't the only one who thought whatever we had between us was different.

I smiled, unable to help myself. "Third week running."

He moved into the room with slow, deliberate steps. "Finished for the day?" he asked, stopping closer than strictly necessary but not close enough to touch. I found myself wanting to lean into him to close the gap between us.

"Yeah." I shifted my weight, suddenly very

aware of my body and how my pussy clenched at the thought of reaching out to touch him. "Saved you guys for last."

His gaze remained steady on mine. "I'll walk you out."

Not a question. Not quite an order either but pretty close. I had to smile at his gruff exterior. As with a lot of these guys, I suspected Rancor was a marshmallow on the inside.

"Thanks," I said, gathering my keys from the counter. We moved through the kitchen and out the door into the late afternoon light. The compound hummed with distant activity off in the distance.

Rancor walked beside me, close enough that occasionally our arms brushed. Each touch sent electricity skittering across my skin. He didn't speak, and surprisingly, I found the silence comfortable. When we reached my car, I turned to face him, leaning back against the driver's door.

"Why do you keep coming back?" His voice was low, rough at the edges. The question came without preamble, direct in a way that startled me.

I blinked up at him. "To deliver your groceries?"

"Here." He gestured vaguely at the compound around us. "Other drivers won't."

I considered lying, giving some bland answer about customer service or professionalism. But standing there, with his dark eyes studying me so intently, I couldn't bring myself to be anything but honest. "The money," I admitted. "The tips are good. *Really* good." I paused, heart hammering against my ribs as I added, "And… I might like seeing you, too."

The words hung between us, more revealing than I'd intended. My cheeks heated, but I didn't look away. Something shifted in his expression, a subtle softening around his eyes and a slight parting of his lips as he processed what I'd said.

"Yeah?" The single word held a vulnerability I hadn't expected from him. Somehow, that made me feel a little better about my admission.

"Yeah," I confirmed, surprising myself with how steady my voice sounded.

Rancor took a slow, careful step closer to me. My breath caught as he moved deliberately into my space, giving me time to retreat if I wanted. I didn't move. Couldn't move. Didn't want to. He leaned in slowly, his face coming toward mine. But instead of the kiss I expected, he dipped his head to the curve where my neck met my shoulder. I felt his breath first, warm against my skin, then the unmistakable sensation of him inhaling deeply, taking in my scent.

The intimacy of the gesture froze me in place. No one had ever done that before. Smelled me with such deliberate intent. It should have been strange. Should have made me uncomfortable. Instead, heat bloomed low in my belly, spreading outward until my fingertips tingled with it.

His beard brushed against the sensitive skin of my neck, the unexpected tickle making me giggle. The sound surprised both of us. His lips curved against my skin in what felt like a smile, and he drew back enough for me to see his face. Sure enough, a small smile played at the corners of his mouth, transforming his features. Making him look younger, somehow. Less burdened. My heart stuttered at the sight.

I didn't think about what I did next. Didn't plan it or weigh the consequences. I simply acted on the pull I'd felt since the first moment I saw him. My arms moved up around his neck, fingers finding the warm skin above the collar of his T-shirt. I pressed myself against the solid wall of his chest and rose up on my toes.

His hands settled just above my waist, large and warm through my shirt. He held me like I was something precious, something that might break under too much pressure. I pulled him down toward me, our faces inches apart, giving him time to pull away.

He didn't.

Our lips met in a kiss that started gentle and tentative. His lips were warmer than I expected, softer. He tasted faintly of coffee and something distinctly his own. My fingers curled against the nape of his neck, into the short bristle of hair there, and I felt rather than heard the low, contented groan rumbling through his chest.

The kiss deepened, his grip tightened at my waist, drawing me closer, while I explored the contours of his shoulders, the strong column of his neck. When we finally broke apart, both breathing hard, Rancor pressed his forehead against mine. Our breaths mingled in the small space between us. His eyes, so dark and unreadable from a distance, revealed flecks of amber among the brown, and a warmth I hadn't expected.

"Cora," he said, just my name, but it carried weight. Like he was testing how it felt to say.

"Rancor," I whispered back, the name strange and perfect all at once.

"Marcus," he said softly. I pulled back slightly, confused. He growled and tightened his grip around me. "Marcus Wheeler. My name."

I smiled up at him. "Would you prefer I call you by your first name?"

He shook his head. "Ain't that man anymore. Just wanted you to know." He lifted his chin to rest on top of my head. He actually trembled as he held me. I got the impression this was something important to him, but I had no idea why.

We stayed like that until reality reasserted itself in the form of distant laughter from somewhere in the compound. I reluctantly pulled back, my hands sliding down to rest against his chest. His heart beat strong and fast beneath my palm.

"I should go," I said, though everything in me wanted to stay.

He nodded, stepping back just enough to give me space to open my car door. The loss of his warmth was immediate, the late afternoon air getting cooler as the sun set.

I slid behind the wheel, started the engine. Through the windshield, Rancor stood watching me, his expression open in a way I hadn't seen before. A look of profound longing painted his face like a beacon. It was funny, because in the romances I enjoyed reading, the hero often wore the exact same expression. I raised my hand in a small wave, and he returned the gesture, that same slight smile touching his lips.

As I drove away from the compound, the taste of him still on my lips, a realization settled over me like a warm blanket. For the first time in years -- maybe for the first time ever -- I'd found people who made me feel something other than the need to disappear. And in Rancor, I'd found a man I desperately wanted to know better.

The thought both comforted and terrified me. I'd spent so long keeping myself safe by keeping everyone at arm's-length so I didn't form connections with others that could be severed easier than they could be forged. Now I was speeding away from a compound full of ex-cons with the lingering sensation of one of them on my skin, under it, seeping into places I'd closed off inside me a long fucking time ago.

And God help me, I couldn't wait to go back.

Chapter Four

Rancor

The soil pushed between my fingers, damp and alive. Dawn painted the sky in shades of purple and orange, filtered through the camo netting that hung above the compound. Sarah's garden had been waiting for me since before first light. The mint had grown wild again, pushing into spaces it didn't belong. Sarah would have laughed at that. *You always try to take whatever room that isn't yours.* She often told me that when she'd wake up with me wrapped around her, my face snuggled against her neck. She would have that smile that lit up everything inside me. I reached for the pruning shears, the weight familiar in my palm.

As I worked, the burn scar on my forearm caught the morning light, paler than the surrounding skin, a reminder of another life. Construction foreman. Husband. Almost a father. I'd been proud of all three. I'd helped turn the warehouses into livable spaces for all of us. I'd done my best to be a good person and the best protector to my family, but my best efforts hadn't been enough.

Truth was, if it hadn't been for Knuckles, I doubt I'd have survived prison. Not because someone would have killed me. I'd actually worked through a plan to kill myself. Knuckles reminded me of the club and how they needed me just as much as my wife had. They were hurting from her death, the death of their unborn niece, and their brother all at once. It wasn't enough to pull me out of my depression, but he gave me something to work toward and the knowledge that I still had people who cared about me in the world.

"You're growin' too fast," I muttered to the mint. My voice sounded strange in the quiet morning. I didn't talk much these days, not even to plants. But Sarah had always talked to her garden. Said they grew better when you acknowledged them.

Working out here settled something restless inside me, something that had stirred yesterday when Cora's lips met mine. Something I wasn't ready to name. I wasn't hung up on my dead wife, though I knew I'd always love her and she'd always be in my thoughts. Sarah wouldn't want me to mourn her forever. Cora wasn't something I'd been expecting, though.

Her taste lingered, even now. Vanilla and coffee and something uniquely her. The warmth of her body against mine had shocked my system like jumping into cold water after years in the desert. I'd nearly forgotten what it felt like to hold someone. To want someone. To have someone look at me with something other than fear or pity in their eyes.

I pinched a leaf of basil between my fingers, breathing in its sharp scent. She'd smelled me. My lips twitched at the memory. Cora had let me breathe her in, and then she'd done the same, her nose pressed against my neck for just a moment. Like she was trying to memorize me.

I set down the shears carefully, wiping soil from my hands onto the worn denim covering my thighs. Six years since I'd buried my wife, waking up alone or in a concrete box with a cellie I despised. And now this woman with eyes like a winter sky had walked into the compound and cracked something open inside me that I'd thought died with Sarah.

"Here you are again." I glanced up to find Knight grinning down at me. "Is it a coincidence you started spending more time here around when a certain delivery driver started showing up?" His voice held no judgment, just the gentle teasing of a brother who knew when something had shifted.

I drew in a breath. "Still need supplies."

"Uh-huh." Knight picked up a small stone from the garden's edge, turning it over in his tattooed fingers. "And it's got nothing to do with the fact that you kissed her yesterday where anyone with eyes could see."

Heat crept up my neck. I'd forgotten how exposed we'd been, standing there by her car. Hadn't thought about the compound's many eyes, too consumed with the feel of her, the taste of her.

"So what if I did?" The words came out more defensive than I intended.

Knight set the stone back down precisely where he'd found it. "So nothing," he said simply. "Glad to see you taking an interest in her. She seems like a good person."

"She's just a delivery driver," I said, but the lie tasted bitter.

Knight shrugged, shoving his hands in to the back pockets of his jeans. "If you say so." His voice softened. "But whatever she is, she's got you looking less like a ghost these days." He took a step back. "And that's something none of us thought we'd see."

I didn't respond. Couldn't find the words to neither confirm nor deny what he saw. Because he was right. Something had changed. I could feel it shifting under my skin, uncomfortable and foreign after feeling nothing but rage and grief for so long. I honestly couldn't say the change was unwelcome, but trying my best not to linger on the possibility my happiness could be taken away again so easily kept me in check.

Knight lingered a moment longer. "Carrie's making breakfast. Food'll be ready in thirty." He took another step back. "In case you want to join the living for a while today."

Then he was gone, his footsteps fading as he moved back toward the main building. I returned to the garden, but I'd lost focus. The mint blurred before my eyes as memories of Cora intruded. The way she'd leaned into me. The small, surprised sound she'd made when our lips met. The feel of her fingers against the nape of my neck. Christ, I hadn't thought about anything beyond the grief in so long, I hadn't bothered to remember the wonderful memories I kept buried deep inside where they could never leave me.

I'd given Cora my name. My real name. Not Rancor. Marcus Wheeler. A name I hadn't spoken aloud in years. A name that belonged to a man who I'd thought had died the night Sarah did. Remembering the feel of Cora's lips against mine made me grateful that man was still inside me somewhere.

As the sun climbed higher, warming my shoulders through my T-shirt, I found myself wondering if Cora would come back today. Wondering if she'd let me taste her a second time.

* * *

Cora

Dark clouds hunched over the horizon as I drove toward the Kiss of Death compound. The afternoon light had turned strange, that eerie yellow-green that always preceded a serious storm. My windshield wipers smeared dust across the glass, and I made a mental note to replace them at some point. Wipers were like roofs. You don't think about them until it rains. I'd checked the weather before heading out, knew a front was moving in, but I'd pushed forward anyway. After yesterday's kiss, part of me had been looking for any excuse not to come back to the compound. The other part, the part that won out, couldn't stay away. I wasn't kidding anyone, including myself. I hadn't looked forward to seeing anyone in my life as much as I anticipated seeing Marcus.

My vehicle rattled over the uneven road leading to the gates. Griffin waved me through the gate without hesitation when I rolled my window down and threw a hand up at him in greeting, now familiar with both me and my vehicle. The compound looked different today, the camo netting overhead swaying in the strengthening wind, casting moving shadows across the ground.

I took a deep breath, trying to steady my nerves. Yesterday, I'd kissed Rancor -- no, Marcus -- with an impulsiveness that surprised even me. I'd spent the night replaying the moment, the feel of his beard against my skin, the unexpected gentleness of his lips, the way his large hands had held me like I might shatter. I'd given into something I couldn't resist, and now I had to face him again, pretending my heart wasn't hammering against my ribs.

I'd barely pulled to a stop near the kitchen building when I spotted him. He stood just outside the door, arms crossed over his chest, watching my approach with that intense focus that made my skin prickle. The dark clouds behind him made him look even more imposing than usual. My throat went dry.

I killed the engine and sat for a moment, gathering my composure. I could keep my cool. So what If I'd only ever been kissed one other time, and nothing so complicated or pleasurable as the one I'd shared with Rancor? Except for the fact that I could still taste Rancor on my lips when I licked them. Simply looking at him now, even from a distance, I could feel his body against mine, could still smell his wonderfully masculine scent.

When I stepped out of the car, the air felt heavy with the coming storm. Rancor uncrossed his arms and moved toward me, each step measured and deliberate. He wore another gray T-shirt, stretched tight across his broad shoulders, and the same worn jeans. His expression remained unreadable, but his gaze softened when he met mine.

"Cora," he said, just my name, a greeting and an acknowledgment rolled into one.

"Hey." I pushed a strand of hair behind my ear, aiming for casual and missing by miles. "Looks like we're racing the weather."

He glanced up at the darkening sky, then back at me. "Storm's coming fast." His voice remained quiet, measured. "Better hurry."

I nodded, moving to the back of my truck. The tailgate dropped with a metallic groan, revealing stacks of grocery bags. Rancor moved beside me, close enough I could feel the heat radiating from him but not touching.

We fell into a rhythm, each grabbing bags and carrying them toward the kitchen. The first fat raindrops hit as we made our third trip, spattering against the dust like small explosions. The wind picked up, bending the trees at the compound's edge.

"Crap," I said, eyeing the remaining bags as the rain intensified. My hair began sticking to my neck, dampening quickly.

Rancor studied the sky, his expression tightening. He moved past me, gathering twice as many bags as before, his muscles straining beneath his shirt. "Storm's gonna hit hard."

As if on cue, lightning flashed, followed almost

immediately by a crack of thunder that I felt in my chest. The sky opened up, rain suddenly pouring down in sheets. Within seconds, I was soaked, my T-shirt clinging to my skin, water running into my eyes.

Rancor set his bags inside the kitchen door on the counter. "Leave it," he called over the roar of the downpour as he shut the door. "Prospects are on the way." He held out his hand. "Come with me."

I hesitated, watching rain pound into the remaining groceries. "But the food --"

"Is taken care of." Another flash of lightning, another boom of thunder. The rain hammered down harder, stinging my exposed skin. Rancor held out his hand. "I'll get you some dry clothes and you can wait out the storm with me." He ducked his head slightly, but not before I saw a stain of red blush on his cheeks above his beard line. "I mean, if you want to."

I stared at his outstretched hand. This was different from a kiss in the compound yard. This was entering his private space. Crossing a line that had nothing to do with physical touch and everything to do with trust.

As if on cue, the door burst open to admit two younger men. A strong gust of wind nearly knocked me sideways and the decision made itself. I took his hand.

His fingers closed around mine, warm despite the cold rain, and he tugged me away from the kitchen, deeper into the warehouse. His grip was firm but gentle as he led me through the massive building to the back of the common room. From there, he took me through another door leading to a long, wide hallway with doors at intervals along the walls.

Rancor -- Marcus -- moved down the hall to stop in front of one of the doors. He fished a key from his pocket. When he pushed the door open, he stood aside, letting me enter first.

I stepped into his space, taking in everything at once. The apartment was sparse but clean, with an open layout that revealed a small kitchen area, a living room with a worn leather couch, and a doorway I assumed led to a bedroom. What caught my attention, though, was the wall of windows on one side, partially covered by a roof overhang to create a sheltered porch. Through the glass, I could see the garden below, not being lashed by rain.

"Bathroom's there if you need it," he said, pointing to a door on the left I'd missed when I'd first entered.

"No. Good. Thank you."

"Come," he said simply, reaching out for me to take his hand. Once again, I did, this time I allowed myself to relax, to let him slip his fingers through mine and tug me gently after him.

He took me through the door onto a covered porch that stretched along the back of the building. The space was sheltered by a metal roof that extended several feet outward, keeping the rain at bay. Two wooden chairs sat side-by-side, facing outward. The small garden looked freshly tended with loving care. It held various herbs instead of flowers or fruits and vegetables.

"Sit." Rancor gestured to one of the chairs. The gray T-shirt clung lovingly to his arms and chest. It was hard not to see how strong the man was. I lowered myself into the chair, not exactly at ease, but the sound of the rain and the rolling thunder was soothing. The scent of rain-soaked earth rose up, mingling with the fragrance of the herbs and fresh-cut grass. The rain was heavy, but the thunder only rumbled, any lightning well off in the distance.

Rancor settled into the chair beside mine, his large frame making the wooden seat look almost too small, yet his presence filled the space without being overwhelming.

We sat in comfortable silence for several minutes, watching the rain fall like a curtain on the garden below. I tried to relax, to ease the tension from my shoulders, but awareness of him beside me kept me rigid. Yesterday I'd kissed this man without hesitation. Today, sitting fully clothed on his porch, I felt more exposed than I had in years.

The garden captivated me despite my nervousness. Even through the rain, I could see the loving way the small bed had been cared for. The juxtaposition of the way he tended the herb garden and the man whose road name was the very definition of deep, bitter anger wasn't lost on me.

I jumped when there was an unexpected clap of thunder amid the lazy rumbling. The rain picked up and the sound was loud enough to make conversation impossible. Despite the first big boom of thunder, I found the sound of the wind and rain oddly peaceful.

Rancor's gaze shifted to me, those dark eyes taking in my jumpy reaction. His expression remained neutral, but something in his posture changed, softened almost imperceptibly. "You're safe here. But we can go back inside if you want."

I looked over at him and smiled. "I like it here. I'm good until you tell me otherwise."

I must have said the exact right thing because he gave me a startled expression before smiling at me, reaching for my hand again. Again, I let him lace his fingers through mine, and we watched the storm raging just beyond the overhang.

Minutes stretched in silence, broken only by the storm's percussion. Thunder rumbled, softer now, moving away from us. The rain continued to pour, but the frantic intensity had eased to a steady rhythm.

"Sarah planted everything," he said, the words emerging from him like he'd had to pull them from somewhere deep inside him. "My wife." I turned to look at him, surprised by this voluntary offering of information. His gaze remained fixed on the garden, raindrops sliding down his profile. "She started with herbs." He gestured toward a section near the center. "Cooking herbs first. Then medicinal. Said a garden should heal both hunger and sickness. The roses came later." His hand moved toward the far edge where climbing roses clung to a trellis. "For our third anniversary. Said we needed something just for beauty." A pause, heavy with memory. "Was gonna add fruit trees next. Had it all mapped out."

The past tense hung between us. Had. Was gonna. I thought about the man kneeling in the soil, tending what his wife had started. Preserving what she couldn't finish.

"It's beautiful," I said softly. "You've kept it alive."

His jaw tightened, the muscles working beneath the skin. "Least I could do." Another pause. "After I couldn't keep her alive. Knight and Oktober helped keep it while I was in prison."

I couldn't help the sharp intake of breath. My grip tightened on his hand, and I thought his hand trembled slightly. Seeing how much pain he was in hurt me. It was easy to see this guy hadn't had an easy go at life the last few years. If this place gave him peace, I'd sit with him as long as he wanted me to.

"Do you tend it every day?" I spoke softly so,

even though the rain had slowed somewhat, I wasn't sure he could hear me, but the situation didn't feel right to try shouting over the downpour.

He nodded. "Morning ritual. Before the compound wakes, generally." His fingers drummed lightly against the arm of his chair. "Helps me… remember. And forget." He shrugged. "Maybe I'm looking for some kind of absolution."

"What happened to her?" I asked, the question slipping out before I could reconsider. "To Sarah." I'd have felt like an ass for pushing him, but I got the feeling he needed to get this out and had been leading up to the conversation but was stumbling along just as much as I was.

Rancor went still beside me, so completely motionless I wondered if he'd even heard me. Then I saw the change come over him -- a darkening, a hardening around his eyes and mouth. When he finally spoke, his voice had dropped to nearly a whisper.

"Carjacking." Each word emerged like it was being torn from somewhere deep inside him. "Wrong place. Wrong time. I was across the street. At the store." His breathing had changed, becoming more measured, controlled. "Came back to find her bleeding out on the pavement."

My heart clenched. "Rancor, I'm so --"

"She was pregnant." His hands curled into fists on the arms of his chair. "Five months. We were gonna name him James. After her father."

The grief in those simple statements nearly broke me. I couldn't imagine the weight of losing not just a partner but a child who never had the chance to be born. The storm inside this man suddenly made perfect sense.

"The guy who did it." Rancor's voice remained

steady, emotionless in a way that spoke of practiced control. "He was a junkie lookin' for money for a fix." His jaw tightened. "Police caught him. Released him a few days later because his daddy had enough pull to get him bail when he never should have been let out of a fuckin' cage." The more he spoke, the less calm he seemed. He broke out in a sweat, his reaction to the memory visceral. I knew what was coming. Could see it in the set of his shoulders, the careful blankness of his expression.

"So I found him myself." No inflection. Just fact. "Beat him to death with my bare hands. Didn't even try to hide it. Waited for the cops to come." A muscle in his cheek twitched. "Got six years in Terre Haute, but I would do it again without hesitation."

The confession hung heavily between. He'd admitted to murder, calmly and without remorse. I should have been afraid. Should have been looking for the quickest way off this porch, away from this man who had killed and had no remorse. Instead, I understood. Not in the abstract way of someone sympathizing with tragedy, but in the bone-deep recognition of what it meant to protect those you loved.

"I ran away from home when I was sixteen," I said, the words emerging from some place I usually kept locked down tight, but I thought I owed it to Marcus to give him a piece of myself. Same as he'd just done to me. "My parents had me late in life. I was supposed to be the miracle for their son, Jace."

"Why you?" Marcus's question caught me off guard. In fact, this might be the most he'd ever spoken to me in one sitting.

"He needed a bone marrow transplant and no one else in the family was a match. Jace was on the national registry as needing a BMT, or whatever, but he had some rare antibodies in his blood that made it difficult to match him with a suitable donor. The only realistic chance he had was with a close relative and there simply were none."

"So they decided to have a baby? Take a chance that child would have whatever your brother needed to survive?"

"Pretty much, I guess. Looking back, I'm not sure they really thought the whole process through."

"Not sure why any doctor would allow something like that to take place. Seems unethical."

I couldn't help but smile. "Marcus, I think you know I like you a lot."

He tilted his head, narrowing his eyes in confusion. "I hope you do."

"I do. So please understand I mean no disrespect when I comment on the irony of the guy who killed someone talking about medical ethics."

Surprisingly, he barked out a startled laugh. "Yeah. I can see the irony."

"And you'd be right about the whole medical-legal-ethics-whatever shit. Obviously, I don't actually remember the whole thing, but my parents weren't exactly quiet about their displeasure with me. I've never actually sat down and questioned them, but I've overheard tearful conversations with Jace and my father when Jace was twenty-three and I was nine. I overheard Mom crying and stood outside their bedroom door.

"I don't remember the details, but I remember vividly when they'd lamented how I hadn't been able to help him, even though it was the sole reason they'd had me."

"Christ," he bit out. "That's a hell of a thing for a

kid to hear."

"She was yelling at my father, and someone was throwing things. She said I was useless because I couldn't save her baby. And lots of other things, but I kind of got sick to my stomach and ran to my room. After that, I stayed out of her way."

"What about your father?"

I shrugged. "He was a busy man. He had to keep my mother in designer clothing and expensive sports cars after all."

"And your brother?" He asked his brief questions with a measured tone, but I could tell by the way he held himself absolutely still he hung on every word I said and that he didn't like what he heard.

"He passed away a few days later. I know she was upset and I tried my best to be where she wanted me to be, but in the background. Seen but not heard. She took every opportunity to tell her friends how disappointed she'd been when I hadn't been able to save my brother. It was a miserable few days for me, but I endured because it wasn't about me. It was about Jace. After that, they sent me to boarding school in London and I saw them maybe three or four times afterward before I took off at sixteen." I shrugged. "So, I left home and never looked back. Nobody looked for me," I continued, my voice steadier than I expected. "With the money my father had, if they'd wanted to find me they could have. They were probably glad I disappeared. One less thing to get in the way of their lives."

He studied me a moment. "You were sixteen when you left?"

I nodded. "Yeah."

"And you were nine when they sent you off to school?" I nodded again, confused. "And you saw them four times in those seven years?"

"I'd love to say I was exaggerating, but if anything, I'm overestimating the number of times I saw them. My parents abandoned me. Sure, I had money and food and a roof over my head, but I was told not to come home because international airfare, round trip, wasn't in the budget. They were already spending a fortune on my education."

"How'd you get back to the States?"

"I saved most of the money they put in my account each month to buy a ticket. Figured Nashville was about as far from New York as I could get. Maybe not geographically, but socially it's a world of difference."

"How old are you, Cora?" He stroked the back of my hand with a thumb, staring at me intently.

"Twenty-two."

"And you've been on your own all this time?"

"Don't sound so shocked." I couldn't help but smile. "I'm perfectly capable of taking care of myself."

"I have no doubt you can, honey. I just don't like the idea of you being on your own. Are you safe?" The longer we sat here, the more chatty he was getting. It was kind of cute because this guy acted nothing like the hardened biker I'd pegged him for. He was a marshmallow if I ever saw one. 'Course, men who were true marshmallows were the ones who were super protective of those they let close. "Just don't like not knowin' you're safe at night."

I smiled, unable to help myself. "You know, Marcus, I think you're the first person in my life who at least said they gave a damn about me."

"I do give a damn about you," he grumbled. "But I also know I'm overbearing sometimes."

"Really?" I raised my eyebrows. "Because you

seem pretty quiet to me."

He stayed silent for a while. I thought I might have pissed him off or insulted him or something, but he never let go of my hand. In fact, he kept up that slow lazy slide of his thumb over the back of my hand. "Did you graduate high school before you took off?"

I shook my head. "No. Spent three years on the streets before I got my GED. That's all I needed to get a job. Which I did. And here I am." I smiled up at him before gesturing to the garden below us. "Never had anything worth protecting like that."

Again, he said nothing for several moments, processing what I'd shared. My story represented the first personal detail I'd revealed to anyone at the compound other than in vague generalizations. Sure, the women were all super-friendly and sweet, but I didn't live here. I might not know much about motorcycle clubs in general, or this club in particular, but I knew a tight-knit family when I saw one. Mainly because I'd spent my whole life wanting that very thing.

When he finally spoke, his voice was gentle in a way I hadn't heard before. "Somebody should have protected you."

Five simple words, but they cut through years of carefully constructed defenses. I blinked rapidly, fighting the sting behind my eyes. The rain had tapered to a light drizzle, sunlight breaking through in wider shafts now, creating rainbows in the mist above the garden.

"I protected myself," I said, hearing the stubborn pride in my voice. "Still do."

Rancor nodded, understanding in his dark eyes. "Doesn't mean you should've had to."

He stood and paced away slightly, resting his

shoulder on one of the wooden posts holding up the porch. I was still in his line of sight. The weight of his gaze drew me in, and I found myself moving before I'd made a conscious decision. I stood from my chair and stepped toward him, closing the distance between us.

He remained where he was, looking at me with an expression I couldn't fully read. He seemed skeptical, but like he desperately wanted what I dangled in front of him. I placed my hands on his shoulders, feeling the solid strength beneath his shirt. His skin radiated heat even through the fabric.

"Thank you," I whispered, "for showing me the garden. For telling me about Sarah."

His hands came up to rest on my hips, steadying me as I leaned into him, stood on my tiptoes, and pulled him gently to meet my lips with his.

This kiss felt different, almost languid but no less intense. It didn't take me long to moan when he swept his tongue over the seam of my lips, asking entrance. I tasted rain on his lips, felt the scratch of his beard against my chin. My fingers tightened reflexively on his shoulders, drawing myself closer.

When we broke apart, his eyes remained closed for a heartbeat longer, as if savoring the moment. The storm had passed completely now, leaving behind that peculiar clarity that comes after heavy rain.

"I should go," I said reluctantly. The last thing I wanted to do was leave, but it was best if I put some physical distance between us for a bit. I needed to make sure I thought about this whole situation clearly before I did anything to get myself hurt. Physically or emotionally.

He nodded, looking almost as reluctant as I felt to end the short interlude we'd shared. "I'll walk you out."

We moved through his apartment in comfortable silence. At the door, he paused, seeming indecisive. Then his expression relaxed and he put his hand on my shoulder. "Wait here. One minute."

I watched as he disappeared back onto the porch, returning moments later with something in his hands. A small terracotta pot containing a leafy green plant with delicate purple flowers sat so small against his large hands.

"Sage," he said, offering it to me. "Sarah's favorite. Heals the soul, she said."

I took the pot with careful hands, our fingers brushing in the exchange. The gesture felt impossibly intimate, him sharing not just a plant, but a piece of her. Of him.

"I've never kept anything alive before," I admitted, studying the small leaves.

"Water twice a week." His voice was soft. "Morning sun. It'll do the rest."

He walked me back through the kitchen to my truck. "Thanks for the shelter," I said, standing beside my vehicle, the potted sage held carefully against my chest. "And the company."

Rancor's hand came up, hesitated, then gently tucked a damp strand of hair behind my ear. The touch sent electricity through me, different from the storm's energy but no less powerful.

"Give me your phone," he demanded. He got this stubborn look about him when he thought he wasn't going to get something he wanted very much. I had to bite back a smile as I handed it to him. He punched in some numbers and there was a buzzing sound from his pants. Yeah. Wasn't touching that one. "Sent my phone a text so you have my number." He held my gaze. "Come back," he said. Not a question.

Not quite an order. Something in-between.

"I will." I smiled up at him, meaning it more than I'd meant anything in a long time. "I don't have anything scheduled, but I would love to spend some time with you."

"Yes." His simple reply made me smile.

I climbed into my vehicle, setting the sage on the passenger seat with care. I started the engine and put the vehicle in gear. As I pulled away, I caught sight of him in the rearview mirror. I wasn't sure I was ready for the path I was going down but found myself wanting to skip along it all the same. And for the first time in my life, the road ahead felt like it might lead somewhere other than *away*.

Chapter Five

Cora

The rain had slowed to a drizzle by the time I left the compound, but the roads glistened like black ice under my headlights. I gripped the steering wheel with one hand while the other rested protectively over the small pot of sage Marcus had given me. I smiled despite the weather, despite everything. The truck's wipers squeaked against the windshield, struggling against the mist that wasn't quite rain anymore but refused to clear.

The headlights behind me caught my attention, reflecting in my rearview mirror and casting my cab in harsh white light. A car had pulled onto the road behind me from a side street. Nothing unusual about that. I flipped my mirror to dim the glare and focused on the road ahead.

Three turns later, the same headlights remained fixed behind me. My shoulders tightened. I had to be paranoid. Two people could share the same route home without it meaning anything.

I took a right turn I didn't need to take.

The car followed.

My pulse quickened. I checked the speedometer, making sure I didn't go even a mile over the limit. My registration was current, my lights all worked, and I hadn't had anything to drink. There shouldn't be a reason for anyone to pull me over, but the whole vibe just screamed cops.

The headlights drew closer, close enough that I could now make out the silhouette of a police cruiser. Just like I thought. My mouth went dry. I'd had enough run-ins with police during my homeless months when I first came back to the states to develop a healthy wariness. They hadn't exactly been friendly to teenage runaways, even ones who weren't causing trouble.

I took another unnecessary turn, this one taking me farther from my apartment. The cruiser followed, maintaining its distance. Just close enough to let me know I was being watched and they were playing with me.

Then the red and blue lights flashed on, painting the wet pavement ahead of me in alternating crimson and cobalt. My heart slammed against my ribs. I pulled off into a gas station parking lot under the flood lights. I didn't have any reason to think there was any danger, except the hair on the back of my neck standing on end. I lowered the window but returned my hand to the wheel, making sure to keep my hands still and visible.

Because I liked keeping a low profile, I did my best to obey the law in all respects. I didn't jaywalk. I didn't drink if I expected to go anywhere other than where I was drinking. I'd never even smoked weed, for fuck's sake. But my hands wouldn't stop shaking, and my throat felt tight with fear. I'd learned to listen to that internal warning.

The officer didn't approach immediately. The waiting ratcheted up my anxiety until I felt my pulse throbbing in my fingertips where I gripped the steering wheel. Through my side mirror, I watched a man finally exit the cruiser. Tall, maybe in his fifties, with broad shoulders and a swaggering walk that spoke of absolute confidence and a healthy dose of arrogance. Just ducky.

"License and registration." His voice was flat, professional, giving nothing away. I got a better look at him now. Sharp features, close-cropped gray hair, steel-colored eyes that assessed me with cold calculation.

"Can I ask why I'm being pulled over, Officer?" My voice came out steadier than I expected.

"Detective," he corrected. "Detective Reeves. And you were swerving." I hadn't been swerving. We both knew it. But arguing would only make things worse.

"I'm sorry, Detective. The roads are slippery." I reached slowly for my glove compartment. "My registration is in here, and my license is in my wallet."

I retrieved the requested documents, leaving the glove box open. His gaze flicked to the potted sage on my passenger seat, then back to me as I handed over my license and registration.

"Been drinking, Ms. English?"

"No, sir. Not at all."

He studied my license. "Long way from town, aren't you? I thought the local delivery apps had put out warnings about those warehouses." My stomach dropped. He knew who I was and what I did for a living. This wasn't a random stop.

"I'm paid to deliver groceries and sundries, sir. Company policy is that we take the next order on the list," I said, keeping my tone neutral. It was the truth; we were supposed to pick up the next order on the list. Didn't mean the rule was always enforced.

"To the Kiss of Death compound," he stated. Not a question. Before I could respond, a second officer emerged from the cruiser. She looked several years younger than Detective Reeves. "This is Detective Olivia Mercer."

Detective Mercer nodded at me curtly. Unlike her partner, she at least maintained the appearance of professionalism, though her gaze held a similar calculating gleam. She hung back slightly, standing at the passenger side of my car, her posture alert but not overtly threatening.

"You shouldn't be in such a remote area as that warehouse graveyard. Especially in this weather." He gestured to the drizzling rain.

"It's my job, detective." I swallowed against the dryness in my throat. "I have to eat and make rent. The weather doesn't change that."

Reeves leaned in closer, resting his arm on my door. The smell of coffee and cigarettes wafted from him. "How long have you been delivering to the Kiss of Death compound?"

"A few weeks." I kept my answers short, not volunteering information.

"Making friends there, are we?" The question came with a smile that didn't reach his eyes. "Or something more than friends, perhaps?" My heart hammered against my ribs. I knew Marcus's past, but I had no idea what this detective's interest was in me or the club. Besides, my first instinct with any kind of authority figure was always going to be to keep my mouth shut.

"I deliver groceries," I repeated. "That's all. I'm not sure how much clearer I can be."

"You ran a stop sign back there," Reeves said suddenly, changing tactics. "At the intersection of Warehouse Row and River Street."

I hadn't run any stop signs. There wasn't even a stop sign at that intersection. "I thought I swerved, sir." Inwardly I winced. Not the time for snark. Not the time at all.

His expression hardened. "Are you calling me a liar, Ms. English?"

"No, I --"

"Step out of the vehicle, please." It wasn't really a request.

"Am I under arrest?"

"Not yet," he said, the threat unmistakable. "But we need to search your vehicle. Detective Mercer, would you assist Ms. English while I take a look?"

"You don't have a warrant," I said, the words tumbling out before I could stop them.

"Probable cause," Reeves replied smoothly. "I believe you might be transporting contraband for your gang friends."

My fingers gripped the steering wheel so hard my knuckles ached. I knew my rights, but I also knew that arguing with cops rarely ended well for people like me. Slowly, I released the wheel with one hand and opened my door. The last thing I wanted to do was give this guy an excuse to manhandle me. Or worse.

Detective Mercer stepped forward, maintaining a polite distance. "Just stand over here, please," she said, gesturing to a spot by the gas pump.

Rain misted down on my already damp clothes as I watched Reeves begin his search. He started with the passenger seat, picking up the potted sage plant.

"What's this?" he asked, turning it in his hands.

"It's sage," I replied. "An herb. For cooking."

"Where'd you get it?"

I hesitated, unsure how to answer. The truth would only reinforce his suspicions about my connection to Marcus. A lie might be worse if he somehow knew the answer already. "It was a gift," I finally said.

"From who?" He set the plant down carelessly, almost tipping it over.

"A friend."

"A friend at the Kiss of Death compound?" He

didn't wait for my answer before moving to the back seat and then the trunk.

Detective Mercer remained beside me, her expression unreadable. "You've been making regular deliveries there," she stated. Not a question.

"Yes." I watched Reeves toss delivery receipts onto the wet pavement. My stomach twisted. "Pretty sure I already said as much."

Reeves eventually returned, empty-handed but clearly disappointed by his lack of findings. "Nothing today," he said to his partner. "But that doesn't mean there won't be something tomorrow." The threat in his words was clear. He turned back to me. "You know what kind of people you're dealing with, Ms. English? Murderers. Traffickers. Men who think they're above the law."

My mind flashed to Marcus in his garden, gently pruning herbs. To Hannah's laughter. To the women at the compound who had welcomed me with open arms. I thought of Detective Reeves searching my vehicle without cause, threatening me without evidence. "I don't deal with anyone, detective." This was getting old and that bad vibe singing in my head was getting worse. "I get paid to do a job. That job involves delivering goods through a legitimate company to anyone who places an order through their app."

Reeves stepped closer, invading my space. "We'll be keeping an eye on you, Ms. English. The kind of people who run with that crowd tend to end up in one of two places. Prison or the morgue. You seem like a smart girl. Make better choices." I lowered my gaze, hoping he took it as submissiveness, but said nothing. "You can go," he finally said, stepping back. "Drive carefully. Wouldn't want you running any more stop signs."

I climbed back into my car. The sage plant had been knocked over, soil spilling onto the passenger seat. The bastard had likely done it on purpose to look for drugs or something. I righted the pot gently, brushing the dirt back into the pot.

In my rearview, I watched the two detectives return to their cruiser. They didn't leave immediately. Instead, they sat there, headlights still on, watching me. I started the engine and pulled back onto the road, my heart still racing.

Only when I'd driven several blocks did their headlights finally disappear from my mirror. My breath came in shallow gasps, and I realized I'd been holding it. I wiped at my face, surprised to find it wet not just with rain but with tears I hadn't realized I'd shed.

The interaction had left me feeling dirty somehow, violated in a way that had nothing to do with the physical search of my vehicle. My mind raced with questions. Why were they watching me? What did they want with the club? And what would happen if they decided to "find" something next time? For the first time since I'd started delivering to the compound, I wondered if I should have stayed away.

I drove in circles for twenty minutes before heading home. The rain intensified again, drumming on the roof of my car with a fury that matched my racing thoughts. Water streaked down my windshield faster than the wipers could clear it away.

Every pair of headlights sent a fresh spike of adrenaline through my system. Every police car made my stomach clench. I took side streets instead of main roads, changed lanes more often than necessary, and kept my speed exactly at the limit.

I stopped at a red light, the glow painting the

raindrops crimson on my windshield. My phone sat in the cup holder, screen dark. I picked it up, found Marcus's number, my thumb hovering over the call button.

What would I say? That I'd been pulled over? That a detective seemed to have a vendetta against the club? That I felt unsafe? Marcus had already told me he'd killed a man and gone to prison for it. He didn't need me calling him with problems he already knew existed. Besides, I didn't want to start this with drama. That's what daytime television was for.

The light turned green. I put the phone down and drove on. The temptation to call persisted. I wanted to hear his voice, to be reassured. But what kind of foundation would that build? Running to him at the first sign of trouble when we'd shared all of two kisses and a conversation in the rain?

By the time I reached my apartment complex, the rain had slowed to a drizzle again. I parked in my usual spot, grabbed the plant, and hurried inside, scanning the parking lot one last time before closing the building's main door behind me.

My apartment was on the first floor. Nothing fancy. One bedroom, a bathroom, a kitchen that opened into a small living area. I locked the door behind me, then locked the deadbolt and chain before setting the security alarm.

I placed the sage plant carefully on the kitchen counter, then headed for the bathroom. I turned on the water as hot as I could stand it before undressing. My damp clothes went straight into the laundry hamper. Steam filled the small bathroom as I stepped under the spray, letting it wash away the rain, the search, the feeling of Reeves' eyes on me.

Under the hot water, my mind kept circling back

to Marcus. Convention said I should be terrified of him. Honestly, though, despite his road name being Rancor, Marcus was a very quiet, kind individual. If someone had hurt a person I loved, would I have done any differently? I didn't know. I'd never loved anyone enough to find out.

After my shower, wrapped in a threadbare towel, I found a place for the sage on my kitchen windowsill, the only spot in my apartment that got decent morning light. I arranged it carefully, my fingers lingering on the small leaves.

The contrast wasn't lost on me. The club was basically a group of ex-cons, yet they had treated me with nothing but respect. They'd tipped generously. They'd welcomed me. They'd made me feel valued and appreciated for perhaps the first time in my life, even if they were paying me to come to them. And I had started coming to visit from time to time with the women.

I dried my hair with a towel, the rush of thoughts continuing. Maybe I romanticized the club. Maybe I was being naive. But I couldn't deny the warmth I felt when I thought about the compound, about the women there, about Marcus and his garden. Not to mention that every single person I'd met in that place treated me with kindness. The few children I'd seen there were happy and seemed well adjusted. And Haven. Every woman I'd had the privilege to meet who took shelter there said nothing but positive things about everyone. Kiss of Death guarded that place like Fort Knox and made it clear they would defend the women and children there to the death.

I pulled on an oversized T-shirt and climbed into bed, my body exhausted but my mind still racing. My phone sat on the nightstand, Marcus's number just a tap away. I reached for it, then pulled back. Not tonight. Tonight, I needed to think. To consider whether the connection I felt was worth the complications it clearly brought.

I fell asleep with rain tapping against my window, the sage plant sitting in silent witness, and Detective Reeves' warning echoing in my mind.

But it was Marcus' face I saw as I drifted off. Marcus, with his gentle hands and careful, halting words. Marcus, who had held me in the rain and given me a piece of his heart in the form of a potted herb.

Whatever trouble came from it, I knew I would go back. I would see him again. Because for the first time in my entire life, someone made me feel like I belonged somewhere. And that feeling alone was worth the risk.

Chapter Six

Rancor

The old Harley's carburetor currently lay in several pieces on my workbench. My work light over the table cast long shadows across the concrete floor. I didn't need much light because there was no way I'd get much done on this thing. All I could concentrate on was Cora.

Three days since I'd seen her. Three days since she'd left with that fucking sage plant and an honest-to-God real-ass smile. For the first time in what felt like a lifetime, real warmth spread through me like a spring thaw.

I'd texted her once, just to make sure she got home safe. She'd responded with a photo of the sage sitting in her kitchen window. Not much, but I didn't like to talk much. Texting always proved to be a special kind of hell for me, but I'd do it for her.

My phone sat dark on the workbench beside me. Cora usually texted before she brought something. We had a scheduled delivery today sometime around three, but I hadn't heard from her. I was trying to wean myself from the phone, but knowing I would see her soon had me wound as tight as a teenager going on his first date. I didn't like that I couldn't control myself with regard to Cora.

The door to my workshop slid open, spilling brighter light across my workbench. I didn't look up, knowing one of my brothers likely came to check on me. "You see what time it is?" Knight asked, his voice pitched low despite us being alone.

I kept my eyes on my work. "Nope." To be honest, I took pride in the fact I hadn't looked at my phone since I'd started on this thing after lunch.

"Didn't the old ladies do a grocery order for today?"

That made me look up. Knight stood in the doorway, his tattooed face serious in the half-light, his colored-in eyes impossible to read. But I knew the set of his shoulders, the way his fingers tapped against his thigh. He wasn't upset exactly. Disconcerted seemed like a better description. Maybe even worried.

"Scheduled for three," I said, setting down the part I'd been cleaning. "She's late? What time is it?" I reached for my phone and glanced at the screen. "Four seventeen," I muttered. "Fuck." I unlocked the screen and checked my messages. Nothing.

"That's not all either. Been some strange cars circling the compound today. Non-club. Non-cop, but moving with purpose."

I wiped my hands on a rag, trying to hold back the sudden surge of unease. "What kind of purpose?"

"The kind that makes the hair on the back of my neck stand up." Knight stepped fully into the workshop, letting the door close behind him. "I've spotted the same sedan three times, different drivers. And a van that's made two passes."

I stood, rolling my shoulders to release the sudden tension. And the very real worry something was wrong with Cora.

"She text you?" Knight asked, watching me carefully.

I shook my head. "No."

"That normal?"

"Not really."

"She's not picked up the girls' order, according to the app. And, of course, no one else will get it." I quickly brought her name up on my phone and called her, not taking my gaze from Knight's. "Straight to voicemail."

Knight's jaw tightened. "There's something else. Tiny saw a police cruiser following a vehicle that matched Cora's description about two hours ago. Heading east on River Road."

I stared at the dismantled carburetor for a long moment, needing to think and not react. Everything primitive inside me wanted to take off at a dead run, find Cora, and annihilate anything threatening her.

"Do you think it's possible she's working with the police, Rancor?" Knight asked in a quiet voice. "She doesn't strike me as the type, but…"

I shook my head. "Can't deny it's Goddamned convenient," I whispered. The pain slicing through my chest at the thought of Cora betraying me nearly brought me to my knees. "Cora started coming here after we were basically blackballed from a fuckin' delivery app. But why?"

"Since when do the police need a reason to keep close tabs on a compound full of ex-convicts?" Knight wasn't given to snark, but even I could admit that was a stupid question.

"Get eyes on River Road," I said, my voice steady despite the pressure building in my chest. "Check the route between here and her apartment. Call Knuckles."

Knight nodded, already pulling out his phone. "What are you thinking?"

"Thinking someone's taking an interest in our delivery girl." I reached for my cut, the leather vest heavy with the weight of patches and memories. "And I don't like coincidences."

"You know this is about. Don't you?" My gaze snapped to Knight's. He'd been able to read me like a book since the day we'd met. Only this time, I hadn't even acknowledged to myself I knew what was going on.

"Maybe. Can you get a look at whoever is in those vehicles?"

"I can try. The windows are tinted pretty dark, but I can at least get a different angle on the street. See if I can figure out better what we're up against. What are you thinking?"

Before I could answer, my phone vibrated. I lunged for it, snatching it up and unlocking the screen. A text from an unknown number.

This is Cora. I apologize for the delay. I had an unexpected errand. I'll be arriving at the compound in approximately 30 minutes with your delivery. Thank you for your patience.

I stared at the message, something cold sliding down my spine. In the three weeks I'd known her, Cora had never texted like this. She sounded formal, stiff, like someone was watching over her shoulder as she typed.

Or like someone else entirely had written it.

Knight appeared at my side, his own phone in hand. "Diesel just called in. Said he spotted her car heading this way, but she's not alone. Black sedan following at a distance."

I made a decision. "Get Knuckles," I grunted. "I may need backup."

"You think she's in trouble?"

"I think someone's using her to get to me, or the club." I started walking toward the main gate, Knight falling into step beside me. I showed him the text. It had come through the delivery app instead of her messaging me directly like she usually did. "And I don't like people fuckin' touchin' what's mine."

The words slipped out before I could catch them.

Knight didn't comment, but I saw the slight lift of his eyebrow. I didn't correct myself. Some things didn't need explaining.

"What's the play here?" Knight asked as we reached the gate.

"We wait," I said, taking up a position where I could see the road approaching the compound. "We watch. And we find out what kind of trouble she's bringing to our door."

Knight's phone buzzed and he glanced at the screen. "Knuckles is coming to us. Said to meet him at the gatehouse."

Perfect. We could control the situation better if we contained it inside our territory. If I could get Cora inside, we could keep everyone else out.

The gatehouse was exactly what the small shelter sounded like. Since we'd started New Beginnings, or Haven as the residents had taken to calling it, Knuckles had made sure to always have the main gate manned by two patched members.

We'd been hunted before. We would be again. But this time, they'd dragged Cora into it. They'd regret the line they'd crossed. If it was the bastard I thought it was, I might have to finish what I started.

* * *

Cora

The back seat of the police cruiser smelled like antiseptic and something sour and acrid I couldn't identify. OK, that was a lie. I knew exactly what it was, but I refused to consider exactly how close I sat to the stink of piss and vomit. Through the window, I stared at my car sitting abandoned in the gas station parking lot as we pulled away. Detective Reeves drove in silence, his eyes occasionally flicking to the rearview mirror to check on me. Beside him, Detective Mercer kept her gaze forward, her profile sharp against the passing streetlights. She had my phone tucked into her pocket. Confiscated "for evidence" she'd said when she'd patted me down.

"Just a friendly chat," Reeves said when they'd intercepted me at the gas station where I'd stopped to fill up before heading to the compound. Nothing friendly about the way he'd flashed his badge, or how Mercer had stood blocking the path to my car. Nothing friendly about the tight grip on my arm as they'd guided me to the cruiser. I'd be lucky if I didn't have his fingerprints in a chain of bruising around my upper arm.

"How much longer?" I asked, hating the tremor in my voice.

"Not far to the station," Mercer replied without turning around. Her tone wasn't unkind, just professionally distant. "Ten minutes, tops."

I'd tried texting Marcus when I first spotted them following me, but they'd pulled me over before I could. The half-written message sat unsent in my phone's memory, now in Mercer's possession. I wondered if Marcus was waiting for me, if he'd noticed I was late.

The police station loomed ahead, gray and utilitarian against the evening sky. Reeves pulled into a reserved spot near a side entrance, away from the main doors.

"This way," Mercer said after opening my door. No handcuffs, at least. Small mercies.

They led me through a series of hallways, each looking identical to the last. Officers glanced up as we passed, their expressions ranging from curiosity to indifference.

The interrogation room was exactly like on TV

and in the movies. A small room with a metal table bolted to the floor and three uncomfortable-looking chairs represented everything. A large, one-way mirror took up most of one wall. The fluorescent lights buzzed overhead, casting everyone in a sickly pallor that made even Detective Mercer's healthy complexion look slightly jaundiced.

"Have a seat, Ms. English." Reeves gestured to the chair facing the mirror.

I sat, placing my hands flat on the table to hide their trembling. "Am I under arrest?"

"No, no," Reeves smiled, the expression never reaching his steel-gray eyes. "Just hoping for your cooperation on a matter of public safety."

Mercer remained standing while Reeves took the chair opposite me, placing a manila folder on the table between us. The folder remained closed, but his fingers tapped against it rhythmically, drawing my attention.

"You've been spending a lot of time at the warehouses," he said. Not a question. "At the compound of the motorcycle club called Kiss of Death."

"I deliver groceries there," I replied, the same answer I'd given during our first encounter. I was beginning to feel I was destined to repeat myself over and over until the end of time. "It's my job."

"Is that all it is?" Reeves tilted his head, studying me. "Just a job?"

The image of Marcus's garden flashed in my mind, of his hands gently pruning the herbs, of his lips against mine in the rain. I forced my face to remain neutral. "Yes."

Reeves exchanged a glance with Mercer, who nodded almost imperceptibly. He opened the folder and slid several glossy photographs across the table toward me.

My blood turned to ice.

The photos showed me at the compound, but not as I remembered being there. In one, my image had been expertly spliced into what looked like a party scene, my posture suggestive as I leaned against a shirtless man whose face was just out of frame. In another, I appeared to be counting money, surrounded by bags of white powder that I knew had never been there. A third showed me climbing onto the back of Rancor's motorcycle, which I'd never been on.

"These are fake," I whispered, my mouth gone dry. "I never -- You made these up somehow."

"Photoshopped? Altered with some fancy AI program? Perhaps," Reeves shrugged, the casual gesture belying the threat in his eyes. "But they'd look convincing enough to a judge. Enough to justify charges for prostitution, drug distribution, conspiracy…"

"That's insane," I said, pushing the photos away. "You can't just fabricate evidence."

"We're not fabricating anything," Mercer spoke up, her voice softer than Reeves' but no less firm. "We're simply preparing contingencies. In case our request for cooperation is denied." Was it my imagination, or did Mercer look uncomfortable with my interrogation?

My hands trembled harder, and I balled them into fists. "What do you want from me?"

Reeves leaned forward, his expression saying he had me right where he wanted me. "Information. Access. Eyes and ears inside a criminal organization that has, thus far, managed to operate just beyond our reach."

Mercer approached the table and placed three

small objects on the surface. They looked like small, innocuous everyday objects. A button, a thumbtack, and what appeared to be a tiny plastic air freshener shaped like a pine tree sat in front of me and I got a sick feeling in my stomach.

"Listening devices," she explained, her tone matter-of-fact. "State of the art."

I stared at the tiny objects, each no bigger than my thumbnail. "You want me to spy on them."

"We want you to help us protect the community from dangerous criminals," Reeves corrected. "Men who've killed, who traffic drugs and young girls. They believe they're above the law."

The faces of the people I'd met flashed through my mind. Hannah's warm smile, the club members who treated me with nothing but respect, Marcus… They didn't match Reeves's description, and none of them would ever hurt a child like he was suggesting, but I couldn't deny what Marcus had told me about his past. He'd killed a man. He'd gone to prison. But context mattered, didn't it? Marcus owned the shit. I couldn't blame him either. I'd have wanted to do the same thing. Would have if I'd been strong enough. So, no. I wasn't picking up what these assholes were throwing down.

"I can't help you," I said, the words barely audible. "They trust me. Besides, I can't lie worth a damn."

"That's exactly why it has to be you," Mercer said, almost sympathetically. "Look, we're not asking you to put yourself in danger. Just place these devices where they won't be found, then walk away. You never have to know what we hear."

Reeves tapped the photos again. "Of course, if you prefer to face charges based on this evidence, that's your choice. Though I imagine it would be difficult to find work with a record for prostitution and drug offenses. Housing too, for that matter."

My carefully built life, the apartment I'd fought to keep, the job that barely paid my bills but was honest work, all of it hung by a thread these two could snip with a single call. I'd been homeless before. I couldn't go back to that. Couldn't face the streets again, the hunger, the constant fear.

"Where?" The question tasted like defeat on my tongue.

Mercer pulled out a small notepad. "The main clubhouse kitchen. Should be easy enough with access. We know you've been inside, so this should be a walk in the park." His smile was anything but reassuring. He looked like an evil villain about to kick a puppy that'd pissed on his Italian shoes. "Under a cabinet or shelf, somewhere not immediately visible. The meeting room where they hold club business. And if possible, Rancor's personal quarters."

My stomach lurched at the last request. "Rancor? I can't get into his apartment. I've never been there." The lie came easily, an instinctive protection of the one private space Marcus had shared with me. Besides, I'd lied before when I said I couldn't lie. I couldn't lie to my *friends* worth a damn. Someone like this fucking bastard, I could lie to all fucking day with a fucking smile on my face.

Reeves studied me for a moment, then nodded. "The first two will be sufficient. For now."

"How am I supposed to get into their meeting room? I've never studied the inner workings of a motorcycle club, but I don't imagine it's much different from TV. They're not going to just talk about their business in front of God and everyone."

Reeves simply shrugged. "You'll figure something out."

"When?"

"Today," Mercer said. "Now. They're expecting you, aren't they?"

I nodded mutely. The devices seemed to grow on the table before me, morphing from tiny objects into massive burdens I was being asked to carry.

Reeves gathered the photos, sliding them back into the folder. "We'll be listening. Not just to what the devices pick up, but to make sure you fulfill your end of this arrangement."

"And if I do this," I said, fighting to keep my voice steady, "you'll leave me alone? Get rid of those photos?"

"Complete this successfully, and we'll discuss a more permanent arrangement," he replied silkily, the non-answer hanging between us.

Mercer collected the devices, placing them in a small plastic bag which she handed to me. "Put these in your pocket. Act normal. You're just doing a good deed."

I snatched the bag, the plastic crinkling under my tight grip. They returned my phone and led me back through the maze of hallways to the side entrance where we'd come in.

"Just remember," Mercer said as she opened the door for me to get into the back of the patrol car, but I stood there, unable to force myself inside the vehicle. "You're doing this for the greater good." She handed me my phone. "I took the liberty of having one of our tech guys clone your phone. Anything you have on there regarding the animals inside that compound, we now have."

I clenched my fists, not looking at the other

woman. "Then you have the same shit you had before you took my phone. I'm doing this to prevent fabricated evidence being used against me." Finally, I met her gaze with a steady one of my own. "Funny. I've been to that compound several times. Never once have I felt threatened. I've also delivered to New Beginnings. The women and children being sheltered there say they've never felt safer."

"You realize that's all a front," Reeves interjected. "Right? They're using those poor women."

"If you truly believe that, why haven't you raided the shelter? Why aren't you doing something to help the women you say you know are abused by the men in the club?"

"They're smart about it," Reeves said without hesitation. "They keep the majority of the building under lock and key. Ever wonder why you can't get past the foyer? They're hiding something. Likely all kinds of abuse."

I shook my head, unable to prevent the humorless chuckle from escaping. "Well, Detective Reeves, between the men in Kiss of Death and the two police officers standing here with me, only the police are blackmailing me into doing something that, if you're telling the truth about this club, is clearly putting me in a life-threatening situation. If I get caught and these guys are the real deal, you're signing my death warrant." I pursed my lips. "All for the greater good."

"We all have to make sacrifices sometimes, Ms. English. This is yours."

"Yeah? What sacrifices are you making, Detective Reeves? I'm the one taking the risk. I've literally not done anything to anyone. You pulled me off the street, threatened me, and now you're trying to pretend you're doing the community a service?" I snorted. "You're a twenty-four-carat gold son of a bitch, Detective Reeves. Karma's a real thing. I sincerely hope you're prepared for the blowback you're earning."

"Trust me, sweetheart," he sneered. "I can handle any blowback. Those thugs are all going to get what's coming to them. Do what we tell you to, and you'll have a long, happy, uneventful life."

"Uh-huh." I slid into the car, fastening my seat belt and staring straight ahead. I glanced up at Detective Mercer. "One woman to another, Detective Mercer, he's going to drag you down into the muck and mire like an abusive spouse. He won't take you down with him. No. He'll shove you overboard and take off with the Goddamned boat."

Chapter Seven

Cora

The compound gates loomed ahead like the entrance to hell itself. But now, instead of fearing what waited inside, I dreaded bringing danger through those gates myself. My hands wouldn't stop trembling, no matter how tightly I gripped the steering wheel. Those devices Detective Reeves gave me sat heavy in my pocket, three tiny betrayals I'd been coerced into carrying. I blinked hard, trying to clear the burning in my eyes. Crying wouldn't help. Nothing would help now except getting through the next hour without falling apart. So here I sat, red-eyed from crying and sick with guilt, driving straight back into the arms of people whose trust I was actively betraying.

I pulled up to the gate, my car's engine sputtering as if it, too, were reluctant to enter. The guards waved me through and I went to my usual spot at the back of the main warehouse. Marcus stood alone outside the building, his broad frame silhouetted against the afternoon sun. Even from a distance, I could see the slight tension in his shoulders relax at the sight of my vehicle. He'd been waiting for me. That realization landed like a punch to my gut. Given everything that had happened with the detectives, it had completely slipped my mind to call him like usual. And I was late.

He approached as I parked, his pace measured and deliberate in that way that had once intimidated me but now felt like a steadying rhythm in my chaotic world. I took a shuddering breath, trying to compose myself before stepping out. The listening devices felt like an albatross in my jacket pocket, weighing me down.

"Cora." Just my name, but the concern in his voice nearly broke me. "What's wrong?"

I couldn't meet his eyes. "Rough night," I managed, my voice sounded as raw as my insides felt. My throat tightened with fear. Dread sat in the pit of my stomach.

His silence stretched between us, a quiet demand I elaborate. I couldn't possibly explain to him I'd been blackmailed and threatened into betraying him and the club. I busied myself with grabbing the first bags from my trunk, but Marcus gently moved me aside, lifting the heavier loads himself.

"You've been crying," he murmured softly, observant in a way that made hiding impossible.

"Allergies," I lied and immediately winced. I'd told Reeves the truth. I really couldn't lie worth a damn.

The compound felt different today -- hostile, like it knew I was a traitor. The camo netting above swayed in the light breeze, casting moving shadows that seemed to follow me accusingly. The kitchen door swung open under Marcus' gentle push. The fluorescent lights hummed overhead, casting a harsh glare on the stainless-steel surfaces. Everything always looked so clean and tidy.

No one else loitered in the area. Just my fucking luck. Marcus didn't like me to carry much inside, leaving me with nothing to do but wait. With no one here, I could put the one in the kitchen where they wanted me to without fear of getting caught. My whole entire being rebelled at the thought and I knew that, if I did this, not only would I be physically ill, but I'd never be able to look myself in the mirror again.

"Water?" Marcus's voice startled me. He stood at the refrigerator, holding out a bottle.

I nodded, accepting it with a trembling hand. The cap wouldn't budge under my weak attempt. Marcus gently took it back, twisted it open, and returned it without comment on my obvious distress. "Thank you," I whispered, the simple kindness making my chest ache. I took a large gulp of the cool liquid, trying to settle myself.

His phone buzzed. He glanced at it, his brow furrowing slightly. "Need to check something. Be right back." He gave me a pointed look. "Stay here. Please."

I nodded, my heart pounding. If I went through with this, it was now or never. As soon as the door swung shut behind him, I pulled out one of the small devices. It looked like a black thumbtack. I scanned the kitchen, panic rising as I searched for a spot they wouldn't find it.

In my panic I dropped the tiny thing. I nearly sobbed in terror. What should I do now? I could leave it and hope it was good enough. Just as the thought entered my mind, the big, industrial refrigerator kicked on. Where the thumb tack rolled too far for me to retrieve. Served me right.

A wave of nausea hit me so suddenly I had to grip the edge of the counter to keep from doubling over. Cold sweat broke out across my forehead and upper lip, and my mouth filled with a metallic taste letting me know I was about to blow chunks.

I lunged for the sink, certain I'd be sick, but nothing came up. Just dry heaves and shuddering breaths that sounded dangerously close to sobs. Water. I needed more water, but not to drink. I fumbled for the faucet, turning on the cold water and splashing my face. This wasn't right. These people had been nothing but good to me. And Marcus? How could I possibly do this to him? Especially to save myself. That made me the worst kind of person.

The kitchen door swung open, and I straightened so quickly that spots danced before my eyes. Marcus stood there, watching me with an expression I couldn't bear to interpret. The room tilted slightly, the fluorescent lights suddenly too bright, too harsh.

"You don't look good, honey," he said, his voice low and gentle. He approached slowly, as if afraid I might bolt. Or collapse.

"I'm fine," I managed, though my reflection in the stainless-steel refrigerator door told a different story -- pale face, red-rimmed eyes, a woman coming apart at the seams. "Just haven't eaten today. Got lightheaded."

He moved closer, his presence both comforting and excruciating. I wanted to lean into him, to confess everything, to beg for help. Instead, I lowered my gaze to my feet, too ashamed to look him in the eyes.

"Cora." Just my name again but loaded with questions I couldn't answer.

"Really," I insisted, not looking up. "I'm fine. Just tired."

A moment of silence stretched between us, heavy with his doubt. Then his hand appeared in my field of vision, large and steady, covering mine where it rested on the counter. The touch was gentle but insistent. "If someone's hurting you," he said, each word slow and deliberate, "I can help. *We* can help you."

The tenderness in his voice nearly shattered my fragile composure. I bit the inside of my cheek hard enough to taste blood, using the sharp pain to center myself, to hold back the confession that threatened to spill out. "No one's hurting me," I whispered. Another lie, but not entirely. Reeves wasn't hurting me physically. He was destroying not only my self-worth, but also any chance I might have had at happiness with Marcus.

He didn't push, didn't demand answers. He just stood there, solid and patient, his hand still covering mine. And that patience was almost worse than any interrogation could have been. I didn't deserve his concern, not when I'd just planted a listening device that would capture his private conversations, betray his trust, and potentially harm him and everyone else here.

Marcus didn't press me with more questions, but his quiet concern was almost worse than an interrogation. He watched me with those dark eyes that seemed to see straight through my walls to the terrified girl underneath.

"I should get going," I mumbled, not meeting his eyes.

"I'll walk you out." Not an order, yet not quite a request either.

Outside, the afternoon sun cast long shadows across the compound. A few club members nodded to Marcus as we passed, their curious gazes sliding over me before looking away. Did they sense the deception clinging to me like a second skin? I couldn't be less cut out for this task, and, I not only resented Reeves and Mercer for putting me in this position, I hated them both. Mercer more than Reeves because she should have been my advocate.

When we reached my car, I reached for the driver's door, desperate to escape, to be alone with my shame and fear. To figure out what the hell I was going to do next. But before I could open it, Marcus's hand gently closed around my arm. Not restraining, just connecting. "Cora." My name in his mouth always sounded different. Softer. Important. "Look at me."

I couldn't. If I looked at him now, with guilt flooding my veins and Reeves' threats echoing in my mind, I might shatter completely. But his fingers lightly touched my chin, tilting my face up until I had no choice but to meet his gaze. The tenderness I found there nearly broke me. His dark eyes held no accusation, no suspicion. Only genuine concern that I knew I didn't deserve.

"Tell me what's going on so I can fix it," he said quietly, his voice barely above a whisper. "You can trust me with your life, Cora. No one will ever protect you as fiercely as I will. I swear on my life."

Trust. The word landed like a physical blow. What did I know about trust? My parents had taught me trust meant nothing. The streets had taught me trust was dangerous. And now I violated the trust of perhaps the only person who had ever offered trust freely. God had a special place in hell just for me, and I fucking deserved it.

"Marcus, I --" My voice caught, the words tangling in my throat on a small sob. I wanted to tell him. God, how I wanted to unburden myself, to explain about Reeves and the fabricated photos, the blackmail, the impossible choice I faced. But what if Reeves could hear us right now through the devices I still had on me? What if confessing put Marcus in danger?

"Whatever it is," he continued, his thumb brushing lightly against my cheek in a gesture so tender it made my eyes burn, "we can figure it out. Together."

A tear escaped before I could stop it, trailing down my cheek until it collided with his thumb. His expression shifted subtly, concern deepening into something fiercer, more protective. I wanted to have him hold me tight, to hold me together. Because, I knew I was on the verge of shattering.

"Who made you cry?" he asked softly, but I heard the edge beneath it, the barely contained rage not directed at me but at whoever had caused my distress.

Another tear followed the first, and I didn't bother wiping it away. Why pretend anymore? I was falling apart, and we both knew it. "I need to think for a while," I finally whispered, the closest to honesty I could manage. "I have to figure this problem out on my own."

His hand dropped from my face, but he didn't step back. "Some problems are too big for that. In case you hadn't noticed, I've got some pretty fuckin' big shoulders. I can manage the load for you."

I let out a broken laugh that sounded dangerously close to another sob. "You have no idea."

"Try me." Two simple words, an offer of partnership that pierced straight through my defenses.

I shook my head, blinking back fresh tears. "I can't. Not yet." Maybe not ever, a voice whispered in my mind. How could I confess to being the very threat he was trying to protect me from?

He studied me for a long moment, his expression unreadable. Then he nodded once, accepting my answer without pushing further. The respect in that simple gesture, honoring my boundaries even while offering help, made my heart ache with a longing so intense it frightened me. "When you're ready," he said quietly, "I'll be here."

I nodded, not trusting my voice.

I climbed into my car, the familiar creak of the door a small comfort in a world that had become increasingly uncertain. Marcus stepped back, giving me space, but his gaze never left mine.

"Be safe," he said as I started the engine.

"Be careful, Rancor." I used his road name, hoping he'd take the subtle hint. I couldn't tell him what was going on, but I could at least plant the seed he needed to watch himself.

His brows furrowed and he said nothing for the longest time. Then he nodded his head slowly. "Yeah, baby. I will."

I nodded again, put the car in gear, and pulled away. My knuckles turned white against the steering wheel as I fought to keep the vehicle steady on the road. What would Reeves do when he realized only one device sat inside the compound and that he probably couldn't hear a Goddamned thing on it? Would he make good on his threats? And what would Marcus do when he discovered what I'd done? The thought of seeing betrayal replace that careful tenderness in his eyes was almost worse than anything Reeves could do to me.

I had two impossible choices. As I drove away from the compound, rain began to fall, gentle drops that quickly became a downpour, matching the storm raging inside me. I drove away from perhaps the only person who could help me, toward a future I couldn't predict and choices I didn't want to make. And I had absolutely no idea what to do next.

Chapter Eight

Cora

Making myself leave the relative safety of my car to enter the café on Music Row felt like climbing the steps to the gallows. Through the rain-streaked windshield I stared at the entrance. Warm light spilled from its windows onto the wet pavement outside, promising comfort I knew I didn't deserve and wouldn't receive as long as this *thing* was hanging over me. I just didn't know what to do.

I spotted Marcus through the glass, his broad shoulders, shaved head, and thick, dark beard unmistakable even in the dim interior. He'd taken a corner table, his back to the wall. Likely so he could have eyes on the door. My stomach twisted as I killed the engine. Somehow, facing him here felt worse than when I'd left the compound yesterday with that damn listening device already broadcasting everything to Reeves. Assuming any noise from the fridge didn't mask conversations.

I sat for a moment, trying to talk myself into continuing on. Marcus had requested to meet here. He'd sent a text with the name of the restaurant, politely asking to meet. Normally I'd have jumped at the chance, but my conscience rode me hard. What I'd done kept me awake, staring at my ceiling all night while guilt gnawed at my insides. I knew what I'd done was wrong.

When I finally pushed open the door of my vehicle, the rain hit me in cold, heavy drops. I didn't bother with an umbrella, letting the rain soak into my hair and dampen my shoulders. Maybe I wanted the discomfort as some small penance for what I'd done.

The bell above the café door jingled as I entered,

announcing my arrival to a room of strangers who barely looked up from their laptops and conversations. The place was kind of a local hangout as well as a popular place for tourists to listen to live music. A musician in the corner strummed something slow and melancholy on an acoustic guitar, the notes mingling with the hiss of the espresso machine and murmured conversations. The air smelled of coffee and cinnamon, of rain-damp clothing and the faint sweetness of pastries warming in the display case.

Marcus watched me approach, his dark eyes giving nothing away. He'd chosen a small table, creating an intimate setting in an otherwise very public place.

"Hey," I said, the word coming out breathier than I intended. I slid into the chair opposite him, wiping rain from my face with shaking hands.

"Cora." Just my name, but it carried a weight, an acknowledgment. If he noticed I couldn't quite meet his gaze, he didn't call me out.

A server appeared at our table, a girl with multiple piercings and rainbow-tipped hair. "Know what I can get you?" she asked, the tablet in her hands to take our order at the ready.

"Two coffees," Marcus said before I could answer. "Hers with cream, no sugar." My head jerked up at that. He'd noticed how I took my coffee. I couldn't remember ever telling him that preference.

"Food?" the server asked.

"No, thank you," I replied, my voice steadier than I felt. The thought of food made my stomach clench tighter.

Marcus's gaze never left me as the server walked away. Behind him, a couple argued in hushed tones over a shared muffin. To our left, a man in a rumpled suit tapped furiously at his laptop keys. Normal people doing normal things, while I sat across from a man I'd betrayed, wondering if he already knew and, if he did, what he intended to do to me because of it. I'd love to say the only reason I'd come was because he'd named a public place, but the truth was, I'd have come anyway. I deserved to be tortured for what I'd done so this had been a form of self torture, I guess.

"You look tired," he said, breaking the silence between us.

I forced a smile that felt like cracked glass on my face. "Didn't sleep much."

"Bad dreams?" There was something in his tone that made me wonder if this was more than casual conversation.

"Something like that." I twisted my hands in my lap, hidden beneath the table. "How are things at the compound?"

He tilted his head slightly, studying me. "Quiet."

The server returned with our coffees, setting them down with a gentle *clink* of ceramic on wood. I wrapped my cold fingers around the warm mug, grateful for something to hold onto.

"Knight's been busy," Marcus continued once the server left. "Security upgrades. New cameras and such." He took a deliberate sip of his coffee, watching me over the rim of his mug.

Outside, the rain intensified, beating against the windows in heavy sheets. I took a sip of coffee to hide my expression. Such a small detail, him knowing how I took my coffee. It shouldn't have mattered, but the weight of guilt pressed harder against my chest at his kindness.

"Your sage still alive?" he asked, the question catching me off guard with its normalcy.

"Yes," I said, an unexpected warmth blooming in my chest at the thought of the plant sitting in my kitchen window. "It's actually doing well. I was worried I'd kill it."

"Sage is resilient," he said. "Hard to kill once it takes root." His words seemed weighted with meaning beyond the plant, and I found myself searching his face for clues. Did he suspect something? Was this entire meeting a test?

A man at the counter dropped his spoon, the metallic clatter making me flinch. Marcus noticed, his gaze sharpening at my reaction. "You seem jumpy today," he observed, his voice deceptively casual.

I shrugged, aiming for nonchalance and missing by miles. "Just tired. Work's been stressful."

"Someone giving you trouble?"

"Something like that." Not exactly a lie, but the deception tasted bitter on my tongue as it rolled out. I really was a horrible liar. Mainly because I hated when people lied to me and, therefore, I tried not to lie to others. Golden Rule and all.

A group of college students burst through the door, bringing with them the smell of rain and the ringing of laughter that seemed to belong to another world entirely, one carefree and minus all the intrigue and evil inhabiting mine. They shook water from their jackets, oblivious to the tension crackling at our small table in the corner.

"I missed you yesterday," Marcus said after another stretch of silence. "After you left."

The simple admission caught me in the center of my chest, a direct hit to whatever defenses I'd managed to construct. I swallowed hard against the sudden tightness in my throat. I had to fight not to rub my chest where the ache tightened painfully.

"I missed you too," I whispered, the truth of it surprising me. Two tears slipped from my eyes and I ducked my head. I had missed him. I'd been looking forward to seeing him again. Of seeing everyone I'd met in the compound. Because, despite everything Detective Reeves had told me, I still had trouble with the fact that every single person in Kiss of Death I'd met had treated me with kindness and respect. The kiss I'd shared with Rancor had been the highlight of my life up to this point.

His expression softened just slightly, the barest hint of warmth in those dark eyes. For a moment, we were just two people sharing coffee on a rainy afternoon, nothing more complicated than that. But the moment passed like a shadow, reality reasserting itself between us. He was still while I fidgeted. If he didn't already know what I'd done, I couldn't hold out telling him if I stayed with him very long.

"Something happened," he said, not a question but a statement of fact. "Between when you texted me and when you arrived at the compound yesterday. Something that changed you."

The coffee turned to acid in my stomach. His perception was too sharp. And too accurate for my peace of mind. I stared down at my hands, unable to meet his gaze. "Marcus, I…" I began, but the words died in my throat. What could I say? That I was spying on him? That Detective Reeves had threatened to destroy the life I'd built for myself if I didn't do what he'd told me? That I'd already betrayed him once and didn't know if I could stop from doing it again because my cushy life was more important than his freedom? Yeah. Didn't sound good to me either. He waited, patient as stone, for words I couldn't find.

When he finally spoke, he measured his words

carefully, like he tried to choose them so they'd have the desired effect. Or maybe my guilty conscience liked playing tricks. "Knight found something interesting yesterday," Marcus said, his voice dropping lower, forcing me to lean forward to catch his words. "After you left." The café noise receded as my focus narrowed to the man across from me, his words landing like stones in still water. "Surveillance equipment. Not ours." He took another sip of coffee, his movements deliberate and unhurried despite the bomb he'd just dropped. He didn't take his gaze from me, studying me hard. Which wasn't unnerving in the least. "Police-grade, according to Knight. Very high-end. Very illegal without a warrant."

My lungs seized, refusing to draw breath. The rim of my coffee cup clicked against my teeth as my hand shook. I set it down before I could spill, the ceramic making a hollow sound against the wooden table. "Where?" The question escaped before I could stop it, my voice barely audible even to my own ears.

Marcus's gaze never wavered. "Kitchen, under the fridge." The exact spot where I'd dropped the device I'd tried to plant. "Strange place for something like that to appear, don't you think? Especially right after your visit." He wasn't accusing, just stating a fact. If he was angry, his expression betrayed nothing. Ice still flooded my veins. He knew. Or at least suspected.

My gaze darted toward the door, measuring the distance, wondering if I could make it before he grabbed me. As if reading my thoughts, Marcus shifted slightly in his chair, his posture relaxed but his position now subtly blocking my easiest path to the exit.

"I need to know if you're in trouble," he said, his voice so low I had to lean even closer to hear him. "Whatever it is, I can help you. Protect you." The offer hung between us, sincere and impossible. My hands trembled harder, coffee sloshing over the rim of my cup onto my fingers. I didn't feel the heat.

"You can't," I whispered, the words torn from somewhere deep and wounded.

"Try me."

I stared at him, at the calm in his dark eyes, at the stillness of his large frame. The rain drummed against the windows, providing a soundtrack to my racing thoughts. How could I explain Reeves and the threats, the fabricated evidence? How could I admit what I'd already done? Marcus seemed to sense my struggle. He leaned back slightly, giving me space to breathe, and changed tactics.

"In Terre Haute," he began, his voice still pitched for my ears alone, "I learned to read people. Had to. When you're surrounded by men who'd kill you for looking at them wrong, you learn to spot trouble before it spots you." He traced the rim of his cup in a slow, deliberate circle. "You watch for tells. The way someone's pulse jumps in their throat when they're lying. The micro-expressions that flash across their face before they can control them. The way fear shows in the eyes before the brain even processes the danger." I swallowed hard, acutely aware of my own pulse hammering visibly at the base of my throat, of the cold sweat breaking out across my forehead, of every involuntary reaction my body was betraying me with.

"Most men in prison," he continued, "they don't know they're about to snap until it's already happening. But their bodies know. I learned to recognize the signs before trouble started so I could get out of the way." His gaze dropped meaningfully to my fingers, which had begun tapping a nervous rhythm against the table. "In prison, knowing who's about to break can save your life."

The musician in the corner hit a discordant note, the sound jarring against the soft melody he'd been playing. Outside, a car horn blared, making me flinch. Every sound seemed magnified, every sensation heightened as adrenaline flooded my system.

"When I first got to Terre Haute," Marcus said, "I was raw. Grieving and angry. Made me an easy target." He pushed up one shirt sleeve slightly, revealing a thin, pale scar running along his forearm, different from the burn scar I'd noticed before. "Got this my second week. Guy came at me in the yard. I didn't see it coming because I wasn't paying attention to the signs." I stared at the scar, physical evidence of the violence he'd survived. My gaze traveled up to the other mark on his face, the one I'd touched that day in the rain. "After that," he continued, "I learned. Watched. Listened. Started noticing the patterns." His voice remained calm, almost hypnotic. My tongue felt thick, useless in my mouth. I tried to swallow but couldn't. "Right now," he said, his gaze holding mine, "you're showing every sign of someone who's cornered." As if to demonstrate, he reached across the table and gently covered my fidgeting fingers with one large hand. The warmth of his skin against mine shocked and grounded me. "I've seen fear like this before, Cora. Usually right before someone does something desperate."

He touched me gently but with firm pressure, his calloused palm rough against the back of my hand. I stared at our hands, his so large it engulfed mine completely, and felt something inside me begin to crack. The weight of secrets, of fear, of choices made under duress pressed down until I could barely breathe.

"You don't understand," I whispered, my voice breaking on the last word. Tears tracked freely down my cheeks now.

"Then help me understand." His thumb stroked across my knuckles, a gesture so tender it made my tears come even harder. "Whatever happened, whatever you did, we can fix it." The certainty in his voice made something twist painfully in my chest.

"It's not that simple." I spoke barely above a whisper, my voice stretched thin with strain.

"It never is." The corner of his mouth lifted in a small, sad smile. "But I've got time. And I'm here to help you if you'll let me."

Marcus waited, his hand still covering mine, patient as always. He didn't push, didn't demand. Just sat there, offering silent support while the rain continued its steady drumbeat against the windows and café life continued around us.

My throat closed around the confession fighting to escape. I opened my mouth, then closed it again. I clutched his hand so hard, I feared I might hurt him. I couldn't seem to let go because, right now, Marcus's touch was the only thing holding me together. The pressure of his steady gaze, the weight of his offer of protection, the knowledge that I'd already betrayed him, all crashed down on me at once, overwhelming in its intensity.

"Marcus," I started again, my voice barely audible over the ambient noise of the café, "I'm afraid."

"I know," he said simply. "But you're not alone." And just like that, the last of my resistance began to crumble. "I'm not here to hurt you, honey. I'm here to help you. Whatever it takes."

My entire body began to shake, not just my hands now but a violent tremor that started deep in my core and radiated outward. The words I needed to say jammed in my throat, forming a lump I couldn't swallow past or breathe around. Marcus's eyes narrowed slightly, reading the fear that must have been written across my face in neon. I opened my mouth, tried again to force sound past the blockage in my throat, but nothing came. Just a strangled, desperate noise that didn't even sound human to my own ears.

"Breathe," Marcus said, his voice steady. His hand still covered mine, warm and anchoring, but it wasn't enough to stop the trembling.

I stared at him, trapped between my impossible choices. If I told him about Reeves, about the threats, about the device I'd already planted, would he help me or would I be signing my own death warrant? If I said nothing, if I placed the remaining bugs as ordered, would I be able to live with myself? I'd told Detective Mercer the truth when I said everyone at the compound treated me better than the police.

The weight of betrayal pressed down on my chest until I struggled with each breath. If I'd been a stronger person, I'd have called up Detective Reeves and told him to shove those other two bugs up his ass. But I was nobody. My parents might have clout, but I didn't. No matter what I did, I would be the loser in this story.

Behind Marcus, rain lashed the windows with renewed fury, as if the storm had been gathering strength just like the pressure building inside me. A flash of lightning illuminated the café, briefly turning everything stark white before plunging back into the warm, golden glow of the overhead lights.

Thunder followed, a deep, bone-shaking rumble that seemed to come from everywhere at once. I flinched, the sound too close to the roar in my own head.

"They made me do it," I finally whispered, the words escaping in a rush of air that left me dizzy. "I didn't want to." I shook my head almost violently, holding on to Marcus's hand like a lifeline. "I swear I didn't want to."

Marcus remained perfectly still, only his eyes moving as they searched my face. "Who?" he asked, the single word carrying the weight of promised retribution.

"Detective Reeves," I said, his name bitter on my tongue. "And his partner. Mercer. They -- they pulled me over yesterday. When I left the compound. They took me to the station and showed me photos they'd fabricated. Of me. With drugs and --" I broke off, unable to continue.

Marcus' jaw tightened, a muscle jumping beneath the skin. "They're blackmailing you." I nodded, the movement jerky and uncontrolled. My hands shook harder in his grip. "The kitchen," he said. "That was you."

It wasn't a question, but I nodded again anyway. Shame burned hot under my skin, making my face flush despite the cold sweat breaking out across my forehead. "I didn't know what else to do. They said they'd destroy my life. That I'd go to prison for drugs and prostitution." The irony of confessing this to a man who'd served six years wasn't lost on me. "I've been homeless before. I can't -- I can't go back to that. I found out a lot about myself when I left London to come back to the U.S. on my own. One was that I could never be homeless for any length of time. I did twenty-four hours in county lockup for vagrancy once and found out pretty quickly I'd never survive in jail either." I took a breath. "I doubt Reeves or Mercer know about my fears, but it felt like they knew what I was afraid of the most and exploited it."

Another rumble of thunder shook the windows. The rain fell in sheets now, a solid wall of water visible through the glass. I could barely make out the shapes of people running for cover on the sidewalk outside. My body wouldn't stop trembling. I felt like I might shake apart, come undone completely right there in the middle of the café with everyone here to witness. Marcus' hand tightened around mine, trying to still the violent shaking, but it was useless. I was coming apart at the seams.

"There's more," I whispered, my voice cracking. "They gave me three. I only planted one. The others --"

My purse, which had been balanced precariously on the edge of the table, chose that moment to slide off. It hit the floor with a soft *thud,* the contents spilling across the worn wooden planks. Rolling out like an accusation, two small objects that looked innocent enough to anyone else but unmistakable to Marcus. The remaining listening devices.

Time seemed to stop. The café noise receded to a distant hum. I watched Marcus' gaze lock onto the tiny betrayals lying exposed on the floor between us. His expression didn't change. Not a flicker of surprise, not a flash of anger. Instead, a stillness came over him more frightening than any rage could have been. The kind of stillness preceding violence in nature.

Slowly, with deliberate movements reminding me of a predator trying not to startle its prey, Marcus released my hand and bent down. He gathered my scattered belongings, carefully setting each item on the table between us. Then, with the same measured control, he picked up one of the listening devices between his thumb and forefinger, straightening to examine it in the light.

Around us, the café continued its normal rhythm. The barista called out drink orders. The college students laughed at something on a phone screen. The musician switched to a new song, something with a faster tempo, clashing with the frozen moment at our table. None of them noticed the crisis unfolding in their midst.

Marcus turned the small device over in his fingers, his dark eyes assessing it with clinical detachment. "Knight said these were expensive," he said, his voice so quiet I had to strain to hear it over the ambient noise and the blood rushing in my ears. His gaze shifted from the bug to my face, his expression unreadable. "Makes sense Reeves would have access to them."

I remained frozen, unable to move or speak, waiting for his anger, his disgust, his rejection. My heart hammered so loudly in my chest I was certain he could hear it across the table. Outside, the storm reached a crescendo. Rain pelted the windows with such force it sounded like hail. Lightning flashed again, closer this time, casting stark shadows across Marcus's face, highlighting the scar I'd once traced in a gentle exploration. Thunder followed almost immediately, the crash so loud several café patrons jumped in their seats.

Marcus set the device on the table beside my other belongings, then bent again to retrieve the second bug. This one he placed beside the first. I waited, breath caught in my lungs, for his judgment. For him to walk away. For him to expose me to everyone in the café as the traitor I was. For something, anything, to break the terrible, weighted silence between us.

When he finally spoke, his voice was low, measured, betraying none of the emotions that must have been churning beneath his controlled exterior. "Reeves has been after me since I got out," he said. "This isn't about the club. It's personal. If Reeves has been watching us all this time, then my interest in you has put you in his crosshairs."

I blinked, struggling to process his words through the fog of fear clouding my thoughts. "What?"

"His son," Marcus said, still not looking at me, his eyes fixed on the listening devices. I wondered briefly if they were active and Reeves was listening to everything we said. Marcus would know and would assume he was listening so, I guess, fuck it. It wasn't like Reeves and Mercer weren't going to figure out I hadn't done what they'd asked. I was at their mercy no matter how I looked at it. "The man I killed. The one who murdered Sarah." He picked up one of the bugs again, rolling it between his fingers contemplatively. "He was Kurt Reeves Jr. Detective Reeves's only child."

The revelation hit me with physical force, driving what little air remained from my lungs. Suddenly, Reeves' fixation, his willingness to fabricate evidence, his determination to use me against the club, all of it made a terrible kind of sense.

"He's using you to get to me," Marcus said, finally raising his eyes to meet mine. "And I led him right to you."

The guilt in his voice, the self-recrimination in his eyes, wasn't what I'd expected. I'd brought danger to his door, betrayed his trust, planted a listening device in his home, and somehow he was taking the blame?

"I'm sorry," I whispered, the words hopelessly inadequate. "I didn't know what else to do."

Marcus swept the bugs into his palm and closed his fingers around them. His expression shifted, hardened into something resolute and dangerous. "You don't have to do anything," he said. "I'll handle Reeves."

The calm certainty in his voice sent a chill down my spine. "What are you going to do?"

Marcus slipped the bugs into his pocket, then reached across the table to brush a tear from my cheek that I hadn't realized was there. His touch was gentle despite the lethal promise in his eyes. "This time, I'm going to protect what's mine," he said simply. "And then I'm going to make sure Detective Reeves never threatens you again."

The storm raged on outside, matching the intensity of what passed between us in that moment. Fear and relief and something deeper, something I wasn't prepared to name yet, hummed in the air between us.

And despite everything, the danger, the uncertainty, the knowledge that things would likely get worse before they got better, I found myself believing him.

Chapter Nine

Rancor

Rain drummed against the roof of my truck as I drove us back to the compound. Cora sat rigid in the passenger seat, her fingers twisted together so tightly her knuckles had gone white. The listening devices weighed heavy in my pocket. They were probably active, so I had no doubt Reeves knew his plan hadn't worked. He'd played her perfectly, exploiting her fears, using her against me. My jaw ached from clenching it, but I kept my face neutral, my movements measured. Showing my rage now would only frighten her more. I didn't want her thinking I was angry at her. She was the only innocent person in this whole fucking mess.

"You don't have to take me back to the compound," she said suddenly, her voice barely audible over the engine's rumble. "I've already caused enough trouble."

I glanced at her. Her face had paled, eyes rimmed with red, hair still damp from the rain. Something fierce and protective surged in my chest. "You didn't cause anything, honey." I kept my voice low, steady. "Reeves did."

Kurt Reeves. The name left a bad fucking taste in my mouth. I'd known from the moment I was released that he'd come for me someday. Eight years hadn't dulled his hatred. Or mine. But I hadn't expected him to find such an effective weapon. Using Cora against me, forcing her to do his bidding when he couldn't do anything to me legally, threatening to destroy her life… It was calculated cruelty. The kind that spoke of a patient, festering rage that matched my own. And now Cora, an innocent person who had done absolutely nothing wrong, got caught in the crossfire of a vendetta that began long before she entered my life. "He was waiting for an opportunity," I said, more to myself than to her. "Watching for a weak point."

Her head snapped toward me. "I'm your weak point?"

I didn't answer immediately, eyes fixed on the rain-slicked road ahead. The windshield wipers beat a steady rhythm, clearing sheets of water only for them to reform an instant later.

Finally, I nodded once, the admission coming easier than I expected. "Yes."

She fell silent again, turning to watch the rain. I needed to call Knight, to prepare the compound for our arrival. I reached for my phone, engaged the hands-free, and dialed.

Knight answered on the second ring. "You good?" He'd been on edge since we discovered the first bug.

"Ten minutes out." I kept my eyes on the road as I spoke. "Everything secure?"

"Locked down tight. You alone?" His question carried layers of meaning.

"Got Cora with me." Out of the corner of my eye I saw her tense beside me at the mention of her name. "She's clean. Reeves had her plant the kitchen bug. Blackmailed her."

A beat of silence on the line. "Figured as much. Looked like she dropped it instead of actually placing it." Knight's voice softened slightly. "She okay?"

I glanced at Cora again, noted the way she hugged herself, shoulders hunched as if expecting a blow. "She will be." I slowed as we approached a flooded section of road. "Reeves fabricated evidence against her, threatening to arrest her for trafficking and prostitution if she didn't cooperate."

"Classic," Knight muttered, disgust evident in his tone. "Knuckles is here. We'll meet you in the common room."

The call ended and silence filled the cab again, broken only by the rhythmic slap of wipers and the steady drum of the rain. Cora's breathing had quickened slightly at the mention of Knuckles. I couldn't blame her. Our president carried his reputation like armor, cultivated it deliberately. Most people found him intimidating even when he was trying not to be. Well, everyone but the old ladies. His wife, Hannah, saw to it the women knew he was a big softy. Yeah. He really wasn't.

"Knight and Knuckles are waiting for us," I said, choosing my words carefully. "They know what happened. They know you didn't have a choice."

She nodded mechanically, but the tension in her body didn't ease. "Are they angry?"

"Not at you. You did nothing wrong."

"Maybe I should have just told you."

I thought about her statement for a moment. "I wish you'd trusted me enough to come to me, but I understand. Reeves knew exactly what to say to make you doubt everything you thought you knew about us."

We turned onto the access road leading to the compound. Even through the rain-blurred windshield, I could make out the increased presence. Two prospects stood guard at the gate instead of the usual one, and I spotted Diesel positioned on the roof of the gatehouse, the outline of a rifle visible beside him. I knew there was at least one other patched member in the gatehouse, but I didn't see who. Seemed Knuckles and Hawk weren't taking chances.

The gate slid open as we approached, Griffin giving me a nod and a two-fingered salute as we passed through. I drove slowly down the main thoroughfare, noting several more brothers around the perimeter. Every face reflected the same focused vigilance. Word had spread. The compound was battening down for a storm that had nothing to do with the rain.

I parked near the main entrance, killed the engine, and turned to Cora. Her face had gone even paler, if that were possible, eyes wide as she took in the heightened security. "They're protecting you," I said, hoping to reassure her. "Not holding you prisoner."

A hint of disbelief crossed her features, but she nodded again. I climbed out, circled to her side, and opened her door. The rain had slowed to a steady drizzle, cold against my skin as I held out my hand to help her down. Her fingers were like ice against my skin, trembling slightly. We walked together toward the entrance, her steps growing more hesitant as we approached the door and her shaking increased. It was easy to see the situation terrified her. For that alone I'd beat Reeves to a bloody fucking pulp.

Inside, the common room was quiet, most of the brothers giving us space. Knight and Knuckles waited near the fireplace, their expressions guarded but not hostile. Knight stood with his arms crossed, his tattooed face unreadable to most, but I caught the concern in the set of his shoulders. I handed him the other two bugs. Knight shoved them into a small box before putting them inside his office only a few feet from us.

Beside him, Knuckles looked deceptively relaxed in an armchair, one ankle resting on the opposite knee. On the low table between them lay several small objects. The listening device, now dismantled into its component parts spread out where Knight had obviously been studying them, likely discussing what he found with Knuckles.

Cora froze just inside the doorway, her hand tightening painfully around mine. I gave her fingers a gentle squeeze, urging her forward. Knuckles rose as we approached, his movement slow and deliberate. I felt Cora tense beside me, bracing for confrontation. But when Knuckles spoke, his voice held none of the harshness she clearly expected.

"Got Hannah to make some coffee," he said, gesturing to a carafe on the table. "Figured you could use something to warm you up."

Confusion flickered across Cora's face, followed by wary suspicion. She glanced up at me, searching for guidance. I nodded slightly, encouraging her to take a seat on one side of the couch. I sat next to her, draping an arm casually over the back of the couch. I brushed her shoulder reassuringly in silent encouragement.

"We've been at this game a long time, honey," Knuckles continued once Cora was settled. "Cops trying to get to us through people outside our compound ain't exactly a new play. You likely got caught in the middle because you kept picking up grocery orders for us and the shelter."

"I'm sorry," Cora whispered, her voice cracking. "I didn't want to --"

Knuckles waved a dismissive hand. "Ain't your fault Reeves is a vindictive bastard with a badge." He leaned forward, resting his elbows on his knees. "The man threatened to arrest you with fabricated evidence. That ain't coercion. That's fucking terrorism."

Knight stepped closer, gesturing to the dismantled device on the table. "Found the one under the fridge in the kitchen yesterday after you left," he explained, his voice softer than usual. "Swept the compound twice since then. We're clean."

"They're police-grade," Knuckles added. "Illegal as fuck for Reeves to place without a warrant, which may be why Reeves needed someone else to plant them." His eyes, normally hard as flint, held an unexpected gentleness as he looked at Cora. "You ain't the first person he's backed into a corner, sweetheart. And you won't be the last."

Cora stared at the dismantled device, then at Knuckles, then at me. The confusion in her eyes slowly gave way to disbelief, then to something like hope.

"You're not… you don't blame me?" Her voice was small, vulnerable in a way that made my chest tighten. Two tears tracked from her lovely eyes. They felt like daggers straight to my heart.

"For what?" Knuckles shrugged. "Doing what you had to when a cop with a grudge threatened to destroy your life? Hell, most people would've done worse, especially to a bunch of ex-cons. No. I wish you knew you could have gone to Hannah, Pippa, or any of the other women, or Rancor. But I understand you don't really know any of us. Not knowing if anyone here would give a good Goddamn about you if he arrested you, you had to protect yourself."

It was Knight who broke the final thread of her composure. He moved closer, crouched down to her eye level. "The fact that you're here right now," he said quietly, "telling us the truth even though you're terrified? That says everything we need to know about you." He gave her a kind smile, which, with his tattooed eyes and face, was slightly creepy.

The dam broke. Cora's face crumpled, her shoulders hunching as she folded in on herself. At first, her crying was silent -- just tremors shaking her small frame, tears streaming down her face. Then a ragged sob tore from her throat, followed by another, until she was gasping for breath between them.

I dropped my arm from the couch to her shoulders and, without thinking about it, pulled her onto my lap and urged her to bury her face against my chest. She came willingly, collapsing into me, as the weight of her fear and guilt poured out. I cradled the back of her head, threading my fingers through her hair as I held her, letting her fall apart against me.

"It's okay," I murmured. Comfort wasn't something I'd offered anyone in a very long time. "You're safe now." Over her head, I met Knuckles' gaze. He nodded at me, a confirmation he had my back because he knew I'd kill to protect this small woman, even if it meant going back to prison. Knight stood, moving behind Knuckles, his expression solemn. Reeves had made this personal long ago. Now he'd crossed a line that couldn't be uncrossed.

As Cora's sobs quieted to shuddering breaths, I shifted, slipping one arm beneath her knees. She made a small, startled sound as I lifted her, but didn't resist, her arms looping around my neck, face still pressed to my shoulder.

"Taking her to my place," I said simply. Knuckles nodded, the gesture conveying both permission and understanding. She needed to know she was safe with me and that I'd be her protector. I knew Knuckles and Knight wanted information from her, but I didn't think now was the time. They had the bugs. They knew Cora wasn't the bad guy. Interrogating her, though necessary, could wait.

I carried her from the common room, her weight slight in my arms. The compound was relatively silent given the absence of people in the common room. With everyone on lockdown, the women and children were in the centermost warehouses in our complex. They were well-protected until Knuckles got this SNAFU sorted out. The brothers who were present minded their own business. It was our way. All of them would have our backs when push came to shove.

Cora's fingers curled into the fabric of my shirt as I carried her through the main warehouse and out the back into the courtyard. The distance was farther than I'd normally want to walk, but the time would give Cora time to settle herself.

I carried her to my apartment, only setting her down to open the door. I kept my arm around her protectively, not ready to let her out of my reach, especially when she was obviously feeling fragile. Her tears had soaked through my shirt. Each one felt like a painful blow. I'd keep her safe. Whatever it took.

Chapter Ten

Rancor

I shouldered open the door to my apartment, carrying Cora across the threshold like something precious and breakable. The space felt different with her in it, smaller and somehow warmer. My living quarters were sparse by most standards. A leather couch sat against one wall, with a large screen TV on the opposite side of the room where the kitchen opened up. A workbench covered in motorcycle parts along the far wall represented the only clutter and I even had that area organized for what I worked on at the time. Everything in its place. I rarely brought anyone here, and never women. This was my sanctuary, the one place I didn't have to wear my mask. Now she saw all of it, all of me, and I found I didn't mind.

Her gaze moved around the room, taking in details I'd stopped noticing long ago. I set her down carefully and she walked gingerly across the room to stand in front of the window that looked out over Sarah's garden, now partially obscured by rain.

"This is you," she whispered, her voice still rough from crying. "I can see you in this room." She nodded to the garden outside. "I can see you there."

I nodded. She seemed so small, vulnerable in a way that stirred something protective in me. Her face was flushed, eyes swollen from tears, hair mussed where my fingers had threaded through it. She'd never looked more beautiful to me.

"Hot chocolate." I knew I sounded abrupt and gruff, but I struggled to hold my anger inside. Fucking Reeves. "You need something warm."

I moved to the kitchen, heating some milk and

tossing in some powdered chocolate mix. I didn't even think about what I did. I only had the stupid mix because of Hannah and Pippa. For some reason, they piled a big basket full of the stuff outside my room a couple weeks ago. I had been going to throw it out because, what the fuck would I do with hot chocolate, but I'd put it away. Now I was glad I had.

When I returned, she'd drawn her knees up to her chest, making herself smaller on the couch. Her shoes were off, placed neatly side-by-side on the floor. The gesture, this small effort to respect my space, didn't escape my notice.

I set the mug down on the coffee table and sat beside her. Our thighs touched, the contact sending warmth through me that had nothing to do with the hot chocolate. She didn't pull away.

"Thank you," she said, reaching for the mug with unsteady hands. I watched her take a small sip, her throat working as she swallowed. A drop of chocolate clung to her lower lip before her tongue darted out to catch it. My stomach tightened at the sight. Now was not the time to wonder what her tongue would feel like lapping a drop of precum from the tip of my cock.

"I knew," I said after a moment of silence. "At the café. Before you told me. I knew something was wrong."

She looked up at me, confusion clouding her eyes. "How?"

"Your hands." I gestured to where her fingers curled around the mug. "They shake when you're afraid. And you couldn't look at me for more than a few seconds at a time." I paused, choosing my next words carefully. "Spent six years learning to read people. Learning when they're about to break."

"Is that why you approached me so carefully?"

Her voice was steadier now, the hot chocolate doing its work. "Why you didn't just confront me about the bug?"

I nodded. "Needed you to tell me yourself. I needed to know if it was coercion or…" I let the sentence hang, unable to voice the alternative.

"Or if I'd betrayed you willingly." She finished the thought, her expression pained. "You thought I might have been working with Reeves all along?"

"Had to consider it." Honesty seemed the only path forward now. "Wouldn't have been the first time someone got close to learn club business." Her face fell, and I realized my words sounded like I'd been suspicious of her from the start, like our connection had been built on wariness rather than attraction. "I never believed it," I added quickly. "Not really. I had to be sure for the sake of everyone in the compound."

She nodded, her gaze dropping to where my hand now rested on her knee. I hadn't consciously decided to touch her, but there it was. My palm rested against the worn denim of her jeans, my thumb rubbing back and forth against the fabric. Her breathing quickened slightly at the contact.

I pulled my hand away, balling my fingers into a fist to keep from touching her again. "Sorry," I muttered.

She shook her head quickly and snatched my hand back, lacing her fingers through mine with one hand and covering the top of my hand with the other. "I like it when you touch me. Even if it's just holding my hand. You ground me."

I nodded. "Your touch grounds me, too. I just need to comfort you."

"You do." She looked up at me with a watery smile.

"I know what it feels like," I blurted out. "To do something you never thought you'd do because someone backed you into a corner. Don't blame yourself for trying to survive. We don't really know each other and haven't built the trust you need to feel like you can come to me if you're in trouble." I shook my head. "No one here blames you for any of this. You're the only innocent person in the whole mess. Me and Reeves both got blood on our hands."

"I still betrayed you." Her voice fell to a whisper. "I feel awful."

"Reeves forced you," I corrected. "Used you. There's a difference." When she dropped her gaze, I continued. "You're the first person since Sarah who's made me feel something other than rage." The confession spilled from me unexpectedly, raw and honest in a way I rarely allowed myself to be. "First time I saw you, standing in that kitchen with Hannah, something… woke up. Something I thought had died with her."

Cora's gaze snapped to mine and her breath caught. "Marcus…"

"I came out of prison feeling like a ghost. And it didn't have anything to do with the six years I spent inside. My wife was my world. I was adding to my world with the child she carried. When they were ripped from me, I thought I'd died with them." I forced myself to hold her gaze, to face whatever reaction my words caused. Her eyes were wide, luminous with unshed tears, but not from fear or pity. I saw in her eyes a longing as intense as my own. "You walked into the compound." My voice roughened. "And suddenly I was solid again. Real."

Her mug made a soft *thud* as she set it on the table. Slowly, deliberately, she reached up, her fingers trembling slightly as they touched my face. I held perfectly still as she traced the scar at the edge of my eyebrow, then the lines at the corners of my eyes, then the edge of my beard along my jaw. Her touch was featherlight, exploratory.

"I've never belonged anywhere," she whispered. "Never had anyone look at me the way you do."

"How do I look at you?" The question emerged hoarsely, strained.

"Like I matter. Like I'm worth protecting." Her fingers paused at the corner of my mouth. "Like you see me."

The air between us grew heavy, charged with something more potent than desire alone. Her gaze dropped to my lips, then back up, a question that needed no words. I'd been careful with her since we met, but the look in her eyes now stripped away that caution, igniting something primal and hungry.

I leaned forward, one hand coming up to cup her cheek. Her skin was warm beneath my palm. Her eyes fluttered shut as I closed the distance between us. When our lips met, it wasn't like our previous kisses. There were no gentle explorations and tentative beginnings. This was deeper, rawer, fueled by more than the truth we'd each laid bare before the other. Her mouth opened beneath mine, a small sound catching in her throat as my tongue slid against hers. I tasted the sweetness of the chocolate drink and the unique taste of the woman who had haunted my dreams since I'd met her. Cora's eager need, as desperate as my own, made the blood surge hotly in my veins.

She gripped my shoulders, her fingers digging into muscle as she pressed closer. The careful control I'd maintained cracked. Each stroke of her tongue against mine, each small gasp she breathed into my mouth, chipped away at the walls I'd built until they crashed down around me with a defeated groan.

For the first time since I'd walked out of Terre Haute, I allowed myself to want something without reservation or guilt. And as Cora melted against me, I knew with absolute certainty that I would do whatever it took to keep her safe. To keep her mine.

Her kiss tasted like surrender and salvation all at once. I slid my hand around to the back of her neck, gripping her in a dominant hold she accepted without protest. I didn't break the kiss, but pulled her onto my lap, needing her closer, needing the weight of her against me. She came willingly, her thighs sliding to either side of mine, settling herself against me with a soft sound that vibrated through my chest. The feel of her straddling me sent heat flooding through my body, pooling low in my stomach and instantly making my cock hard.

Cora tugged gently at my beard as she explored my mouth with increasing boldness. The hesitation from earlier had vanished, replaced by hunger that matched my own. She rocked slightly against me, whether intentionally or not I couldn't tell, but the friction against my cock drew a low groan from deep in my chest.

Her lips curved against mine in response, pleased by my reaction. I felt her smile more than saw it. Then I was lost. From the night Sarah died to the moment Cora walked into my life, I'd merely existed, not really wanting to continue on but not knowing what else to do. Now, I had purpose, someone to protect and cherish for the rest of my days. God help me, I couldn't let her go even if I wanted to.

"Marcus," she breathed against my mouth, the sound of my name on her lips. Telling her from the beginning to call me Marcus instead of by my road name had been impulsive on my part. Now, I thought maybe I'd known all along Cora was the woman for me. Hearing her say my name separated her from every other woman in my life other than Sarah. After Sarah passed, no other woman had ever called me anything other than Rancor.

I slipped my hands under her shirt, finding the warm skin of her back. She shivered at the contact, goose bumps rising beneath my fingertips. I traced the ridge of her spine, the subtle curve of her waist. The softness of her skin against my calloused palms felt like a kind of absolution.

She pulled back slightly, eyes half-lidded, pupils dilated so wide the blue was just a thin ring around black. Her lips were swollen from our kiss, cheeks flushed with color that had nothing to do with tears now. I'd never seen anything more beautiful.

"I want…" she started, then faltered.

"What?" I urged, my voice rougher than I intended. "Tell me what you want."

"You," she whispered, the single word carrying such weight I felt it settle in my chest like a stone. "Just you." She swallowed and I saw the vulnerability hovering just beneath her expression. "Please make love to me, Marcus." With deliberate movements, she reached for the hem of her shirt, drawing it upward. I caught her wrists, stopping her.

"Me," I murmured. I sounded like a fucking caveman, but I honestly couldn't get the words out. I wanted to unwrap her, to claim my present like a greedy toddler on Christmas morning.

She nodded, seeming to understand my primitive mindset. She raised her arms above her head as I grasped the fabric, lifting it slowly to reveal inches of pale skin. I took my time with her, every new inch a slow reveal. The gentle sweep of her belly under my hand, the hard edge of her ribcage, the black lace of her bra stretched across pale skin… all of it combined to create something hard and combustible inside me. Each layer sparked something hot and sharp, and I let myself savor the feelings surrounding me both inside and out. I drank her in, all of her, every single detail, not wanting to rush, not willing to miss a thing. When I finally pulled the shirt over her head, her hair fell in tousled waves around her shoulders, static making strands cling to her cheeks.

I brushed them back, tucking the silky strands behind her ear with careful fingers. Even this small gesture felt intimate in ways I hadn't experienced in years. She watched me with wonder in her eyes, like she couldn't quite believe I was touching her this way.

"Your turn," she said softly, reaching for the hem of my shirt. When she tugged the fabric over my head and tossed it aside, her breath caught. I knew women appreciated the heavy muscles of my torso. I'd never really cared before now. The way she looked at me made me want to puff out my chest in pride. She didn't find me lacking physically.

She explored my chest and shoulders, the featherlight touches driving me crazy with the sweetest torture. She paused over one ragged scar that ran from my left shoulder halfway down my chest.

"Shiv," I explained before she could ask. "Third year in."

Something flashed in her eyes. Not pity, but a fierce protectiveness that caught me off guard. She leaned forward, pressed her lips to the scar in a gesture so tender it made my throat tighten. "I hope you gave as good as you got."

I smirked. "Better than."

"Good. No one gets to hurt you again, Marcus. Not me, not Detective Reeves, no one."

I framed her face in my hands, forcing her to look into my eyes while I did the same with her. "You could never hurt me unless you leave me, Cora. And I'll deal with Reeves. I knew this whole situation with him would come to a head one day. His attack on you is making me force the situation, but the conflict was inevitable the moment I got out of prison."

"Please don't do anything on my behalf, Marcus. I won't be the cause of you getting into trouble."

"Don't worry about me, baby. Now that I've got you in my life, I'm not going to do anything to jeopardize my good luck."

Before she could say anything else, I stood with her in my arms, forcing her to wrap her legs around my waist and hold on tightly as I strode down the short hall to my bedroom. I was most definitely making love to Cora, but I was doing it in my bed.

We finished undressing, our motions faster the more clothing we shed. "Need you," I croaked out. "Come here."

She came to me without hesitation, her bare skin gleaming under the soft light of my bedside lamp. I lifted her into my arms again, feeling the glorious press of her bare skin against mine. I laid her down on my king-size bed carefully, the sight of her pale body against my dark sheets stirring something possessive in my chest.

"You're sure?" I asked, needing to hear it even as my body ached for hers.

"I've never been more sure of anything in my entire life," she answered, reaching for me.

I lowered myself over her, bracing my weight on

my forearms to keep from crushing her smaller frame. Her legs parted, welcoming me between them, the heat of her against my hardness drawing another groan from me. I captured her mouth again before moving down her body with my lips, teeth, and tongue.

I trailed light kisses over her shoulder, down the edge of her collarbone and across her flat stomach. Her skin was like silk under my mouth, and the feeling made me shudder with desire.

Moving back up her body, I buried my face in the hollow of her neck, breathing in her sweet scent as she turned her head to the side to give me all the access I wanted, even as she arched against me. "God, Cora," I groaned against her soft skin. "You're so fucking beautiful."

She wiggled under me, pressing herself closer still until the hard length of my erection ground against the soft lips of her pussy. I had to bite back the urge to sink into her wet heat. The only reason I managed was because I was dying to taste more of her before I fucked her. I wanted to worship her body in a way no one ever had, for her to scream my name so much she'd never forget who she belonged to.

"Marcus," she moaned. "Touch me." Her breathy demand was all I needed to hear. I slowly licked a line from the pulse point of her neck down to one achingly hard nipple, teasing it with my tongue before taking it between my teeth and sucking gently. She arched off the bed with a cry that vibrated through me.

"More." I found her breathy demand sexy as fuck. So I gave her what she wanted, kissing and licking and suckling until both nipples were puckered, red, and swollen. Each moan of hers added fuel to the fire in my blood.

"Fuck," I muttered against her skin. "Too much."

"Not enough!" Her sharp cry made me groan against her skin. She tilted her hips up in invitation.

"You drive me insane, woman." Though my tone of voice was harsh, the kisses I trailed down her stomach were reverent and gentle. I wanted nothing more than to eat her up, but I needed to pace myself. Otherwise, I wouldn't last. And in no reasonable world that is sane and just would I ever come before seeing to her pleasure.

I trailed kisses down her stomach toward the treasure between her legs. Her scent surrounded me now, intoxicating me more than any other drug on earth ever could. She tasted so fucking good beneath my lips that every nerve ending in my body sizzled like lightning just waiting for the final strike.

The first touch of my tongue on her bare pussy had Cora screaming and arching up to meet me. I wrapped my arms around her thighs so to keep her open to me and just held on for the ride.

Right before my eyes, my sweet, gentle Cora turned into some kind of wild thing. Sweat erupted across her body as she thrashed and screamed when I found her clit with my tongue. I sucked and flicked the little bundle of nerves over and over, wanting her mindless and on the verge of coming.

"Marcus! Oh, fuck!" Nails dug into my scalp as she urged me closer, trembling thighs tightening around my head. I doubled down, sliding two fingers inside while I worked that sensitive nub with my tongue. Slick walls clenched around my fingers, everything about her body confirming those breathless pleas. "Please, Marcus. I need you to fuck me! Now!"

I gave one last, lingering lick before crawling up the length of her. Sweat-glistened skin, a heaving chest, the flushed, desperate look beneath me made a groan tear out of my throat. How the hell was I supposed to survive this?

I reached for the nightstand drawer and grabbed a condom. Hastily tearing open the package, I rolled the thin barrier over my cock before covering her with my body. Our mouths met in a hard, hungry kiss as I thrust my tongue between her lips. I positioned myself at her entrance, the head of my cock nudging against slick heat.

"Look at me," I commanded, my voice so strained I barely recognized myself. Her eyes fluttered open, pupils blown wide with desire. "I need you to watch me so I can watch you. Need to see your eyes while I shove my cock inside your sweet pussy."

She whimpered but complied. I could tell the dirty talk turned her on and made a note to revisit the revelation later. Right now, though, I needed to concentrate on the matter at hand. Which was to, A) not hurt her, and B) not come the second I slid inside her.

When I finally pushed inside her, the tight heat of her body nearly undid me. I had to grit my teeth and breathe through my nose to keep from filling the condom with my cum the second I moved. She was so fucking tight, her body gripping mine like she was made for me. I stilled once I was fully seated, giving her time to adjust.

I watched her face as her eyes widened in shock first, then her eyelids dropped lower, heavy with desire. Her pussy squeezed my cock in time with her heartbeat. I began to move then, setting a slow rhythm that soon had her arching beneath me, matching me move for move. She dug her nails into my shoulders again as I increased the pace. I knew I would wear her mark and wanted to smile. I welcomed the sting, relished the evidence that she needed me.

My usually quiet nature fell away as we moved together, my voice roughening with groans and whispered praise and more than my fair share of dirty talk against her ear. She responded with her soft cries growing louder, less inhibited as pleasure built inside her. I shifted my angle, driving deeper, watching with fascination as her composure shattered completely.

With one long, loud wail of pleasure, Cora came in a hard, wet rush. I had no hope of doing anything other than following her. She clung to me, lifting herself up to meet every one of my thrusts with one of her own. She moved faster and harder with each pass until she controlled the pace of our lovemaking.

I panted, sweat coating my skin as I fucked Cora harder and harder. Each time I thrust into her, a grunt erupted from my throat. Cora answered every single one with her own cries.

Finally, I shoved myself as deep as I could, my back bowing as I bellowed to the rafters. I had no idea how the poor condom managed to hold my load because it felt like I came in a flood. Never in my life had I experienced the pleasure I found in this woman's arms.

I collapsed on top of her, gasping for breath even as I pinned her to the mattress. For long moments, all I could do was take one breath after another. Somewhere inside my fucked-up head I knew I needed to roll off so I didn't crush her. I was so much bigger than she was I doubted she could comfortably take my weight for long. But I couldn't seem to do anything more than breathe.

It took me a few seconds to find the strength to push off the mattress to roll off Cora. When I did, she whimpered and clung to me, holding me to her with arms and legs wrapped around me.

"I don't want to hurt you, baby," I murmured. "Ain't goin' nowhere. Just rollin' over so you can breathe."

"I can breathe just fine." Her voice was hoarse from her screams, and I had a surge of pride. I'd done that to her. I'd made her shout my name.

I gave her what she wanted for a few minutes. When she finally relaxed her hold, I rolled us slowly. My cock had softened and slipped out of her, but I still needed to deal with the condom. Reaching to the nightstand, I snagged a few tissues and cleaned myself up as best as I could before tossing the mess in the trashcan beside the bed. I snagged another couple and gently wiped between Cora's legs. She murmured sleepily but didn't protest further.

Once I'd discarded the tissues, I wrapped both arms around her and sighed. Had I ever felt this contented? I couldn't say for sure about Sarah, but I knew one thing with absolute certainty—I loved Cora. The feeling wasn't the same as what I'd experienced with my wife, but I knew love when I felt it.

I reached down, pulled the rumpled blanket over us both. She made a small, contented sound, burrowing closer to my chest. I tightened my arms, keeping her secure against me.

Outside, the rain had stopped. Through the tall windows, I could see stars emerging from behind breaking clouds. The world beyond these walls still held threats, but for now, in this moment, with her soft weight against me and her breath warming my skin, the outside world and its dangers seemed distant, maybe even manageable.

I pressed my lips to the top of her head, breathed in the scent of her hair. She murmured something indistinct, already mostly asleep. I let my own eyes drift shut.

I didn't know what would happen tomorrow, but I knew whatever came at me, I wanted Cora to be at my side. And I'd beg, borrow, cheat, steal, or kill to make that dream the sweetest reality.

Chapter Eleven

Cora

I woke to the weight of a muscled male arm across my waist, heavy and warm like an anchor keeping me from drifting away. For a moment, I didn't move, afraid that the slightest shift might break whatever spell had been cast over us. Morning light peeked over the distant mountains, painting a golden stripe across the rumpled sheets where it shone through the group of tall windows along one wall. I watched dust motes dance in the beam, feeling Marcus's steady breath against the nape of my neck, each exhale a reminder that this wasn't another dream.

I turned my head slightly, just enough to see his face in profile. Sleep had softened the hard lines that usually defined him. Even his thick, dark beard couldn't hide the slight relaxation around his mouth or the temporary absence of the tension that seemed to live in his jaw. A scar I hadn't noticed before curved along his hairline, pale against his sun-weathered skin.

As if sensing my gaze, his eyes opened -- no gradual awakening, no blinking into consciousness. One moment he slept, the next he was fully alert. Dark eyes fixed on mine with an intensity that sent a current racing down my spine, leaving goose bumps in its wake.

"Morning," he said, his voice a low rumble that I felt more than heard, vibrating through me where he had me wrapped tightly in his arms. He lay partially over me on his side so I could see his face clearly.

"Morning," I whispered back, suddenly aware of my tangled hair, my naked body, and the vulnerable state I found myself in. At least, I thought I should feel vulnerable. I was in bed with a man I barely knew. I was naked. I was surrounded by the biggest bunch of hard-asses I'd ever come across. Strangely, instead of being scared, I felt protected and wanted.

He didn't move his arm from my waist, but his thumb began a slow sweep across the bare skin of my stomach, each pass igniting nerve endings I hadn't known existed until his touch found them.

When he shifted slightly his beard brushed against my shoulder, the rough texture a striking contrast to the softness of his lips that followed. I shivered, not from cold but from the sensations he created within me from the mere stroke of his calloused fingers.

I breathed him in, this man who'd become my unlikely sanctuary. And it was more about Marcus than this place. I had the feeling that I'd never feel as safe, protected, and relaxed as I did when Marcus was with me.

"You sleep okay?" he asked, propping himself up on one elbow to look down at me. Before I answered, he leaned in to place a lingering kiss on my lips and I sighed in pleasure.

I nodded when he pulled back, not trusting my voice as my heart performed acrobatics against my ribs. My hands trembled slightly as I reached up to touch his face, needing to confirm he was real, that this wasn't some elaborate fantasy my desperate mind had conjured. The solid warmth of his cheek and the coarseness of his beard beneath my palm sent relief flooding through me in a dizzying rush.

"I slept better than I have in years," I admitted, surprised by the truth of it. Last night could have easily gone the other way for me, but the one thing I felt deep in my bones was that these were good people. Marcus was a good man, and so were the other people

I'd met here.

His eyes tracked every minute change in my expression, reading me with the same careful attention he seemed to give everything that mattered to him. I wondered what he saw. My pulse quickened under his scrutiny, probably visible in the hollow of my throat. His gaze dropped to the fluttering there, then back to my eyes, missing nothing. I swallowed hard, suddenly thirsty in a way that had nothing to do with water.

"Water?" he asked, as if plucking the thought directly from my mind. "Coffee?" His voice remained that measured, quiet tone I'd come to recognize as uniquely his. He didn't move and I didn't want him to.

I shook my head.

A slow smile spread across his face. "You thirsty for something else?"

I shrugged, trying to be all nonchalant about it. I had exactly zero experience with sex other than trying a small amount of self-pleasure which hadn't been all that fulfilling. Definitely had no idea what to do with the whole morning-after bit. What did he expect now? I knew what I wanted, though. "Maybe?"

His grin widened and he slid his hand up my waist to cup my breast. "Good. Me too." He brushed his thumb across my nipple, sending a jolt of pleasure straight to my clit. I gasped, arching into his touch. The confident way he handled my body made me feel both vulnerable and powerful at the same time. "I like the way you respond to me," he murmured, his voice deeper than before. "You were made for me."

I couldn't argue with that assessment. Every place he touched seemed to bloom with heat. When he dipped his head to replace his fingers on my nipple with his mouth, I cried out, wrapping my arms around his head and holding me to him.

The wet heat of his tongue circling my nipple had me squirming beneath him. He used his teeth, just the barest scrape, and I nearly came. "Marcus," I breathed, my hips lifting of their own accord, seeking friction against him. I arched my breast to his mouth, needing him to keep sucking.

He looked up at me, his dark eyes nearly black with desire. "Tell me what you need, Cora."

"You," I answered simply. "I need you to fuck me."

He moved over me then, supporting his weight on his forearms as he settled between my thighs. I felt his cock pulsing between us. Marcus growled low in his throat, the sound primal and possessive. The hard length of him pressed against me, hot and insistent, making my hips rise instinctively to meet him.

"Condom," he murmured against my neck, his beard tickling my sensitive skin.

I nodded, though a part of me wanted nothing between us. He reached toward the nightstand, fumbling in the drawer without taking his eyes off me. When he found what he sought, I took it from him, tearing the packet open with trembling fingers.

"Let me," I said, pushing against his chest until he rolled onto his back. I straddled him, feeling bold in a way I never had with anyone else. The sight of Marcus stretched beneath me, his powerful body at my mercy, sent a thrill through me. I positioned the condom at the tip of his cock, rolling it down his impressive length with deliberate slowness. His muscles tensed under my touch, jaw clenching as he watched me through hooded eyes.

"You're killing me," he groaned when I gave him a teasing stroke.

I smiled, feeling powerful in a way I never had

before. "Good."

I positioned myself above him, feeling the blunt head of his cock press against my entrance. Slowly, I sank down, taking him inch by inch until he filled me completely. The stretch was exquisite, bordering on too much, but the burn never quite gave in to pain. I gasped as I settled fully onto him, my hands braced on his chest for support.

"Fuck," Marcus breathed, gripping my hips so tightly I knew I'd wear his fingerprints as bruises. The thought sent another rush of heat through me. "You feel so fuckin' good wrapped around my cock."

I began to move, finding a rhythm that had us both panting. Rising and falling on him, I watched his face contort with pleasure, his gaze never leaving mine. Each time I rose and fell, taking him deeper, the coil of pleasure inside me wound tighter.

"That's it," he encouraged, sliding his hand up to my breast. He squeezed and kneaded gently before using both hands. The ragged groan ripped from him sounded suspiciously like surrender. I could relate because I was pretty sure I'd surrendered to Marcus the first time he kissed me.

"That's it," he encouraged. "Ride me. Fuck me and come on my cock." The way he looked at me, like I was something precious and cherished and so desired it pained him, was the nail in my coffin. I'd never felt this level of connection with anyone. Not family. Not friends.

I leaned forward to kiss him, my breasts brushing against the hard plane of his chest as I continued to fuck him. The friction sent shivers across my skin as our tongues met in a dance that matched our bodies. He tasted like sleep and desire, a heady combination that made my head spin.

"You're so beautiful." His ragged whisper against my lips made me break out in a sweat. "So perfect."

I quickened my pace, chasing the building pressure. When Marcus reached between us to thumb my clit, circling with just the right amount of pressure, I cried out, my rhythm faltering as my pussy clamped down on him as I came.

"That's it, baby," he encouraged, his voice rough with need. "Come for me. Let me feel you milking my fuckin' cock."

My scream was followed closely by his rough shout. I collapsed on top of him, my pussy still pulsing every time his cock did. All I could do was breathe as Marcus held me against him, his arms tight bands around my slight body.

"Fuuuuck," he groaned. "You've killed me."

I laughed softly against his chest, feeling the rumble of his laughter join mine. He rubbed lazy strokes up and down my back, sending pleasant aftershocks through my sensitized skin. He was still inside me, semi-hard and pulsing occasionally, made me feel deliciously full.

"Much as I'd love to stay in bed and fuck you the rest of the day, we have things to discuss."

I sighed with resignation. "Yeah. I knew it was a temporary interlude. We probably should have already talked."

He slid from the bed with a fluid grace that belied his size and moved to the bathroom. I couldn't help but watch as he moved naked across the room, muscles shifting beneath skin marked by scars telling the story of his life.

He returned with a glass of water and handed it to me. I accepted the glass and took a healthy swallow.

"Thank you," I said, the words so inadequate, but I wasn't sure how to express the depth of the gratitude I felt for him. And that wasn't all. I knew I was falling for the tough biker.

"You're welcome," he replied simply, settling back onto the bed under the covers beside me.

As I set the glass on the nightstand, he reached out, brushing a strand of hair from my face with a gentleness that made my breath catch. I leaned into his touch without conscious thought, my body making decisions my mind was still struggling to process.

"You good?" he asked, the simple question carrying layers of meaning.

Was I good? My life had been upended, I was being blackmailed by a cop with a vendetta, and I'd spent the night with a man who had killed someone and served time for the deed. Oh, and that cop with the vendetta? The person the man I was currently fucking had killed was that cop's son. By any rational measure, I was anything but good. Yet the strange truth was, I felt more centered, more myself, than I ever had. Something about Marcus -- about us -- felt right in a way nothing else ever had.

"Yeah," I said, surprising myself with the certainty in my voice. "I think I am."

His eyes softened, the barest hint of a smile touching his lips as he nodded. Outside, I heard the compound coming to life. The rumble of a motorcycle in the distance reminded me of my situation and exactly how fucked I could be. But here, in this room, time seemed suspended, creating a pocket of calm amid the brewing storm.

I knew we couldn't stay here forever, but for now, in the gentle morning light with Marcus's steady presence beside me, I allowed myself to simply breathe, to exist in a moment that felt like the beginning of something I'd never dared to hope for.

Reality hung at the edges of our bubble, waiting to intrude with all its complications and dangers. Marcus shifted beside me, his expression turning more serious as he sat up against the headboard. The sheet pooled around his waist. When he spoke, his voice carried the weight of decisions that couldn't be postponed any longer.

"We need to talk about what happens now," he said, his tone measured but firm. "About keeping you safe."

I pulled the sheet higher over my chest, suddenly needing the thin barrier it provided. Not from him, but from the conversation we were about to have. "I know," I said, my voice smaller than I intended.

His dark eyes held mine, unwavering. "Reeves won't stop. You need to understand that. He's been waiting years for a way to get to me, and now he thinks he's found it." His hand moved to cover mine where it clutched the sheet. "Considering what happened the last someone I loved was hurt and how it directly affected Reeves, I'd have thought the bastard would have learned a lesson. But I know he hasn't."

The weight of his words settled in my stomach like lead. I hadn't asked for this, hadn't wanted to become a pawn in some vendetta that started long before I entered the picture. Yet here I was, caught in the middle of a conflict I barely understood.

"I want you to stay here," Marcus continued, his thumb brushing over my knuckles in a gesture that had already become familiar. "At the compound. With me."

My pulse quickened. Stay here? I didn't want to be that too-stupid-to-live naked girl in the slasher movie who ran into the tool shed filled with all kinds of big-ass saws and knives rather than the running car, but I knew I was going to stay with Marcus. Part of me I hadn't known existed until I met this man whispered that I'd never felt safer than I did within these walls.

I took a breath, trying to think rationally and not with my heart. Which was damned near impossible considering I was wired to follow my heart. "For how long?"

"A week. To start." His expression remained unreadable, but something in his eyes softened. "Long enough for me to deal with Reeves. For us to figure out what we want from each other." His fingers tightened slightly over mine.

I glanced away, unable to hold the intensity of his gaze while my thoughts tumbled over each other like clothes in a dryer. My free hand found the edge of the sheet, fingers working the fabric between them in nervous motion.

"I can take you to your apartment," he continued. "You can pack what you need. Couple of the brothers will come along. Make sure we're not followed so Reeves can't blindside you again."

"What about my job?" I asked, latching onto the practical concern. "I still need to work."

"Are you required to work to keep your job?"

I shook my head. "No. It's just kind of work when you want."

"Good. We can play it day by day. If I can't convince you to take a few days off, I can at least make sure you're safe when you go." The simplicity with which he approached these complications should have annoyed me. Instead, it was strangely reassuring.

I shifted, finally meeting his eyes again. My pulse throbbed at my wrists, at my temples, marking time in a rhythm that felt too fast. "Marcus, I barely know you," I said, the words catching in my throat. "And yet…"

"And yet?" he echoed, the two simple words somehow encapsulating everything between us.

I took a deep breath, steadying myself. "I've spent my life since I ran away making careful choices, trying to keep myself as safe as I could without smothering myself. Those choices led me to a life where no one would have noticed if I disappeared." My voice grew stronger as I continued, finding truth in the words as I spoke them. "But being with you feels like the first correct choice I've made. Everything is moving so fast," I admitted, my fingers now fidgeting with the edge of the pillowcase, "but I can't fight what I want with every fiber of my being. So I'm not going to try."

His eyes flashed with hunger and a possession that should have frightened me. Instead, I felt an answering hunger deep in my belly. He moved his hand from mine to my cheek, calloused palm warm against my skin as he brushed my lower lip with his thumb.

I leaned into his touch, but couldn't resist adding, with a sudden flash of humor that surprised even me, "But if you break my heart, I'll cut yours out with a spork."

The laugh that erupted from him caught me completely off guard. Not the quiet chuckle or subtle smirk I'd witnessed before, but a full, deep belly laugh that transformed his entire face. Lines I'd never seen before appeared around his eyes, his head tipped back against the headboard, and the sound… God, the sound was like music I hadn't known I'd been waiting to hear.

"A spork?" he managed, his shoulders still shaking with mirth. "Why a spork?"

"Maximum inefficiency," I replied, finding myself smiling in response. "I'd want it to take a while."

Another burst of laughter, and the knot of tension I'd been carrying for so long I'd forgotten it was there suddenly loosened. The relief was so immediate I nearly gasped. Seeing this side of Marcus, unguarded, genuine humor, felt like discovering a secret garden behind a wall of thorns.

When his laughter subsided, he studied me with new eyes, as if seeing something in me he hadn't noticed before. "I won't break your heart, Cora." The humor was gone, replaced by something solemn, almost reverent. "That's a fuckin' promise."

I believed him. Despite everything logic told me, despite knowing him for such a short time, I believed him with a certainty that felt like coming home.

"Okay," I said simply. "I'll stay."

He reached for my hand then, intertwining his fingers with mine. Our hands looked right together, his large and scarred, mine smaller though not fashionably delicate. Marcus leaned forward, his free hand cradling the back of my neck as he drew me to him. The kiss was different from those we'd shared before. Not so desperate and hungry, but soft with deep meaning. Like a promise. His lips moved against mine with deliberate tenderness.

When he pulled back, his forehead rested against mine, our breathing almost ragged in the quiet morning light. Whatever came next, we would face it together. And for the first time in my life, I thought I might have found the future I'd always dreamed of.

Chapter Twelve

Rancor

My phone buzzed against the nightstand, shattering our quiet moment with its harsh vibration. I reached for it, already recognizing Knuckles' code of three short bursts that meant he'd called church. Cora's warmth pressed against my side as I thumbed open the message, my jaw tightening as I read. "Fuck," I muttered.

"What is it?" Cora asked.

I showed her the screen.

Common room. Now. Bring your woman.

She read it, her eyes widening slightly. "Your woman?" I watched her process the words, a tiny furrow forming between her brows. I'd promised to protect her, and now the club was demanding her presence at what was certainly going to be a strategy session about Reeves.

"Yeah, baby." I had to smother my grin. "That's you."

"They want me there too?" she asked, uncertainty threading through her voice.

I nodded, already swinging my legs over the side of the bed. "This is good. Means they're bringing you inside the circle." I reached for my jeans, pulling them on without bothering with underwear. "Knuckles doesn't invite outsiders to meetings."

She sat up, clutching the sheet to her chest, her hair falling in tangled waves around her shoulders. "And now I'm not an outsider?"

I paused, one arm through my shirt sleeve. "You were never an outsider, Cora. Not since the first time you came to the compound. When you came back the next time the old ladies ordered, you were one of us."

The words came out rougher than I intended. "But now, you're officially under club protection. Knuckles is acknowledging that to everyone by inviting you to join us."

"You're sure I'm not in trouble?"

I chuckled. "No, baby. If you were in trouble, you wouldn't get a warning. And since you're mine now, Knuckles will see to it everyone in this club protects you the same as they would the other old ladies. Once we make it official, he won't have to make a grand gesture. Anywhere you wear your property cut, everyone will know you're under the protection of Kiss of Death MC."

The explanation seemed to satisfy her. Her features relaxed and she smiled up at me. "Thank you, Marcus. For everything."

"You're very welcome. And thank you for the same." I leaned in and gave her one more soft kiss.

She dressed quickly while I shrugged into my club colors over my T-shirt. I watched her dress, her hands steady despite the tension I could feel radiating from her. When she finished, I reached for her, pulling her against my chest for a moment. She felt small in my arms, but not fragile. Never that. This woman had more strength than most men I knew. Maybe not physically, but she was mentally tough as nails. And I knew she wasn't afraid to fight. She just needed a direction and a goal. Reeves had her off-balance before, but not now. She might be unsure in this new world, but my woman would fight tooth and nail against anyone who threatened what she considered hers. Same as me.

"Whatever Knight found," I murmured against her hair, "we face it together. You understand?"

She nodded against my chest, then pulled back to

look up at me. "I'm ready."

The walk to the common room took us past several brothers. Diesel nodded to us from his position near the main entrance. Hawk stood outside the common room door, his posture deceptively relaxed while his gaze constantly scanned out the windows. The increased security wasn't lost on Cora. I felt her press slightly closer to my side as we approached.

"Rancor," Hawk acknowledged with a slight nod. His gaze shifted to Cora, assessing but not unkind. "Ma'am."

"Hello, Hawk. Call me Cora. Ma'am makes me sound old." She wrinkled her nose delicately.

Hawk chuckled. "Just mindin' my manners. Carrie would have my hide if I accidentally insulted you."

"Well, I'm not the formal sort. Carrie knows that." All the women had made a point to make Cora feel at home. Though she hadn't been around Carrie as much as some of the others, Cora genuinely liked the other woman.

The common room had transformed from its usual relaxed atmosphere into something resembling a war council. The long wooden table that normally hosted card games and meals now dominated the center of the space, surrounded by grim-faced club members and a couple of the old ladies. Hannah sat beside her husband, Knuckles, her usual warm smile still bright as she waved to Cora despite the situation. Pippa sat beside Gunnar, who had been drafted as de facto VP. He'd yet to accept the designation, but still put in the work. Gunnar said he didn't want the responsibility. Pippa said he didn't want to have to pretend to actually be responsible.

Knuckles gestured to two empty chairs across

from him. "'Bout fuckin' time," he grunted, but there was no real heat in the words. He even managed a wry grin. His gaze held mine for a moment, communicating what his words didn't. A frisson of trepidation danced up my spine. Whatever Knight was about to say was bad.

I guided Cora to the chairs, my hand on the small of her back in what I hoped was a reassuring gesture. She moved with surprising composure, her chin high despite the palpable tension in the room. Pride surged through me at her strength.

"Knight," Knuckles barked once we were seated. "Show them."

Knight nodded, tapping a few keys on his laptop. The projector hummed to life, throwing images onto the white wall behind him. My stomach turned cold at what appeared.

Cora's face stared back at us from surveillance photos that had been expertly altered. In one, she appeared to be handing a package to a known dealer in East Nashville. In another, she stood inside what looked like a warehouse, surrounded by crates labeled with the Kiss of Death insignia. Documents filled the next slides. Bank statements showing large deposits, text message exchanges discussing "product" and "shipments," all of it seeming to implicate Cora, as well as Kiss of Death, in some kind of drug trafficking ring.

"Jesus," Cora whispered beside me. I reached under the table, finding her hand and gripping it tightly.

Knight's voice cut through the stunned silence. "Reeves has been busy. These have been uploaded to Nashville PD's secure server in the last forty-eight hours. He's building a case against Cora as our mule."

Knight clicked to another slide showing official-looking paperwork. "And this is a warrant request, not yet submitted but drafted, for a raid on the compound. He's claiming Cora's information led them to evidence of large-scale drug operations here."

Knuckles slammed his fist onto the table, making several coffee mugs jump. "That fuckin' pig," he snarled. "Using a woman to get to Rancor. Low even for a cop with a hard-on for revenge."

My fingers tightened around Cora's hand, but I kept my face impassive. The rage building inside me was a familiar beast, one I'd spent years learning to cage. Now it prowled restlessly, sensing freedom was near. But acting on blind fury wouldn't help Cora.

"How long do we have?" I asked, my voice steady despite the inferno raging beneath my skin.

Knight shrugged. "Three days, maybe four, before he submits the warrant request. Once it's approved --"

"We need solutions," Knuckles cut in. "Not fuckin' timelines."

Tiny, who'd been silent until now, leaned forward. "We could disappear her. I got contacts in --"

"No," I interrupted, the single word slicing through the room. "We're not running. Not from this. Reeves wants me. If he gets what he wants, he'll leave you guys and Cora alone."

Knight cleared his throat. "I have another idea. One that buries Reeves instead of us." All eyes turned to him as he pulled something from his pocket. He laid a small, round object that looked like an ordinary button on the table in front of him. "We get him to confess. And we record him."

"How the fuck do we manage that?" Hawk asked from his position by the door.

Knight's tattooed lips curved into a smile that didn't reach his eyes. "Rancor arranges a meeting. Face-to-face. Reeves is arrogant. He'll think it's a surrender and that he's won. Men like him can't resist gloating."

I nodded slowly, understanding forming. "And I wear this," I said, gesturing to the button.

"Exactly. Military-grade recording with audio and video. It's also a tracking device. Picks up everything within fifty feet. I've got the equipment to filter through the background noise." Knight's eyes met mine. "You get him talking about what he's done to Cora, how he fabricated evidence against her and the club, his plans for the raid. I can take it from there," Knight said. "If IA won't do anything, I'll take it to the press. Media just loves a good scandal."

Cora's breathing had grown rapid beside me, her pulse visible at her throat. I placed my free hand on her lower back, feeling the shallow rise and fall of her ribs.

"It's risky," Hannah said, speaking for the first time. "Reeves could arrest him on the spot."

"Not without blowing his own plan," Knight countered. "He needs the raid to plant whatever evidence he plans on 'finding' here." He made air quotes. "He has to have some kind of evidence before he can justify an arrest, and to find evidence, he needs to get into the compound. For that, he needs the warrant."

"Meaning he can arrest Marcus, but it's not likely the charges will stick until he collects incriminating evidence he's likely going to plant during the raid when he executes the warrant." Cora's assessment was spot on.

Knuckles studied me across the table, his expression unreadable. "Your woman's smart, Rancor.

She's gonna be good for you." He gave Cora an acknowledging nod. "Your call, brother. It's your woman he's using as a pawn."

I felt Cora tense at those words but kept my eyes on our president. "I'll do it," I said. "Let him think he's got me backed into a corner. His ego won't let him pass up the chance to rub it in."

Knuckles gave a sharp nod. "Get on it."

Knight passed me the button-shaped device across the table. "Battery lasts a week of continuous recording. Secure it to your vest and the bastard will never know it's there."

Minutes later, after a quick test to make sure the device was working the way Knight wanted to, I reached for my phone. I thumbed open a new message to Reeves, knowing he'd kept my number all these years, probably hoping I'd slip up and give him something to use against me.

We need to talk. Tonight. Just you and me. The old Byers warehouse district, loading dock three. 9 PM.

I hit send, knowing he wouldn't refuse. Not when he thought victory was within his grasp.

Cora found my hand with hers under the table, her fingers cold against my skin. I squeezed gently, a silent promise that everything would be OK. Whatever happened next, I would bring Reeves down. For her. For us. For the future I was only just beginning to believe might be possible.

The spot was one meeting place of many we had set up throughout the city. This particular one was close to the compound. The location alone would be irresistible to Reeves. Any chance to get close to the compound would be one he'd take. Add to it I'd be out in the open and Reeves couldn't resist.

I'll be there. Leave your whore at home.

Oh, he'd pay for that remark. But not until I was ready. To do this, I needed a clear head. I couldn't afford to be so blinded by anger and hate I lost my cool.

* * *

Now, the warehouse district stretched before me like a giant's graveyard. Abandoned loading docks and empty buildings looming as silent witnesses to what was about to unfold. I pulled my bike into a shadowed alcove next to the meeting point, my boots crunching on broken glass and gravel as I dismounted. The night air carried the scent of rust and stagnant water, fitting for the rot I was about to confront. I checked the recording device disguised as a button on my jacket, waiting until the tiny red light in the back switched to green and blinked three times before going dark. The tiny earpiece Knight had insisted I wear sat snug and nearly invisible. "We ready?" I murmured, knowing Knight and Cora were listening from the surveillance van parked several blocks away.

"All good." Knight's voice came through. "Audio-visual's crystal. We're tracking you without interference."

I moved through the shadows. My heartbeat remained steady, my breathing controlled. This wasn't rage driving me now. What I felt was colder, more focused. More dangerous.

Loading dock three stood half-collapsed at the far end of what had once been a textile factory. Moonlight sliced through broken windows, casting prison-bar shadows across concrete stained with decades of industrial spillage. I positioned myself in the center of the open space, refusing to hide in darkness like Reeves surely would. Let him see me waiting.

I didn't have to wait long.

"Wheeler." Reeves' voice echoed against corrugated metal as he stepped from the shadows, exactly as I'd expected. He called me by my last name. His face looked older than I remembered, deep lines carved around a mouth twisted into what he probably thought was a smirk of victory. "Or should I say Rancor? That's what your little gang calls you, isn't it?"

I kept my expression neutral, giving him nothing. "Reeves."

He circled me slowly, keeping distance between us. He was stupid, but not *that* stupid. "I was surprised to get your message," he said, voice dripping with false casualness. "The mighty Rancor, reaching out to the cops. Must be desperate times at the compound."

"You know why I'm here." I followed him with my gaze only, refusing to turn my body as he circled. "It's not the club you're after. It's me. Always has been."

Reeves stopped his circling, his smirk widening into something ugly. "Not just you anymore. Your little delivery girl is quite the prize. Who'd have thought you'd give me such a perfect weapon?" He laughed, the sound bouncing hollowly off concrete walls. "You think you can protect her? I own her future now."

I let my shoulders tense, giving him the reaction he wanted. The more confident he felt, the more he'd reveal. The best part was, it didn't look like I was going to have to try very hard to get him to admit what he'd done. Give him enough rope, and I was confident he'd hang himself. "Leave her out of this. She's innocent."

"Innocent?" He barked another laugh. "Not according to the evidence. Did you know she's been moving product for you for months? That she's been laundering money through that cute little delivery service? The photos don't lie, Wheeler. Neither do the financial records." He pulled out his phone, swiping through images I knew were fabricated. "By this time tomorrow, she'll be in booking. Day after that, arraignment. By the end of the week? Just another inmate number."

My fists clenched at my sides, rage building despite my efforts to contain it. "Those are fake. You manufactured all of it."

"Prove it." He shrugged, pocketing his phone. "That's the beauty of digital evidence these days. Once it's in the system, it might as well be gospel. And I've spent months building this case, making sure every pixel is perfect, every document properly filed." His voice grew louder, more animated as his excitement built. "You think anyone will care when she cries frame-up? They never do. System's designed to crush people like her."

"Why?" I asked, needing to get him to specifically admit to the fabrication. "Why target her?"

His eyes narrowed, something feral flashing across his features. "Because you took something from me. My son. My only son." Spittle flew from his mouth as his control slipped. "Six years wasn't justice. It was a fucking vacation. Now you get to watch while I take apart your life piece by piece, starting with that bitch who thinks she's in love with you."

There it was. Now all he needed was a little nudge. "So you're falsifying evidence to frame an innocent woman." I kept my voice level, despite wanting to rip his throat out. "Planting bugs. Threatening civilians. That's not police work, Reeves. That's a vendetta."

"Call it what you want," he snarled, stepping

closer. "I call it justice. I've spent years watching you, waiting for the perfect moment. I tried putting a target on you in Terre Haute, but someone on the inside managed to shut down the contract. But when she showed up at your compound, all wide-eyed and trusting when you came around, I knew I had you. She was exactly your type, and she made it easy by thinking she could fix you or some shit. She took you on and I had you both right where I wanted you." His voice dropped to a vicious whisper. "You can't protect her, Wheeler. I *own* her now, just like I'll own you rotting in a cell, knowing you couldn't save another woman you loved."

"How were you planning on getting evidence to back your doctored photos?"

"I've got a warrant application in the works. We'll raid that little clubhouse of yours and get the evidence I need to put both you and your little whore away for a long fucking time."

"No, you won't. Because we don't have anything in there to find. We're all ex-cons who have no interest in going back to prison."

Reeves shrugged. "Oh, once I get inside, I guarantee you there will be enough evidence to put everyone in the whole Goddamned place in prison."

I snorted. "You're not seriously considering planting evidence. No way you're good enough to make a whole SWAT team look the other way while you carry out your vendetta."

"SWAT will do exactly what I tell them to. Which you might want to keep in mind since they all have big guns and are itching to use them. I doubt any of them would think twice about accidentally shooting a bunch of murderers."

I tilted my head inquisitively, hardening my

expression to one I knew Reeves would recognize as me meaning business. "Let me get this straight. I don't want there to be any misunderstandings."

"I'm all ears, Wheeler. Ask me any fucking question you want." The smirk on his face said he knew he'd won. He was practically celebrating. Arrogant prick deserved every fucking thing he had coming.

"You're saying your SWAT team would have no problem shooting first and asking questions later if you told them to?"

Oh, yeah. Reeves thought he had me. The threat was clear. "That's exactly what I'm saying, you stupid fucking cunt." He bit out the words between clenched teeth, getting as in my face as he could, given he was a good head shorter than me. If I'd wanted to kill the son of a bitch, I could have easily done it. But I'd promised Cora I wouldn't. At least, not yet.

Knight's voice whispered in my earpiece: "We have it all. Get out."

I gave Reeves a cold smile, one that made even the hardest cons step back. "Thanks for the information," I said, turning to leave.

"Where the hell do you think you're going?" Reeves demanded, confusion replacing his triumph.

"He's going home, Detective Reeves. You, however, are coming with me." The new voice cut through the cavernous space like a blade. Detective Mercer stepped from a side alley, flanked by two uniformed officers who remained a respectful distance behind her. Her expression was professionally blank, but I caught the satisfaction in her eyes.

"What the hell are you doing here, Mercer?" Reeves spat, his face contorting with shock and rage.

Mercer ignored him, addressing me directly.

"Mr. Wheeler, we have enough. Thank you for your cooperation."

Reeves looked between us, understanding slowly dawning. "Cooperation? What the fuck is this?"

"This," Mercer said calmly, "is the conclusion of an eight-month Internal Affairs investigation into your misconduct, Detective Reeves. Specifically, your harassment of civilians, fabrication of evidence, and abuse of police resources for personal vendettas. And personal gains." She gestured vaguely toward my jacket. "What you just confessed to ensures you'll be fired and likely serve prison time."

Reeves' face drained of color before flooding red with fury. "You fucking bitch!" He lunged at Mercer, but I stepped between them, instinctively protecting the woman. The uniformed officers moved quickly, restraining him before he could reach either of us.

"I'm happy to add assaulting an officer to the charges," Mercer said calmly as they cuffed him. She turned back to me. "You're free to go, Mr. Wheeler. We may need a formal statement later, but for now I suggest you return to your compound and reassure Ms. English that the threat against her has been taken care of."

I studied her face, looking for any sign of deception. Finding none, I nodded once and walked away, Reeves' cursing fading behind me. I didn't look back. Didn't need to see him broken. The recording in my pocket was enough.

A block away, Knight's unmarked van sat in the shadow of a defunct water tower. The side door slid open as I approached, revealing Cora's pale face, Knight beside her with headphones around his neck. I climbed in, and Cora immediately threw herself against my chest, her arms wrapping around my waist.

"You heard?" I asked, holding her tightly against me.

She nodded against my chest. "Everything. God, Marcus, he was going to --"

"But he won't," I cut in gently, tilting her face up to mine. "It's over, Cora. Reeves is done."

"And Mercer?" I asked Knight as we pulled away from the curb. "You trust her?"

"Yep," Knight said without hesitation. "She's working with Lana Thompson, the lawyer who helps women at the shelter. I called her when we set up the meet with Reeves."

"Well, you could have warned me, you motherfucker," I grumbled.

"Now, what would have been the fun in that?"

I pressed my lips to Cora's forehead, feeling her trembling subside. "Bit cool but the bike's waitin' if you want to ride with me."

She grinned. "Yeah. I think I'd like that."

"Good. Let's go home."

Chapter Thirteen

Cora
Three Months Later…

The stupid dress I wore felt like a straitjacket, clinging to my body in all the wrong places. I tugged at the neckline for the tenth time, willing the fabric to give me just a little more room to breathe. Beside me, Marcus shifted his broad shoulders inside a suit jacket that should have struggled to contain him but was perfectly tailored to his large frame. His jaw worked beneath his thick beard. We made quite the pair outside *Jeff Ruby's Steakhouse* in Nashville. The place was ridiculously expensive, but the food was phenomenal. I'd only eaten there once. The day my parents told me they were shipping me off to Europe for school. I hated the place on principle.

Six years since I'd spoken to them, six years of building a life they'd never understand, and now here I stood like a lamb dressed for slaughter. I had no idea how they'd found my phone number, but they'd called a couple days before to set up this meeting and had told me not to bring my new "friends." They'd known all about Kiss of Death and voiced their disapproval aggressively. I hated exposing Marcus to what I knew would be very judgmental people, but he'd insisted on coming with me, not caring if my parents wanted him there or not. I couldn't be mad at him for defying my parents' wishes because I knew If I made it through this evening without throwing up, it would only be because Marcus grounded me with his presence and his touch when I needed it.

"You keep fidgeting with that dress, I'm gonna tear it off you right here," Marcus muttered, his voice low enough that only I could hear.

"Don't tempt me with a good time," I replied, trying to match his lightness, but my voice trembled. "I'd rather be anywhere but here right now."

"Say the word, baby, and we're outta here."

The valet stand bustled with activity, sleek luxury cars pulling up one after another. A Ferrari. A Bentley. The kind of wealth that once surrounded me like air, so ubiquitous I hardly noticed it until I walked away. Now it felt suffocating and so alien I couldn't imagine going back to that life.

Marcus turned to me, his large hands sliding around my waist and pulling me close. His touch steadied me even as anxiety twisted my stomach into painful knots. "We get back on my bike, go home, and I can lick every inch of your creamy skin until you beg me to fuck the shit outta you." His whispered voice was sin in my ear. I wanted to take him up on that promise. God, how I wanted to. But the weight of unfinished business pressed down on me like a stone. I was also sure he wouldn't let me ride without a helmet back home the way he had here to preserve my hair. I had it up in a high ponytail divided into three sections I'd curled so they lay in spirals down my neck and behind my shoulders. We'd gone slow enough the wind hadn't been much of a factor and though the air was decidedly cool, we'd ridden slowly down the crowded streets. The brisk temperature had helped me focus on the meeting to come.

"I need to face them," I whispered. "I don't really know why, but I feel I need to do this."

Since leaving London six years ago, I'd rebuilt myself piece by jagged piece. I'd slept on park benches and in shelters. I'd worked jobs that left my feet aching and my spirit crushed. I'd learned to survive on my own terms, not theirs. But somewhere deep inside, a part of me still cowered under my father's disapproval and my mother's cutting remarks. That part of me needed to die tonight.

"These people hurt you," Marcus said, his voice dropping into that quiet register that made everyone else strain to hear him but somehow reached me with perfect clarity. "They'll probably try to manipulate you."

"Oh, I know they will," I said softly. "It's what they do."

The muscle in his jaw jumped beneath his beard. His instinct to protect me, to shield me from pain, was written in every line of his body, in the way his gaze constantly scanned our surroundings.

"I don't like this. They hurt you, and I'm not sure how I'll react."

"I know," I said with a smile. Marcus was nothing if not protective. Just the other day Marcus had growled at the older gentleman who owned a coffee shop I frequented because he'd bought my coffee. Thankfully, the man, who had to be pushing ninety, had merely patted Rancor's arm and told him to treat me right. Rancor had shaken his hand and promised to do just that. "But I'm not the same person who ran away from them. I'm stronger now." I reached up, placed my palm against his bearded cheek. "Because of you. Because of what we've built together."

The gold band and the single diamond solitaire on my finger caught the light from the restaurant's entrance, a reminder of promises Marcus and I had exchanged just two weeks ago in a simple ceremony at the compound. The memory of that day flooded me with warmth, pushing back against the chill of apprehension.

"I just worry they'll try to take you away from me," Marcus admitted, his vulnerability striking in a man who showed it so rarely. "People like that, with money and connections, they think they own people like me."

I shook my head firmly. "They can't take what isn't theirs to begin with. My heart, my future, those belong to you and me. No one else."

Around us, Nashville's elite streamed past in designer clothes, their conversations a blur of business deals and social climbing. None of them spared us a second glance, though we stood out like wolves among sheep. Marcus in his suit that couldn't quite disguise the predator beneath. Me in a dress I'd bought specially for this night, wanting to armor myself in the trappings of the world I'd left behind. Kind of ironic given we were going into a place where the bill for the two of us was likely to top five hundred dollars.

"I have to face them. I need to look them in the eye and show them I survived without them. That I'm happy despite them."

Marcus brushed his thumb across my cheek, wiping away a tear I hadn't realized had fallen. "Then we do it together," he said. "But the first sign they're hurting you, we leave. That's the deal."

I nodded, swallowing past the lump in my throat. "I love you so much."

He smiled, taking my hand in his, our fingers interlacing. He brought my fingers to his lips. "I love you, too, honey."

We turned together toward the restaurant entrance. The gleaming glass doors reflected our images back at us, distorted and strange. I barely recognized myself in the tight black cocktail dress, my hair swept up in an elegant twist. Marcus looked dangerous even in formal wear. The tattoos crawling up his neck, peeking out from his dress shirt, added to his predatory aura. He got more than his fair share of admiring glances from every single woman in the entire place. A few men too.

Just before we stepped inside, Marcus leaned down, his breath warm against my ear. "When we're done here," he whispered, "I'm going to take you home and peel this dress off you so slowly you'll beg me to tear it. Then I'm going to taste every inch of that gorgeous body until you forget these people ever existed."

Heat bloomed across my skin, starting at my neck and racing upward. Then downward. In that moment, I found strength in the promise of his touch, in the life we'd started far from the toxic world of my past. Funny, I had to find this kind of peace in a motorcycle club with a compound full of ex-cons and the women who loved them. Kiss of Death was more my home now than my parents' house had ever been.

I smiled up at him, a genuine one for the first time since we'd arrived. "That, Marcus Wheeler, is the best incentive I've ever heard for getting through a miserable dinner."

His answering smile was slow and wicked, just a slight curve of lips beneath his beard, but it hit me like a bolt of lightning. We stepped through the doors together, his hand at the small of my back, a united front against whatever awaited us inside.

We were led through the restaurant's main dining room, where crystal chandeliers cast prismatic light across white tablecloths and silver place settings. "Your party is already seated," the hostess told us. She paused at the threshold, eyes flickering between me and Marcus.

When her gaze lingered a little bit longer than I liked, I cleared my throat loudly. I waited until her gaze snapped to mine. "I'm about to spend the most miserable forty-five minutes of my life at the table with two people I've not seen or heard from in six years. They're going to berate, ridicule, and try to bully me into doing whatever it is they want from me. Believe me when I tell you I'd love nothing more than to take your skank ass to task for making eyes at my husband just to get thrown out and have an excuse to leave them sitting here all fucking night."

Marcus barked out a laugh before quickly muffling the sound with a cough no one believed. "How about we escort ourselves the rest of the way," he interjected smoothly. "They probably already look like they've had a couple too many tequilas with lemons instead of limes."

With one last glare at the shocked woman, I put my shoulders back and marched through the double doors of a private dining room where my parents awaited.

The room was a smaller version of the main dining area, with a single table set for four beneath a chandelier. My father stood at the head of the table, rigid in a bespoke suit that probably cost more than our entire wardrobe. My mother remained seated, her back straight as a ruler, hair still the same perfect blonde as when I left, most likely courtesy of New York's most expensive colorist.

The room contracted around me, air suddenly too thick to breathe. They looked exactly the same, untouched by the six years that had transformed me completely. Time had frozen for them, preserving their wealth, their status, their unshakable certainty that the world existed to bend to their will.

My father's gaze swept over us, lingering on Marcus with the same expression he might use when finding something unpleasant stuck to his shoe. "Well," he said, voice clipped. "You finally decided to grace us with your presence."

"Hello, Father," I replied, hating the way my voice automatically shifted, adopting the polite, deferential tone I'd spent years unlearning. "Mother."

She didn't rise to greet me, just inclined her head slightly. "Cora." Her gaze traveled from my face down to my dress, lips tightening. "You've gained weight. Not in a healthy way." She gave an indignant sniff, like my very presence offended her. I hadn't seen them in six years, and that was her opening line. I bit back a hysterical laugh. Some things never changed.

"This is Marcus," I said, refusing to acknowledge her comment. "My husband."

The word fell between us like a grenade. My mother's perfectly manicured hand flew to her throat. My father's face flushed a dangerous red.

"Sit down," he barked, not looking at Marcus, not acknowledging my introduction. "We have matters to discuss."

We moved to the table, Marcus pulling out my chair with surprising grace before taking his seat beside me. His thigh pressed against mine beneath the table, a warm anchor in the cold sea of my parents' disapproval.

"What exactly is this?" my father demanded once we were seated, finally addressing Marcus directly. "Some kind of joke? Showing up with this… person?"

"His name is *Marcus*," I said, ice crystallizing in my voice. "And I just told you, he's my husband."

My mother reached for her water glass, hand trembling slightly. "We've been worried sick," she said without a trace of actual worry in her tone. "This little rebellion has gone on long enough, darling. It's time to come home."

"Rebellion?" I repeated, the word tasting bitter on my tongue. "I'm twenty-two years old, Mother. I've been on my own for six years. This isn't a phase or a temper tantrum. This is my life."

"Six years," my father scoffed, waving away half a decade as if it were nothing. "Six years of playing poor or whatever this is. Slumming." He gestured vaguely toward Marcus without looking at him. "Did you think we wouldn't find you? That we wouldn't eventually bring you to your senses?"

"I never hid," I said quietly. "And, obviously, you could have found me at any time you wanted."

The waiter appeared, nervous eyes darting between us as he sensed the tension. "Would you care to order drinks?"

"Scotch," my father snapped. "Macallan 25. Neat."

"Bring me the driest white wine you have," my mother added.

"Water for us," I said, not wanting anything to dull my senses for what was to come.

When the waiter retreated, my father leaned forward, his expression hardening. "Let me be clear, Cora. This ends now. You're coming home with us tonight. Your mother has already arranged for your old room to be prepared. Your therapist is expecting you Monday morning."

I stared at him, genuinely stunned by his delusion. "That's not happening."

"Don't be difficult," my mother snapped, her voice taking on the syrupy quality she used when trying to manipulate me. "You've had your adventure, dear. Proven whatever point you needed to make. But this has gone on long enough. Look at you, in that cheap dress, with this person." Her eyes flicked dismissively toward Marcus. "What would your grandfather say if he could see you now?"

Marcus remained perfectly still beside me, his silence more powerful than any words could be. I could feel the tension radiating from him, the controlled power of a predator deciding whether to strike.

"The Cora we raised would never embarrass us like this," my father continued, acting as if Marcus weren't present. "That trust fund we set up for you was meant to set you up properly, not finance whatever sordid lifestyle you've been living. Do you have any idea what people say about you? About *us*? Your mother can barely show her face at the club anymore."

"How tragic for her," I murmured, earning a sharp look from both of them.

"Enough sass," my father barked. "You're coming home tonight. End of discussion. We'll get this marriage annulled, if it's even legal, which I seriously doubt. Your mother has already spoken to several suitable young men who are willing to overlook this… indiscretion."

The waiter returned with drinks, setting them down with trembling hands before retreating quickly. My father took a long swallow of his scotch, then fixed me with the look that used to make me shrink into myself.

"I expect you to be grateful," he continued. "After everything you've put us through, we're still willing to welcome you back. Still willing to restore your place in this family. Most parents wouldn't be so forgiving."

"*Forgiving*?" The word escaped me in a whisper. "Is that what you think this is?"

"Of course, it is," my mother said. "We're offering you a clean slate, Cora. A chance to put this ugliness behind us and return to your real life."

That was when Marcus finally spoke, his voice so quiet they had to lean forward to hear him. "Her real life," he said, each word measured and precise, "is with me. Has been for a while now."

My father's head snapped toward him, eyes narrowing. "No one asked for your input. This is a family matter."

"*I am* her family," Marcus replied, his tone carrying the dangerous undertone I recognized as carefully controlled rage. "The only family she needs."

"Security," my father called over his shoulder, not taking his eyes off Marcus. "We need someone removed from our private dining room."

I sat frozen, unable to speak as years of conditioning battled against the person I'd become. My face settled into a mask of boredom, a defense mechanism I'd perfected in childhood, but my hand gripped Marcus's under the table so tightly my knuckles were likely white with the tension.

"You've always been such a disappointment." My mother sighed, shaking her head. "Always so willful, so determined to embarrass us. We gave you everything, and this is how you repay us?"

"We expect you to come to your senses now," my father added, his tirade building steam. "Pack whatever meager belongings you care about and say goodbye to… this person. Our driver is waiting outside to take you home. I've already contacted the board at English Financial. There's a position waiting for you, provided you demonstrate the proper attitude. It's more than you deserve, but that's what parents do. They forgive. They provide. Now it's time for *you* to show some gratitude."

They finally paused, breathing slightly heavier from the exertion of their self-righteous speeches. Their eyes fixed on me with identical expressions of expectation, waiting for my capitulation, my apology, my surrender. The silence stretched between us, taut as a wire.

I looked at my parents' disdain-filled faces and felt something inside me finally giving way, like a knot suddenly unraveling in my gut after years of tension. My entire life, I'd been taught to swallow my words, to speak only when spoken to, to agree and apologize and accommodate. The invisible chains they'd wrapped around me since childhood suddenly felt gossamer thin, their power existing only in my mind.

I glanced at Marcus beside me, his steady presence a reminder of who I'd become, of the strength I'd found in his arms and in myself. Then I turned back to my parents, smiled, and spoke the words I'd been holding back for most of my life.

"Go fuck yourselves." The second the words fell from my lips, a weight lifted from my soul. My words landed in the silence like stones dropped into still water. My voice didn't shake or rise, didn't betray the thunder of my heart beneath my ribs. I simply stated it as an order, a dismissal of everything they represented.

My father's mouth opened, then closed, then opened again, no sound emerging. For once in his life, Charles English was speechless. Beside him, my mother's face drained of color, her perfectly painted lips forming a small 'o' of shock as her wine glass tumbled from her hand to spill on the table in front of her.

"Excuse me?" she finally managed, her voice barely audible.

"You heard me," I replied, still smiling, "but I have no problem saying it again. Go. Fuck. Yourselves. Both of you. Preferably with something rusty and painful."

My father recovered, his face flushing purple. "How dare you speak to us that way! After everything we've done for you!"

"*What* exactly have you done for me?" I asked, rising slowly from my chair. Marcus stood with me, his hand finding the small of my back. "Controlled me? Belittled me? Made me feel worthless unless I was fulfilling your expectations?" I shook my head. "That's not love. That's ownership. And I am *not* your property."

"Sit down this instant," my mother hissed, eyes darting to the door as if worried someone might overhear. Always more concerned with appearances than reality.

I grinned. "Make me."

My father slammed his palm on the table, causing the silverware to jump. "You ungrateful little bitch. After everything we've sacrificed for you!"

"The only thing you ever sacrificed was my happiness," I replied, feeling lighter with each word. "And I'm done paying that price."

I turned away from them, tugging gently on Marcus's hand. He followed my lead without hesitation, matching his stride to mine as we walked toward the door.

"If you leave with him, you're cut off," my father called after us. "No more safety net, Cora. No more family name to fall back on."

I paused at the doorway, looking back over my shoulder. "I've been without your money for six years, *Father*. Haven't missed it. Not once. Not even when I was sleeping in homeless shelters." I smiled again, genuinely this time. "And as for the English name, I traded up. I'm Cora *Wheeler* now. And no matter what happens between me and Marcus in the future, I will never be Cora English again. That name - your name -- is *dead to me*." I only added that last part because my mother often used to say I was dead to her whenever I did something she hadn't much approved of. Saying it before she could might be petty, but the satisfaction was immeasurable.

We stepped through the doorway before they could respond, leaving them sputtering in outrage behind us. The main dining room stretched before us, a gauntlet of curious faces. I felt Marcus's arm slide around my waist, his body slightly ahead of mine in that protective stance that had become so familiar.

"You okay?" he murmured, his voice for my ears alone.

"Never better," I replied, meaning it.

We walked through the restaurant with unhurried steps.

A different hostess appeared at the front door, her false smile strained. "Was everything to your satisfaction, Miss English?"

"It's Mrs. Wheeler," I corrected her. "And it was exactly what I needed, thank you."

Outside, the night air hit my flushed skin like a blessing, cool and clean after the stifling atmosphere within. To my surprise, Marcus' motorcycle waited at the curb, its gleaming black body an incongruous sight among the luxury cars. The valet, a young man with a smug expression, pulled the keys to Marcus' bike from his pocket and tossed them to Marcus.

"Out front for a quick getaway," he said to Marcus, gesturing at the bike.

Marcus slipped something into the young man's hand that made his eyes and his grin widen. "Thanks, man," he said.

Without hesitation, I reached down and slipped off my heels, holding them loosely in one hand. The pavement was cold beneath my bare feet, but the discomfort felt clarifying.

Marcus swung his leg over the bike, the movement smooth despite his formal clothes. He held out his hand to me, his dark eyes reflecting the city lights. "Ready to go home, wife?"

Wife. The word sent a shiver through me that had nothing to do with the night air. I took his hand and climbed behind him, my tight dress riding up my thighs as I straddled the machine. The cool leather seat pressed against my skin, the engine's vibration already thrumming through the frame beneath me.

"Cora!" My father's voice cut through the night, sharp with command. He stood at the restaurant entrance, my mother a pale shadow behind him. "Don't you dare leave like this!"

Marcus kicked the bike to life, the engine roaring with sudden violence that drowned out whatever else my father might have said. The sound reverberated in my chest, primal and fierce, a mechanical growl that matched the wild freedom blooming inside me.

I wrapped my arms around Marcus' waist, pressing my body against his back, feeling the solid warmth of him even through his jacket. My bare legs extended on either side of the bike, exposed to the night air in a way that would have scandalized my mother, but I couldn't bring myself to care.

As we pulled away from the curb, I looked over my shoulder at my father. My mother now stood by his side. All she needed was a set of pearls to clutch and a fainting couch and she'd be the epitome of the dramatic Southern woman.

Maybe it made me a bad person, but I shot them both a cocky smirk and flipped them the bird as Marcus popped the clutch and took off onto the streets of Nashville with a surge of power.

The wind whipped through my hair, giving me a sense of freedom I hadn't realized I'd been needing. The cold bit at my exposed skin, racing up my legs and along my arms, but I welcomed it, needed it to clear my head after the suffocating heat of confrontation.

I pressed my face against Marcus' back, breathing in the scent of him beneath the lingering traces of unfamiliar cologne. His body moved with the bike, muscles shifting beneath my hands as we leaned into a turn, the city blurring around us in streaks of light and shadow.

For the first time since I'd received my parents' message demanding this meeting, I felt like I could breathe fully. Each inhalation filled my lungs with cold, clean air, washing away the last traces of the perfumed prison I'd left behind. Each exhale carried away another fragment of the girl they'd tried to shape me into, the perfect daughter, the obedient heir, the empty vessel for their ambitions.

We sped through Nashville's streets, the wind's icy fingers combing through my hair, tugging my dress, painting my skin with goose bumps. I didn't care. The cold was a price worth paying for this freedom, this wild escape that felt like flying.

I tightened my arms around Marcus. He briefly covered my hand where it rested against his stomach.

No words were needed between us. He knew, as he always seemed to know, exactly what I was feeling in this moment.

Freedom tasted like night air and victory, like the promise of Marcus's skin against mine once we were home. And for the first time in my life, I knew I was exactly where I belonged.

Chapter Fourteen

Rancor

We arrived at my quarters in the Kiss of Death compound with my heartbeat still racing, the night ride having done little to cool the fire Cora had ignited in me with her defiance. I shoved the door shut behind us, locking it because no way in the fucking world was anyone going to interrupt me tonight. Freedom looked good on Cora. Victory, even better.

"God, that felt good," she breathed, her voice still carrying that edge of defiance that had cut through her parents' expectations like a blade. She paced the floor barefoot, the hem of her black dress swishing around her shapely thighs.

I loosened my tie, watching her move. Her trembling hands clenched and unclenched at her sides, not from fear this time but from the aftershocks of adrenaline. Her lips curved with stubborn pride as she ran her fingers through her hair where it had come loose from the high ponytail that had started the evening.

"You were magnificent," I said, my voice rougher than I'd intended. The sight of her flushed with her victory, her eyes bright, was the most erotic, amazing, beautiful thing I'd ever seen.

She turned to face me, the dim light in my apartment catching on the subtle shine of her dress, highlighting every curve. "I've wanted to say that to them for years," she confessed. "Every time they made me feel small, every time they treated me like a possession…" She shook her head, a strand of hair falling across her cheek. "In a way, I think them sending me off to boarding school made me realize my relationship wasn't normal or healthy. Especially when they just left me there. I wasn't the only kid there with parent issues. Wasn't even the only one who never went home. But the experience was enough to make me realize I could have more if I was willing to strike out on my own."

I'd taken down men twice my size in prison without hesitation, faced down rivals and cops with an unblinking stare, but nothing had ever moved me like watching this woman find her voice. The woman who'd somehow become my anchor, my reason, my fucking salvation in a world that had taken everything else from me.

"You told them exactly who you are," I said, shrugging off my jacket and draping it over the back of a chair. "Who you've always been."

Her eyes tracked my movement, darkening slightly as I rolled up my sleeves, exposing the forearms marked with memories in ink and scars. The energy between us shifted, tension crackling in the air like static before a storm.

"And who am I, Rancor?" she asked, her voice dropping lower, the question carrying weight beyond the words themselves. She didn't often use my road name, but I got the feeling she was now as a symbolic way of finishing the break with her old life. As much as I loved hearing my real name on her lips, I found I liked my road name even better. Especially now, given it represented a new life for us both. Though my second life hadn't started out the way I wanted it to, the current destination was more than I ever thought I'd have again.

I stepped toward her, deliberate and measured, the way I approached everything that mattered. "Mine," I answered simply. The word hung between us, heavy with all it implied. She wasn't my possession, she was my life, the person I wanted and needed to protect most in this world. Did I miss Sarah? I would always miss her. But I knew she'd want me to be happy. I had to believe she was smiling down on me from heaven.

A visible shiver ran through Cora as I closed the distance between us. I settled my hands on her hips, the expensive fabric of her dress smooth and cool beneath my fingers. I felt her heat through the barrier, her body responding to my touch with an immediacy that never failed to humble me.

I turned her to face me fully, pinching her chin with my thumb and finger to tilt her face up until her eyes met mine. "You're the woman who just told her entire past to go fuck itself," I said, my tone dropping to that quiet, measured cadence that always preceded something fierce. "You're the woman who chose a future on her own terms. Who chose me." My thumb traced her lower lip, feeling it tremble slightly beneath my touch. "You're my wife. My fucking heart walking around outside my chest."

Her breath caught, the sound small but unmistakable in the quiet room. I watched her pupils dilate, black consuming blue until only a thin ring remained. She swayed toward me, her body seeking mine instinctively.

I pulled her into a bruising kiss, swallowing her gasp as our lips collided. The gentleness I usually reserved for her burned away beneath the heat of need. My fingers dug into the fabric of her dress as I bunched it in my fists. I backed her against the wall with deliberate force. The small *thud* of her body meeting the drywall sent a jolt of satisfaction through me.

She gripped my head, her nails scraping against my scalp, kissing me back with a fervor equal to my own. I felt her teeth against my lips, the sharp nip more demand than request. I growled low in my throat, pressing her harder against the wall, pinning her with my larger frame.

"Did you feel powerful, telling them to go fuck themselves?" I murmured against her mouth, my beard scraping the delicate skin of her jaw as I moved to her ear. I bit the lobe gently, relishing her sharp inhale. "Because watching you do it made me want to fuck you right there in the parking lot."

Her breath came fast against my neck, her chest rising and falling rapidly where it pressed against mine. "Yes," she admitted, her voice ragged with want. "God, Marcus, I've never felt so free."

I captured her mouth again, my tongue claiming hers with possessive intent. Every slide of our lips, every shared breath, felt like sealing a pact we'd made long ago. My hands slid down her sides to her thighs, finding the hem of her dress and pushing it upward, exposing the silk of her skin to my calloused palms.

She arched into me, her body a living flame against mine. I lifted her easily. She wrapped her legs around my waist as I supported her against the wall. The position aligned our bodies perfectly. I shoved her skirt over her ass, the hard ridge of my erection finding and pressing against her pussy through the silk panties she wore. The other layers of fabric suddenly seemed an intolerable barrier.

"I need you," she whispered, the words broken and raw. "Need you to fuck me, Rancor!"

The second she uttered those words using my road name, I lost my Goddamned mind. "Hang on," I bit out before I hooked my finger in the elastic of her panties and guided my cock to her entrance.

With one shift, hard shove, I buried myself deep

inside her cunt. The wet, hot heat of her pussy surrounding my bare cock was unlike anything I'd ever felt in my life. I actually saw stars on the edge of my vision.

"I've got you, baby," I promised, my voice rough with a passion I had no hope of containing. "Always. My woman. The warrior."

"I need this fucking dress off!" She tightened her legs around my hips but shoved me back, trying to reach behind her. Probably for the zipper. When she gave a frustrated screech, I wrapped my arms around her, found the tab and tried to slide it down her back. The Goddamned thing hung and I tugged a little bit too hard. The satisfying rip of the delicate fabric under my grip probably wasn't pleasant to her as it was to me. She gasped, not in protest but in approval, her eyes darkening further as I exposed more of her skin to my hungry gaze. "Fuck," she breathed as I ripped it further, exposing the black lace beneath. "Hated this fucking dress from the moment I put it on."

"You're mine," I growled, needing to repeat myself until we both believed it to our very souls. I grazed my teeth over her neck, leaving marks she would feel long after this night ended, visual reminders of my claim on her. Not because I owned her, but because she had chosen to give herself to me. The thing that surprised me most was that, though I didn't believe she was my possession, I knew deep in my soul she owned me.

"Yes," she agreed, no hesitation in her voice. "And you're mine. Every goddamn inch of you."

I began to move then, thrusting my hips, fucking her hard. The need to plant my seed inside her was the most pressing desire I'd ever had in my life.

"Say it again," I demanded, my breath hot

against her ear. "Tell me who you belong to."

Her nails dug into my shoulders, leaving half-moons of pressure through my shirt that I knew would mark my skin. "You," she whispered, her voice breaking with need. "I belong to you, Rancor. Only you."

I fucked her with powerful movements, claiming her with my body the way she'd claimed my soul the first Goddamned day I met her. She screamed, the sound raw and primal, her head falling back against the wall as my movements drove her up and down the flat surface. I prayed I wasn't hurting her since I didn't seem to possess the self-control to slow down.

Thankfully, when I looked into her lovely eyes, I saw only hunger, the same hunger I knew reflected back at her.

I set a punishing rhythm that had us both gasping. Each thrust drove us higher, the force of my movements pressing her harder against the wall. Her black dress hung in tatters around her waist. Cora reached between us and grasped the edges of my shirt, yanking hard. Buttons scattered around us but the only thing that mattered to me was getting her tits out of her bra so I could mash against her chest to chest.

"Look at me," I commanded, slowing my pace just enough to make her whimper in protest. Her eyes snapped to mine, pupils blown wide with arousal. "I want to hold your gaze while you come on my cock. Just for me."

She nodded frantically, her breath coming in short, sharp pants that matched the rhythm of my thrusts. I slid one hand between us, finding her clit with practiced ease. The first touch had her arching against me, a strangled cry escaping her lips.

"That's it, baby," I encouraged, my voice rough

with exertion and need. "Fuckin' come. I've got you."

The tight clench of her body around mine told me she was close. I increased my pace, driving into her with relentless force, feeling my own release building at the base of my spine. The sight of her, head thrown back in abandon, skin flushed with pleasure, lips parted on my name, pushed me closer to the edge.

When she finally came, her entire body tensing around mine, I followed her into bliss, my release tearing through me with an intensity that left me gasping. We clung to each other, shuddering through the shared pleasure, the wall at her back the only thing keeping us upright as I leaned into her. I gasped for breath as I rested my forehead against hers. I remained inside her, unwilling to break our connection just yet.

She kissed me, a soft, lingering press of her lips against mine as a small joy-filled laugh escaped her. "Well," she murmured, "that's one way to celebrate telling my parents to fuck off."

I chuckled, the sound rumbling from deep in my chest. "Just getting started, wife," I promised, carefully withdrawing from her body and lowering her feet to the floor. Her legs trembled beneath her, and I felt a surge of masculine pride at having reduced this strong, defiant woman to such a state.

I swept her into my arms, carrying her the short distance to our bed. She went willingly, her arms looped around my neck, her head resting trustingly against my shoulder. I laid her down with more gentleness than I'd shown minutes before, the sight of her sprawled across our sheets sending a fresh surge of desire through me despite my recent release.

She reached for me, her arms open in invitation. I followed her down, covering her smaller body with mine. This time, when our lips met, the kiss was softer, the urgency replaced by something deeper, more tender.

"I love you," I murmured against her mouth, the words still new enough to feel like a revelation each time I spoke them. For years after Sarah died, I'd believed that part of me had died with her. Cora had proven me wrong, awakening feelings I'd thought forever lost.

Her hands framed my face, thumbs tracing the contours of my cheekbones with reverent care. "I love you too," she whispered back. "So much it scares me sometimes."

"Don't be scared, honey. I will guard your heart with my life."

"I know." She stroked my face as she pulled me back for another kiss.

I sank into her again. This time the sensation was no less intense for its gentleness. I moved, watching her face as her pleasure built slowly. This wasn't the raw, animal coupling of before, but something equally powerful for the love it conveyed.

With a soft cry, she came, milking my cock again for the seed I needed to plant inside her. I shuddered as I came, groaning against her neck as I held myself inside her as deeply as I could, never wanting to be free.

After, as our breathing slowed and the sweat cooled on our skin, I wrapped my arm protectively around her, drawing her close against my side. She came willingly, her body molding to mine so she fit perfectly.

"No regrets?" I asked, my voice low in the quiet room. "About us? About your parents?"

She tilted her face up to mine, her expression open and unguarded in a way she rarely was with anyone but me. "Not a single one," she said firmly. "My only family is right here." She pressed her palm against my chest, directly over my heart. "Everything I need, everything I want. It's all right here."

I covered her hand with mine, feeling the steady thump of my heartbeat beneath our joined fingers. The peace I found in her arms was something I never thought I'd experience again.

Cora was my love. My wife. My everything. I'd lost so much and had dwelt on those losses for a long time. Now, all I wanted was to embrace the second chance I'd been given.

"Tell me you love me again," I demanded.

I felt her lips move against my chest as she smiled. "I do love you, Rancor. With all my heart." Her voice was thick with fatigue, and I knew neither of us would last much longer.

As sleep claimed us, cradled in each other's arms, I felt a sense of completeness I'd longed for my entire life. In Cora, I had found my anchor, my sanctuary, my reason to believe in second chances and the enduring power of love.

Marteeka Karland

International bestselling author Marteeka Karland leads a double life as an action romance writer by evening and a semi-domesticated housewife by day. Known for her down and dirty MC romances, Marteeka takes pleasure in spinning tales of tenacious, protective heroes and spirited heroines. She staunchly advocates that every character deserves a blissful ending.

Marteeka finds joy in baking and gardening with her husband. Make sure to visit her website to stay updated with her most recent projects. Don't forget to register for her newsletter which will pepper you with a potpourri of Teeka's beloved recipes, book suggestions, autograph events, and a plethora of interesting tidbits.

Marteeka at Changeling: changelingpress.com/marteeka-karland-a-39

Want more? Wanda Violet O. is Teeka's Dark Erotica side.

Bones MC Multiverse

Contemporary MC and Crossovers

- Bones MC
- Shadow Demons
- Salvation's Bane MC
- Black Reign MC
- Iron Tzars MC
- Grim Road MC
- Bones MC Legends
- Kiss of Death MC

Print and Audio

- Bones MC Print Duets
- Bones MC Audio
- Salvation's Bane MC Audio
- Iron Tzars MC Audio
- Grim Road MC Audio
- Kiss of Death MC Audio

Changeling Press LLC

Contemporary Action Adventure, Sci-Fi, Steampunk, Dark Fantasy, Urban Fantasy, Paranormal, and BDSM Romance available in e-book, audio, and print format at ChangelingPress.com – MC Romance, Werewolves, Vampires, Dragons, Shapeshifters and Horror -- Tales from the edge of your imagination.

Where can I get Changeling Press Books?

Changeling Press e-books are available at ChangelingPress.com, Amazon, Apple Books, Barnes & Noble, Kobo, Smashwords, and other online retailers, including Everand Subscription and Kobo Subscription Services. Print books are available at Amazon, Barnes and Noble, and by ISBN special order through your local bookstores.

ChangelingPress.com

www.ingramcontent.com/pod-product-compliance
Lightning Source LLC
La Vergne TN
LVHW020525100826
845148LV00010B/1343